Ms Perfectly Fine

Ms Perfectly Fine

KATE CALLAGHAN

No part of this book may be reproduced or stored in a retrieval system or transmitted in any form or by any means, electronic, mechanical, photocopying, recording, or otherwise without express written permission of the author.

The characters and events portrayed in this book are fictitious. Any similarity to real persons, living or dead, is coincidental and not intended by the author.

Edited By: Emma O'Connell
Formatted By: Enchanted Ink Publishing
Proofread By: RaeAnne at Lavender Prose
Cover By: Pru Schulyer

Copyright © 2023 by Kate Callaghan. All rights reserved.

ISBN: 978-1-7397537-7-1
ISBN: 978-1-7397537-8-8

WWW.CALLAGHANWRITER.COM

Readers! Please note that this novel contains themes including (but not limited to):

stalking, trauma, chronic pain, anxiety, survivor's guilt, and self-isolation. This is an adult romance with mature content and not suitable for those under 18.

Whether you have emotional scars, physical ones, or both, **you** are **worthy** of *being loved*.

Note from the author

I didn't think I'd ever write a book with no fantasy, but here she is. I also never thought I would write a book that touches on chronic pain. When I started writing *Ms Perfectly Fine,* I didn't think I would ever publish it. Despite suffering with chronic pain myself, I didn't know if I could write about it and do it justice—but I wanted to try. There are so many of us out there who suffer in silence and are forced to be "fine" in order to live in this world.

Sometimes, people don't need to be cured or fixed; they just need to be seen and heard. I didn't want Autumn's pain to define her, and I didn't want to cure her, because for many of us with chronic pain, there *is* no cure. Autumn has built a safety bubble around herself in her routine and adjusted her life so she can do what she loves, but it's still a struggle—and like many of us, she's got a little too comfortable in her routine. She has overcome so many challenges. Elijah is her next hurdle. He bursts her bubble and forces her out of her shell. He wants to be part of her world, no matter how many obstacles she puts in the way.

Her pain does not define her, but it's part of her. For both Elijah and Autumn, I wanted this to be a story of forgiveness, acceptance, and self-love.

Autumn & Elijah's Playlist

No One Can Fix Me | Frawley

Midnight Rain | Taylor Swift

Skin | Rihanna

Changes | Lauv

@ My Worst | Blackbear

The Great War | Taylor Swift

Be Your Love | Bishop Briggs

Body | Julia Michaels

Must Have Been The Wind | Alec Benjamin

Enemies | Lauv

Born Without A Heart | Faouzia

Autumn's piece

Winter, 1. Movement | Antonio Vivaldi

Nina's piece

Winter (L'Inverno) Op. 8 No. 4 Minor: Allegro Non Molto

Ms Perfectly Fine

KATE CALLAGHAN

Prologue

10 Years Ago

Snow crunched under Autumn's fingertips as she regained consciousness. Her breath fogged in front of her as she lay on her back, telling her she was outside in the cold, but she felt cradled by waves of heat emanating around her body.

Did I black out? Did I faint during the performance? She had never passed out before, especially not during a piano recital. *Even if I did pass out...where am I?*

Glancing around, she took in the broken wooden beams everywhere, trembling as she realised that she was no longer on the outdoor stage, but beneath it. *The stage collapsed?* Her brain tried to piece events together. She remembered playing, and then—nothing.

Something was looming over her. She realised it was her piano, but it was no longer whole, crushed by the weight of the beams she guessed had once made up the roof.

A terrified cry escaped her. She was trapped. She panted, fearing that what remained of the stage would come down on her. *The piano is taking the weight. Relax. Someone will find you.* The inner voice soothed her, keeping her from descending into panicking, but whimpers still escaped her.

If you're afraid, you're alive, the voice reassured her, and Autumn made an effort to stay her breathing. *Where's Mollie?* she thought frantically. Her friend had been right beside her before this had happened. *She must be further back. I hope she's okay.* The silence worried her. It seemed to taunt her, as though the stage was cut off from the rest of the world.

The snow melted beneath her back, and her dampening clothes caused her to shiver. Her soft cries only drained her further, and she remembered that her mum always said to take a breath when scared. Autumn attempted to take a deep breath only to finally learn where the heat was coming from. A cluster of fallen stage lights in the near distance had caught fire. Panicking, she inhaled sharply.

Smoke invaded her lungs, inspiring a coughing fit that highlighted her injuries. Instinctively, she covered her mouth, but the movement swelled an agony in her back that caused sparkles to form in her vision. Tears poured down her cheeks, not only because she was terrified, but because the smoke stung her eyes. Every part of her body hurt, making it impossible to pinpoint where she was injured.

"Help!" she cried out, desperate for this nightmare to end, but no one answered.

"Please! I'm under here!"

Again, unanswered, and the smoke was growing thicker.

Slow movements. I have to get out of here. Autumn tried to move her legs; the relief of being able to wriggle her toes was overwhelming. Attempting to sit up, she cried out and collapsed as she discovered that a piece of wood had broken off from either a beam or the piano and was pinning her down. *I need to pull it out if I'm to get out of here!* She gripped the wood and was blinded by pain. The heat of the flames mixed with the icy cold of the snow disorientated her. All she wanted was to go home.

"Mum, please help me," Autumn cried out with all the strength she could muster—though it only came out as a whisper—feeling her tears roll down her cheeks.

Just when she thought all hope was lost, she saw torches flashing through the debris, followed by the echoing shouts of strangers. She waited for Mollie to cry out, but no one called. *Mollie, please call out to them. Please say something!*

She faded in and out of consciousness, and her breathing grew shallow. The beeping of radios and muffled shouts above her were a blur of sounds.

"Autumn! Mollie! Call out if you can hear us! Bang something if you can't!"

Relief coursed through her veins. They were coming for her, but she didn't have the energy to respond. There was nothing she could hit to make a sound, and the pain radiating through her spine was taking the last ounce of energy she had.

"Over here! We've found one of the girls! Keep the parents back," she heard.

They found Mollie. She's safe.

Please, I'm here, Autumn pleaded silently, but her adrenaline waned, and her eyelids grew heavy.

Chapter One

Autumn

Sweat trickled down Autumn's forehead as she pressed her palms into her eyes, hoping to scrub away the memories. Ten years of counselling and still the same nightmare.

Her chest felt heavy, as if someone was sitting on her, preventing her escape. It was always the same dream, although sometimes her mind liked to play tricks by changing her age or the season. Last night, it had settled for the original. *Sixteen. Winter showcase.*

"Just breathe," she chanted, and removed the sheets from her body.

On the edge of the bed, she looked out of the large-paned windows to the blooming cherry blossom tree in the front garden, trying to ground herself back in the present. She scrunched her toes in her white, fluffy carpet as relief finally washed through her veins.

"If I don't start sleeping, I'm going to keep messing up in rehearsals," she said to herself, placing a hand over the scar on her aching back where the wood had once pierced only inches from her spine. The thought of performing her piano solo in four weeks had obviously triggered her memories, her subconscious plaguing her to recognise what her conscious mind begged to forget. Her former therapist had told her it was all part of the healing process, but a process that lasted ten years would drive anyone to the edge.

Maybe I should have waited another year before I accepted the offer to perform, she thought, pulling herself from the beige sheets. Some people might call her bedsheets, ivory walls, and cream carpets boring, but she liked to keep things simple.

"You don't need another year. You've been hiding long enough," she told herself. She'd worked too hard to let her demons take over, especially when she was so close. The Spring Showcase was her comeback to the solo stage. She had spent the last few years in the orchestra, hidden and safe, but she was ready for the next challenge. She owed it to herself—and to Mollie, who was now nothing more than a shadow in her nightmares. Autumn's fingers grazed her neck, feeling the sorrow of calling out for her friend in the dream. A call that would go unanswered forever.

Tears welled in her eyes, but she rubbed them away.

"One day at a time. Breakfast and rehearsals—I can do that," she said, looking into the mirror on the white dresser and pulling back her auburn fringe with a cat-eared headband. It was still cold, so she tugged on her fluffy striped socks and pulled her favourite lilac dressing gown around herself. The soft sensation helped her body relax.

One step at a time. The first few steps of the day were always the toughest, but once her muscles warmed up and relaxed, the pain sank into the back of her mind. Never completely gone, but easier to ignore.

Across the narrow landing in her mint-tiled bathroom, splashing water on her face washed away the last traces of her anxiety. The clock on the wall read seven a.m. She didn't have a clock in her bedroom because hearing it tick on sleepless nights drove her insane.

Like clockwork. Her body was well used to her rigid schedule even though for today's rehearsal, she didn't have to get up for another hour. *It's my turn to pick up the coffee order for everyone. I should have plenty of time,* she thought while she brushed her teeth.

Suddenly, her feet tingled. *That's a new sensation.* The ground tiles shook, and she realised it wasn't her body but her house that was vibrating. *What the hell?* She spat the toothpaste in the sink and hurried out of the bathroom to hear voices echoing up the staircase of the two-storey townhouse.

Uncle Tim? Did he order contractors to come in and forget to tell me? It wouldn't be the first time he had forgotten to tell her about some work being done. Then again, she wasn't in a position to complain—he'd rented the house to her at a more than charitable price since she'd first moved to the city. Tim called it a family discount, but he wasn't really her uncle; he and Autumn's father used to run an investment firm together before her parents settled in the country after her accident. When Autumn had got a job in Wickford six years ago, she couldn't afford to live on her own, and she was too shy to live with others. She didn't like people seeing her in pain. Not because she was ashamed, but because people—not all, but some—tended to treat her as though she were contagious. Tim's offer had been a life-saver. It wasn't like he needed the money; he owned most of the commercial property in Wickford.

Still, he could have given her some warning if he was going to do some renovations. He usually called to tell her. She went to her bedroom and looked for her phone to call him, but only her earphones and a book lay on her bedside table. Autumn groaned when she noticed her phone charger was also missing. *I must have left it in the kitchen when I was practising.* She rarely used her phone; she didn't have social media, and her parents only rang on Fridays for their weekly check-in, when they tried to talk her into returning to the comfort of her library job in their small town of Islacore and away from the stage.

The banging intensified, forcing Autumn from her thoughts. Creeping downstairs, she went to peek at what was going on. She hated talking to people she didn't know, but not as much as she didn't like people in her house.

"Why do I get the feeling it's going to be one of those days I regret getting out of bed?" she muttered, tightening the dressing gown around herself. She thought about getting dressed, but she didn't want anyone coming upstairs while she was half-naked. She wouldn't survive the mortification, and if she didn't know why they were here, it was only rational to assume they didn't know she was there. *Tim must have given them a key to get in.*

The vibration started again, but this time it was accompanied by faint drilling. She found her lavender front door wide open and two women coming out of her sitting room, carrying her couch in their arms. They wore matching uniforms, and she read **WE MOVE IT SO YOU DON'T LOSE IT** on their backs. *At least they aren't burglars...*

"I don't mean to be rude, but what are you doing in my house and with my furniture?" she asked.

The women only looked her over as though she was bothering them. "Sorry to disturb you—we were told the house would be empty," one said.

Autumn's jaw dropped. *Who the hell told them I wouldn't be here? It certainly wasn't Tim. I've already paid him rent this month, and I've never mentioned moving out.* She was so stunned, she almost missed the rest of what the blonde woman said.

"The owner told us to remove the furniture from the front room to make room for the desk and his bed. We shouldn't be too much longer. Sorry to have disturbed you so early." She said it as though the explanation should make perfect sense, but Autumn was even more confused. *The desk—his bed? Whose bed? Tim can't be moving in.*

"Please put my couch back where you found it. This is *my* house. There is no *his* anything," Autumn said, trying to sound calm, placing her hand on the couch.

"Orders are orders. Take it up with the boss," the other mover said, shoving past Autumn and bringing the couch down the steps of the terraced house.

Stomping towards the first-floor sitting room, Autumn found her TV covered in plastic wrap and the rest of her furniture already missing. *Where is my furniture?* she thought, taking a breath, trying not to let the sudden invasion of her home overwhelm her. Most of the panic was currently overridden by her confusion and desire to know what the hell was going on. A large desk with multiple monitors had taken its place, and the floor was littered with motorcycle helmets and what looked like Star Wars figurines. *This stuff definitely doesn't belong to Uncle Tim,* she thought, looking from someone drilling holes in the wall to the block of shelves she guessed would house his figurines resting against the wall, ready to be put up. She fisted her hands as the drilling continued to grate on her nerves. *Fucking sleeping pills. I must have slept through them coming in. The one time I take them!*

A man in the same moving company's overalls reached for her TV, and she placed a hand on his forearm.

"Don't even think about it! Who owns all this?" she demanded. "Where are you taking my things?"

The older man looked at the strange belongings. "No need to be alarmed, miss. The boss told us to put the old furniture in his storage unit across town and bring the new in. We have a bigger TV in the van. No point in keeping this one," he tried to reassure her. Over his shoulder, Autumn saw that the drilling was for not just shelves; speakers now hung from the corners of the ceiling.

"I don't need a bigger TV. Can you please give me the name of who ordered you here?" she asked, then was distracted by a different man lifting her vintage stereo. She blocked his path, her arms extended, and he frowned. "Put that down, or you will regret the day you set foot in this house!"

Her words must have struck a chord because both men stepped away from her personal items and left the front room, but not before she noticed them exchanging annoyed glances. *They think I'm being unreasonable!*

Once she'd driven the contractors out, Autumn closed the door to the front room with a sigh of relief. At least some things were safe inside. *The rest can be rescued,* she figured, noting the two moving vans sitting outside her front door.

"We're only trying to do our job, miss. If you have an issue, speak to the owner," one of the men grumbled as they headed back to their van.

Autumn groaned in frustration. *The owner? Whoever 'he' is isn't the owner!* She took a breath to collect her thoughts. "Excuse me, can I please ask where the owner of these belongings is?" she asked one of the workers who had just entered her home, carrying a coffee machine that looked far too complicated towards the kitchen.

"Follow me. Mr Wells is in the kitchen. Sorry about the lads—one of the girls told me you weren't expecting us. I'm sure once you talk, you'll have this whole matter sorted," she answered, leading Autumn towards the kitchen with a glance at her cat headband. When the helpful mover turned, Autumn took off the ears and gritted her teeth in embarrassment.

Mr Wells? I've never heard Tim mention anyone by that name. There's no way he sold the house while I'm still living in it. Autumn headed through the wood-floored hall to the open-plan kitchen. A man whom she guessed to be in his early thirties stood against her kitchen island with a phone to his ear, wearing a suit tailored so well to his build that it could almost be considered sinful. Autumn might have thought him attractive if he hadn't invaded her home at dawn and furthered her misery on an already tough morning.

"Thank you for your help," she whispered and waited for the mover to put down the coffee machine before she approached the stranger. "Mr Wells? Sorry to bother you, but could you please tell me why you are here in my home?" she asked, trying to sound reasonable.

Mr Wells looked at her dressing gown before turning his back on her, though not before his amused smile caused her embarrassment to turn to anger.

"Sorry, I was interrupted. What were you saying?" Mr Wells continued with his conversation, annoyance evident in his deep voice as he continued his conversation about some game.

Autumn gaped at his audacity. *Is he seriously going to pretend that I'm not standing right here?* Any lingering attraction immediately turned to loathing thanks to his attitude. She rose up on her tiptoes, bringing them face to face. His dark eyebrows pulled tightly together as he frowned at her. He had a small scar on his lip, a flaw in his handsome face.

"Are you just going to ignore me?" she hissed, not caring about being polite anymore.

"I'm on the phone. Do you mind?" he mouthed.

"And movers are removing *my* things on *your* orders! What are you doing in my—"

"I'll have to call you back. I'm dealing with a small issue," he said into the phone. His dark brown eyes fixed on Autumn as he hung up, and she didn't need to be told she was the 'small' issue.

She relaxed her shoulders, trying to compose herself. Then she saw her piano and the plants sitting on top of it from the corner of her eye, and rage coiled within her. *How fucking dare he!*

"What are you doing in my home?" she barked, loudly enough for those working in the kitchen to hear. They stopped working to stare at her, and she pointed towards the door, telling them silently to GET OUT. She spied her phone on the counter. Maybe she should call the police, or at least check to see if Uncle Tim had anything to do with this invasion.

Mr Wells straightened and looked down at her. "You must be Autumn. Tim told me I'd be sharing the house for a time, but it seems Tim forgot to tell you."

She folded her arms. "Forgot to tell me what? Why would we be sharing the house?" she demanded, tired of being left out of the loop.

He actually looked apologetic, offering her a charming smile and extending a hand towards her. "I thought you knew I'd be coming. My name is Elijah Wells, and we'll be sharing because I rented half the house." He extended his hand towards her, but she ignored the gesture and charming smile.

"I wish it was nice to meet you. Maybe it would have been if you hadn't invaded my house with no warning! I wasn't informed you were coming. I'm sorry to disappoint you, but there is no way we are sharing the house."

Elijah didn't seem fazed. "Pardon my *invasion*, but it was a last-minute decision. I'm afraid my being here isn't up to you. Tim offered me the house for a few months, and since you're apparently going on tour soon, he didn't think it would be an issue." He circled her as he spoke, but she refused to be intimidated.

"The tour isn't for another five weeks. My leaving is only a *might* at this point—nothing is confirmed. I don't think either of us wants to be sharing the house indefinitely," she pointed out. Why would Tim even offer the house to this man? She was only considering going on tour with her company the week after the showcase *if* the showcase went well and she somehow survived her solo. And even if she did go on tour for three months, she still planned on coming home.

"How do I even know you're telling the truth? I've never even heard Tim mention you, and I've known him pretty much my whole life," she added. He could just be some psycho! *A tall, dark, handsome psycho. But when did hotness ever stop someone from being dangerous?*

Elijah squared his shoulders, clearly growing tired of their conversation. "Tim and I are old acquaintances. I just came back from abroad and I needed a place to live and work while I get my company off the ground. He was kind enough to offer this place. Let's say he owes me a favour."

That only left her with more questions. *Acquaintances? Tim wants me to share my home with some random guy he owes a favour to? And he wants to work from home, which means he'll always be here. This isn't happening.* Her worst nightmare was coming to life, even if it came wrapped in a pretty, tailored package.

"I don't care what Tim owes you. He never told me you were coming, and trust me, you don't want to live with me—" She was cut off by more drilling.

"Whether I want to live with you or not is beside the point. I've already paid for six months, and then I'll be out of your hair. If you don't like it, take it up with Tim. He's the landlord, so it's his decision, not yours," Elijah said.

Autumn realised he had backed her up against the counter. She considered shoving him, but she didn't want to touch him or his immaculately ironed shirt. "He might own the house, but this is my home. I won't share it with a stranger," she ground out as he leaned over her, a smile creasing his scarred lip.

"Once we get to know each other, I think I could grow on you. You might even be gone by next month. After that, you'll never have to see me again." His gaze fixed on hers confidently, as if she'd already agreed. If he hadn't been so smug, it might have worked.

"Whether I leave or not is up to me, and stop looking at me like that, it won't work," she said, breaking eye contact. "You can't work *or* live here. I have to practise, and—" She stopped. *I don't owe him any explanation. I cover my rent; why would Tim do this?*

The drilling started again, and she couldn't think. "Can you ask them to stop for a minute?"

Elijah shouted for them to stop, and they did so immediately. She was surprised he'd listened. *Maybe he won't be too unreasonable.*

"Why would a grown man want to share with a stranger when you don't have to?" Autumn asked, wanting, *needing* him to see reason.

He shrugged. "I don't have to explain myself to you, but since you've been blindsided...I'll admit I'd be happier in my own place, but my company is developing, and renting business space in the city is expensive and hard to find. I moved home rather quickly and didn't have time to search for a place to live. Since Tim is an investor in my company, he offered me the house—or half, I should say." Elijah plugged in the coffee machine by the fridge while he spoke, and Autumn was glad for the space he put between them. She ran her hands through her hair. She understood his reasoning, but she didn't want the solution to his problems to be the cause of her own.

"I understand that Tim wanted to help you, and I wish you all the best in your search, but Tim never talked to me about this arrangement, and I like my privacy. Trust me, you don't want to live with me. I play the piano at all hours, and you won't be able to work," she said, though it came out more as a plea. "Surely, there's someone you can stay with?"

"Nope. But if you really have a problem, leave. I won't keep you," he said, opening *her* fridge. Her anger rose to new levels as he took her watermelon slices.

"Make yourself at home," she gritted out.

He took a bite, wiping the juice from the corner of his mouth. "Don't mind if I do." He winked. "I'm happy to share." He offered her a slice of her own food.

There is no way he's staying here. She crossed her arms, silently rejecting the offer.

"Forgive me, just trying to lighten the mood. I have a lot to get done today, and since I've explained myself, if you wouldn't mind leaving us to it?" His eyes landed on her bare legs. "You should probably get dressed; there are quite a few movers here today."

"I'm a grown woman! You can't tell me what to do," Autumn snapped, trying to find her composure. If he did live here, she'd never feel at ease.

"Then you should act like one. Accept the situation. Let the movers get on with their work. This matter is between us," he reasoned.

She wanted to throw the mug on the counter at him, but it was her favourite. Anger clearly wasn't getting her anywhere, so she softened her attitude. "I can't move out. This place is close to the theatre where I work."

"Then we should both stay. I can see that my sudden arrival has been a shock between us, but Tim told me you're like a daughter to him. He assured me how nice you were," Elijah said. She noticed his gaze lingering on her hair, and she wondered if he was trying to figure her out as she was him.

"I'm nice to those who don't invade my home without warning," she countered coldly, picking up her phone. "You'll leave my home before the day is out, so stop putting holes in my walls."

"Our walls," he corrected her.

"Not for long. Tim will get this straightened out. In the meantime, *no* permanent changes to potentially shared spaces. No drilling in the kitchen. Even if I allow you to live here, which I'm not going to do, you don't get to just change the layout of my kitchen without at least politely asking me about it." She moved around him, but he reached for her hand.

"Wait!" He blocked her path as she dodged his grasp and made to leave.

With a sigh, she crossed her arms, giving him one last chance.

"Let's not get off on the wrong foot. I should have introduced myself before I moved my stuff in. I honestly thought Tim would clear it with you." Elijah extended his hand once again, and a strand of hair fell over his forehead. "Can we start over? Elijah."

Autumn got the feeling he was used to getting what he wanted. If his looks didn't win others over, then his charm probably did.

"Autumn Adler," she replied, taking his hand. She didn't want him to think she was unreasonable. "I've rented this place for nearly six years. Alone. Tim probably didn't tell me because he knew I wouldn't agree," she added, and realised Elijah was still holding her hand. He dropped it gently.

"I understand your want for privacy, and I promise to stay out of your way, but there's more than enough room for the two of us. I'll find a place once my latest deal closes, and you'll never see me again," he promised.

She shook her head. They were going in circles.

"How about we split the house? You rent the top floor—I won't go upstairs," Elijah suggested. "This is a two-floored terraced house, right? I'll keep to the ground floor front room, and we'll share the communal spaces. C'mon, I'm only using the front room—as an office *and* a bedroom." He looked at the sliding doors that divided the front room from the kitchen. "Close the doors and I disappear. You said you need to practise; I won't move your piano, since it's in the communal space, and I'll give you space to practise. Tim told me you were a pianist."

His plan was reasonable, almost considerate. *It's only one room, and I could just ignore him...* She almost opened her mouth to agree, but then she pictured it. Getting up on a particularly anxious morning and having to practise with a stranger in the next room listening instead of the blissful solitude she was used to. Having a particularly bad pain day and feeling like she couldn't get dressed but she had to because she might run into her housemate. Never being able to sit in the kitchen with a cup of tea without wondering if he'd walk in.

"No. I'm sorry, but I have my routine and I can't have it disturbed," she said flatly.

He groaned, and for the first time, she saw a crack in his charm. "It's my understanding that you don't have a contract with Tim. I do," he said bluntly.

She didn't like how he was looking at her. It was too piercing. She hated that she was the first to look away.

"I practise at all hours, and it'll affect your business," she argued.

"Noise doesn't bother me." Elijah shrugged again, crinkling his suit as he folded his arms.

"It's your noise that bothers *me*," Her tone was harsher than she'd intended, but surely he could see how invasive his request was. From the computer and multiple screens to the tailored suit and motorcycle helmets, it was obvious he could afford a place of his own.

"I'll stick to my space. We share the rest and do our best to stay out of each other's way," Elijah said flatly, walking away from her as though the conversation was over.

"There's only one shower, and it's on *my* floor. You don't plan on showering in the foreseeable future?" She smirked when he stopped in his tracks.

"I get the feeling you're an only child," he muttered under his breath.

Autumn glared at him for making assumptions about her, even if they were true. "How many siblings I do or don't have has nothing to do with our living arrangements," she snapped, wondering where he was going with such a statement.

"It's not going to help the situation because, clearly, no one taught you how to share," he explained. "You're overcomplicating matters when this is really quite a straightforward arrangement." He undid the top button on his shirt. Good, she was getting under his skin.

"You come into my home at seven in the morning, remove my belongings without permission and start drilling with no warning, and *I'm* complicating things?"

"Boss? Where do you want these installed?" A young man walked past her with tech she didn't recognise, looking startled by her presence.

"With the computers, front room," Elijah told him, and the guy looked between them before disappearing into the other room.

"What's with all the tech? What are you, a hacker?"

"No, they tend to stick to books and movies. I run a game development company. We have one game so far and another in the works, hence why I am here in your delightful company."

Autumn knew what it was like to make sacrifices for a dream. She could respect him a little for that. "You think you can run it from one room?"

"How I run my business is none of your concern." He smiled, exposing his white teeth.

Did he step out of a damn romance novel with that smile? If only he had the personality to match it! She pushed the thought from her mind. She was growing tired of the back-and-forth, though it seemed like he was enjoying the argument. "I don't care how you run it so long as you don't run it from here. So long as it doesn't involve you taking my furniture and putting it God knows where. That's my property, not Tim's! Don't think about removing another item without my permission." *I've never lived with anyone before, and I'm certainly not going to start with him.*

Her phone vibrated in her hand. It was a text from Nina; she was on her way. Autumn needed to get ready to leave. She didn't want Elijah to answer the door. Another glance at her phone showed her all the messages from the orchestra group chat ordering their coffee; she'd forgotten it was her turn to pick up the orders. She quickly texted Nina, asking her to pick them up.

"I have to leave, but"—she silenced her phone—"don't get too comfortable. We'll continue this discussion later."

"You're leaving? We haven't finished! And don't worry, your furniture and belongings are safe in my storage unit. They'll be returned once we go our separate ways—in mint condition," Elijah said, raising an eyebrow.

"Feel free to converse with yourself. I have rehearsals," she said, not offering any more information. "Keep to your own floor. Don't move my stuff *anywhere*—not until I talk to Tim—and while I'm out, no major changes at all until this is sorted. Otherwise, you're wasting everyone's time, including your own, if we come up with a different solution." The morning's confrontation had caused her shoulders to tense. The last thing she needed was a tension headache to round out her already aching back from her fitful sleep. She liked her life calm and predictable; he was a threat to that.

"I'm sure we can figure this out! I'll be here when you get back," Elijah called as she left him to get ready, almost running into his movers.

"Please get your plants off my piano!" she yelled back. He dared to laugh, apparently finding her temper entertaining. His positive outlook on their current predicament only furthered her irritation. It had taken a lot of careful consideration to arrange her furnishing just how she liked it. Everything was easily accessible and in its rightful place, so she never had to think or worry about where her things were when she was having a bad pain day.

Before she'd even reached the stairs, the drilling was vibrating through her once again.

Chapter Two

Autumn

Autumn returned upstairs and dressed in a simple black wrap dress. *Why the hell didn't Tim talk to me before inviting a stranger into my house? Did he think I was overstaying my welcome? The last time I dropped off my rent to his office, he seemed a little off, distracted... Maybe there's more to this than I know.* She swept her hair up in a gold claw clip, the morning sun illuminating the golden highlights in her auburn hair. *I pay my rent on time; I've never had a noise complaint...* She stared into the circular mirror on her dresser, applying her favourite fire-engine red lipstick. Checking out her window, she decided it was still too chilly to go without tights, so she grabbed them from her dresser and yanked them up over her thighs and full hips.

Once she was ready, she checked her May schedule taped to her mirror and groaned in frustration. With today's rehearsal schedule, she wouldn't have time to stop by Tim's office today; she'd have to call him after practice. She picked up her sheet music with the corrections from the day before from her unmade bed, fighting the desire to stop and make it neatly. Elijah's sudden appearance had thrown her careful morning routine into chaos. She hastily turned off the fairy lights on her headboard and the bookshelves above it.

If Tim wanted me out, surely he would have warned me so I could have found other arrangements. I could have moved in with Nina for a time...but what would I do with my piano? She wondered if her day could get any worse.

Downstairs, the drilling enveloped her once again. All she wanted to do was get back into her pyjamas and throw everyone out of the house, but she had to get to rehearsals. There were only four weeks left until the showcase, and she couldn't miss it just because some stubborn wall of muscle decided to bulldoze her morning.

"Do you mind?" she hissed, dodging a mover who passed her in the hallway as she attempted to put on her boots and long black coat. The worker merely grunted in response and left the door open. Cherry blossom petals wafted in through the open door. Autumn was excited for the warmer months, looking forward to getting out of dark colours and into her favourite pastels. Today, however, black was most fitting. She was in mourning for her privacy.

In the kitchen, Elijah was nowhere in sight when she grabbed her painkillers and a heat pack from the kitchen medicine cabinet. She hesitated upon closing the pastel pink cabinet door, afraid he would discover her prescriptions, supplements, and adhesive heat strips. *How much has Tim told him about me? I doubt he would have told him about my accident.* She shook away the worry of him knowing more about her than she did about him. There wasn't time to move her medicines to the upstairs bathroom—she kept everything so well stocked that her supply would carry anyone through the apocalypse. *He'll probably be too busy organising his own things to notice mine. If he's still here when I get back, I'll move them.*

She walked down the steps to the stone path dividing her front garden, which was in awful need of care. Then again, Autumn liked the wild look and how everything was covered in cherry blossom petals. Beyond the garden gate, she noticed a slick black motorcycle in the small parking space she had never used. *Makes sense, considering the number of motorcycle helmets.* There was always something a little sexy about a motorbike, she admitted mentally, only to have it ruined by the sound of the door opening behind her.

"Autumn!" Elijah called out. He stood at the top of the steps with his arms folded.

She gripped the small iron gate at the end of the pathway. *What could he possibly want now? Maybe he wants my bedroom while he's at it!*

"You don't need to wake the neighbours," she hissed. She really didn't want them poking their noses in. The older women who lived next door were always trying to set her up with their son. Then again, if they saw her with Elijah, they might stop asking about that.

"You weren't planning on leaving without saying goodbye, were you?" he said, and any thought of using him to her advantage was eclipsed by her desire for him to disappear.

"That's exactly what I was planning to do," she retorted, pulling her tote bag higher on her shoulder.

"Before you make your escape, what's your alarm code? Tim didn't know, and I have to go out for a meeting," Elijah explained, following her down the path.

She smirked, pleased to have the upper hand—though judging from Elijah's relaxed demeanour, their co-habitation didn't bother him nearly as much as it was bothering her.

"Figure it out. I have to get to rehearsals," she said, and though she prided herself on being a reasonable person, she turned her back on his deep frown. It was oh, so satisfying. For the first time this morning, she smiled, and considered skipping down the path.

"Autumn!" Elijah called again.

Delighting in his irritation, Autumn waved smugly before closing the gate behind her. Once she was clear of the intruder, she wondered how he'd got in with the movers without the alarm code. *I set it last night. It was raining pretty hard, though; maybe there was a blackout?* It wouldn't have been the first time.

Her thoughts were disrupted when her phone rang.

"Hey, you almost here?" Nina's warm voice was like a comforting hug after the morning she'd had.

"I'm only around the corner—be there in a second. I've sent you the coffee orders for everything. I'll pay when I arrive," Autumn said, avoiding the puddles on the path from last night's spring shower. "You won't believe the morning I've had."

Nina chuckled. "I can't wait to hear what made *you* late. Don't worry, I got the list. I'm in the queue now."

Autumn didn't want to tell her about Elijah until she got her morning coffee. Hanging up, she dipped under the deep blue awning which protected her favourite coffee shop, Brewtiful Beans. The smell of coffee mixed with aftershave and perfume greeted her as the usual crowd of suits waited for their drinks. She gently nudged her way through, searching for Nina. The smell of freshly made pastries made her mouth water and stomach growl. She realised she hadn't eaten, which was a terrible idea with the painkillers she planned to take after such a tense night. There wasn't time to queue, so she rooted in her bag, relieved to find an emergency protein bar. *I can eat on the way.* Finally, she spotted Nina with the trays of coffee at their usual table, waving a pink doughnut box to get her attention. Autumn had never loved her friend more. Doughnuts were far nicer than protein bars.

"What would I do without you?" she exclaimed, mocking a bow.

"You sounded stressed, so I figured some doughnuts were in order," Nina said, embracing her. She was a hugger, and this morning Autumn returned the embrace eagerly. She loved that her friend knew her so well.

"Since when do you love my hugs?" Nina asked when Autumn didn't pull away early as she usually did.

"I needed one after the morning I've had," Autumn admitted, giving her one last squeeze.

"Bad pain night? Rehearsals yesterday went a bit long. I wouldn't be surprised if that caused it," Nina said, zipping up her faux-fur lime jacket. She was the queen of bold fashion choices; the outfits combined with her jet black pixie cut and tattoos made it impossible not to notice her.

"No, it wasn't the rehearsal, just a nightmare." Autumn diverted her attention to the pink box and pulled out a cookies-and-cream doughnut, taking a generous bite before picking up the coffee with her name.

"You haven't had a nightmare in a while. Could be the solo?" Nina suggested.

Autumn nodded, taking a gulp to let the sweet vanilla syrup perk her up. Coffee and doughnuts were the perfect end to a horrible morning. *I wonder if the invader's coffee machine makes coffee as good as this. I could always keep the coffee machine and get rid of him.*

"Probably, but this time it was hyper-realistic. I could even hear myself trying to calm myself down," she said, warming her hands on the cup. "Usually I get so lost in the memories, I can't tell it's a dream."

"You need some time off. All you do is play, and your body probably needs a break. You've been doing back-to-back musicals and now rehearsing for the show," Nina pointed out, stacking the trays of coffee.

"I'm perfectly fine. It was one night. If I couldn't manage, I would tell you," Autumn countered. "Once the showcase is over, I'll give my body a break." She knew she was pushing it, but she needed all the practice she could get.

"Uh-huh. What about the tour?" Nina said, picking up the trays. Autumn avoided her knowing gaze.

"I haven't decided whether I'm going yet. I want to see how the showcase goes first," she said. Anyway, it wasn't entirely up to her; their conductor wanted to make sure she was up for it too.

"So long as you're happy, I'm happy," Nina said as Autumn held the door for her.

Nina was one of the few people she never felt the need to hide her pain from. The first day they'd met, Autumn had collapsed during an audition due to the overworked nerves in her back. She'd hit her head, and the conductor had insisted on calling an ambulance. Autumn hadn't expected Nina to stay with her, but not only had she done so, but she'd never made her feel like her pain was a nuisance. Nothing bonds or tests a friendship faster than a night in A&E.

"Thank you, and thank you for saving my butt this morning. I'll transfer you the money for the coffee in the car," Autumn said, wanting to change the subject before they reached Nina's vintage beetle.

"No rush, but I have to ask—if the tour isn't stressing you out, what happened this morning? Now, where did I put my keys?"

Autumn waited patiently. Nina losing things was a frequent issue, but usually, they turned up. She took a sip of coffee. "I have an invader."

"I need more information. Animal or human? Continue." Nina's eyes narrowed as she placed the coffee trays on the car roof and continued to root in her bag. "Wait, please tell me this isn't about rats or spiders. I need my coffee first if we're going to be discussing rodents." Nina shivered, and Autumn shook with laughter, knowing how much her friend detested all manner of things creepy and crawly.

"My landlord, Tim, rented out the first floor of my house to some guy he invested in," Autumn explained. "I would have preferred rats." Now it was Nina's turn to laugh.

Autumn looked through the car window and noticed that the keys were on the seat. She pulled on the handle, and the door opened, much to Nina's surprise.

"I thought I locked it!"

"The keys are on the seat," Autumn pointed out, and Nina frowned.

"I must have got distracted when I texted you." She sighed. "Thank God it wasn't stolen!"

Autumn felt theft wasn't likely since the old Bug was more suited to the scrapyard, but she would never say that to Nina. The car was her friend's pride and joy.

Nina took the keys from the seat. "Mystery solved. Now, back to your invader. This is amazing—you're literally living my rom-com dream! I didn't think this stuff actually happened in real life."

"How is sharing a house with a complete stranger a dream for you?" Autumn demanded, brushing her hair away from her face as the wind picked up.

"If you read more romances, you would understand," Nina told her, raising her eyebrows suggestively. "The sexual tension, the mystery..." She winked, and Autumn tried not to roll her eyes.

The only tension between us is frustration. She thought of him standing over her, the charged atmosphere...no, that had been irritation, not attraction.

"I love a romance as much as the next person, but waking up to drilling and a stranger in my home is not what I'd have in mind for Prince Charming's arrival," she said, placing the box of doughnuts in the back seat.

"You could use a good drilling," Nina muttered, the engine rattling as she turned the key.

Autumn would have thrown a doughnut at her, but she wouldn't waste such deliciousness. The last thing she wanted to do was talk about her dating life. "This isn't a movie, this is my life! Right now, a stranger is moving into my house!"

"Fine, I'll stick to serious questions. What does he do?" Nina asked, raising her defined black eyebrows. "Is he attractive? Single?"

Autumn groaned. "He does something with games. From the one conversation we've had, he's arrogant, smug, he knows how much his smile is worth, and I don't plan on falling for his bullshit charm."

Nina smirked as they set off for the theatre. "So he *is* charming and attractive!"

"No, he *tried* to charm me. I wasn't going to let him get away with ordering movers into the house without telling me he was coming."

Nina was clearly amused by the situation. "Okay, so he lacks manners. Maybe you got off on the wrong foot. I'm sure he was surprised to find a hostile redhead in his house."

"I'm not hostile, and if I was, I was justified," Autumn said, gripping her coffee so tightly the lid popped off.

Nina held her hands up in submission before quickly placing them back on the steering wheel. "Okay, yes. He handled it wrong. Does this non-charming guy have a name?"

"Elijah." Autumn's mind drifted to the white shirt that emphasised his broad shoulders.

"Did you get his last name? We should look him up. He might have socials we can stalk—might be able to find something to use against him," Nina pointed out. Autumn appreciated her willingness to help.

"Wells, but no prying. The less I know about him, the better. He won't be staying long if I have anything to say about it," she said, looking out the drizzle-covered passenger window.

"Maybe him staying isn't the worst thing. You need someone to shake up your life," Nina said, eying her hesitantly.

"I like my life just how it is. I have my piano, I have you. What else could I need?" Autumn argued.

"There's more to life than work."

Autumn didn't want to hear it. Her pain therapist told her the same thing, but she didn't want to have another setback by adding more to her life. She was content, and that was enough.

"I'm fine. Happy, even. Please, let's not have this conversation again." This morning had been hard enough as it was.

Nina pursed her lips. "I'm sure he'll be gone soon enough. Once you've set your mind on something, nothing can stop you," she said as they pulled into the busy car park at the back of the theatre.

They headed in through the back entrance, moving through the dark passages until they reached a rush of voices and broken music as the others warmed up.

"You're here! I was about to call," Aimee said once they came through the red velvet side curtains. Aimee was the lead cellist, with a caffeine habit that rivalled everyone else's.

"No need to send out a search party for your coffee. One Americano with extra shots," Autumn said, handing her the tray with Aimee's coffee. Autumn loved Aimee's wigs, always changing from one day to the next; today, her pink hair was braided to perfection.

"Sasaki wanted me here early to go through one of the movements alone. I swear I never want to hear Vivaldi's movement again," Aimee said as Laurna came up beside her and kissed her cheek, her violin still in hand.

"Once you have your coffee, you'll love it again."

Aimee shook her head. "There's not enough coffee in the world."

Laurna took her chai tea from the tray. "I think you love caffeine more than me," she said, and Aimee squinted in consideration.

"Of course I love you more; you supply me with caffeine," Aimee teased, and Laurna rolled her eyes.

"I know how you feel. Sasaki has been at me about the Winter movement," Nina began.

They only had a few more moments to chat, but Autumn was thankful for the distraction as they neared the performance. Staring out at the empty audience to the empty boxes, she was looking forward to feeling part of something bigger than herself when they played. She'd been part of Wickford City's Chamber Orchestra, which comprised about fifty members, for almost six years. She never tired of the theatre that had stood for over one hundred years and would probably still be standing long after they all finished their careers.

Only half the team were in today, and they quickly devoured their coffees and pastries before their conductor, Mr Sasaki, appeared from the wings of the stage in his open waistcoat, glasses perched at the end of his nose.

"Morning, everyone. If we could take our places, we can get started," he said, taking centre stage.

"Morning, sir," was echoed in response as everyone dispersed and took their chairs on the tiered stage. Autumn took one final sip of coffee before she sat at the piano and laid out her sheet music.

"Could you lead us in, Autumn?" Sasaki said, and she eagerly obliged, letting her fingers graze the keys. Losing herself in the melody, she was determined to focus and forget all about Elijah Wells and his infuriating smirk.

Chapter Three

Elijah

"That didn't go to plan," Elijah sighed, leaning over the gate, unable to resist the urge to smile as he watched the small, fiery creature storm off down the road.

Tim had assured him Autumn wouldn't mind sharing the house since it was only for a short while. *Then again, she probably wouldn't be so hostile if she hadn't found a strange man in her kitchen. How was I to know she wasn't going on tour? I certainly didn't plan on sharing with her indefinitely.* He hadn't expected Tim, a stickler for details, to not inform Autumn of his arrival. *Could Tim have done this on purpose in a terrible attempt at setting us up? Doesn't seem like something he would do. Perhaps he simply made a mistake.*

He scrubbed his freshly shaved jaw. He was annoyed at himself for reacting to her barbs, but he hadn't been able to resist. Her temper intrigued him as much as her striking green eyes—how she wasn't afraid to stare him down. *Hopefully, once she calms down, we can talk again*, he decided, reaching for his phone as he made his way back to the house.

"You could have warned me I would be sharing a house with a she-demon," he said when Tim picked up the phone after a few rings.

"Is that any way to greet your father? No 'Good morning. Thank you for giving me a place to live when you suddenly decided to return home and ask for a healthy investment?'" Tim said.

Elijah dropped the phone to his side for a second to keep calm. *Estranged* father, more like. He was the product of his father's extra-marital affair, which wasn't exactly publicised in his social circles. It was why he'd taken his mother's name, Wells.

"You get as much out of this arrangement as I do. I take it you didn't tell Autumn about my arrival?" One of the clauses to receiving the investment had been that he had to live in this house. He suspected it was because his father wanted to keep him close even though they had spent their lives at a very comfortable distance.

"I take it that Autumn is the she-demon? She is the daughter of one of my oldest friends. There's nothing demonic in her nature," Tim answered.

"Then her being blindsided this morning is a misunderstanding and you did talk to her about my moving?" Elijah asked pointedly, moving to the front room, which was to be his office. It was an absolute mess, half-emptied boxes and clothes everywhere. Two movers, who'd finished putting up the shelves on the grey walls, left him to talk in private. They had also returned Autumn's couch from the truck since he'd forgotten to order his own. He hoped it would win him some points with her.

Tim cleared his throat, and Elijah waited for the excuse.

"Are you still there?" he asked when it didn't come, dropping into his desk chair. Turning on the computer, he waited for the screens on the far wall to glow.

"I didn't get a chance to speak with her. I thought you were moving in next Friday. When we spoke last, you said your flight didn't get in until next week."

"Since we last spoke, it *is* next week," Elijah said with a sigh, running his hand through his hair. "It was one of your terms that I stay here, but I can leave..." He did want to get out from under his father's thumb. However, he was in the process of closing the biggest deal of his life with Nirosoft, and the last thing he needed to be doing was boxing up and searching for another place to live.

His father's silence was followed by a quick curse. "No, we agreed. I'll fix this. I'll call her," Tim began, then paused. "She'll be in rehearsals now. If I interrupt her, it will only worsen the situation. I'll text her later and tell her this was my decision."

"Fine. I wouldn't have taken the house if she disagreed to my being here," Elijah said, and Tim chuckled.

"She's very passionate about her privacy, and not a fan of people. Give her some time, and she'll warm up. I think you'll be good for her."

"I'm not here to be set up. I'm here to work," Elijah protested. He supposed it might be fun to wind her up. But his mind drifted to her pressed up against the counter, her eyes staring up at him defiantly, and his body definitely wanted to do more than wind her up.

"I wasn't suggesting a set up. Autumn is like a daughter to me, and I think it will do her good to be around others. Did you tell her about our situation?" Tim inquired.

Elijah felt like a cold bucket of water had been thrown over him. Tim might be *like* a father to Autumn, but he was *his* actual parent.

"No. I don't think she needs to know. I know how you like to keep your personal matters private. I wouldn't want her to have a poor opinion of you," he said, clenching his jaw as he heard Tim sigh in relief. He wished his father cared more about their relationship than the opinions of others, but after thirty-two years, he wasn't expecting any miracles.

"Good. I don't want her to misunderstand," Tim said.

Sure, he might have looked after his son financially growing up, but it had been mostly in exchange for his and his mum's silence. The day he'd graduated, Elijah had left Wickford to put as much distance between them as possible. If it hadn't been for one of his investors pulling out at the last minute, he wouldn't be at his father's mercy now.

"I'm sure you'll figure out a way to make it work. Agree to cohabit? You're both adults," Tim said.

Elijah rolled his eyes. "I don't think she'll agree to anything I ask for, unless it's to go for a long walk off a short pier," he said, swivelling in his chair. He didn't have the time to pack up his life once again while he was working on the biggest deal of his career. His company was relying on the sale of his latest game so they could pay off their investors.

"I'll talk to her, and I'm sure once she understands we didn't mean to blindside her, she'll be more accommodating," Tim said.

"The sooner you talk, the better. I don't want to be the villain in anyone's story." Elijah stared through to the kitchen and remembered to take the plants off of her piano. He would put them in the conservatory Autumn apparently only used for fake plants. He considered it a crime to waste such a beautiful space on plastic. "What about her own family?" he asked.

Tim hesitated, which piqued his curiosity.

"They live in the countryside. They are rather close," Tim said, and it was clear from his tone that he wasn't going to elaborate. "If you want to know more about her, then ask her."

I don't think she would answer if I did. Elijah noticed a box of Autumn's belongings in the corner of the room. Unable to resist the urge to pry, he wandered over. Inside was a photo of two girls in their teens. One was clearly Autumn—the red hair was a dead giveaway—and she had her arm around a girl with thick glasses and dark hair. *Mollie and Autumn* was scrawled on the back.

Feeling like he was invading her privacy, he put it back in the box and pushed it under the couch.

"She's protective of her space, but she's all bark. We had a deal, and I won't let you back out," Tim said. "I would hate to have to pull my investment."

Elijah sighed. He regretted taking the investment, but once the deal was closed with Nirosoft, he'd pay him back and that would be that. "There's no need for that. I'm not going anywhere," he said, hoping Autumn would understand that he was just as cornered as she was.

"Good. Now get settled. I don't want this matter to distract you from your work," Tim ordered, always thinking about the bottom line.

"You don't need to worry about my work ethic," Elijah said dryly. "But before you go, the alarm wasn't set when I came in this morning. I have a meeting later, and I don't want to leave without setting it. You don't know where she would keep any information like that, do you?"

"Sorry, I haven't a clue. Odd that she didn't set the alarm last night; she's usually very careful," Tim said, sounding concerned. Elijah frowned in disappointment, hunting around the kitchen for the fiftieth time in case he stumbled across a sheet of paper with the information on it. Tim was still talking, but Elijah only came back to the conversation when he said," She didn't tell you before she left?"

"No, she didn't, and took great pleasure in leaving me in the lurch. I don't want to leave without setting it after the whole street has seen movers," he admitted, frustrated. He smoothed his hands over his suit trousers, dusty from the move. He was only wearing the damn thing to meet with his investors; he much preferred his jeans and hoodies.

Tim laughed, enjoying his misery. "Sorry, son. I didn't think she would react this way, but I'm sure you'll figure it out. I have to get to a meeting. I'll send you the number for the alarm company." He hung up, and Elijah noticed one of the movers at the door to his office.

"We're all finished here, but I wanted to let you know that the lock on the back door is broken. Do you want me to call someone to come and fix it?" he asked.

Elijah's phone dinged with the number for the security company. "Yes. Thank you for noticing and for all your work this morning," he said. Inspiration struck. If he was fixing one lock, why not solve his own problem? "If Autumn doesn't want to tell me, then I'm going to have to go around her," he said to himself, knocking the bobblehead of Darth Vader on his desk. He placed it with the rest of his bobblehead collection on the wall over the plush grey couch. Picking up his signed motorcycle helmets, he organised his office as best he could as he rang his business partner. Francis didn't answer, so he left a message.

"I can't make it to the morning meeting. Could you stop by the house once you've finished the pitch? I'll send you the address."

༄

"Having a good day?" Francis asked, coming up the path to greet Elijah that afternoon.

"It's been interesting, I don't know about good," Elijah said, watching the locksmith finish up. The alarm company had already changed the code, and the locks were the final touch.

"Do you want me to make you a spare? I can have it sent to you later," the locksmith said.

"Yes, just one." Elijah would have to give one to Autumn, but he looked forward to making her sweat a bit first.

"I'm all finished here, so I'll get going. I'll drop the spare key 'round later," she said, packing up her gear. Elijah was impressed by how little time it had taken.

"Thank you," he called after her, and she waved goodbye.

"What are you up to?" Francis said, studying his best friend and business partner.

"Changing the locks." Elijah grinned, almost giddy. He couldn't wait for Autumn to get home. *She thinks she's won, and now she'll have to grovel.*

"Why?" Francis asked.

Elijah closed the door behind his friend. "One of the locks was broken, so I figured I might as well change them."

"I get the feeling that's not the whole reason," Francis said, pulling off his tan coat and hanging it on the coat hook in the hall.

"The woman I'm sharing the house with neglected to give me the alarm code, which is why I couldn't make the meeting and had to make you come here," Elijah admitted.

"And does *she* know you're changing the locks?"

"No, but she will." Elijah smirked, and Francis shook his head.

"This is her?" Francis asked, looking at a picture on the wall. Autumn in front of her piano, with an orchestra behind her.

Elijah nodded.

"She's pretty, and she's done a great job on the house," Francis said. He loved interior decorating. Elijah figured it was the creative in him.

"Oh, she's beautiful, but hostile as hell. Tim has been

renting the house to her for the past few years. I thought he cleared my living here with Autumn, but he didn't," Elijah said, leading him to the kitchen. "Now I'm the arsehole who invaded her home."

Francis chuckled. "You're locking her out? I'm curious, but if I'm witnessing a crime, then I don't want to know more. I can't believe you missed the meeting with Nirosoft just so you could wind up your new housemate!"

"I wouldn't have missed it if Autumn had given me the alarm code," Elijah muttered, but he was distracted by the burritos Francis produced from the brown paper bag in his hand. "Please tell me you remembered the vegan cheese?" He was starving, having neglected breakfast in all the chaos.

"I wouldn't bring such an offering just to torment you. Since you couldn't make it to the breakfast meeting, I figured you hadn't eaten yet," Francis said, taking a bite of his own while Elijah made coffee.

"How did the meeting go?" Elijah asked hesitantly when Francis wouldn't meet his eye.

"Nirosoft wants to see a demo by the end of the month before they consider purchasing the game for their online stores," Francis informed him.

A sinking feeling settled in his gut as he opened the fridge. Unfortunately, Autumn only had dairy milk, though she seemed to have every flavour—strawberry, banana, the collection went on.

"Two *weeks* to fix the rest of the bugs? I didn't consider they might screw us on the timeline. We have a contract!" Taking out the regular milk for Francis, Elijah closed the fridge door. He hadn't unpacked his own mugs, so he looked for Autumn's. Opening one of the pale pink cabinets, he found a colour-coordinated medicine cabinet. He didn't get a look at what was in the baskets, but it troubled him.

Is she sick? Maybe that's why she's so opposed to me living here? He closed the door before Francis saw what it contained. He already felt like he had stepped too far over the line.

One cabinet over, amongst an impressive collection, he noticed two mugs: one with a preppy panda and another with a lazy lizard. *At least she has a sense of humour,* he thought, wondering which one she used the most. Judging from the faded cartoons, they both got a lot of use.

"Could have used your charm at the meeting. I just do the drawing; I shouldn't be negotiating anything. Clearly, the locks were more important than the meeting," Francis said into his coffee.

"They're only chancing their arm. We can get it done."

"You're the boss," Francis said as they ate. "But you should have been at the meeting. We can't risk any hiccups this late in the game."

Elijah finished his burrito. "There wouldn't have been a hiccup if it hadn't been for Autumn," he insisted with his mouth full. "If I left and Autumn got home before me, my stuff would be on the street, including our work, and I'd be locked out!"

"I like her already. A woman who can resist the Wells smile? Can't wait to meet her. Hearing your charms have been resisted will make Aiden's day. Todd isn't sleeping much."

Elijah grinned, suddenly delighted he was sharing the house with Autumn and not a two-year-old. Aiden liked anyone who gave as good as they got. Elijah still wondered how he and Francis had ended up together; they were polar opposites. Francis was a mixed-race atheist with a splash of anarchy to his personality. Aiden had been a good Catholic boy in the closet who'd never stepped a foot out of line—that was, until he fell in love. When he'd been a rookie officer, he had arrested Francis for graffiti. *Who knew an arrest could lead to love?* Ten years later, Aiden was a detective and Francis had traded his graffiti for game graphics.

"Delighted I can provide some entertainment. Now, less talk about *her*, please," he pleaded.

"Okay, but I have to ask—what are you going to do when she comes home and finds she's locked out? I don't think she'll be any more lenient to your cause."

"I'll share the code *and* key when she gets back from rehearsals," Elijah said airily. Francis didn't look convinced. "Show me the new sketches. Did you add the longer tentacles to the sea monster?" Elijah looked at the folder tucked under his friend's arm.

"I struggled to try and make it original. I worry it might look too much like a kraken," Francis said, opening his folder.

"Hmm. Add more eyes and teeth and have fewer suckers on the tentacles," Elijah advised as they studied the designs on the counter.

Francis jotted the notes on the paper. Thankfully, they were getting to the final touches on the game they had been working on for the last two years. However, being in the home stretch brought new excitement and anxiety.

While they discussed the details of the final boss the player would face, Elijah added his own mugs and utensils to Autumn's packed kitchen. When he opened the cupboards, there were a lot of ingredients, giving him the impression she liked to cook. He didn't have much skill in the kitchen, unless you counted microwaving meals.

"Don't put that there," he barked as Francis went to put his coffee cup on top of the piano.

Francis started, but thankfully he didn't spill on the hardwood floors. "Jesus, Eli, you made me jump!"

"If you'd put that down, I don't think we would have survived until tomorrow."

"It's just a piano."

"No, it's like her child or something. The movers put my plants on it, and I thought she was going to throw me out of my own house!"

"You just met her, and she already has you wrapped around her finger," Francis said smugly, putting the mug on the glass table.

Elijah shook his head, though he was worried his friend might have a point. He barely knew her, and yet he couldn't wait for her to get home—even if it was just to fight with her again. *If that's not toxic, I don't know what is,* he thought, vowing to make a conscious effort to be on his best behaviour when she returned.

"I'm just saying, if you touch or mark the piano, I don't want to find out what she would do to my computer," he said darkly.

Francis is right, I should have been there. I don't want a repeat of what happened this morning with the alarm code to occur again. I'll have to convince Autumn that we can live amicably, or both our lives will be thrown into chaos. He couldn't remember the last time something or someone had managed to displace work from his mind this thoroughly. Autumn's effect on him unsettled him more than he cared to admit.

Chapter Four

Autumn

After rehearsals, everyone went out for dinner, but Autumn stayed to avoid going home, not wanting to face her intruder. She craned her neck, trying to work out the cracks after a long day of sitting. Checking her phone, she noticed a text from Tim. *It's not like him to text instead of call. The only time he doesn't call is when he's busy with work.* She didn't understand why he couldn't take the time to discuss something that had altered her daily life. She checked her watch and realised it was too late now. Tim never did like confrontation; he much preferred to sweep things under the carpet. When he cared about something, he would move mountains to help, but when he made his mind up, he became an immovable mountain himself. If he'd agreed to let Elijah stay, she worried he wouldn't rescind the offer.

She hesitated before opening the text, afraid that it would be bad news. She got up from her stool to pace, then clicked on the notification.

> **Tim:** Sorry for the late notice and the shock this morning. Mr Wells was supposed to arrive next Friday, but according to my assistant, this Friday is next Friday. I have let the front of the house for a short period. I apologise for the inconvenience. I have already returned half the rent to your account as you now rent only one floor. There will be communal use of facilities. I hope you can embrace this short-term situation. It might be good for you to have some company. If you have any issues with the new tenant, please contact my assistant.

Autumn stared at the screen, not sure how to respond. Bewilderment turned to anger as she read it again. *Good for me to have some company? Am I a stray dog?! If I wanted company, I would get a pet!* She dialled his number but it rang out, telling her he was avoiding her call. She took a breath, trying not to let the situation overwhelm her. She didn't know why he was acting so strangely or why he suddenly thought she needed company. *There's clearly to be no discussion on the issue.* Having no say in the matter caused her to sweat a little, but Tim had always looked out for her in the past; there had to be some explanation. *He's done so much for me over the years; maybe I can give him some grace,* she thought, trying to calm down. *Clearly, he wants Elijah to stay. What if I challenge him and I'm the one who ends up having to leave?* She didn't want to even consider it.

Giving up, she started to play, immersing herself in the music to wash away her stress. She loved being alone in the theatre. It was as though all those who had come before her were speaking to her, guiding her silently through the notes. There was no other place in the world she would rather be.

Her parents couldn't understand; they thought the pressure was too much for her body. After the accident, they'd never wanted to see her on stage again. Understandable, considering they had witnessed one collapse on top of her, not knowing whether she was even alive under the wreckage. However, the only thing that had got her through learning to walk again was getting back on stage. Regaining sensation in her feet after weeks of physio meant feeling pedals beneath them again. It had been who she was for as long as she could remember, and she felt nothing without it. She'd survived. She wasn't going to waste the second chance.

"I thought you would still be here. The concert is in four weeks; you don't have to worry so much. Keep your focus, and get some rest. Staying after practice every day isn't necessary," Conductor Sasaki said, interrupting her. Autumn stopped playing as he approached. He was getting greyer by the day—he was older than her father.

"What are *you* still doing here? You work just as late as I do." She smiled, closing the lid on the keys. He was a strict conductor, like many others, but he knew her limits. He'd ensured her return to the stage once she'd recovered went smoothly. Losing her now would put the show at risk since many came to their shows to see her play.

"Trying to find sponsors for the showcase. Funding is lower than I would like for the season," Sasaki admitted, sounding tired. *Just because you love what you do doesn't mean it doesn't take its toll.* She didn't like to see him worry.

"If you want, I can play some extra shows. And I've had offers to put in some guest appearances with other orchestras out of the city. I could try and raise some awareness for our next performance," she offered.

He shook his head. "No, if you work any harder, you'll be putting the rest of us to shame," he said, placing a reassuring hand on her shoulder.

"And if the theatre closes, then we'll be out of work," she retorted.

He laughed, a rattle caused by more years of smoking than she had been alive echoing from his chest. It worried her more than she would admit. He was her biggest champion, and the mere thought of losing him made her panic.

"Let me worry about the showcase and the theatre; you focus on your work. I know you are struggling to connect with the Winter Movements. You need to figure out what is troubling you." Sasaki always saw through her doubts.

There was nothing for her to say; she felt that she'd been chasing the music of late, when usually it came to her. "I'll figure it out. I think I'm just overthinking."

He merely raised his dark brows. "Are you sure you are ready for the solo? It's not too late to back out."

"It's just…old demons. Give me a few more days, and I'll have my nerves under control. I'm not backing out." Would he give her seat to someone else?

Sasaki, seeming to read her expression, waved his hands. "There is no need to worry; the seat is yours so long as you truly want it."

Autumn swallowed and considered what he was saying. She was troubled by how much faith he had in her, but if she couldn't trust herself, she would trust the man who had brought her back to the stage when everyone had said she shouldn't.

"What if it's not perfect? What if my solo return is a bust?" she asked, rubbing her thighs. She wanted to be as good as the greats, if not better.

"Autumn, you will never be satisfied, not even with perfection." He was right, but it didn't stop her from trying. "When I heard you were playing again for that local theatre in Islacore, there was no doubt in my mind that you would be back. However, the girl who went under the stage isn't the same girl they pulled out. You have scars, emotional and physical. I think if you embrace them, you will be unstoppable."

"If only it were that simple. I try to overcome them, but managing my health and my life can be overwhelming. Aren't we supposed to strive for perfection?" she asked him, turning in her stool.

Sasaki hesitated, straightening his waistcoat.

"Perfection is my job, but I know there is beauty in mistakes. If you can put your emotions into your music, I think it will help you," he said, making it sound like the easiest thing in the world.

"I don't have anything trapped in me," she argued, though she knew it was a lie.

"You are a pressure cooker of talent, and if you won't use it, then you won't be able to break through with this piece or any piece," he told her.

She wanted to argue, to deny it, but it was true. She couldn't control the music; instead, it was controlling her.

"I'll try," she sighed.

"Good, and be gone with you. I have to lock up."

Autumn pulled herself from the cushioned stool.

"I don't think she would ever leave unless you forced her to," Nina said from the audience seats. Autumn didn't know when her friend had returned, but it was getting late. The sun had been replaced by the cloudy night sky above the glass roof.

"And that's why she is my favourite," Sasaki said.

Nina pouted. "You aren't supposed to have favourites."

"No, but I do, and when you master the Autumn Movement, you might be in the running."

"Challenge accepted," Nina said, and Autumn knew she meant it. Nina never liked to be considered second best. She had had a late start to learning the violin, so she always felt like she was behind everyone else, but that hadn't stopped her from being the lead violinist for the last three showcases.

Sasaki's phone rang, and he left them to it with a quick wave.

"You didn't have to wait for me," Autumn said. She had sat for too long. The backs of her legs were aching despite taking small breaks between movements. Thankfully, the heat patch she had applied at lunch was keeping the spasms at bay. She reminded herself to take a muscle relaxant when she got home to stop it from getting any worse.

"Didn't have to, but wanted to. Need a ride? We tried to wait for you at the restaurant, but you didn't show and we were hungry," Nina said.

Autumn frowned. "I didn't know you were waiting!" She grabbed her woolly grey cardigan from her bag, wanting to keep her muscles warm. Her bath at home was calling, but the excitement was replaced with dread when she remembered who else was waiting for her. Sasaki had distracted her with thoughts of the showcase, but now she was thinking of her intruder, and with Tim being no help, she was on her own.

"I tried to call you to get some food, but you didn't answer," Nina said.

Autumn glanced at her phone. There was a missed call from Nina, an hour ago. If she had a penny from every phone call or message she'd missed while she was playing, she'd be a millionaire.

"Can we get going?" Garrett called, loudly enough for everyone to hear. Autumn tried to hide her disdain for Nina's boyfriend, waiting by the doors at the other end of the auditorium. She decided to make her own way home.

"You go ahead; someone is eager to see you," she said, nodding towards Garrett, who didn't even bother to step in.

"Are you sure? I think it's going to rain," Nina said, though her smile said she was happy to go.

"I need the walk after sitting for so long," Autumn said, forcing a smile. She would rather walk in the rain than sit in a car with Garrett. There was just something about him that she didn't quite like, but Nina was on the rebound after her girlfriend had moved back to the states, so Autumn was keeping her mouth shut as long as she was happy. Nina jumped on stage, giving her friend one last squeeze before heading to Garrett, who looked just as pleased to leave without Autumn.

"I'll see you in the morning. Let me know how it goes with your mystery man!" Nina winked, backing away towards the door.

"If you don't hear from me, then you know we murdered each other," Autumn joked half-heartedly. Elijah was the last thing she wanted to talk about. Besides, she wasn't in any position to be judging relationships; the most intimate relationships she currently had were with her physiotherapist and the vibrating wand on her nightstand. Then again, both were exceptionally loyal, there when needed, and helped relieve her pain.

"Call me if you need help with the body!"

Garrett gave a half-hearted wave before placing a possessive hand around Nina's waist, and then they were gone. Autumn finished packing up her sheet music and searched for her umbrella, but she had forgotten it in her haste to escape the house.

"I can drive you." Heather, Sasaki's assistant, appeared from the side of the stage, making Autumn jump.

"God! Where did you come from?" Autumn exclaimed, placing a hand on her chest. Heather was petite and quiet as a mouse. She rarely talked to anyone, always in Sasaki's shadow. Autumn could count on one hand how many times they had talked since she had joined the team two years ago. Autumn put it down to her age and that she might just be shy.

"Didn't mean to frighten you. I was helping Sasaki with billings," Heather said, pushing her glasses up her nose.

"I wouldn't want you to go out of your way," Autumn said.

"It's fine, I'm headed that way." Heather followed Autumn's gaze to the rain pounding on the glass roof.

It was at times like this that she wished she had a car. She knew how to drive but didn't have a car because she lived so close, and walking helped her stretch out anyway. She only took the lifts from Nina because it was on her way in the mornings, and it meant they got to catch up before rehearsal.

"If it's not too much out of your way…" Autumn shrugged, hating to be a nuisance.

"Not at all. I was heading out anyway. Are you ready?" Heather said, pulling at the end of her mousy brown ponytail.

"Yes, I'll meet you outside," Autumn said, turning off the stage light. When she turned around, Heather was already gone. The office light down the back of the theatre was still on, so she figured Sasaki hadn't left yet. Autumn wondered how Heather knew where she lived, but she would have access to her personal file, so she probably knew where everyone lived.

As she left the theatre, Heather pulled up to the front curb, and Autumn hopped into the car out of the rain.

"Thank you for this. I would have been a drowned rat by the time I made it back," she said, trying to make light conversation as they waited in traffic.

"What are friends for?" Heather replied, and Autumn smiled softly. She wouldn't necessarily have considered them friends; they saw each other around the theatre, but she rarely attended any of the drinks or events following their showcases to socialise. "I heard you worrying about your solo piece," Heather added, keeping her eyes on the road.

She was listening? Autumn wasn't sure how to feel about her eavesdropping on her conversation with Sasaki, but she didn't want to make the drive any more awkward.

"It's been a few years since I've performed solo. Just nerves," she said.

"I wouldn't have thought you get nervous. You make the stage look like your home," Heather said.

"It is my second home, but it doesn't mean I don't worry about my performance," she said, trying not to sound defensive.

"You should trust Sasaki. He wouldn't give you the solo if he didn't think you could do it." Heather's words were supportive, but there was something in her tone which made Autumn uncomfortable.

"Do you play? Many of those who've worked with Sasaki before have gone on to become performers," Autumn commented, trying to find some mutual ground and divert the attention away from herself.

Heather shook her head. "No, I haven't a musical bone in my body. It was my sister who got the musical genes."

Autumn wondered why she would choose to work for a conductor.

"I majored in events management. After college, I saw an ad for the PA position and since I grew up around music, I thought why not!" Heather beamed.

It was the first time Autumn had seen her excited. "Does your sister still play? Perhaps I know her."

Heather shook her head. "No, not anymore. She wasn't lucky to have made it like you." She quickly corrected herself before Autumn could reply. "Not that you aren't talented! You probably wouldn't have noticed her. She wasn't a prodigy like you."

"I'm sure I would have; the city's classical music world is quite a close-knit group. What was her name?" Autumn asked.

Heather turned on the radio. "Sorry, I love this song!"

Maybe she doesn't like talking about her sister? Not all siblings are close, Autumn mused, though as an only child she could only guess. They spent the rest of the short journey listening to the radio. It was better than forcing conversation. *Hopefully, Elijah will have done the smart thing and left.* She clasped her hands on her lap as they turned into her street.

"It's the white house in the middle," she said.

Heather pulled up to the curb. Autumn's stomach dropped when she saw that all the lights were on. *He's still there.*

"You leave the lights on? You should conserve energy. It's not good for the environment," Heather said with a hint of passive-aggression.

"They're on a timer. Better not to come home to a dark house," Autumn lied, not wanting to tell her about her new living situation. She worried that if Heather knew she was living with a guy, everyone would find out. She didn't want to have to explain that she was living with a stranger she knew little to nothing about.

"Suppose you can never be too careful when you live alone."

"Thanks again for the lift. I really appreciate it. See you tomorrow." Autumn opened the car door, and Heather handed over her bag.

"Night," was all she said before Autumn closed the door, afraid Heather would hear the music radiating from her house.

I can explain the lights, but not the metal music! she thought, rushing up the path. Reaching the door, she realised Heather hadn't left. Autumn waved. What was she waiting for? Heather waved back and drove away.

~∞~

AUTUMN OPENED HER FRONT GATE, using her cardigan to protect herself from the rain. *Does he want the whole street to know his taste in music?* She guessed it was a pathetic attempt at claiming his space. However, she was too cold to care about his motives; she just wanted to get out of the rain.

Placing her key in the lock, she frowned when it wouldn't budge. *What the fuck?* She tried to twist it again, only to curse as her bag slipped from her shoulder and its contents scattered over her front step.

For the love of.... She crouched to pick up her belongings, banging on the door with her other hand. *He'd better answer the damn door.*

The music stopped, and once everything was back in her bag, she rose to see Elijah standing by the door in low-hanging jeans and an open shirt. His hands were in his pockets while he watched her get drenched. *Not a care in the freaking world. He's clearly making himself comfortable in my home. Who just struts around someone else's home half-naked?*

"My key won't work—let me in!" she shouted, dropping her cardigan from over her head. It was growing heavy, and she was already soaked; there was no point in trying to protect herself.

"I know," he called back, smiling devilishly.

For a second, Autumn forgot about the rain, unable to stop her gaze from travelling from his defined chest to the trail of hair where his hips met his jeans. She couldn't remember the last time she'd seen a guy naked in person, and not one who looked so... Her train of thought was cut off when he waved at her, and she diverted her gaze, trying not to blush. Without a word, he left her to continue banging. Seconds later, he reappeared in the front window and slid it open. *At least I don't have to shout through the door, but he could have done the decent thing and let me in.* She tried to remain calm.

He offered her the umbrella she had forgotten to bring with her that morning.

"I don't need an umbrella. I need you to let me in," she hissed, snatching it from him.

"Changing the locks. How could you be so petty?" she asked, clutching her folder to her chest, afraid her sheet music would get wet.

"Me, petty? I wasn't the one who strutted out of here without giving me the alarm code," he replied, a glint of mischief in his rich brown eyes as they raked over the dress clinging to her curves.

"I don't strut," she bit back as his eyes settled on her hips.

"Yes," he said, tilting his head. "You do."

She could see how much he was enjoying her distress. She had never met anyone who could infuriate her so much.

"If you're done looking at me like I'm a piece of meat, can you *open* the door?" she hissed, afraid her neighbours would call the police if she shouted.

His deep laugh only made her resent him all the more. Elijah leant out the window, unfazed by the rain catching his hair.

"Apologise for not giving me the alarm code and causing me to miss an important meeting. Then I'll let you in." He sighed, crossing his strong arms over his body.

"Are you serious? You invaded my home and you want an apology?!" Autumn demanded, wrapping her arm around herself.

Elijah nodded, and she noticed his stubble from the day. *I prefer him without it,* she thought, then she told her subconscious to shut it.

"Just open the door," she pleaded. *I can't afford to get sick before the performance.*

"Tim told me he talked with you," Elijah countered, and she hated that he was acting like the voice of reason.

"A text doesn't count as talking to me," she snapped. "You should be the one apologising to me for ruining my morning and now my evening."

"I'm sorry for intruding on you this morning. Now it's your turn," Elijah called over the rain.

She sighed. "I apologise," she muttered half-heartedly, and he tutted.

"Say it like you mean it."

Autumn was two seconds away from throwing a rock through the glass, but she didn't want to have to pay for the damages.

"I'm sorry." She forced a smile, and he disappeared. "Open the damn door!"

She was about to bang on it when it whipped open and she stumbled, thumping his bare chest. He frowned, looking down at her hands on his skin.

"No need to resort to violence," he murmured, a faint smile playing on his lips.

She jumped back as though he'd burnt her. Then she noticed the towel in his hand. It wasn't one of her fluffy blue ones, but white; it must be his. Not that she cared whose towel it was—she just wanted to get dry.

"I didn't know where you kept yours, so I grabbed it when I got the umbrella."

His words softened her anger a little, though she didn't want to show it. Why had he bothered to go and get her a towel and umbrella instead of just letting her in?

At least I know he didn't intend to harm me. Clearly, he's just an idiot. She dropped the umbrella and snatched the towel from him.

"So I shouldn't expect a thank you?" he drawled, watching her dab her face and neck dry. The towel was soft and warm on her skin, but she wasn't going to thank him. She was too worried about how being stuck out in the rain would affect her pain.

The last thing I need is to miss a rehearsal because of a flare triggered by his stupid games. It had only been a few minutes, though, so hopefully a good soak in the tub would help.

"Thank you for making a bad day worse." She grimaced, shaking out her long hair and coating him in raindrops, and he winced. "You should put on some more layers—would hate for you to catch a cold," she said, looking unashamedly at his bare chest. *I can admire the view while still hating him,* she thought, though she hated that any part of her positively responded to him. She assured herself that it was merely the presence of his warm body so close to her freezing one that made him so enticing.

Elijah took a step towards her. "If you're cold, I can just turn up the heat."

She slipped out from between him and the door. "Locking me outside and then flirting? Do you have any basic social skills? You know what—I don't care. Just give me a key and then I can spend the rest of the night pretending you don't exist!" she ranted, drying her hair with the towel.

"Please isn't in your vocabulary?" he asked, raising his eyebrows.

All she wanted to do was end the conversation and get in the bath, so she just extended her hand.

"I made you one, and the new code is written inside the keypad. Now neither of us has to be worried about being locked out," he said, looking in the bowl on the table by the door.

"I wasn't worried about being locked out until you locked me out," she barked. For a moment, she considered leaving him where he stood and calling Nina to come and get her, but she didn't want him to win. She couldn't let him drive her out of her home.

He placed the key in her hand. His fingers brushed her palm, sending shivers up her arm. *It's only because he's warm, and it was freezing outside.*

"I apologise. It was a rash decision. I didn't change the locks entirely to spite you, and I didn't know it was going to rain. The lock on the back door was broken. I was having it fixed, so I thought I might as well change the front locks," he said, pulling at the back of his neck. She wondered if he now regretted it. She hoped he did.

"The back door lock was broken?" She looked to the back of the house.

"Didn't you know? The movers spotted it when they were putting things in the shed."

"I don't go out the back often, but it was fine last week," she told him, wondering how it had happened. She was too tired to care right now, and there was no point in dwelling on it since he'd already fixed it. The movers had probably broken it by accident and not wanted to admit to it. "Goodnight, Elijah." She headed upstairs to the bathroom before he could say anything else to infuriate her. She wanted to put as much space as possible between her and his naked torso.

"I ordered you a pizza," he blurted out, and she stopped on the stairs in surprise, narrowing her eyes at him.

"What?"

He shifted nervously. "Don't think too much about it. There was a double deal, and I did blindside you this morning..."

She was amused by his discomfort, and if she got food out of it, all the better.

"I didn't know when you would be back, so I put it in here to keep it warm," he went on, and she resisted the urge to smile. She refused to be won over so easily.

"What's on it?" she asked, trying to keep her voice neutral. She was damp and sore, and pizza sounded perfect. Following him into the kitchen, she watched him take a boxed pizza from the oven.

"There was one in the freezer with pepperoni, so I figured it would be a safe bet," he said, opening the lid. The smell made her mouth water.

"Thank you. It's my favourite," she muttered, too tired and sore to keep up her defences.

"Don't mention it," he said, like it was nothing. "Consider it a peace offering."

"You don't get to call for peace when you started the war," she retorted, knowing he was merely trying to get on her good side.

"Suit yourself. I look forward to the next battle." Elijah saluted before heading into his room, sliding the doors to the kitchen closed behind him.

"You shouldn't be," she said, staring at the closed door. *If he wants to play pranks, then it's only fair I return the favour.*

Taking the pizza, she noticed lights on in the conservatory. She walked over to the glass doors and noticed that a new green couch had been added, along with a glass coffee table. The stone wall was decorated with strings of new fairy lights. A fresh floral smell met her senses, and she admired the brightly coloured hanging plants. *They are pretty,* she admitted. She loved flowers, but she didn't have the time to maintain them; it was the same reason she didn't have a pet.

It was so quiet that she was almost fooled into thinking that Elijah had left the house. She went to his door and considered thanking him for making the conservatory look so pretty, but she didn't want to encourage him to stay, so she headed upstairs.

She'd planned to have a bath, but she didn't have the energy to wait for the tub to fill. Instead, she stripped off her soaking, chilled clothes and stepped into the shower. Under the sound of the water, she let the heat soak into her muscles. Rubbing the tension from her shoulders from hours of playing, she vowed not to let Elijah continue to get under her skin. Then she thought of his hands rubbing her shoulders, the warmth radiating off him in the hall, and she opened her eyes.

I'm not going to be fooled by his muscles or charm, she thought, turning off the water. Dressed and snuggly in her favourite robe, she tried to ignore the music drifting up the stairs. *I should have asked him to keep it off, but I'll ignore him, and continue life as normal; confrontation is the last thing I want. I'm not going to let him run me out.*

Climbing into bed, she opened the pizza box and ate happily. Warm and comfy, she was determined to have a better day tomorrow.

Chapter Five

Elijah

"Maybe I shouldn't have left her out in the rain. I didn't know it was going to rain, and I didn't plan on leaving her out there. Why didn't I just open the damn door instead of winding her up?" Elijah scolded himself, throwing himself into his office chair.

He stared at the ceiling, hearing Autumn padding around upstairs. Though he'd wanted a reaction from her, he hadn't been expecting his own. The rain coating her long, fair eyelashes and her pink, freckled cheeks, her green eyes ablaze as she watched him in the doorway—the memory brought a smile to his lips. Despite being delighted by her outrage as he'd watched her pick up her belongings, pathetically trying to protect herself with a well-loved cardigan, he couldn't help but want to help her.

"I did let her in eventually. I'm sure she has some friend she could stay with if she really didn't want to be here," he said to himself, thinking of how her clothes had clung to her curves, outlining every part of her in a way that had made him want to reach out and grab her. Seeing her so drenched and miserable sparked some guilt; he hadn't known it was going to rain heavily. He had meant to open the door when he saw her coming up the path, but it had been too good an opportunity to pass up. *How was I to know she would look so good wet?* He ran his hands through his hair, pushing the thoughts aside. Lingering on that memory was dangerous.

"At least she ate the pizza." He realised how confusing his actions might appear to her. One minute he was locking her out, and the next, giving her dinner; his emotions towards her were giving *him* whiplash.

No tiny redhead is going to mess up my plans.

He lost himself in lines of code until he saw the clock hit four and his eyes felt like they were going to fall out of his head. His bed wasn't made yet, so he collapsed onto the couch. The only blanket he could find was in the sitting area in front of the kitchen. He didn't know why she was so upset with losing the front room when there was a couch and a TV in the open-plan kitchen.

It smelt like her. The whole damn house smelt like her. *She's inescapable.* It was pastel yellow and furry. *Where did she even find this? It looks like someone skinned Big Bird from Sesame Street.* But he made do. With the computers off, his eyes delighted in the darkness.

∿

"What the...?" Elijah cursed in a daze as music echoed through the wall.

He pulled the blanket over his head, trying to ignore Autumn's playing, but it sounded like she was trying to kill her piano. The sheer speed of the notes vibrated in his ears.

"What is she playing at this ungodly hour?" he groaned, putting on his slippers. He stood too quickly, and speckles blurred his vision. Rubbing his eyes, he found his phone on the desk, then recoiled in horror. *Two hours—I slept for two hours!*

He opened the sliding doors to the kitchen to find Autumn scribbling something on a piece of paper on top of the piano.

"What are you doing?" he asked, his morning voice rough.

She didn't even look up as she sipped from her mug. He walked over as she went back to playing and cleared his throat to get her attention, but she didn't react.

Has she been possessed? Unable to resist, he pulled her stool out from the piano. Her head snapped around, her fair eyebrows pulled together in a scowl.

"What are you doing? I'm practising," she growled, trying to pull herself back towards the keys.

There was no way he was letting her play, for both his and the piano's sake. He turned her around to face him and pointed to the clock on the wall. "It's six a.m. Your schedule on the fridge says you don't have practice until nine."

Autumn folded her arms across her chest. "If you had your own place, you wouldn't have to worry about *my* schedule," she said, leaning forward until their faces were inches apart, neither one backing away. "That's my work schedule, which doesn't include my practice schedule."

"I worked late—"

"And I rise early," she countered.

"I think you deserve a lie-in," he muttered. Without his morning coffee, he didn't have the energy to argue. "Are you going to stop playing and go to bed if I ask nicely?"

The corner of her mouth twitched with a smile. "Not a chance."

"Okay, then you leave me no choice." Before she could respond, he leaned forward and threw her over his shoulder.

"Hey! You can't—" she panted, slapping his back. "You can't do this! You said I could practise whenever I wanted!"

He held her tight, his arm around her thighs. *This morning is looking up.* Then he realised that being so close to her, feeling her body against his, might not be the best idea.

"Not before dawn. I think that's enough practice for one morning. We could both do with sleep—the extra hours might put you in a better mood," he said as she tried to squirm out of his hold.

"I was in a perfectly fine mood until you interrupted," she insisted, trying to wriggle out of his grasp.

"Judging from how you were playing, I very much doubt it," Elijah said, dropping her lower down his back a little. The threat of the fall forced her to cling to his waist.

"You'd better not drop me," she squealed as he walked down the hall. "You can't tell me when I can *and* can't practise!" Her voice was muffled.

"No, I can't, but I can stop you from waking me at six o'clock!"

She stopped wriggling when he started up the stairs.

"You can't just manhandle me like this," she argued.

"The more you fight, the more I'm enjoying this," he told her, his voice low, and she stopped moving.

"Pig," she grumbled.

Elijah chuckled, kicking open her bedroom door before he dumped her on the unmade bed. "Stay put and get some sleep, or, for the love of God, let *me* sleep," he said, his hands in prayer position.

"Stay? I'm not a dog," she snapped. "I was practising—this is my job. I told you living together wouldn't work. If you don't want a morning call every day, then I suggest you find other accommodation."

"No, you were getting revenge because I locked you out in the rain. The poor piano was the victim. If you were practising, it wouldn't have sounded like you were trying to break the keys."

Autumn glared at him. She tried to stand, and he placed his hands on either side of her on the bed. He watched her swallow as she stared up at him.

"With compliments like that, I'm not surprised you're single," she said.

"How do you know I'm single? Or is that just wishful thinking?" he asked, his interest piqued.

She leaned away, but she couldn't go far. "I don't care. God help the poor woman who gets stuck with you!" she said, folding her arms.

"Right now, that's you," he said.

She placed a hand on his chest, trying to push him away. However, he watched her blush as her hand settled on his bare chest.

A tense silence fell between them. Being so close to her, in her room, felt like the last place he should be. He followed her gaze from his chest to his face, and he wanted to brush the strand of hair that had fallen over her face, but he couldn't bring himself to move. She couldn't know the effect she was having on him. He wouldn't let her have the satisfaction, not until he knew she wanted him as much as he wanted her. *Christ, what is she doing to me? I hardly know her,* he thought, straightening up.

Thankfully, she spoke first.

"You might be able to take over my house, but this is *my* room. Get out," she ordered, her chest rising and falling quickly. He wished he could harness her energy for something they would both enjoy.

"Fine, I'm leaving," he said, staring down at her, "but unless you want me to tie you to the damn headboard, stay put and *away* from the piano." He winked, hoping she would defy him. He would love any excuse to tie her up.

However, he was quickly disappointed when she covered her bare legs with her duvet. He'd been too distracted by their fight to even notice the tiny shorts she wore.

"Fine, you win. But I did warn you about my playing, which you decided to ignore," she said, reminding him of how he'd said it wouldn't bother him. Then again, he hadn't expected her to be playing before the break of dawn. When their eyes met, he saw her plotting her revenge, and he wasn't ashamed to admit he was looking forward to it.

He closed the door and went back downstairs, feeling too wound up to go back to sleep. *She's going to be harder to win over than I thought.* His stomach rumbled. Hunting through the fridge, all he could find was a heap of chopped vegetables in assorted containers. He had never seen so much meal prep. *She clearly likes her life organised.* The top shelf contained a box labelled *Breakfast*. Lifting out a pink container, Elijah found overnight oats labelled 'Vegan' topped with fruit and nuts. *She might get angry if I eat this, but she has a couple more,* he thought, trying to resist, but it smelt so good. *One bite won't hurt, and I did get her dinner last night...* He took a small mouthful.

Before he could stop himself, the container was empty. *Definitely good with food,* he thought, licking some honey from his lips.

He had some time to kill, and he didn't think he could get back to sleep. He might as well have let Autumn continue playing. But when he went into the hallway, he couldn't hear her moving around. If she had gone back to sleep, he didn't think she would appreciate him waking her up.

He found himself staring at the walls in the corridor. *The pastel blue isn't really my taste, and downstairs is my territory,* he thought. *I think it's time for a change. Since she woke me up, I might as well put the time to good use.* The movers had put the paint he'd ordered in the shed with the tools he needed, and now seemed like as good a time as any. *If I put my stamp on the place, she might start thinking of it as our place instead of hers.*

It was a lot of effort for a temporary home, but no matter where he lived or how long he stayed, he always liked to make it his own. Otherwise, he couldn't settle in.

Two hours later, the first coat of deep grey was finished, and he'd removed his headphones to get some water. The painting had worked out some of his pent-up energy from their argument, and at least he would get to sleep once Autumn left for the day.

"What did you do to my hallway?"

Elijah heard Autumn before he saw her. *Speak of the tiny devil...* He smiled to himself as he left the kitchen to find her standing wide-eyed on the staircase. She was already dressed, and he found himself missing her little pyjama shorts with music notes. Light tresses framing her face, her hair was wrapped in a messy bun secured with a pencil, which gave him the adolescent urge to free it.

"This is my floor. I can decorate how I see fit, and it could use a fresh coat of paint. Since you saw to it that I was up early, I thought why not get started," he explained, stepping onto the plastic sheeting that protected the wooden floor.

"Your home? I think you mean *my* home." She smiled innocently, which terrified him. "Did you have to pick such a dark colour? It took me ages to pick that blue."

He almost felt guilty, but then he remembered his wake-up call. "I think it enriches the house, and it brings out the silver frames around the artwork," he said, surprised by her lack of reaction.

Autumn said nothing, stepping over the cans. Elijah followed her, concerned by how calm she appeared.

"Why are you following me? Don't you have some painting to finish?" she asked, taking a bottle of wine from the fridge. He sat on the other side of the kitchen island.

"I'm letting the first coat dry. Wine for breakfast? Not the first time I've driven someone to drink." He took in her smile. Not the reaction he'd been expecting, but seeing how her face lit up made his chest tighten in a good way.

"You haven't driven me to anything. It's a gift for my friend," she said, opening the door to the pantry. He wondered what her friends would be like. Was it for a guy or a girl? What was she like around them? He apparently only brought out her fiery side.

"A special occasion?" he asked, trying to learn more about her.

"Yes," she replied, stretching up to the shelf above the ironing board to remove a gift bag for the wine. Elijah watched her knitted jumper rise, exposing her waist wrapped tightly in her high-rise jeans.

"A birthday?" he asked, noticing a patch on her lower back. *Is she covering a tattoo?* he wondered, then looked to the medicine cabinet. He'd nearly forgotten about his discovery, but he wasn't going to snoop into her private life. Some lines you don't cross. Even he had boundaries.

"No, she's been given a solo in our next showcase," Autumn said before he could ask about the patch.

"Singer?" At least he knew it was for a girl, and he was relieved there wasn't a special guy in her life. She turned around and caught his eyes on her lower back.

He quickly looked away when he realised he had been caught staring. Autumn pulled down her sweater, and he focused on the bowl of fruit in front of him.

"Violinist." Autumn put the bottle in the gift bag and put it in the tote bag on her shoulder.

"Are we having a civilised conversation?" he asked.

She sighed, tucking a loose strand of hair behind her ear. "Why do you have to ruin it? It might surprise you, but I'm perfectly capable of having a civilised conversation. I only struggle with those who turn my front room into a man cave." She took a pre-made protein drink from the fridge.

"Don't worry, I've kept your furniture in storage. I'm even paying for it to be stored," he said.

Autumn stared at him blankly. He wasn't sure if she was happy or annoyed by that fact.

"How generous of you. But if you ever live with another woman in the future, I suggest you ask before you move her things," she said, taking a gulp of the dark green liquid from the glass jar. He knew it didn't taste very good, but it didn't seem to bother her. He might steal her other prepped meals, but he would leave those to her.

"I know my living here is an inconvenience to you, but I…"

"Need to make your next fantasy game? If you had your own place, you'd have all the space in the world *and* you wouldn't waste money storing my stuff," Autumn said, then froze as though she had said too much.

Fantasy game? She looked me up. I never told her I design fantasy games. Tim could have told her, but I doubt it.

"You Googled me?" he asked, leaning on the counter.

"So what? I wanted to know who I was sharing a house with," she retorted as though it were no big deal, though she was blushing slightly.

"Has no one told you not to Google yourself? It's never the best way to judge one's character." Surely, nothing too bad could have come up. Maybe some critics talking about his last game, about how he'd left the company in Canada to start his own.

"I'm not worried about my character, I'm worried about yours," she admitted, though she wouldn't meet his eye.

"What did you learn?" It made him almost giddy to know she was interested in him in any way. *What is wrong with me? Why should I care at all what she thinks about me?* He scolded himself, but he couldn't help it.

"Thirty-two. Single, or there was no information on that. Head designer at Nirosoft until last year, when you left to start your own company, Kyloware. Judging from the figurines I almost stepped on yesterday, the name stems from your love of Star Wars. Your first solo shooter game was a success, and you sold it for millions, only to reinvest it in your own company." She recalled the information like she had read it from a catalogue.

"You're right about the name. And I'm single, just to clarify."

"I don't care. Those were just the headlines. I just wanted to make sure you weren't a complete psycho," she said.

Elijah couldn't help but laugh. *Fair enough.*

"Did you Google me?" she asked, fidgeting with the glass in her hands.

"No, I prefer to get to know people the old-fashioned way," he said, and she scoffed.

"I wouldn't hold my breath." She put the empty smoothie cup in the sink. "And since you're single, I'd prefer it if you didn't bring women home. It's bad enough having you here."

"Same goes for you. I don't need to see some guy in his boxers first thing in the morning," he countered, not liking the thought of any guy being close to her except him. He barely knew her, and yet he didn't want anyone else getting to know her.

"You don't need to worry about that," she said, pulling on a cropped leather jacket which had lain across the chair beside him. "Open all the windows. I don't want the house to stink of paint when I come home." There was no sting in her words.

"Have a good day," Elijah said sweetly.

She hesitated in the doorway. He eyed her curiously.

"By the way, I should say thank you," she said. He frowned, confused. "You were right about the grey; it really highlights the framed portraits."

Elijah lost his smile. "You like it?" he asked, surprised he'd done something that didn't cause her misery. The way her eyes brightened was different from when she was angry but still as satisfying, if not more so.

She walked back towards the stairs, not looking where she was going, and he followed her. "Why wouldn't I? Sorry, but your plan failed. You saved me having to paint. It's a much richer tone than the blue – I owe you one."

Elijah couldn't believe it. *She played me. Or maybe our taste isn't so different...* He suddenly noticed she was about to put her foot in the tray of paint. "Watch your step!"

She grabbed for him as she fell. He tried to catch her, but slipped on the plastic sheeting; on the way down, he successfully knocked over the bucket of paint. Autumn lay cradled in his arms. He'd protected her fall, but they were lying in a puddle of paint.

A moment of silence passed before either spoke. It was Autumn who broke the silence.

"You can let go now," she huffed. He hadn't realised he was gripping her to his side. She sat up, and he stifled a laugh as he looked her over.

"Good thing you like the colour, because you're covered in it," he said, lifting the bucket of paint to his side.

She looked down at her jeans, whining, "These were my favourite!"

"You should have looked where you were going. That's karma for gloating," he chuckled.

She glared at him, then smeared her paint-covered hand down his face, neck, and T-shirt. She laughed, a sound that he wanted to hear again. But he dodged her next swipe and rolled over, pinning her down and forcing her to lie in the puddle.

"Truce?" he asked.

She nodded, breathing heavily beneath him. "Truce."

He offered her a hand up, which she accepted, so he must be making a dent in her resolve. They stared at each other, admiring their handiwork. Then he realised she would probably be late for rehearsals.

"You should change before you go," he said, and her face dropped.

"Oh my God, I'm going to be so late!" She ran up the stairs, leaving him with a mess.

"Don't worry. I'll clean up," he called, but there was no reply, only faint cursing as he heard either her bedroom or the bathroom door slamming.

Elijah picked up the paint bucket and avoided touching anything else with his paint-covered hands. Since he had to wait for her to leave to use the bathroom, he used a kitchen towel to wipe his face and carefully removed his T-shirt. A few moments later, he heard the front door open and close.

"Not even a goodbye or a thank you," he mumbled to himself, but he had to admit he was just as much to blame for the mess as she was.

Once he cleaned himself up and the hallway no longer looked as though a paint bomb had gone off, he sat down to work. Plenty of emails were already waiting for him. A few hours had passed when a message came in on his phone.

> Tim sent me your number. Thank you for cleaning up the mess. A :)

Elijah smiled at his phone like an idiot. No woman had ever had this effect on him. He thought about replying, but he figured it was better to let a good thing lie.

Chapter Six

Autumn

"Elijah painted?" Nina said, sitting on the damp park bench. It was a nice day for a walk, so they'd decided to have lunch in the park at the heart of Wickford.

"Yep, but he only did it because he thought it would piss me off," Autumn said, wiping the bench with her sleeve to get rid of the droplets from the oak tree above. It was nice to be away from the rush of office workers.

"And it didn't? You made me trek to *how* many paint stores to pick out that specific shade of blue?" Nina exclaimed, unwrapping her BLT sandwich.

"It wasn't that many stores!" Autumn watched a family playing not far from them and took a generous gulp of coffee.

Nina gave her a knowing look.

"Okay, it was more than a few," she admitted. "When I woke up and smelt the paint, my stomach dropped. I thought he'd pick an awful colour to wind me up, but it was actually nicer than what I already had. About halfway down the stairs, I caught him dancing—painting, but dancing," she said, laughing at the memory. It was certainly not what she'd expected to find in her hallway at eight a.m., but it had been better than a bunch of movers in overalls.

"That's adorable." Nina sniggered with her mouth half full. "Does he know you caught him?"

"No. He had headphones on, so he didn't hear me. I waited until he went into the kitchen and then called out. I didn't want to frighten him." She also hadn't wanted him to know how long she'd been watching him.

Autumn did everything herself—put up her own shelves and hung the paintings she bought at the local artists' market—and she prided herself on that independence, but seeing Elijah putting effort into the house had made her feel surprisingly at ease. As opposed to every other waking moment, when he was driving her crazy. She still hadn't forgiven him for tossing her over his shoulder like a ragdoll; even thinking about it made her blush.

"So he isn't all bad. Do I sense there might even be an inkling of understanding between you?" Nina teased, finishing her sandwich.

"I think if we can keep some distance from each other, then we should be fine," Autumn agreed, choosing not to tell her friend about what had happened in the earlier hours of the morning. "I don't have much choice since Tim won't answer my calls. I won't get to talk to him until our monthly meeting on Monday."

"It's only a few more days. It's okay to have more people in your life. You can manage more than you think," Nina said.

"This isn't about managing. I just want to protect myself."

"From him, or from your own feelings?" Nina asked, trying to meet her eye.

Autumn didn't know how to respond. It had been easy to let Nina into her life because they worked together; they'd been forced together. Now, the same was happening with Elijah. She wished it were easy for her to accept a new person in her life, to be carefree and go with the flow. But with all she'd been through, she found comfort not in people, but in controlling her surroundings. There was so much she didn't have a say over—her memories, her pain—but she *could* control who came and went from her life for the most part. Her home was her bubble, the one place she could remove her mask and be unashamedly herself. To cry or yell or weep in the shower until the water ran cold. The thought of someone witnessing her rawest self terrified her.

If we weren't forced to live together, would we have got on? Not even in a romantic sense, but as just friends? Sharing a home with him meant she had no way of controlling what he did and didn't see. She didn't know if he would accept her, pity her, or dismiss her. The worst part was, she didn't know which of the three she feared most.

Nina placed a hand on her shoulder, disrupting her thoughts. "Sorry. I didn't mean to put you on the spot. This isn't about Elijah; I worry you close yourself off, and I don't think it would hurt you to take a risk or two."

"I know you mean well, but you'll never understand what it's like to live in my body. I've worked for years to reach a baseline, but I'm still expected to go further. I'm doing the best I can. Between the stress of rehearsals and now Elijah, it's about as much as I can manage." She swallowed, trying to stop the tears from welling up.

Nina wrapped her arms around her. "I didn't mean to pressure you. Sometimes I forget how much you go through because you hide it so well. If you're happy, then I'm happy. We should get back," she said gently.

"I don't mean to hide it. I'm so *bored* of the cramps and spasms and sleepless nights—I bore myself just thinking about it! So talking about it just exhausts me. I'm fine, really. It's just been a crazy few days," Autumn managed to say, gathering up the rubbish from their lunch.

"You don't have to be fine. Not with me," Nina promised, taking her arm as they left the park. Autumn didn't want to leave. She wished they could hide in the park a while longer, but they couldn't be late for afternoon rehearsals.

When rehearsals were over, Autumn played the first part of her solo for Nina. She stopped when she saw Nina wince. Something was off. She was playing the right keys, but it didn't fit.

"I know it's not the strongest, but I was interrupted before I could settle into it," she said, thinking of how Elijah had stopped her. *Even he said how terrible it sounded! I should be able to do this in my sleep. He thought it was bad enough to be considered revenge.*

"I think it sounds fine. You're just being hard on yourself," Nina said, sitting on the stool beside her. Thankfully, no one was in the theatre to hear her tripping up.

Even if she was still messing up, she had to admit that her back felt a lot better with the extra rest this morning, even if she didn't agree with Elijah's methods. *He must have noticed the medicated patch on my back, but he didn't ask.* She also knew that he must have seen the medicine cabinet since he'd added his own single packet of migraine tablets. Since he'd respected her privacy, she respected his and didn't ask about it.

"Fine isn't what I was going for," she said, closing the lid of the piano harder than she should have. "Of all the shows, why am I messing up my first solo return?"

"Sasaki thinks you're ready, and so do I, but you might need more time," Nina said gently.

"I don't want more time. I want to get back on stage without needing extra support!" Autumn twisted her hair into a claw clip.

Nina rose from the stool to pack her things. "Maybe the problem is that you're pushing too hard. You're so focused on getting it perfect that you aren't enjoying it," she suggested.

"If my *intruder* hadn't interrupted me, then I would have been able to practise more today."

"Forget about Elijah. This is more about you than him. You're playing, but where is the heart?"

Autumn studied the notes on the paper in front of her. *Heart?* Nina's comment confirmed her fears: something was missing.

"Still practising? I hope you aren't neglecting yourself," Sasaki said, appearing from the wings.

Autumn grabbed the sheet music from the third movement and shoved them into her bag before he could scold her for straining herself. "No, we were just messing around. I can assure you, I'm taking care of myself," she said, putting on her jacket.

"Well, enough messing for one day. I want to hear the third movement before the end of the week," he said, looking over his glasses.

She felt her throat tighten at the short time frame. It was a good thing she worked well under pressure—mostly.

"I'll give it my all," she said, straightening her back only to wince.

Sasaki gestured for her to come closer. "Is your back holding up? I know you're already under stress about the movement. I don't want you putting practice before your health."

She didn't want to lie almost as much as she didn't want to see the concern in his eyes. "I'm fine," she said, trying to sound convincing.

"Really?"

"Perfectly," she lied.

"If you say so, but I want you to rest. No solo is worth it."

She knew he was talking as her friend, not the conductor who was relying on her for the showcase.

"That's not necessary—"

Sasaki tutted. "You practised late last night. I don't want your pain to cripple your talent," he said.

Autumn sighed. He was right; when she pushed herself, all she did was make everyone's lives hard. *If I leave now, it gives me more time to work on my piece at home. He can't stop me from practising there.*

"Do you want me to come over later and help? We can go through it together," Nina whispered, reading her mind as they left for the theatre. Autumn wished she didn't know her so well.

"No, this is something I have to figure out for myself," she said. *Finding my heart, apparently.*

Nina gave her a tight squeeze before they parted ways.

Autumn made it home just before the rain started. She removed her shoes at the front door, flexing her back as the ache set in. *Nothing an ice pack and lying on the floor can't fix,* she thought. Thankfully, her key had worked, and Elijah's office was quiet. She would have thought him gone, but his motorcycle was parked outside.

She tiptoed past his door to the kitchen, not in the mood to talk to him after a long day. She was tired, sore, and hungry. She didn't need to add irritation to the list.

"Did he think I wouldn't notice?" she grumbled, rifling through the half-empty fridge as she hunted for her dinner. Some of the meals she had prepared were either eaten or half-consumed. Even her vegan dessert yoghurts were gone!

Elijah had also filled the side shelves with every assortment of alternative milk she could think of, which she didn't actually mind so long as he didn't touch her favourite strawberry milk. There was nothing prepared for dinner, and she couldn't bring herself to cook. She went to the cupboard for one of her emergency packets of ramen and saw that Elijah had filled the shelves with microwaveable meals. *Clearly, he doesn't like to cook. Why is he eating mine and leaving his own? If he won't eat them, maybe I should. He's only eating my vegan meals, and I want those for my meat-free days.* She'd found meat and dairy weren't great for her inflammation, so she tried to round out her meals as best she could without restricting her diet.

She closed the cupboard and fridge door to go and confront him. *If he wants to be rid of me, he's going to have to do better than eating my food.* She opened the sliding doors to find the front room dark. It felt strange; she didn't even recognise it as a room in her house.

"Elijah?" she called from the doorway. Stepping into his territory felt like giving him more power, and she didn't want to give him any leverage. When he didn't answer, she guessed he had his headphones on. She knocked on the door, but he still didn't answer. *He must be doing this to annoy me. The silent treatment? Are we children?* Her irritation propelled her into the room.

"Elijah!" she snapped, moving deeper into the sitting room.

She stopped when she realised he was passed out on his desk. On closer inspection, he stirred slightly—just asleep. She didn't want to disturb him.

With the computer glow over his features, he looked far more relaxed than she had ever seen him. No scowl or false smile; he still hadn't shaved, giving him a more rugged look than the clean-shaven suit she'd first met. He wasn't wearing the paint-covered T-shirt she had left him in that morning, and she couldn't help but notice his defined back.

Stop staring—it's just a back! Not wanting to be a creep who watched people sleep, she averted her gaze, glancing up at the two dormant screens. She wanted a sneak peek at what he stayed up at all hours doing, but she was afraid if she hit one of the keys, it would make a sound. Instead, she tiptoed over the creaking floors to the table beside his desk and studied the multiple sketches of dragons and sorcerers in different colours and styles. *These are incredible! Did he do these? Or does he have someone draw for him?* Leaning closer, she studied the deep colours and intricate details on the dragon's scaly tail and the wizard's beaded cloak.

"You should wait until I'm out before you start snooping."

Autumn jumped back, mortified at being caught. Elijah was stretching his arms above his head. *At least I wasn't staring at him.*

"I wasn't snooping," she protested, looking at *her* empty dinner container on the desk.

"Mmm-hmm," he said, crossing his arms over his chest.

"I have to ask. Are you allergic to wearing T-shirts?" she snapped.

"You're in *my* room," he pointed out. "I could be wearing less, but I think that would make us both uncomfortable."

"Thank you for the consideration," she said, wanting to get off the topic of his naked body. She pulled at her sleeves. "I only came to ask you to leave my shelves alone."

He yawned, clearly still half-asleep. "Your shelves?"

She decided she preferred him unconscious. "Yes, my food." She picked up the container from his desk and waved it in front of his face. "You ate the food I prepped for the rest of the week."

Elijah shrugged, leaning back in the chair. "Sorry—all the painting worked up quite the appetite." Before she could snap at him, he raised his hands in defence. "It's been a long day, but I promise I'll try my best to keep to my own food." He did appear to be somewhat sorry.

"Good. Thank you," she said, grateful for his lack of fight. She wanted to make a quick exit since they'd almost escaped each other without quarrelling, but when she reached the door, Elijah cleared his throat. She turned around to see him watching her go.

"You're a great cook—some would say irresistible." He smiled.

She glared at him. "You're a grown man. I'm sure you can show some restraint," she snapped.

She was about to slide the door closed when her phone rang in her back pocket. It was her mum, who always worried if Autumn didn't answer immediately. She picked up.

"Hey, Mum! Sorry, I just got in."

"Autumn, please close the door," Elijah requested, but when she ignored him, he moved towards the door to close it himself. He opened his mouth to speak, but she didn't want her mum to hear him.

"Hold on, I'm just putting my things down," she said, covering Elijah's mouth with her hand. Indignantly, he pushed it off.

"Did I hear someone else?" her mum said, and Autumn's stomach knotted.

"Nope, just the TV," she lied, her eyes pleading with Elijah to be quiet.

"The TV knows your name?" Mum asked. "Have you met someone? It's been a while since I heard you were with someone. I'm so glad you stopped seeing that drummer. You can't build a strong relationship with someone who is out of the country."

Autumn held the phone away from her ear, having already heard the argument countless times.

"A drummer? I didn't take you for the bad boy type," Elijah whispered, and she waved him away.

"I haven't met anyone. Can I call you back later?"

"Are you safe? Do you need help?" Mum said. Autumn heard the instant panic in her voice.

She sighed. "I'm safe," she admitted, looking at Elijah, who raised his eyebrows.

"Then who is in the house?" Mum yelled down the phone.

Elijah snatched the phone away when Autumn hesitated.

"Hi, Mrs Adler. I'm Autumn's friend."

She shook her head frantically, begging him silently not to reveal their living situation.

"Please don't worry. I'm only here to paint; your daughter is perfectly safe with me," Elijah lied, pretending to zip his lips shut.

Autumn felt her shoulders relax. *If Mum found out we're living together, she'd be on the doorstep tomorrow with more questions than I've answered.* She didn't need to give her parents another reason for them to want her to return home. They hadn't been all that happy when Tim had offered her the house in the first place, even though Tim and her father were childhood friends and had been business partners in the past. Her dad thought it was too much of an imposition.

Elijah put her mum on speaker, but he didn't give Autumn back the phone.

"Isn't it a bit late to be painting? You shouldn't be sleeping with the windows open, not with your back," Mum started.

Autumn caught Elijah's frown and grabbed the phone. She turned off the speaker before Mum said too much.

"I'm fine," she ground out. "We were just finishing up here. He's packing up. Can I call you later?"

"I'm going out with your father later. It's quiz night in the pub, and the prize is a two-day stay at Richmond's spa!"

Autumn felt a little hurt. She had bought them a stay at a hotel in the city for Christmas last year so they could come and visit, but they still hadn't come. Every time she had a show, they were busy, or a pipe had burst, or the chickens had escaped. She didn't press the issue, but she wanted to see them, and between rehearsals and recovery time, she didn't have time to get the four-hour train ride home. She moved into the kitchen and away from Elijah, but to her irritation, he followed.

"Good luck. Can I speak to Dad? I want to invite you both to my next show."

The line went quiet.

"He's out in the garden. I'll get him to call you later," Mum said.

Autumn knew that was code for him not wanting to talk. They usually ended up arguing, which usually resulted in Autumn feeling guilty, followed by an apologetic text from her dad with a vague promise to talk soon.

"Sure. I'll text you the details. I wanted to give you both plenty of notice for the last Friday in May." Autumn forced a smile. She didn't want Elijah to hear her own parents making excuses not to see her.

"We'll try to make it," Mum said. Though Autumn hoped she meant it, she knew better than to get her hopes up.

"Your mum sounds nice," Elijah said from across the kitchen island when she hung up after a quick *Love you*.

"She is," Autumn said, taking a seat at the counter.

"What does she do?" he asked, making a cup of coffee.

Autumn considered not answering, but she thought of Nina's advice in the park. *If we* are *going to be sharing the house for the next few weeks, sharing a little won't do any harm.*

"Mum's the head librarian in our town. There are probably more books than people in Islacore; it's a small village on the coastline," she said, wondering why she'd given him so many details.

He looked impressed. "Clever woman. She must be why you have so many books."

Had he been going through her things?

"I wasn't snooping around," he said before she could ask. "There was a whole shelf I had the movers put into storage." He removed a mug from the cupboard.

"Most of those were gifts from her. If you speak to her again, make sure not to mention you put them in storage—she wouldn't be so nice then," she warned him, glad he hadn't seen the ones in her room. Most of the books above her bed were chronic pain and stress management guides, which she swore she was going to get around to reading one day. The romances alongside them were far more weathered. "The only thing she loves more than me and my dad is books. She was head of historical archives at Wickford University, but that was before my dad retired and we had to move." She didn't mention that her accident was the reason they'd decided to leave the city. She'd never asked her mom how she felt about the move. It had been her dad's idea to sell his shares in the investment company to Tim, or that's what she had been told. At the time, she'd still been in rehab learning to walk, and it seemed redundant to ask now.

"Did you go to Wickford?" he asked, and she shook her head.

"No, I went to a community college. You?"

"I studied in Canada. I couldn't wait to get away from home," he said, looking into his coffee as though he didn't want to go into more detail.

"Must have been hard to be away from your family," she commented, wondering if he was close to his parents.

Autumn liked to think she was close to hers, even if they didn't always see eye to eye.

"My mum got remarried, and I figured leaving would give them some space," he said.

"You didn't like the guy?"

"No, he's great. My mum is happy, and that's all I care about." The way he said it and the way the corners of his eyes scrunched gave Autumn the impression his mum might have had a hard life. "What did you study?" he asked, taking a sip of his coffee.

"Library and information science."

"I would have thought you'd study music."

"No. I worked with my mum in the library on the weekends, so I figured it was a safe bet. It only lasted about six weeks—wasn't for me," she admitted. "I love to read, but I never inherited Mum's obsession with books. Instead, it was Dad's love for music that settled in my bones. He was the one who took me to my first lesson."

"Then how did you end up back in the city, playing in an orchestra?" he asked, sitting across the counter from her.

Autumn studied her hands, not wanting to tell the whole sad story. "My old conductor found out I was playing for a small theatre. He convinced me to come back and work for him, and here I am."

"How long have you been playing?"

"Since I was three. My dad had a piano. He loved playing old songs, and still does, I think. It was something we did together."

Silence drifted between them. She wondered if she had said too much, but when she looked up from the table, he seemed lost in thought.

"I'm jealous they supported your passion. My own father would sell his organs to get me to take over the family business," Elijah said quietly.

Autumn pressed her lips together sympathetically.

Even though her parents didn't understand her reason for going back to the stage, they didn't interfere either.

"They did before. Not so much now, but they let me be. Game design wasn't on the cards?"

"Definitely not," he said, his eyes going wide.

"What was?" she asked, glad it was her turn to ask the questions.

"Finance, investments. Managing other people's money, mostly," he said.

"Wasn't for you?"

He grunted. "No, never."

"What got you into games?" she asked, microwaving one of his meals. She needed to silence her grumbling stomach, and the spaghetti Bolognese did look good. It was also dairy-free—he must need to avoid it.

He watched as she twirled her fork in the spaghetti. She waited for him to say something, but it wasn't like he could argue about her eating his food after he'd eaten hers.

"When I was in boarding school," he told her, "most of the other kids went home for the weekends. I didn't, and gaming became my home. I loved the concepts and stories behind them, and I was good with computers."

Hearing the passion in his voice, Autumn could tell he wanted his company to work as much as she wanted to return to the stage. Even if she didn't like how he had handled their current situation, she admired how he'd gone after what he wanted.

"Piano was the same for me, minus the boarding school. It was the one place I could escape to. It came naturally, and it was something I could do with my dad," she said.

"I envy you. I don't think I've ever had a personal conversation with my father that didn't end in an argument or a debate."

She smiled. She understood the feeling more than he knew. "Why did you decide to go out on your own? The article I read said you were on track to take over Nirosoft."

Elijah looked either surprised or pleased that she was interested in his life, she wasn't sure which.

"I wanted to build something on my own, and I had done all I could for the company. I wanted a new challenge," he said.

"Understandable, but why come back? Why not stay in Canada?"

"A fresh start, and my investors are here," he said, looking at his watch. "Actually, I should get back to work—I have an overseas call."

"Makes sense. I was going to bed anyway," she said, suddenly nervous. *I didn't mean to ask him so many questions. I didn't think he would be so easy to talk to.* The ease of the conversation was unsettling.

"Can I give you something so you won't think I'm invading your privacy?" he asked, hesitating by the door.

"Depends on what it is," she said, her eyes narrowing.

"I used one of your heat patches. My shoulder was killing me after working all night, but I got you a new pack when I went out for a run," he said, returning from his office with her favourite brand in hand.

Autumn took the pack, waiting for him to ask why she needed them. She was suddenly afraid of telling him about her past—that he might look at her like she might break at any moment as so many others did. But the question never came.

"Thank you," she said sheepishly, placing them back in the medicine cabinet. "You can use them if you like. You don't have to ask."

"Okay. If I do, I'll replace them."

"Okay," she said, not able to meet his gaze. "Night," she added before heading to her room. She needed to put some space between them because, suddenly, she felt far too comfortable in his presence.

Chapter Seven

Elijah

"Why do I get the feeling this isn't a good call?" Elijah said when Francis' name lit up his phone. He'd only gone to sleep five hours ago.

"I hate to do this, but I need you to fill in for me at Gamecon."

"You're a key speaker, I can't just fill in!" Elijah said, suddenly wide awake. "It will affect Kyloware's reputation if we leave them in the lurch!"

"I know I was the one who told you we should go for it, but we don't have a choice. Todd's running a fever, and I have to take him to the doctor. It's Saturday, so if I don't take him today, I'll have to wait until Monday, and I don't want to risk it. I can't put him in the car for hours if he is sick, and if I leave it until Aiden can take over, then I won't be able to make it in time for the illustration panel," Francis explained in a rush. It sounded like a million things were happening in the background.

"Can't Aiden take him to the doctor? I don't know anything about drawing, let alone what I need to tell others."

Elijah wished they hadn't signed up this year. Their schedules were packed.

"Aiden has to be in court to give evidence on a case. He can't show up."

There was no other option but to take his place. Elijah tossed the sheets from his body. He would need to get on the road early to escape the traffic of those leaving the city for the weekend.

"This is the price I have to pay for being single," he grumbled under his breath. But he knew he couldn't be selfish; plus, Todd was his godson, and he hated the idea of him being sick. "You need to put your kid first. What do you need me to do?"

"Let me cry for all the freedom you have," Francis snarked. Elijah's phone pinged. "I've sent you everything you need to know. You only have to talk about our game with a few creative details. Just read what I wrote and you should be fine."

"What if they have questions?" Elijah asked, hastily making his bed.

"Show them the latest trailer. A teaser of our game should kill any remaining time. I would cancel, but if we want to hold our slot for next year, we need to stay in their good graces," Francis said.

Elijah didn't really want to release the trailer so soon—not until the contract with Nirosoft was secure. He would have to play it by ear.

"Fine. I can be on the road in an hour. What time is the lecture?"

"Today at four. It's a long drive to Port Harlow, so get going," he said.

Elijah agreed before hanging up. He grabbed his jeans and favourite graphic sweatshirt that featured the dragon king from their last game on his way to the bathroom.

He'd left his stuff in the bathroom last night, sure Autumn wouldn't throw it away, but his aftershave and razor no longer sat on the sink. He checked the wicker basket, but they weren't there either. When he opened the mirrored cabinet, he smiled to himself as he noticed that she had moved her own bits and pieces to the top shelves and placed his own on a separate shelf. *Progress.* She'd also put his toothbrush in a separate cup. It shouldn't have brightened his morning as much as it did, but he felt a spring in his step. He thought about knocking on her door to thank her for making the space, but he figured he should let her sleep.

Once he was freshly shaved, he headed back downstairs and put on his watch. Grabbing his overnight bag, he made sure to pack a spare suit and laptop. *If I leave now, I'll make it just in time.* Clicking into the itinerary Francis had sent him, he saw that once the panels were over, there was a casual buffet for the speakers, followed by bottomless drinks in the hotel across from the event hall. He noticed his former boss Mr Harcroft, the CEO of Nirosoft, was named on another panel talking about upcoming releases. *It'll be a good opportunity to network with other buyers and show Harcroft other companies are interested in the game,* he thought, hoping it would seal the deal.

It was only when he'd finished packing that he realised he would be leaving Autumn alone. *She won't kick me out while I'm gone, will she? I doubt Tim would side with her if she pulled such a stunt. I think after our conversation last night, we have a better understanding.*

In the kitchen, he noticed that Autumn was snuggled up on the couch, asleep, with the TV on standby. *She must have come down in the middle of the night.* Elijah tiptoed, hoping the floorboards wouldn't creak as he made his way over to her. It was too early for her to be up yet, and he didn't want to run the risk of irritating her when they were so close to being civil with each other. He spotted a fluffy white blanket lying on the rug on the floor beside her. The room was chilly first thing in the morning, so he gently lifted it over her; she snuggled it reflexively under her chin. He grimaced, afraid the gesture would wake her, but she only smiled a little and turned over. *How can she be so fierce when she's awake and yet so cute when she's sleeping?*

On the kitchen island, he took one of her notepads and settled for leaving her a note to let her know he would be gone for the night. He was anxious enough about being on a panel for illustration; he didn't have time to think about what she might do in his absence. Out of time, he couldn't help but steal the overnight oats she had prepared in the fridge and the neatly sliced watermelon to make the drive far more tolerable. *I promised I would stop stealing her food, but her anger will keep her thinking of me,* he thought, wondering why she made some food vegan but still had meat and dairy too. *Out of sight, but not out of mind.* Tucking the containers under his arm, he grabbed his overnight bag from his room and turned off his computer.

Closing the front door behind him, he felt a crunch under his foot. He glanced down at a single long-stemmed rose beneath his foot.

There were no rose bushes in the front garden, and he doubted the cherry tree was suddenly blooming roses. He picked up the flower, noticing how perfect it was. The petals were almost *too* symmetrical. The note accompanying it read: *Another year together; our past will determine your future.*

It must have been delivered to the wrong house, he thought. The message didn't sound all that loving, but maybe it did to whoever was meant to receive it. He turned over the card but found no name or contact details for the sender. Eyeing his watch, he decided he didn't have time to check with the neighbours. *I doubt a single rose is important.* At the end of the path, he put it in the compost.

Down the street, he got into his Jeep, deciding it was too long a drive for his bike, even if the skies were clear.

Chapter Eight

Autumn

When Autumn woke up, she noticed her favourite mug on the glass table with a note stuck to it. Shrugging off the blanket, she guessed Elijah must already be up, since the underfloor heating warmed her bare feet. She stretched her arms overhead, trying to work out the sore kinks in her spine. *What is he up to now?* she thought, scowling as she pulled the note off and the tape residue stuck to the mug. Her sleepy eyes adjusted to scribbled words as she made her way to the fridge.

A,

Had to go to a conference. Gone for the weekend, try not to miss me too much. Thank you for making room in the bathroom, I appreciate it.

P.S. If you change the locks, you will be paying for the broken door. Enjoy the peace, it won't last for long.

E. :)

Miss you? In your dreams. At least we managed to survive the first couple of days together. She scoffed, sticking the note to the fridge, unsure of why she didn't throw it away. Making room for his belongings suddenly felt very intimate, though it had been an unconscious decision. She just hadn't wanted his things lying around, and if she'd thrown them away, it would have started another argument.

She reread the part about changing the locks and rolled her eyes. *I wouldn't sink so low.* Then she toyed with the idea of hiring a moving truck and getting rid of all his stuff. *It's only fair, considering he put my things in storage.* Finishing her smoothie bowl, she concluded it would be a waste of time and money. There was no getting rid of him unless he decided to go. *He would only get amusement out of seeing me irritated. Whenever I'm angry, he has that smile—the type of smile that makes you forget why you were angry in the first place.* She refused to give him any excuse to use such a weapon.

After breakfast, she read in the conservatory for a while about a swashbuckling prince and his cursed lover, then realised she should probably water his plants while he was gone. The plants didn't deserve to die because their owner was a pain in the arse. She found the task rather peaceful and decided to leave the conservatory door open so she could smell the fresh flowers as she practised. Once the nerves along the scar down her spine started to spark, she forced herself away from the piano and took the opportunity to stretch without having to worry about Elijah walking in on her.

Having the house all to herself, she thought she would revel in the freedom. However, as she finished her stretches and rolled up her yoga mat, she found the house strangely quiet—not that she was ever going to admit that to him. There was no faint music drifting from his office or the sound of his heavy footsteps on the wooden floors. She'd never felt lonely living on her own, but having the house to herself again felt a little strange. A little too quiet, as if the house were suddenly too big. *It's only been a few days;*

there's no way I could possibly miss him. All he's done is invade my space and drive me crazy, how could I miss that?

A knock on the door disturbed her thoughts. She hadn't ordered anything; Elijah might have, but it seemed strange to have a delivery so late in the afternoon. When she opened the door, whoever had knocked was gone, and two roses had been left on her doorstep.

Freezing in dread, she stared at them.

Who the hell is doing this? It's been three years! How long until they stop sending them? Stepping over the roses, she hurried down the path to find no car or delivery van on the street. As always, there was no note.

I don't want to touch them, but I can't leave them here to rot. Elijah would find them. With a steadying breath, she picked them up, then hissed as one of the stems pricked her finger. *Why haven't they been dethorned?*

She closed the door and put the roses in the bin in the kitchen. Licking the blood from her finger, she walked to the kitchen and removed a bandage from her medicine cabinet. She dropped it when another knock on the door startled her.

Maybe whoever has been sending the roses is tired of being ignored. Sudden terror washed through her at the thought, and she wished Elijah was home.

Another knock. Clearly, they weren't going away. Putting her fears aside, she grabbed an umbrella from the stand by the door and concealed it behind her back. She opened the door to find Nina staring back at her with puffy eyes and a tissue pressed up against her nose.

"Sorry," Nina mumbled, "I tried to call."

Autumn felt her shoulders relax only to be startled by the fact that Nina wore pink sweatpants and a matching oversized hoodie. She didn't think she had ever seen her so casual. *Something must have gone very wrong.*

"What happened?" Autumn ushered her friend inside, putting the umbrella back before she noticed. She pulled her phone from her back pocket, but it was out of battery.

"We fought. Can I stay here tonight?" Nina bawled, reaching the kitchen.

"Fought with who?" Autumn frowned, plugging in her phone while Nina took off her trainers by the island. "And of course you can stay. Just tell me everything."

Nina began to sob uncontrollably. Seeing her so upset broke Autumn's heart. She embraced her friend, letting her get the tears out of her system. After a few minutes, the sobs dissipated. Autumn stroked her back until her breathing evened out. Nina leaned out of her embrace, and Autumn handed her some tissues from the counter.

"With Garrett. He said I don't take our relationship seriously because I still have pictures of Sophia and me."

Autumn's heart sank, and she made Nina and herself a cup of her favourite sweet tea. "Those are memories; you shouldn't feel bad about keeping them."

"I shouldn't have hidden them." Nina sniffled and cupped the warm mug. "You're in them too, and so is Aimee. I just worried that if he saw them, he would feel weird about it, so I kept them in my cupboard."

Autumn was surprised she'd felt the need to hide a part of herself from her boyfriend. Nina was the most self-assured person she knew. It was horrible to see her confidence slipping.

"I said I don't have feelings for her anymore, but he doesn't believe me," Nina went on, her voice cracking.

"Do you? You can tell me—I won't judge. Sophia was your first love, and you only separated because of distance. It would make sense if you still had some lingering feelings." Autumn could see how much guilt was eating at her.

Nina moved to the couch on the far side of the room and tucked her legs beneath herself. "I'll always love her, but I'm not *in* love with her anymore." Nina clutched a cushion to her chest like she was trying to protect herself from her feelings.

"Is there something else?"

Nina didn't meet her eye. "She's getting married."

The strain in her voice told Autumn everything she needed to know. Not that she would ever say it out loud, but she would much rather Nina cried about Sophia's engagement than waste tears over Garrett.

"Are you upset about Garrett, or that she is engaged?"

Nina sighed and buried her face in her hands. "Both."

"A box of tissues and some ice cream coming your way," Autumn said, grabbing them from the counter and the freezer. Sometimes there was nothing to do except to be there. "Wanna cry and watch TV?" Autumn asked, plonking down on the couch beside her.

"Nothing with romance," Nina sniffled.

"How about a horror?"

Nina leant over the couch, scanning Autumn's collection of films. She had a whole shelf dedicated to horror. "The more violent, the better."

It broke Autumn's heart to see her so down. When it came to her heart, Nina was always so loving and vulnerable. She gave people her all; Autumn was often envious of her ability to be so vulnerable. She was terrified of experiencing such hurt. She felt like she had already had enough pain in her life, she didn't need to add heartbreak to the list.

Nina settled on a gruesome zombie flick. They snuggled up on the couch. Halfway through someone being eaten, Autumn realised Nina had arrived minutes after the roses.

"When you were driving up, you didn't see anyone outside the house, did you?" she asked, getting them some water.

"No, should I have? Were you expecting someone?" Nina didn't take her eyes off the screen except to get another scoop of cookie dough ice cream.

"No. I thought I heard someone knock," she said, putting the topic to rest. She didn't want to worry Nina.

They ordered takeaway for dinner, and they were only twenty minutes into their third horror film when she noticed Nina had drifted off. Autumn covered her with a blanket and let her sleep off her tears. Everything would seem better when she woke up.

Chapter Nine

Elijah

Once the stress of the lecture was over, Elijah found himself queuing for reception at Harlow Hotel, since he hadn't been able to check in earlier. As it was Saturday night, the hotel lobby was bustling with those who had attended Gamecon. After hours of small talk, he was running out of steam, and he just wanted to get to his room and rest. Then again, he never managed to sleep in hotels thanks to footsteps in the corridor, the sound of the TV from the room above, or a couple having far too good a time nearby. No matter how tired he was, his mind never quietened.

A heavy hand landed on Elijah's shoulder, and he turned to see his old boss, Mr Harcroft. His beard was greyer than when he had last seen him, but his suit was no less expensive. "Your speech was impressive, although we were expecting your creative director. I didn't know you knew so much about illustration."

"Harcroft." Elijah shook his hand. "I'm afraid there was a family emergency, though Francis was looking forward to coming." He took a step forward as the queue moved.

"His talent is impressive. It still troubles me to have lost both of you," Harcroft said, and Elijah caught the flash of a grimace. Clearly, he was still bitter about it. "No hard feelings. After all, we are acquiring the game, so it's like you never left."

"I wouldn't be where I am today without Nirosoft, but I'm sure the Canada office is coping just fine without us. Our last game was so successful, and I believe we can do even better this time," Elijah said. His ten-year plan relied on it. He would use the capital he'd gained from selling his games to build a company to not only rival his strongest and oldest competitor, but crush them. *If I have to bite my tongue in the meantime, so be it.*

"I hope you're right," Harcroft said, raising his glass. He practically had dollar signs in his eyes. Elijah had no choice but to cheer. "I was hoping to see the trailer today. With the demo on schedule for the end of the month, I hope you aren't cutting it too close." He took a sip of champagne. He wanted them to get the game launched by Christmas.

"Not today—we want to keep customers guessing. End of the month, then we can sign on the dotted line," Elijah assured him. He was afraid that Nirosoft might pull out to spite him for leaving and taking their lead designer with him, but once the game was sure to make money, he doubted Harcroft would give up the golden goose.

"Judging from the profits on your last game, I shall have my pen at the ready," Harcroft said before he was called away to a group of people waiting outside the hotel bar.

Elijah reached the counter to give his name and groaned when he discovered there was no reservation under the name.

"Try Francis Henderson, Kyloware," he said, hearing the customers behind him grumble about the wait.

"Sorry, sir, there must be a mix up. I don't have any listing," the receptionist said, clicking on his keyboard. "But I have a master suite available. Otherwise, I can recommend another hotel one town over. With the conference, everywhere local is booked."

Elijah didn't want to pay for a bad night's sleep. *I've seen Harcroft and I don't have to give another lecture tomorrow, so there's no point in hanging around.*

"Don't worry about it," he said, slipping his wallet back into his pocket. The receptionist appeared surprised by his lack of irritation, but Elijah was too tired to care. *I'm only forty minutes from Mum's, and I have to pick up Brinkley anyway.*

"Thank you for understanding. Here's a voucher if you would like to visit us again," the receptionist said quietly, slipping him a voucher.

Elijah moved aside and let the next customer go ahead before heading for the revolving door.

～

"Mum, you home?" Elijah opened the front door to his childhood home. His stepdad's car wasn't in the drive, so he figured his mum was alone for the weekend.

He felt far more comfortable at home than he did in a busy hotel. When he didn't get any response, he walked through the Pepto-Bismol-coloured corridor to the kitchen. He didn't even get a chance to say hello before Brinkley, his four-year-old golden retriever, started barking and slobbered all over him.

"Where's Mum?" he asked, scratching his furry friend's ears. It was past eight, but there was no way his mum was in bed yet.

Brinkley barked and ran out of the kitchen to a garden that rivalled those on the cover of *Country and Home Magazine*—not that his mum would even let her garden be photographed, in case anyone tried to steal her gardening secrets. The sun had already set, but the garden was lit up with lamps.

Elijah heard his mum gently scolding Brinkley. "Stop barking, or the neighbours will give out again!" When he turned the corner, he found her knee-deep in the soil. Despite the lack of sun, she was still wearing a giant sun hat.

"Isn't it a bit late for gardening?" he asked, realising how much she had aged in the time he'd been away. Her dark hair was still long but streaked with grey, and she had more lines around her eyes—deep brown like his own—as she smiled up at him.

"Never," she said, taking off her gloves. "The prodigal son returns! I'd have thought I'd never see you again if it wasn't for Brinkley." She wrapped her arms around him.

"I was in another country! And thank you for minding Brinkley while I got settled. I'm sure she's been up to mischief." Elijah glanced over his mum's head to see Brinkley sticking her snout in the freshly laid soil.

"I can't plant anything without her digging it up twenty minutes later, which is why I'm still out here this late," she said, ushering Brinkley away from her bulbs.

"It's a retriever's job to retrieve," Elijah joked, hoping she hadn't caused too much chaos.

"The fun part is that she takes the bulbs and buries them somewhere else. In a few weeks, I'll have some plants in some funny places," she said, obviously slightly irritated. "But it's impossible to be annoyed at something so cute."

Elijah understood the sentiment. It was how he had ended up with Brinkley in the first place. A few years after he'd moved to Canada, he'd seen her in a shelter window and couldn't bear to leave her behind. The first moment she'd snuggled into him with no fear or hesitation, he just had to bring her home.

Thinking of Autumn, he wondered how she would react to Brinkley. *Just like her, Autumn is all bark and no bite.* Though he should probably never compare Autumn to his dog—then she might actually bite.

"Are you going to stay for dinner? I have a vegetable stew on," his mother said, placing her sun hat on the kitchen counter as the timer sounded.

The smell in the kitchen made his mouth water. He'd missed her cooking while he was away. She'd learnt everything from old cookbooks they'd found together in a thrift store; it was something to do since they couldn't afford to do much. He would do his homework and she would cook his favourite meals, making clever substitutions for the more expensive ingredients.

"Sounds great. You have me for the night. I'll drive back in the morning," he said, watching as she removed the stew from the oven.

"Great! Frank is at a wine auction for the restaurant, so it's nice to have company," she said, filling two bowls with stew.

"How is the restaurant? And Frank?" They sat at the wooden kitchen table.

"He's good, and excited about opening the new restaurant. I'll tell him you asked after him," she said, warmth in her eyes. "I'm more interested in how things are with you. How are you getting on with the house?"

"Fine, but there were some…hiccups," he admitted, savouring the delicious gravy.

His mum glanced up from her stew, waiting for him to continue.

"It's about a woman," he hedged, afraid to tell her the full situation.

"How exciting! When can I meet her?" his mum said, getting the wrong idea.

"Ha. Don't start planning the wedding. We barely know each other. I, um, rented out her house."

"With her still living in it?" His mum dropped her fork in her stew.

"A friend offered it to me, so I took it. She...might not have agreed," he explained, "but I didn't know she hadn't agreed until after I moved in." He didn't want to have to tell her about Tim's investment. She would warn him against taking anything from his father, and though she was right about his attaching strings, Elijah needed the investment more than his pride.

"Have you apologised? I'm sure she was upset."

"Not exactly." He was starting to feel he was wrong to have accepted the offer in the first place, and yet he didn't want to leave. He just wasn't sure if he didn't want to leave the house or leave *her*. No woman had ever affected him this way; he wasn't sure how to handle it.

"You should have. You might have rented the place, but it was her home. What if the same happened to you?" his mum said, pouring herself a glass of wine without offering him one. He suddenly felt like he was being scolded.

"I don't want her to hate me. I want us to get along. I don't want to spend the next few weeks fighting," he confessed. He wasn't proud of his behaviour so far, and he wanted to make both their lives easier. He swore to himself that he would try and do better. He just didn't know where to start.

"I would go with a gesture, a peace offering."

"A peace offering. I can do that. But I don't know what would be appropriate in this situation," he grumbled. "What if I make it worse?"

"I don't think you could make it worse. She was living her life and now she has to adjust to a stranger! Even a simple gesture would go a long way."

She might be right. Tim had mentioned Autumn wasn't all that sociable. *Perhaps the idea of living with someone caused her more anxiety than I realised.*

"She likes music and plays the piano," Elijah said, not wanting to give her name. *I don't want her to be my enemy, but I don't want her to be my friend either. I want her. All of her.* The thought surprised him.

"What type? You could take her to a concert?"

"Classical, and I don't think a concert would win her over considering that she's a performer."

"A performer? I'm intrigued. An accomplished woman who makes you nervous. I want to meet her all the more," his mother said, finishing her dinner.

He rolled his eyes. "Not helping," he grumbled.

"I don't know what to tell you. I suggest you find a way to make up for the misunderstanding," she said, as if it were the easiest thing in the world.

"I'll figure something out," he said, wishing he could drive home. *If I'm not going to leave and neither is she, then I'm going to have to figure out a way to make her see that I'm not a complete arsehole.*

"I have every faith in you. Matters of the heart are always complicated," she said while he put their empty bowls in the sink.

Before he could argue that his heart had nothing to do with it, his phone rang. He checked the caller ID. Autumn.

"Speak of the devil," he said, but when he answered, crying came from the other end. "Autumn? Is everything okay?"

All he could hear was crying on the other end. Thoughts raced through his mind. Why would she call *him* if she was upset? Maybe something had happened to the house.

"Autumn? Are you okay?" He moved away from the sink to grab his jacket. She still didn't say anything. All he heard were muffled sobs.

"Answer me! Are you safe?" he asked desperately, but before there was any response, it sounded like the phone was dropped. The line went dead. Elijah's chest tightened. He was still over an hour from home.

"Is everything okay? You've gone awfully pale," his mum exclaimed, leaning against the sink.

"No. I think something happened back home," he said, trying to call Autumn back. It still rang out. "I have to go. Can you put Brinkley and her stuff in the car while I try to call my..." He hesitated. *What do I call her—my friend? Feels wrong. Acquaintance feels worse. Maybe just 'housemate?' It doesn't matter!*

"Of course—don't worry," she reassured him, leaving him to make his calls.

He still couldn't get through. He thought of the friend he'd seen picking Autumn up, but he didn't have her number. He tried ringing Tim. No answer. He pulled on his coat and went to the car. Brinkley was already secured in the back seat with her cushioned bed beneath her.

"Sorry, Mum. I'll come back next week," he promised.

"Is there anything I can do?" she asked. He could tell she was trying to conceal her disappointment.

"It's probably nothing," he said, not wanting her to worry even if his heart was hammering. "I'll let you know when I'm home."

Elijah drove back faster than he should have, unable to stop his mind from racing. Had the house been broken into? They often were after moving vans were seen.

Thankfully, he made it to their street without getting stopped for speeding. As he slowed, he noticed a car outside at the gate with its lights off, though the brake lights gave away that someone was in the car. Elijah tried to get a better look, getting close enough to make out the registration before the headlights turned on and the car pulled away from the curb, cutting him off.

It could have just been someone who was lost, he told himself, parking a little down the street, but a sinking feeling settled in his gut. Something felt off.

"Stay here, girl. I'll be back in a few minutes," he said, leaving the windows open a crack. He locked the car with Brinkley inside; not knowing what he was walking into, he didn't want to add another variable or risk her getting hurt. Opening the front gate, he saw the lights were on and there was no sign of immediate trouble. He hurried up the path anyway, eager to get inside and make sure Autumn was safe.

Chapter Ten

Autumn

Autumn nodded along to the music she was blasting in the kitchen when, suddenly, she thought she heard a voice. Turning it down, she realised it was Elijah. Dumbfounded by his sudden appearance, she stared at him as he stood panting in the doorway.

"Are you okay?" he demanded.

She realised she was still tipping the salt into her leek and potato soup. She groaned, placing it on the counter.

"I'm fine. Although I did just put way too much salt into my soup—you frightened me coming in like that!" she said, turning to the saucepan, wondering if she could salvage it.

"You're fine?" He sighed out the words.

"Why wouldn't I be fine?" Why was he so panicked?

"Why didn't you answer your phone?" He looked her over, inspecting every inch. She felt awkward in her sweatpants and Taylor Swift Reputation tour T-shirt—her favourite meal prep outfit. It was also her favourite outfit on moderate pain days because she could leave her sweatpants low on her hips for maximum skin exposure to her heat blanket and ice packs.

"It's charging. I had the stereo on. I thought you weren't coming back until tomorrow?" It was very late to be driving.

"But you were crying? I thought something had happened?" he asked, closing the gap between them. He stared into her eyes as if checking for any trace of tears.

"Crying? Not today, anyway—you were away, so I had no reason to." She tried to make light of the situation, but he glared at her.

"You called me and I heard you crying. I thought something had happened, so I drove like a madman to get back here because you wouldn't pick up the phone."

"I didn't call you…it must have been someone else," she said, confused. "I'm sorry to tell you, but you aren't exactly the first person I would call if I was."

He muttered something under his breath, running his hands through his hair. Then she remembered Nina had been crying first when she came over, and then before she'd left because Garrett had finally called her to apologise.

"I think it was a misdial. Nina was over—"

Elijah shook his head. "Don't worry about it," he said, clearly relieved. "I saw someone pull away from the house when I drove up. Must have been her."

"Oh, Nina left about an hour ago. But this is a main street; someone probably got the wrong house." She thought about the rose and the mystery knocker, and suddenly, she was relieved she wouldn't have to spend the night alone in the house. She wondered if she should tell Elijah, but he already looked stressed enough.

"Forget it. It's fine." Elijah rubbed his eyes.

Guilt made Autumn fidget. She felt bad that he had rushed back so late because of a misunderstanding, but she didn't know why he was so worried about her. It wasn't like they were close. Still, seeing him so concerned warmed her heart. *Anyone else probably would have hung up and continued with their day.* She shifted nervously, not knowing what to say.

"Have you eaten? The soup is almost ready," she said, trying to mend fences, but he seemed distracted.

"No thanks. I'll be back in a while. I have to get something from the car." He left without another word.

She checked her phone, still charging on the counter, and saw his five missed calls. She checked her outgoing calls and there it was: *Elijah.* She cringed at her mistake. *I must have dialled him when I was plugging it in.*

When she'd fixed the soup, she left a bowl for Elijah on his desk and covered it with a plate and a Post-It with his name. *Maybe I should leave him a note apologising for the misdial,* she thought, but the words wouldn't come when she tried to write it.

She accidentally knocked over a notepad, and a series of rough sketches fell out. An octopus with sharp teeth, then a castle with high towers. The last made her breath catch. *It's me!* Or an animated character that had a very similar profile. The red hair was a dead giveaway. Autumn couldn't help but smile. *Is he basing a character off me? Better not be the villain.* She didn't know if he had drawn it, as the other drawings were signed in the corner with an F.

She put the sketches back where she had found them, unsure of how to feel about it. *It's an animation; he could argue it was anyone. Forget about it, we've already had one awkward encounter this evening. I don't want him to think I've been snooping. Again.*

Autumn heard the front door open. She quickly closed the door to his office, but when she stepped into the hall, a golden mound of fur came running towards her only to skid on the wooden floor and crash into her legs.

"Who are you?" she wondered as the golden retriever wriggled on the floor, trying to get her to rub her belly. She knelt down and looked at her collar. Brinkley? *Where the hell did you come from?* It took less than a second for her to fall in love with the gentle giant.

Glancing up, she noticed Elijah was watching them with an amused smile.

"I'm sorry for worrying you earlier," she said, and he nodded.

"No worries; I overreacted." Elijah pulled at the back of his neck. Luckily, her new furry friend nudged her and broke the tense silence.

"You seem to have brought home company. You didn't think to ask before you brought him home?"

She didn't want to fight, but having a housemate was a big enough change. Now there was a pet as well? She loved dogs and had always wanted one, but they were a massive responsibility. With her flare-ups, she worried she wouldn't be able to give it the care it needed.

"*She* is Brinkley. She was with my mum until I settled in. I picked her up on the way back from the conference." Elijah walked past Autumn and into his office. Brinkley brushed her head against her hand as if urging her to follow, and she tried not to look at his toned body as he started to unbutton his shirt.

"I could be allergic to dogs," she pointed out, focusing on her clasped hands. *What is* with *this guy always taking his clothes off? I might not be allergic to dogs, but I'm beginning to think he's allergic to clothes!*

"You aren't, but you're right. I should have asked first," he said sheepishly.

"Yes, you should have, and I could be." Her gaze snapped up at his tone, and she forced herself to ignore the way he'd crossed his arms over his chest. *What is it about a man's forearms?* Brinkley rubbed her head against

Autumn's legs, which made her smile. She bit her lip to stop herself.

"But you aren't." Elijah smiled too, studying her reaction.

"How do you know?" There was no way he could know for sure. She was being petty, yes, but he brought it out in her.

"Because when you came home the other day, you were petting the dachshund next door," he said.

"You were watching me?" She didn't care if he had been, she just didn't like him being proved right.

"No, I just happened to see." He stepped towards her, and she backed up towards the door.

"You didn't think that I might not want more than one animal in my house?" she retorted, not wanting to give him the upper hand.

Elijah rested his elbow on the door frame, leaning over her. She swallowed, finding it hard to ignore her attraction to him at this distance.

"Want me to show you just how much of an animal I can be?" he drawled, tilting his head towards hers.

"Cute. Save your charms for someone who cares." Her words sounded far more affectionate than she had expected or wanted. She cleared her throat, rubbing Brinkley's head to stop her nuzzling for attention. "Goodnight, Elijah," she added, turning her back on him. Brinkley left her side and sat by Elijah's legs.

He closed the door, and Brinkley immediately began to bark on the other side. Sighing, Autumn knocked on his door, already hearing music within.

Elijah opened the door. "Back so soon?"

"I assume she doesn't like the door being closed on her. Please keep the door open so her barking doesn't wake me."

"My door is always open, to both of you," he said.

Autumn rolled her eyes and headed back upstairs,

pausing as she felt his eyes on her. "You could say thank you," she said.

"For what?" He frowned.

"For watering your plants and accepting your furry friend."

Elijah looked at Brinkley, who was now following her. "Thank you. I'll keep my door open so she can come and go."

She thought of the drawing she had found. She wanted to ask about it, but then he would know she had been in his things. "Thank you," she said. "Wasn't so hard, was it?"

"If you'll excuse me, I have work to do." He closed the door. Brinkley barked.

Is he serious? Her eyes widened at the audacity. "Keep the door *open!*" She wondered if he was getting revenge for their early misunderstanding. She'd apologised, so she didn't know why he was being petty.

"Autumn, I don't have time to fight. One night of peace from you would be greatly appreciated," Elijah said, opening the door again.

"I'm not saying you can't work. Your dog keeps barking—just keep the door open like you said you would," she insisted. His mood was giving her whiplash.

"She's a dog. She'll bark when she wants, whether the door is open or closed," Elijah said.

"Are you thick? You just said you would leave it open because she's trying to get in to you. I have rehearsal in the morning, I need to sleep!"

"I'll keep the door closed, otherwise, you'll hear me working."

She noticed a soft smile form on his lips as he looked up at her. *Again with that damn smile. He's enjoying this!*

"You're doing this on purpose," she accused him.

Brinkley barked again as her voice rose. Elijah winked, closing the door.

"Why is your owner so unreasonable?" Autumn asked while Brinkley circled her. She considered knocking at the door again, then glanced at the piano in the kitchen. "Fine. If he's working, I'll work too."

She opened the lid of the piano and patted the seat. Brinkley got the message, jumping up beside her for a quick snuggle.

"I think we are going to be great friends," Autumn told her.

Brinkley kept her nose close to the keys, watching as her hands worked effortlessly across the keys. For the first time in a while, she was playing *and* happy about it.

After a few minutes, Brinkley began to howl, trying to join in. Elijah's curses rang through the house as the terrible sound echoed.

"Autumn!" Elijah stood at the door, tensed shoulders telling of his irritation.

"Sorry! Can't hear you," she shouted, playing louder. Brinkley tried to follow. Elijah winced as the high note pierced his ears, coming into the room.

"I'm working, and you're upsetting Brinkley!"

"'She's a dog, she'll bark when she wants,'" she quoted him, pausing, and Brinkley placed her head on her lap. "I was so inspired by your work ethic that I decided to practise. Thank you for the motivation."

She turned back 'round to play, but Elijah braced his hands on the keys on either side of her. Brinkley hopped off her chair. She was trapped, his hard gaze boring into her.

"Don't make me toss you over my shoulder," he whispered against her ear, "again."

She swallowed.

"You wouldn't dare," she breathed. Her heart was hammering in her chest.

His cheek nearly met hers. "Try me. Maybe you like the feel of your body against mine?"

She went to speak, but no sound came out.

Elijah's sudden gasp broke the tension, and Autumn realised that Brinkley had gripped his trousers in her mouth, pulling him away. Autumn sprang to her feet before he could get close again. Brinkley released her owner once Autumn was clear and sat at her feet.

Elijah frowned at his dog. "Traitor," he mouthed.

Autumn knelt down and rubbed her ears. "Who's the best girl?" she enthused, ignoring him.

"You're nice to *her*," Elijah muttered.

"Who couldn't love this face?" She glanced up at him. "You, on the other hand, are not so loveable."

Elijah shook his head and closed the lid on the piano. "Truce?" He extended his hand with a sigh.

"Truce." Autumn took his hand, but Elijah pulled her towards him. Her body was crushed against his as he leant against the piano.

"But just in case—" he said, quickly snatching her sheet music.

"Give it back!" She reached up, their faces only inches apart. The scar on his lip was more defined up close. She wondered what had caused it, then felt angry that she even cared.

A sly smirk reached his eyes, and she blushed; her body was so close to his that she could only think about the contours of him against her. He dipped his head, and when she went to reach again for her work, she lost her balance. He caught her, and their lips brushed.

They both froze. His lips pressed against hers tasted like electricity.

Autumn pulled away, avoiding his gaze. Her whole body screamed at her for refusing his touch, but her mind told her to run.

"K-keep it," she stammered, wondering why she suddenly felt so cold without his touch.

"It's yours," he said, offering her back her work.

She took her sheet music, his fingers grazing hers. Clearly, neither of them wanted to address the kiss, and she wasn't going to be the first to bring it up.

"I'll stop playing so loud in the morning if you keep it down in the evenings. Keep your door open so that Brinkley isn't barking," she offered.

His eyes narrowed, clearly suspicious.

"That way, we can both get some sleep and we won't be disturbing each other's work," she added.

"I can make that work," he said, nodding in agreement.

"Night, Elijah," she grumbled, turning her back on him only to hear the soft padding of paws following her. "You, stay with him."

Elijah laughed when Brinkley continued to follow her. "I don't think she's going to listen."

"Fine! C'mon, girl." At least if the dog was with her, she wouldn't be making noise trying to get to Elijah.

"You let everyone into your bed so easily?" Elijah teased. Autumn refused to look back.

"Anyone except you," she told him.

His low chuckle irritated her, but it was kind of nice to hear him laugh since the stress of their situation was clearly getting to the both of them. She didn't hear his door close as she headed upstairs. Maybe they were making progress.

Brinkley hopped up and snuggled into Autumn's duvet.

"Move over," she said, but Brinkley didn't budge. "How has this become my life?"

She had spent most of her life avoiding pets and plants because she found it hard enough to deal with her own day-to-day stuff. Now, because of Elijah, the two things she'd never let herself have were taking over her home. He was forcing her to face the boundaries she had placed on herself. She wasn't sure whether she was grateful or annoyed about it.

With a fluffy love bug beside her, she couldn't be angry at him. When she lay down, Brinkley rested her head on her stomach.

"Maybe you'll keep the nightmares at bay," Autumn said, stroking her head.

A thought struck her. *I don't think I've even had a nightmare since he moved in. It must be a coincidence,* she thought, chewing her lower lip. It reminded her how soft his lips had been against hers.

She shoved her face into the pillow.

Chapter Eleven

Elijah

"It's only been a week and even Brinkley's switched sides. I thought bringing her home would help us mend fences. Instead, I feel like I've drawn battle lines!" Elijah said, pacing Francis' sitting room. He'd left out the part where they had kissed accidentally.

"Are you sure you aren't simply embarrassed because you raced home like a madman to find out she was fine?" Francis said, feeding Todd, whose giraffe-covered onesie was also covered with strawberry rice pudding.

Elijah glared at his friend, though he might be right.

"I did what any decent human being would do if they heard someone in distress," he claimed, but he didn't know what had made him so unreasonable afterwards. Instead of picking a fight, he wished he had simply thanked her for accepting Brinkley and for watering his plants—even though she'd given them way too much. *Either she was trying to do a nice thing, or she flooded them to piss me off.* He preferred to think it was the former.

"You're upset because your dog prefers her company to yours," Francis said calmly. It was hard to focus on their conversation because Todd was more interested in flicking his food at his dad than eating it.

"Not helpful." He paced faster. *I'm doing a terrible job at trying to win her over.* "I had to get out of the house. It's Autumn's day off, and she's playing the piano non-stop. I can't focus. When I left, she was staring at the keys as if waiting for them to speak to her. I tried to ask if she was okay, but I figured it was best not to interrupt. I even tried to bring Brinkley with me, to give her some space, but she refused to move out from beneath her stool when I called."

"It sounds like you're worried about her," Francis said.

"Worried she might kill me in my sleep! She gets up at the crack of dawn every morning and blends smoothies right beside my bedroom. I never thought someone so small could make so much noise," Elijah said, rubbing his eyes. Between work and Autumn, he was exhausted.

Francis coughed, clearly trying not to laugh.

"Why are you looking at me like I've lost it?" Elijah asked, tossing his folder on the desk.

"She did warn you about her playing. Maybe this is the reason she lives alone."

"I'm not moving out. If you aren't going to be sympathetic, just focus on feeding your kid," Elijah huffed.

Todd looked between them, giggled, then flicked his spoonful of rice pudding at Elijah. The creamy mess landed right on his blue T-shirt. Francis laughed and kissed his boy, who was clapping at his achievement. Elijah glared at the little demon.

"You did that on purpose! Even you're taking Autumn's side," he said with mock sternness, kneeling in front of the little guy.

His phone vibrated in his pocket with a call. He didn't even get to say hello before Autumn spoke.

"You took my food again? Why? How can you be so petty?" Autumn demanded.

Elijah looked at the containers he had brought with him for their lunch. He had bought the same containers she used, and clearly, she hadn't checked the back of the fridge, where she would find hers safe and sound. Francis rolled his eyes. *Did she make this?* he mouthed.

Elijah shook his head and placed a finger to his lips. Francis shook his head.

"You're both as bad as each other." He got up, taking the containers to the kitchen and leaving Elijah to entertain Todd.

"Your cooking is excellent, and you woke me up this morning making it, but I didn't—" Elijah didn't get to finish before the line went dead. He grinned, knowing how embarrassed Autumn was going to be when she found hers in the fridge. *I thought I was doing something nice buying her more of her favourite Tupperware!*

Francis popped his head back into the room. "Video conference in five. Don't want to keep Tim waiting." He tossed Elijah a clean shirt before leaving to get set up. It was tighter than he liked, but he couldn't hold a meeting with pudding on his T-shirt.

Elijah picked Todd up and carried him to Aiden in the kitchen. "Careful, that spoon is a weapon," he warned, handing him over. Aiden had dark circles under his eyes, and his tie hung loosely around his neck; he looked like he was getting as much sleep as Elijah was.

"Only when it comes to his favourite uncle," Aiden said, placing Todd in his highchair. The kitchen table was littered with papers from whatever case he was working on. Francis worked from home to save on childcare, and Aiden took his work home from the station when he could, but being a detective often took him out.

"You working on a big case?" Elijah asked, looking at various mugshots.

Aiden nodded, rifling through his papers. "A series of break-ins. Lots of paperwork, but at least I can do it here. The last place was a flower shop, except they only took some flowers. Could be an insurance scam. Have to wait and see."

"Don't get him started talking about the case or you'll never get away," Francis teased, coming back in, and Aiden blew him a kiss.

"Don't you both have a meeting to get to?" Aiden went back to his paperwork while they headed to Francis' office.

"Ready?" Francis asked.

Elijah nodded and clicked into the online meeting. Tim appeared on the other side of the screen, sitting at the head of the table as Francis listed off the estimated profits for the game and informed them of where their money was being allocated. The board members along the table seemed pleased and were eager to hear of their recent work. Elijah doubted they even knew what Francis was talking about—his father's company usually dealt in real estate, not tech—but they played along as if they did.

Elijah hadn't told his father yet that he was selling to Nirosoft so that he could break away from his investment. That was a private, in-person conversation. He had no desire to humiliate his father, only to stand on his own two feet.

"How's the game progressing? I'm—*we* are taking a risk in investing in this venture. I expect to be informed of updates more frequently," Tim said, and the call was silent for a moment.

"We are currently finishing the demo for testing," Elijah informed him, keeping it vague. Tim was clueless about their true progress. It was another reason he'd moved into Tim's house—to hide in plain sight. He didn't want his father to discover they were further along than expected. He needed time to sign with Nirosoft, but if Tim and the board got wind of it beforehand, they would pull their shares and he wouldn't be able to pay back his other investors.

"I'm pleased to hear that we are right on schedule," Tim said.

"I can assure you and the board that you will see your investment returned, with interest," he said, knowing this was all the board needed to hear. He had funded the majority of the game's development himself; it was a risk to put in so much of his capital, but he didn't want his father's board to have too much control.

The meeting ended with both sides happy, and he felt like a minor weight had been lifted from his shoulders, at least until the next meeting. But by then, Nirosoft should have signed on the dotted line, and he'd be returning their money.

"Francis, could you give us a minute?" Tim said as the other directors left. Elijah nodded, letting Francis know it was okay to leave. Francis was the only one in his life who knew his true identity as Tim's son.

"Everything okay? You seemed rather tense," Tim noted, something he never would have said in front of the others.

"I want to ask you about Autumn," Elijah said, his shoulders slightly more relaxed now that they were alone.

"What about Autumn?" Tim said, his eyebrows pinching together.

"Why is she staying in your house?" Elijah asked flatly.

His father straightened his tie, and Elijah sensed his discomfort. "Her story isn't mine to tell. Her parents are family friends, and she needed a place to live in the city. The townhouse was empty, so I figured why not help her get back on her feet? Autumn pays her way; there's no more to the story."

"A twenty-something can pay her way in one of the most expensive neighbourhoods in the city?" Elijah pressed, hoping for more information.

"She was—*is*—a music prodigy, but after an incident, she couldn't play. When she decided to return to the city, I helped her as a favour to her father, who used to work with me. Even if she is a couple of years younger than you, age doesn't determine success," Tim said.

"An incident?" Elijah couldn't imagine how it would feel if someone took his computers away. He was relieved Autumn had been able to find her way back to her passion.

"Enough questions. Let her be—she isn't your type anyway," Tim said, placing his hands on the desk.

"That's not why I'm asking!" Elijah snapped. *Isn't it?* He ignored the question.

"I suggest you focus on your work. If you want to know more about Autumn, ask her yourself."

Before Elijah could ask any more questions, the video call ended.

Chapter Twelve

Autumn

That evening, Autumn was wiping the steam from the mirror when Brinkley moved from lying beneath the sink to the door and started barking. Autumn finished adding some of Charli's oil to her back, which was feeling a little better after the hot shower.

"I think your dad's home," she whispered, opening the bathroom door and letting some of the steam out. Brinkley slithered out, going to greet Elijah. Autumn quickly got dressed and headed downstairs, excited for him to discover his surprise.

"What's all this? I think you got a bit too much," Elijah said, gesturing to all the food on the kitchen table. Autumn bit her lip to stop herself from smirking. The T-shirt he wore was far too tight and exposed every sinew—not that she was complaining.

"All organic, from Hewett's Market. Should be plenty to cook for two," she informed him.

"Doesn't Hewett's charge like ten euros for a punnet of strawberries?" he asked, taking a bite of the ones she had washed earlier.

"That's the place," she agreed, "but I figured since I'm cooking for you and to keep *that*"—she motioned to his form, which earned her a raised eyebrow—"the way it is, I should probably get the best ingredients. Since you can't resist my food, I figured I should concede."

His eyes narrowed suspiciously. "Thank you," he said cautiously, smiling.

She smiled back. "Oh no, thank *you*." She winked. "The receipt is on your desk." She watched the colour drain from his face before he went to his office. "Five, four, three, two..."

"You used my card! How could you spend so much on groceries?" he cried out.

"Only the best for you. If *I'm* doing the cooking, I think it's only fair you pay for the ingredients," she called back.

He came out of his office, waving the receipt at her. "You didn't think to ask?"

"I thought it would be a nice surprise. You get what you want. I even cooked dinner for you tonight." She wished she hadn't. Standing to cook after a day's practise meant she needed an ice pack more than she cared to admit.

He crumpled the receipt in his hand and stormed past her. "I need to cool off. I'm taking a shower."

She followed him up, but he closed the door on her.

"I thought you'd be happy to pay, considering I'm doing all the cooking." She leaned against the door, hearing the water run.

"Go away, Autumn."

She smiled to herself. Brinkley lay by the door, patiently waiting for her owner. Autumn knelt and scratched her ears. "Don't worry, he'll be out a lot sooner than you think."

"*Autumn!*"

Elijah's shout made her feel all warm and fuzzy. She was beginning to enjoy the sound of her name on his lips. *Two victories in one day.* After practice, she'd used the last of the hot water to warm her aching muscles.

She heard rustling inside the bathroom and grumbled words she couldn't make out.

"In my defence, I didn't know you would be showering," she said through the door.

Elijah threw open the door, wearing a towel wrapped dangerously low around his hips.

Autumn ran her hands through her wet hair. "It takes a while to wash my hair," she said innocently.

Elijah stared down at her so fiercely she thought she would shrink. She diverted her gaze down, only to realise her mistake.

"You're shameless," he said, and she had to drag her gaze from the V at his hips that dipped below the towel.

"Sorry, I was admiring the view." She smirked.

"Some things are better experienced than admired," he drawled, stepping closer—too close.

Autumn swallowed, trying to breathe so her heart would stop beating in her ears. "Learn to enjoy it. Cold showers are meant to be good for you," she said, not daring to think of what else they could experience together.

"I think we need to add to our peace agreement," he said, not allowing her to escape. His eyes drifted to her lips, and she thought he was going to kiss her. A part of her even wanted him to.

"What would that be?" she breathed, trying to move back but unable to.

"How about we agree on a time that will leave us with enough water for both of us?" he bargained, looking over her curves with hungry eyes.

She smiled, trying not to react. "How about you move out and find a place with a shower all for yourself?"

"I'm not going anywhere," he whispered against her ear.

Autumn folded her arms across her chest to conceal her body's reaction. "Then learn to enjoy the cold water."

"You're right." He squared his shoulders. "I think the cold is quite refreshing. What's a little cold water? I'm sure the dinner you prepared for me will warm me up."

Her joy disintegrated as she watched him return downstairs. She hadn't thought her victory would be so short-lived.

Autumn collapsed on her bed, screaming into a pillow. *What do I have to do to see the back of him?* She tried to erase the image of him in a towel from her memory. Putting away what she had bought, she had found the rice pudding she had made and realised Elijah hadn't stolen it, but the food had been already bought, and she'd figured he still deserved punishment after all he had put her through. *Just because he didn't steal my food this time doesn't mean he won't in the future.*

Suddenly, any thoughts of Elijah disappeared as she was overcome with a series of spasms rippling through her back and into her legs. *I shouldn't have stood for so long cooking!*

"No, no, no," she panted, forcing herself to breathe through the spasms, waiting for them to subside. *This is what I get for neglecting my stretches,* she thought bitterly, wishing she had found the time every day as she was supposed to.

Resting against her headboard, she attempted to reach for the muscle relaxers in her bedside drawer, but a twinge caused her to knock the tub to the ground. A sob and angry growl escaped her gritted teeth as she picked it up, but when she pried open the cap, she realised she had forgotten to fill her monthly prescription. She'd never done that before, but she'd been so distracted by everything going on...

The shockwaves began again, and frustration won out. Autumn gripped the closest smashable object closest to her, a mug, and hurled it at the wall as hard as she could, desperate for any release, even if it was only anger. She heard Brinkley pawing at the door, but she couldn't find the strength to stand. She had to wait for the next spasm to subside.

Luckily, she found some painkillers in her top drawer. They wouldn't kill the pain, but they would get her moving again. She swallowed two and watched the time on her phone, waiting out the agonisingly long twenty minutes until they kicked in.

Chapter Thirteen

Elijah

"Was everything all right at home? You worried me when you ran off last time!" Elijah's mum exclaimed when he picked up.

"Just a misunderstanding. No need to worry," Elijah said, feeling bad for not having called sooner. He put her on speaker so he could finish his email.

"I'll take your word for it. I hope it won't be too long before we get to see you again."

"Once I finish this game, I'll come home more," he promised.

"I'll hold you to it. This is still your home."

"I know. Tell Frank I said hi. I sent him tickets to the next Vixens game. Season tickets were a gift when I left Nirosoft," he said. He was happy to give them away; he had no interest in football, but his stepfather was a huge fan.

"You didn't have to do that! He'll be ecstatic. You could go to a game some other time," his mum said, and he heard in her voice how much she wanted Elijah and Frank to be close. It wasn't that they didn't get along, but Elijah had already been a grown man when she'd remarried; it was strange to have a new dad in his twenties.

"Sure. When I have time, I'll give him a call."

"Okay. Tell your girl I said hi," she said, obviously baiting him for details.

Elijah stopped typing and leaned back in his chair. "My girl? I don't think she would agree with you." It still made him smile.

"No man leaves in such a hurry unless he's worried about someone."

"Didn't *you* tell me it was rude to pry?"

"I would call it concern, not prying. And it's a mother's job to worry."

It didn't matter how old he got, she still could make him feel like a kid.

"I've got to go. Your father and I are going for dinner," she said, and hung up after a quick 'love you.' She always referred to his stepdad as his father, and though he'd never got used to it, he didn't have the heart to correct her.

Elijah had just finished the email to his contract lawyer when Brinkley nudged his leg.

"Not now. We'll play in a bit." Elijah scratched her head, trying to calm her, but Brinkley jumped up on him in response. "What is it? Do you want to go for a walk? Food?"

Elijah removed his headphones only to hear a bump followed by a smash from above. Brinkley ran out while Elijah stared at the ceiling. *What could she be doing now?*

Brinkley came back and barked urgently, giving Elijah little choice but to follow her upstairs. He knocked on Autumn's door, but there was no reply.

"Autumn, are you all right?"

His words went unanswered.

"If you ignore me, I'm coming in," he called, resting his hand on the handle.

"I'm fine. Go back downstairs," she said, peeking out of the doorway. He could see how pale she was. When she'd left him, she'd been basking in her victory, but now she looked like all the blood had been drained from her.

"I heard something," he said, trying to see if she was okay without asking.

"I dropped a mug. Nothing to worry about." She wouldn't let him see inside the room.

"Do you need me to get a broom?" His concern prompted him closer, but she only closed the door a fraction more, so he stopped. "Are you sure you're okay? You're pale."

"No, it didn't shatter. With compliments like those, you could wound a girl," Autumn said, but there was little humour in her voice.

"Did you cut yourself?"

Judging from her groan, she was growing tired of his questions. "I'm tired. I'm going back to bed—I suggest you do the same." She started to close the door, but he glanced down and saw her foot bleeding.

"You aren't fine! Let me get you a plaster," he said.

"I can look after myself. I managed for years without you," she ground out before closing the door in his face. He jerked back so it didn't hit him.

Why was she so reluctant to accept help? *It's a plaster, not a marriage proposal.* Something had to be wrong. He'd never seen her look so broken down, but he couldn't push her into sharing something she wasn't comfortable with. He raked his hands through his hair.

"The first-aid kit is out here if you want it," he said eventually. "Call me if you need me."

She didn't respond. He clenched his fists, wanting nothing more than to bust her door down and find out what the hell was going on, but Brinkley was already playing guard dog.

"C'mon, girl," Elijah said, but Brinkley only rested her head between her paws. "Are you going to stay there all night?"

Brinkley twitched an ear.

"Good girl. Be my eyes and make sure she's all right," he whispered, stroking her ears.

At movement inside the room, Elijah retreated to the stairs, out of sight. He waited there until he heard Autumn let Brinkley in and get the first-aid kit. Once she was taken care of, he went back downstairs. *Even if she won't let me help her, I can still make sure she's okay,* he thought, hating to see her look so defeated.

THE FOLLOWING MORNING, ELIJAH WAS brushing his teeth when he noticed that the first-aid kit was back in its place and a broken mug was in the bin. He brought the lined woven basket downstairs to empty it and found the medicine cabinet open. He closed it, noting that the colours were out of order. *She must have been in a hurry. I wonder if she was rushing because she was late for rehearsals or because she wanted to avoid me after last night.*

He placed his mug on his desk and spotted Autumn at the end of the path. There was something familiar about the girl she was talking to, but she was mostly blocked by the tree. It must be her friend Nina.

Brinkley barking for her breakfast distracted him, and when he returned to his room, they were gone.

Chapter Fourteen

Autumn

Autumn stepped out into the morning sun and limped down the path to the front gate. Nina's last text had said she was running late.

Autumn's rough night's sleep was written in dark circles which no amount of concealer was going to cover. Waiting for Nina, she fumbled in her bag for her next lot of painkillers. A car pulled up suddenly, and she dropped her bag. The sudden movement caused her to wince.

"Morning. Sorry to surprise you like this," Heather said, getting out of the car to help her pick up her bag. Autumn sighed in relief. Bending wasn't her friend right now.

"You're fine. I wasn't expecting you." Autumn offered her a reassuring smile while she put her bag on her shoulder.

"Nina rang Sasaki to say she would be late for rehearsal because her car wouldn't start. He had an early meeting, so I offered to pick you up." Heather smiled far too brightly for so early in the morning.

"I could have walked." That would help with the stiffness, but then again, she didn't want to inflame her nerves any further.

"Nina said you wouldn't be able to," Heather said, looking her over as though she would crumble to the floor. Autumn figured it was easier to accept the lift than it was to argue, and she didn't want to appear ungrateful since Heather had gone out of her way to help her.

"Thank you. I really appreciate it."

"No need to thank me. I'm always happy to help you."

They found Sasaki in the ticket office. He was on the phone.

"Good morning," he mouthed.

Autumn went to the dressing room and put down her bag. Though she had rushed out of the house to avoid Elijah's questions about last night, she'd managed to grab a heat patch before she made a quick escape. Once it was secured, the heat greeting her aching back like a warm hug, she was ready to tackle morning rehearsals.

Before she could greet Aimee, waving at her from the other side of the stage, she noticed Heather whispering something to Sasaki. The way his concerned eyes lingered on her, she had no doubt it was about her. She didn't even get a chance to put her sheet music down before their conductor waved her over.

"I don't think this conversation needs to involve me," Heather said sweetly. Autumn got the sinking feeling she wasn't going to enjoy what was coming.

"Let's talk in private," Sasaki said, leading her to the wing of the stage.

"Busy morning?" Autumn asked, trying to divert the attention away from herself.

"No changing the subject. I can tell from the way you are walking that your back is troubling you." He frowned, looking her over like she was a wounded animal. It made sense, since she felt like she had been hit by a truck, but he didn't need to know that.

"My back is fine. I'm walking funny because I broke a mug and stepped on a shard," she explained.

His eyebrows rose, waiting for the rest of the story.

"It's a spasm. Nothing to worry about," she said, but the way he sighed told her he wasn't convinced.

"First the spasms, then you'll be on bed rest for a few weeks. We can't take that chance," he said, already ushering her towards the dressing room.

"I can play! Give me an hour to practise with the others and then I'll go."

"I may be your friend, but here I'm the conductor, and you will go home. Tomorrow, we'll talk again. I don't want to see your darling face until Monday," Sasaki said, handing Autumn her bag from her dressing table.

"Heather said something, didn't she?" she asked. Usually when she protested, he gave in, but clearly, Heather had sealed her fate.

"She only mentioned that you were taking something in the car; she was concerned," Sasaki admitted.

"What I take or don't take is none of her business. It could have been vitamins," she argued.

"Was it?" he asked, folding his arms.

"No, but still, that's not the point. Heather should have minded her own damn business!"

"She was right to be concerned. A couple of days off won't kill you, and leaning on painkillers isn't the way to cope. You don't want to have to white-knuckle it through the performance. If you are struggling, I can call Marcus Lerou. He just finished touring and would be happy to help if you want to minimise your role," Sasaki suggested.

Autumn's stomach tightened as though she'd been punched in the gut. She'd heard of Marcus; he was what the tabloids called 'the next Autumn Adler.' She hated the thought of being replaced, and she wasn't going to let it happen. If he took her spot, then he really would be replacing her. That hurt more than her back, which was currently sending pins and needles into her left leg.

Taking a levelling breath, she tried to remain calm. "You don't need to call anyone. I can manage just fine. People have bought tickets to see me, not Lerou," she reasoned, trying not to let the hurt affect her voice.

"The audience paid to see your solo, and you can keep your solo. You won't be disappointing anyone. For the rest of the show, however, we might need to look at other options," Sasaki said, his tone telling her it wasn't up for discussion.

"I said I can handle—"

"I will just call him. He'll be on stand-by. As much as I want you to play the whole show, you aren't the only one on that stage, and I won't cancel the show because I failed to have a substitute ready," Sasaki said firmly.

There was little point in arguing with him. He had seen first-hand what happened when she ignored her symptoms and pushed herself too hard. She also knew that after years of being in pain, her increased tolerance meant the pain only grabbed her attention when it was on its way to getting out of hand. It wasn't fair! After everything she'd done to try and ensure the pain didn't control her life, here it was again, coming between her and her goals. And there was nothing she could do about it. Her jaw tightened with all the words she wanted to say, but as they reached the performers' entrance, he pushed it open.

"No more arguing. Home now," he ordered.

Even if his threat came from a place of concern, she hated not having a choice. She lifted her hands in defeat.

"Okay, I'll go."

"See you on Monday. And no practising at home either. Don't make me have to do spot checks, because I will!" He closed the door on her.

Alone, a laugh escaped her, and a whirlwind of relief and upset collided within her. She couldn't cry. She headed for the street and spotted Nina walking down the street towards her.

"Sorry I couldn't pick you up. My car wouldn't start," Nina said in a frenzy, and then her eyes drifted to the bag on Autumn's shoulder. "Where are you going?"

"Bad night. Sasaki is giving me the weekend off." Autumn tried to keep her expression neutral. The last thing she needed was for Nina to report that she was upset and make Sasaki think she couldn't handle the pressure.

"You aren't going to play for four days? I think hell might be freezing over." Nina chuckled. Autumn nudged her, though she was grateful to smile.

"I can resist," she said, already thinking about practising at home. With Elijah home, she was sure interrupting him would only stir another argument, and she didn't have the energy. She was already annoyed at herself for slamming the door in his face last night when he had only been trying to help.

Heather came out and called out to Autumn. "Sasaki wanted me to give you this. It's the corrections we're running for today's practice, so you aren't missing anything for Monday," she said.

Autumn frowned at the sheet music. "Thanks."

"I hope you don't blame me," Heather said. "I just thought he would want to know. He treats you like his own daughter, and none of us want to see you lose your seat."

"What makes you think I'll lose my seat?" Autumn asked. Sasaki had said nothing of the sort.

Heather waved her hands. "Nothing! You won't. Feel

better. You should get inside, Nina, everyone is waiting." She hurried back inside before Autumn could tell her where to shove her *feel better.*

"I think that's the most I've heard her talk since she started working here," Nina said, watching her disappear into the theatre.

Autumn was looking at the scratching of red pen all over the sheet music.

"How am I supposed to make the changes if he won't let me play?" she grumbled, leaning on her friend, who wrapped a comforting arm around her.

"The more you rest now, the more time you have to figure it out. Maybe Elijah can help you around the house."

Autumn shrugged out from her embrace. "He doesn't need to know about this." Although she was grateful for his help last night, she didn't want to get used to it, even if her heart was softening towards him.

"You haven't told him about your back? He lives with you," Nina said, surprised.

"Why would I? He merely rents a room downstairs." Autumn knew there was more to them than that. She could feel it; something had shifted the night he had rushed home to check on her. No matter how much she wanted to put him from her mind, he was always there. Irritating and infuriating but intoxicating, like the aftershave her bathroom towels now smelt of.

"If he's only a housemate, why do you have that look?" Nina asked, disrupting her thoughts.

"What look?"

"The look you get when you want the last cookie but you're resisting."

"You can keep your cookies."

"Okay, but you can't hide it forever. He might understand why you have such a stick up your—" Nina cut herself off as Autumn raised her eyebrows.

"Goodbye, Nina."

She called her physio, Charli, on her way home. Thankfully, Charli had a cancellation and could schedule a home visit this afternoon.

"Have you been doing your stretches and applying the oil I gave you to help your muscles relax?" Charli asked, massaging out the knots in her lower back as Autumn lay on her portable massage table. The sitting area in front of the kitchen had been turned into a meditation room with Charli's relaxing music and aromatherapy candles.

"No to the stretches, but I have been using the oil since the painkillers destroy my stomach. It's been helping; I swear you could sell it by the litre." Autumn's words were slightly muffled as Charli's magic thumbs worked on her tense muscles.

"You need to stretch before you play! I'm glad you're doing one thing I suggest. I've told you before that I'll never sell it. It's an old family recipe and it will stay that way," Charli said, working on her scar tissue. Autumn almost pitied her hands for having to work on her. "Have you tried swimming yet? It will take pressure off the joints. You said you would give it a go once the weather started to warm up."

"I will once the show is over and I have more time," Autumn said, running out of excuses. She hated wearing a swimsuit. Even though her scars could be covered with one with a high enough back, it always made her feel exposed.

"If you refuse to help yourself, you're only going to set yourself back." Brinkley came skidding into the room with her favourite frog toy in her mouth. She jumped up on the physio. "She's so cute! When did you get a dog? You don't have time to stretch but you have time to keep a dog?"

Autumn sighed. "Brinkley came with Elijah. The guy I told you about on the phone—the one who moved in without my permission. I put Brinkley in the office, but she must have opened the door."

Brinkley tried to jump up on the table to get to her. Charli tossed the purple frog across the room, and Brinkley followed it.

"Elijah? I was wondering when you were going to mention him. Who bought the plants?" Charli asked, looking through the glass wall to the overgrown conservatory.

"The plants are also his doing. I'm beginning to think he has an obsession with living things," Autumn said, feeling like she should name the knots in her shoulders after him.

"Would that include you?" Charli hinted.

Autumn lifted her head from the doughnut hole. "If you count 'obsessed with driving me crazy,' then yes, that would include me," she said, glad he was out for the day.

"I get the feeling he's why you are so tense." Charli squeezed her shoulders, and Autumn dropped her head back in the hole.

"He has everything to do with it," she groaned.

"And you can't make life easy for yourself and try and get on with him? It might be more beneficial to you and your healing if you let go of trying to control everything."

"Easier said than done. If you met Elijah, you would understand," Autumn muttered. "I'm well aware of my control issues, but when my body feels so out of control, I can't help but want to try and control everything else!"

There was one thing she really couldn't get a handle on: Elijah and how she felt towards him. One minute she wanted him out, yet he had tried to help her last night when she needed it most, even though she'd been dismissive and rather rude. She kept finding herself watering his plants and wondering what he might like to eat when she did the food shop.

"You've shut yourself in for so long, and it sounds like he's found a way to bring the outside world to you," Charli said.

"Maybe," Autumn said, conceding an inch—only because she hadn't lectured her too much about neglecting her stretches.

"How are rehearsals going?"

"Good, for the most part. I wish my body could keep up."

"Why not focus on where you are rather than where you want to be?" Charli suggested.

Autumn didn't have an answer for her. They settled into a comfortable silence, and she let Charli work, forgetting about the performance, Elijah, and the pain.

Chapter Fifteen

Elijah

"Honey, I'm home!" Elijah called, walking through the front door and putting his keys on the small table by the stairs.

No response, and judging from the soft music coming from the kitchen, Autumn hadn't heard him come in. *She clearly doesn't have an issue using my credit card or the stereos I installed...* He dumped his gym bag and followed the sound through his office to the kitchen, but he stalled at the crack in the sliding door when he saw a woman standing over Autumn's bare back. *She must be getting a massage.*

Elijah wanted to give her some privacy, but his eyes travelled from a sprinkling of freckles on her shoulders to a circular scar to the right of her mid-back. It was highlighted by her pale skin. It must be more than a few years old, but judging from the size, whatever had caused it must have also caused her a great deal of pain. The thought tugged at his heart.

"All finished. Take a light walk to help with the circulation around the scar tissue, but not with Brinkley because she might pull," Charli warned.

Elijah looked down at Brinkley, who'd noticed his return. Thankfully, she hadn't barked and announced his arrival.

"You got it, boss—I mean Charli," Autumn said.

Elijah smiled. *I'm not the only one she's sarcastic with.*

"And please do your stretches. You need to keep your muscles flexible, otherwise the muscles will strangle the nerves and start to seize more frequently. The last thing we want is for your nerves to compress again. I have more medicated patches for you; use them," Charli said, handing them over.

Elijah thought about what he'd seen on her back that first time. *It wasn't a plaster, but a patch.*

"I got it. Stretch, walk, and relax." Autumn saluted, easing herself off the cushioned table with her back to the older woman. She pulled on an oversized grey T-shirt, covering the athletic shorts she had on beneath. Elijah's breath caught in his throat when he realised it was one of his. Seeing her in it, how it flowed over her curves, caused him to react far more than he would have expected.

"You're tiresome. Next time, don't leave it so long before you call. Sasaki was right to bench you for a couple of days," Charli scolded.

"Yes, yes, I won't touch the piano," she said, though it sounded less than convincing.

Elijah winced, afraid the door would squeak as he slid it closed. He waited for Autumn to see Charli out and go upstairs. Then, opening the front door quickly, he sneaked out.

"Hey," he called out in a whispered shout to the woman just about to open the gate. Charli jumped, but luckily she didn't scream. "Sorry. I didn't mean to startle you. I'm Elijah." He kept his voice low. Even though Autumn was upstairs, he was afraid of being caught.

"You must be the intruder. I didn't realise you were in

the house, but I think that was the point," she said, offering him her free hand.

"I prefer Elijah to 'intruder,' even if Autumn doesn't," he said, taking her hand.

"Charli, her physical therapist. It's great to put a face to a name."

He wondered what Autumn had said about him. *Hopefully, it wasn't all bad.* Elijah cleared his throat, not sure where to begin. "Can I ask you how she is? She hasn't told me anything."

Charli waved a hand, silently telling him not to continue. "Sorry, I can't do that. She's my patient, and I would be breaking her confidence," she said, offering him a sympathetic smile.

"The other night, I heard something. I thought she fell, but she said she was fine," he said, following her to her car.

"Sounds about right. In rehab, she was known as Ms Perfectly Fine," Charli said, then looked horrified. "I shouldn't have said that."

"Rehab?" How long ago had she needed treatment? Her back injury must be a lot more serious than he'd thought. *The medicine cabinet is a big hint. She must have slammed the door in my face last night because she didn't want me to see she wasn't so fine.*

Charli's eyes were wide. "Please keep that to yourself. Autumn is terribly private. It's my job to keep her secrets." She rested her hand on his shoulder, a plea for his understanding. "It's up to Autumn to tell you as much or as little as she wants. I understand you aren't in a relationship?"

"We might not be romantically involved, but we live together. If something happens to her, I want to know what to do."

She looked unsure. "If you want to help her, there is something…"

"What?" Elijah stepped closer, eager to help.

"Right now, she needs some distraction. Something that doesn't involve the piano. I've been trying to convince her to go swimming, but she won't listen," Charli said. He could see how worried she was about Autumn.

"If you can't convince her, what makes you think I'll be more successful?" He knew it would be an impossible sell.

"I think she'll want to prove you wrong, so you might be the fire she needs. She's wanted a dog for years, and somehow, you got her to accept Brinkley," she told him.

So that's why she was so quick to allow her to stay. "Any suggestions?"

"Surprise her, and don't tell her where you're going so she can't back out," Charli said.

Elijah had his work cut out for him. *How am I supposed to get her to go anywhere without telling her where? But if she goes, then it shows she's starting to trust me.* Such a thought was all the motivation he needed.

"Swimming won't hurt her or make her worse?" Elijah needed to know he wouldn't be furthering her pain.

"No, it will help her. I wouldn't do anything to put my client at risk, but don't push her. The sea would be great, but she always says it's too cold. The salt water would do her good and the cold won't do her any harm, but there's also the Wickford community pool. Let her do it herself. She has the weekend off, so I would try before she gets back to rehearsals," Charli said, putting her folded table in her car.

"Okay, I'll see what I can do." He didn't know how he was going to get her to go swimming. He could barely get her to stay in the same room as him. "I don't have any meetings tomorrow, so I could try and surprise her in the afternoon."

"Good luck," Charli said. "I'm glad you're with her."

Her words caught him unawares as he opened the car door for her. "Why?"

"She could use a little fire in her life," Charli said with a wink before starting the engine.

Elijah wasn't sure what she meant, but it was clear that to hear the rest of her story, he would have to win Autumn's trust.

HE CLOSED THE DOOR LOUDLY behind him, as if he was coming back for the first time.

"I'm home!" he called, following the music to the kitchen.

The sight of her stopped him in his tracks. Her auburn hair, free from its usual bun, flowed down her back as she swayed to the music. His T-shirt moved with her as she shook salt into the wok she was cooking in. She looked relaxed. *Whatever Charli did must have helped.* He knocked on the marble counter, as she was oblivious to his presence.

"I didn't know you could move like that," he teased, moving behind her.

She jumped, jerking the wok off the heat. Afraid it would fall into her, Elijah shoved the pan away with his forearm. He hissed as the hot metal burned his flesh.

"Jesus! It's hot!" Autumn yelped.

He didn't need her to tell him. His forearm was stinging. Autumn's soft features hardened as concern drifted into her eyes.

"You scared me! Why did you push the pan?" she snapped, taking hold of his arm and examining the reddening skin.

"I didn't want it to hit you," he explained, shaking his hand, trying to stop the tingling burn. He hadn't touched it for long enough to do any real damage. "It's fine, but I do need to get to the sink."

He tried to get to the sink, but she didn't let go of his arm. He picked her up out of the way so he could get to the sink she was blocking. She didn't protest, much to his surprise.

"Sorry," she muttered as he turned the tap on.

"It's fine," he said with a wince, putting his forearm under the cold water.

"You need to keep it there for five minutes," she ordered. "You don't want it to blister."

He was too busy staring at her holding his hand to notice what she was saying.

"Better?" she asked when he didn't respond, and he nodded. "You can't shove hot pans."

"I think I've had enough of a scolding. Can you get the first-aid kit while I keep it under the water?" he asked, wanting to give her something to do to stop her from fretting so much.

She climbed up on the counter to reach the top shelf of the medicine cabinet; he noticed a long, thin scar beside her knee as she went through the basket she pulled out. The scar was old, but he could see how the faint white line ran jagged and wondered how she'd got it. *Was this from the same incident as her back or another one?*

His eyes caught hers, and she followed his gaze to her knee.

"I fell trying to skateboard when I was seven. It's nothing," she said.

He nodded. *Not the injury she went to the rehab centre for.* He flexed his elbow. The burned skin felt tight already.

"How'd you get yours?" Autumn asked, focusing on his burn. He didn't know what she was talking about until she pointed to her upper lip.

"Dad clocked me when I crashed his wedding anniversary drunk. We…don't have the best relationship," he replied easily, moved by the sadness in her eyes.

She didn't say anything to fill the silence, and he guessed she regretted asking. It didn't help that she knew his father—she just didn't know he was Tim. Surprisingly, he appreciated the silence. She didn't try and make it better, she just accepted the information and went back to rifling through the open box. He quite enjoyed being injured if it meant seeing this caring side of her.

"I only have burn cream. Do you think you need one of those gel patches? I think it's too late to go to the chemist," she said as he tried not to let her concern make him so happy.

"The cream will be fine," he reassured her, watching her shoulders relax. He offered her his arm since he doubted from her creased brow that she would let him do it himself.

"The water helped; it doesn't look too bad," she said, dabbing the tender skin with cream. "Thankfully, it's only a surface burn."

Her touch was so gentle, contrasting with everything else he had seen in her. Her hair fell in front of her face, and he couldn't resist brushing it behind her ear. She mumbled a thank you. How her nose scrunched as she finished applying the cream made his heart clench.

"Do you think it needs a bandage?" she asked.

"No, I think it will be better to let the air at it," he said, and she didn't argue. "I'll have a big enough blister tomorrow."

"You might get lucky," she said, only to still a second later.

He smirked, catching her blush.

"Not *get lucky*—I meant you might not get a blister," she stammered. It was the first time he had seen a genuine smile reach her eyes.

"Are you hungry?" Autumn asked, lifting the lid of the boiling water and switching off the hob. Steam wafted up around them, and the sweet, spicy scent made his mouth water.

"What were you cooking?" he asked, trying to draw out their conversation.

"Stir-fried noodles. There's plenty, if you're hungry. Or would you prefer to steal it when I'm not looking?" She sounded unsure, as if any ounce of kindness between them would crumble her façade, but he was sure now that there was a big heart under there. *Does it really take that much concentration to make noodles, or is she just avoiding looking at me?*

"Funny. I won't steal them since you are willing to share—and since I bought them. I could eat," he admitted while she drained the noodles in the sink. "I'm sorry for stealing your meals. I'm so used to ordering food, but yours are much better."

Autumn glanced over her shoulder at him, her eyes wide as she registered the compliment.

"I might have overreacted about the food, but I did think you stole the rice pudding. You could have told me it was still in the fridge." She tapped her nails against one of the bowls. "I can pay you back for the groceries. It was petty."

"You hung up on me before I could explain. Don't worry about it; getting to eat your food is payment enough," he said as she slid a bowl over to him. "However, we have one matter to deal with, since we're on the subject of stealing."

Autumn slurped up some noodles. "And what would that be?" Her eyes narrowed.

"My T-shirt?"

"Oh. Sorry. I didn't want to have to go upstairs and I found it in the dryer; but I took out the rest of your clothes and put them in your office. Is that payment enough?" she asked.

"Seeing it on you is payment enough," he said under his breath.

Clearly, Autumn heard him, because she was suddenly very focused on her bowl and not him. "I was in the middle of a true crime doc if you want to watch it," she offered, rocking from one foot to the other. Was she hurting?

"Sure. I've finished my work for the day, if you don't mind the company."

"Not if you don't hog the whole couch," she said, and he followed her to the TV.

"I'll be on my best behaviour." He meant it; if he was going to convince her to go with him to the beach tomorrow, he had to err on the side of caution. The trust between them was fragile, and he didn't want to ruin it.

They settled on the couch, a safe distance between them. He wished he was the fluffy blanket she wrapped herself in, but even sitting together was progress.

"How's the arm?" she asked, finding her place in the documentary.

"Fine, thanks to you." As they watched, he kept sneaking glances at her. It was only when she drifted off that he really understood how badly he was falling for a woman he hardly knew.

Chapter Sixteen

Autumn

Sitting at the kitchen counter, Autumn was finishing her breakfast when Elijah appeared and placed two bags on the counter, already fully dressed for the day. *I was beginning to think he considered it a crime to wear a shirt,* she thought as he looked at her with eyes she swore saw straight through her.

"Going somewhere?" she asked, putting her bowl in the sink.

"Yes, we are," he said, putting his hands in the pockets of his black jeans.

We? Why would he think she was going somewhere with him? "I can't. I was going to call Nina—"

Elijah grabbed her phone and placed it in his back pocket. Autumn would have tried to get it back, but she didn't want to get too close to him—not when his aftershave smelt so good. "Yes, you can, and you said you owe me for the groceries."

Her eyes narrowed. She'd thought they'd solved this issue. "But you said you forgave me."

"I did, but you still owe me," he repeated, looking down at her. She hated having to look up at him.

"I don't owe you anything."

"Fine. Then I owe *you* for the food, for accepting Brinkley, and for watering my plants—or drowning them, I should say." He took the bowl she was drying from her hands so that she had to pay attention. "I promise you'll enjoy yourself."

She ignored the part about drowning his plants, not wanting to argue. Staring at his hopeful expression, she glanced at the burn on his arm. *He did try to help me. One day out of the house won't hurt, and I'm not allowed to practise anyway.*

"You aren't going to bring me somewhere and leave me there, are you?" She studied him sceptically.

He placed his hand over his heart. "On my honour"—he winked—"we are going to one of my favourite places."

"What if I don't want to go to your favourite place?"

"How about this? You do this with me today, and I'll do something *you* want."

She perked up. "Really?"

"So long as it doesn't involve my moving out," he added.

To her surprise, that hadn't even occurred to her. She wasn't about to admit that, though. "Bummer, but fine. I don't want to be a ghost in the house all day, and I'm supposed to move around today," she agreed, then caught herself before she revealed too much. "I just mean, it's not good to sit around all day."

"That's the positive attitude. Here you go, then," Elijah said, placing a helmet on the counter.

Autumn backed away as if it would jump off the counter and bite her. "No way," she ground out, "am I getting on your bike."

"You'll be *perfectly fine*," he said, mocking her favourite phrase. "Trust me." He sounded genuine, and curiosity overpowered her fear.

"Okay, but this counts as two things."

He nodded eagerly. "Whatever you say, boss."

She picked up the helmet. "Do I need to change?" she asked, looking over her leggings and oversized hoodie. She still had her white trainers on from taking Brinkley for an early morning walk, even though Charli had told her not to. Brinkley had been on her best behaviour.

"Nope, you're perfect," he told her. Before she could gather her thoughts, he grabbed the bags and ushered her towards the door.

Autumn clung to Elijah far tighter than necessary, but he didn't seem to mind as he sped down the streets and out of the city. The wind whipping past chilled her, and she couldn't resist slipping her hands inside his jacket to feel the warmth of his body. She felt his stomach tense, but she had no shame when it came to numb fingers.

Along the coastline, he pulled onto a side road which led them to the beachfront and a set of rocks that a few teens were using to jump into the water.

"What are we doing here?" Autumn asked, removing her helmet. She admired the beautifully sunny day and the sound of the water crashing on the shore. Watching the light reflect off the water was far more relaxing than being stuck indoors staring at the piano all day.

"For you," he said, handing her a bag and pointing to a stone building not far from where they'd parked. "You can get changed in there."

"You can't be serious. You want me to get in the sea?"

He smiled. "Did you think we were going to just watch the waves?"

"I can't swim."

"Yes, you can."

"I have my period," she lied.

"No, you don't; you keep a very detailed calendar on the fridge." She glared at him and he shrugged. "It's not my fault you leave such personal information out in the open."

"It's going to be freezing!"

"The water will be chilly at most. It will be fine," he insisted. "I wonder how many more excuses you have saved up."

She gripped the bag to her chest, glancing at the waves crashing on the shore. "What if I just say no?"

"Then you lose your bargaining chip and the trip will have merely been a waste of your time." Elijah crossed his arms over his chest, daring her to back out of their deal.

"Fine," she huffed, "but I'm only dipping my feet in."

He nudged her towards the stone structure. "Whatever you say, princess. Those are the changing rooms."

"I'm not a princess," she grumbled, marching off in the direction he pointed. *The sooner I give him what he wants, the sooner we can leave.*

"Then stop acting like one," he called.

"You are so going to regret owing me," she muttered under her breath.

The steel cubicles were in better condition than she'd expected, but she was still stung by his comment. *Princess? A princess wouldn't have tolerated his presence. A princess would have had him beheaded for his first insolent comment.*

She pulled out a soft pastel blue towel from the bag and tried to suppress a smile when she noticed a matching swimsuit. *Did this guy actually go out and buy me a swimsuit? How creepy can you get?* She was surprised he hadn't got her a bikini just to piss her off, though she was grateful he hadn't. Even if the costume had a V in the front, the back would hide her scars.

The thought of him in a store shopping for her made her chuckle in spite of herself. She suspected a shop assistant had done the picking. *He could have asked me if I had one of my own and saved himself the trouble.* But she probably would have told him she didn't.

Resting a protective hand on her back, she swallowed her fears, unsure of whether she could actually put on the suit, let alone get in the water. *One step at a time,* she thought, slipping off her clothes.

The swimsuit fit better than she had expected. It rose high on her hips, which made her legs look much longer than they were and showed off her figure. *I'll give him points for style and colour.*

"Why would he go to so much trouble?" she wondered aloud. She stuffed her towel through the handles of the bag and headed out.

Elijah was sitting in the sand in trunks that matched hers. *He had to pick the same colour? We look like a couple!* His arms were wrapped around his knees, exposing every muscle in his back, and Autumn wondered if he was a swimmer. She stilled when he turned around and did a double take, feeling a little self-conscious.

"What? Don't like the suit you picked for me?" she challenged him.

"You'd look great in anything, but so long as you like it, I'm happy," he said, standing and dusting the sand off himself. "I was worried it wouldn't fit, but Nina said it should be fine."

Her head snapped up. "You spoke to Nina about this?"

Elijah scratched the back of his neck, realising he had been caught out. "She called when you fell asleep last night. I thought I'd ask. She didn't even ask why I wanted to know."

"I'm sure she'll have plenty to ask me," Autumn said under her breath. The sun warmed her skin, and she no longer minded being at the beach. "How did you know my favourite colour?" she asked, then realised when he tipped his head. "Nina."

"She's awfully talkative. She said anything pastel would be a winner."

"What else did she say?" she asked warily.

"That was it; we weren't talking long. Afraid she'd spill your secrets?" A mischievous grin lit up his eyes.

"Never." She dropped her bag in the sand. "Okay, so you've got me here. Now what?"

He pointed towards the rocks the teens had been jumping off of.

"No way. I'm not jumping." She backed up into him, and he held her steady. His touch was gentle, and she knew she could easily move away. However, her nerves caused her to remain in his hold. She shivered as his hands travelled up her arms to her shoulders. The gesture both comforted and distracted her.

"I don't think you'll walk in without chickening out," he explained.

"I'm not a chicken," she scoffed, resting her hands on her hips, but he was already heading for the rocks. Thankfully, the teens were already out of the water and getting ready to leave, so she wouldn't have to worry about them watching.

"Thought you weren't a chicken," Elijah taunted.

Autumn stomped past him and towards the rocks. She climbed a large one and lingered on the edge, waves lapping up the sides and kissing her feet. It looked deep enough to jump in, and the drop wasn't high, but she couldn't bring herself to step off. Taking risks was foreign to her, and they were never worth the consequences, in her experience. She worried about jarring her back, but a quiet, rebellious part of herself wanted to do it—wanted to stop worrying about what might happen and just enjoy the moment.

Elijah stood beside her, surprisingly patient.

"I'm going to do it," she barked, even though he didn't deserve it.

"I know."

She had to give him points for being so calm. "I'm not a chicken."

"I know."

"Stop saying I know!" Her chuckle wobbled with nerves.

"How about I go first?" he offered.

She shook her head. She wanted him beside her. "No, I can go."

"How about together?"

She stared up at him. He was holding out a hand. "Really?"

"On the count of three," he said, his fingers weaving through hers.

"One," she breathed.

"Two." He smiled, and seeing him so at ease calmed her nerves.

"Three." She held her breath as they leapt from the rocks.

The water cocooned her body. The cold embraced her, and a rush of happy relief brought her to the surface.

"Elijah," she called, dipping her head back into the water so her hair fell down her back and out of her face.

"I'm here," he said, coming up behind her. She spun around to face him, letting the current float her.

"It's so freaking cold! You said chilly," she said accusingly, trying to keep the water out of her mouth.

"You'll get used to it. Just breathe," he assured her. She didn't know why she'd believed him.

They swam further from the rocks, and it wasn't long before the numbing effect relieved her aching joints after the long ride.

"How are you feeling now?" Elijah asked. "If you're in pain, we can get out."

Why would he think that? "Better. I'm not in any pain—or I'm too numb to feel anything," she told him, looking at the rock they'd jumped from.

"Not so scary after all," he said, following her gaze.

"I wasn't scared." Something brushed past her leg. Autumn lunged for Elijah with a squeal, wrapping her arms and legs around him. "Something touched my leg!" she gasped, clinging to him.

He held her waist as she searched the waters for whatever it was. With one hand, he reached down and pulled up a few strands of clumped seaweed. "Terrifying," he teased.

She slapped his chest. "It could have been a jellyfish!"

"Don't worry, I would have peed on you."

"Gross." She didn't let go; her arms remained around his neck, and his hands held her thighs. From the shoreline, they probably seemed like any adoring couple. Her eyes met his, and she had never seen him smile so broadly.

"Are there usually jellyfish this time of year?" she asked, and he laughed.

"Probably."

"Are you serious?" she demanded, wriggling closer.

"Don't worry. I've got you," he said, and somehow she trusted him. "Relax. Nothing will sting or bite you."

"Not even you?" she quipped, and his eyes darkened.

"Not unless you want me to."

She rolled her eyes. "Really cute."

"I can let you go if you're all right."

"No, don't let go," she said, still afraid of what might be lurking around them. "I'm not afraid, I'm just cold." She could feel every warm ridge of his body against her own, his hands on her thighs. She was amazed at how well they fit together.

"Why are you afraid of the water? We live so close to the ocean, it's a pity you don't come here more often." Elijah's tone was conversational, and she guessed he was trying to distract her.

"I'm not scared of the water, it's the stuff in it."

"Don't worry, there aren't any sharks in these waters," he said, laughing.

"*Please* don't say shark! Can you distract me so I'll stop thinking about what might be in here?"

Elijah took a deep breath. When he spoke, it sounded like he was ripping off a plaster. "I'm Tim's son. He's investing in my company. One of the reasons I have to stay in the house is that he wants to get to know me."

Autumn gaped at him. It took her a moment to gather her thoughts. "You're Tim's son?" she repeated, needing to make sure she had heard him correctly. Elijah nodded, and she couldn't stop her next question. "How have I never known about you? I've known him pretty much my whole life! He worked with my dad for years. Surely, he would have mentioned if he had a son…"

"I doubt your dad knows. I'm not his wife's son. You know how much he cares about his reputation. I was—am—a stain on it, but now that I've made a name for myself, he doesn't mind accepting me into his life."

Autumn noted his dismissive tone, as if his father's lack of acknowledgement didn't bother him, but he couldn't hide the hurt in his eyes.

"He should be proud to have you as his son. You might be a pain in the arse, but you have a good heart, and you work damn hard," she said.

"Thank you—minus the pain in the arse part," he said, gently squeezing her thighs, and she rolled her eyes. He looked like there was more to say. "There's something else I want to admit," he went on. "I…spoke to Charli yesterday.

She didn't tell me anything, only that I should try and bring you swimming."

She drew back, feeling a little too exposed. She felt him studying her reaction as though he was waiting for her to let him in on her secrets. She appreciated his honesty, so she took a breath and tried to gather her strength to discuss the parts of herself she wished to bury. There was no shame in her concealment; she did it to protect herself from the opinions of those who couldn't begin to understand what it took to piece her broken self back together. However, the fact that he hadn't run when he'd seen her with Charli and instead taken the initiative to help her, gave her some hope that he would understand...or at least had the desire to try.

"I was wondering why here, of all places, but she's been trying to get me here for the guts of a year," Autumn said slowly. There was no point in keeping it from him anymore. *If he's met Charli and is talking to Nina, he is getting closer to the truth.* "I was in an accident when I was younger. I was performing a duet at a concert with my best friend, Mollie." She swallowed the lump in her throat and forced herself to continue. "The stage collapsed. I was injured, and Mollie...she didn't make it."

"I'm so sorry, Autumn," he said, hugging her tightly. She thought she would feel suffocated, but instead, all she felt was comfort.

"No one knows how it happened; the stage just collapsed. It was an old outdoor theatre in winter...it just happened," she said, letting the water wash away the memories. She had long given up asking why; anger only fed her pain.

"I wish I'd known sooner." His words were almost a sigh.

"Why? You would have treated me differently. Fighting with you and not being treated like a porcelain doll is the closest thing to normal I've experienced in a long time."

"I'll happily argue with you anyway, but I would have known what was wrong the other night and been able to help."

His sincerity nearly stopped her heart. There was no look of judgement in his eyes, no pity—only concern.

"The other night was just a bad spasm from all the practice. My conductor gave me a few days to recover," she admitted.

"I'm glad you got some time off. Nothing is worth your suffering. How old were you when it happened?"

She didn't mind talking about it with him as much as she'd thought she would. "Sixteen. I haven't been in the sea since Mollie passed. She was the best violinist I've ever met—don't tell Nina I said that—but an even better swimmer. She wanted to compete, but her parents wanted her to play. They thought there was more of a future in it." Now that she had opened up, it felt like she couldn't stop. "After she died, I couldn't face the water without her. I wouldn't even do water therapy when I was learning to walk again. I think…if reincarnation exists, she would want to be a fish," she told him, hoping Mollie was out in the ocean somewhere, at peace.

"I'm sure she would be proud of you for getting back on stage," Elijah said.

"I would have given anything to swap places with her," Autumn confessed. His arms around her tightened, as if he feared she would slip away.

"Don't say that," he breathed against her neck. Autumn eased back but he kept his hand on her waist. "Who would drive me nuts if you were gone?"

She smiled through her tears. "You would have the house all to yourself."

Her words caused a flash of hurt in his dark eyes. "Why would I want that?"

His gaze drifted to her lips and back to her eyes. Suddenly, the water felt too hot. Autumn watched a droplet fall from his hair to his lips. Usually a pale pink, they were tinged with blue from the cold, but they had never looked better.

Elijah tipped his head towards her. Feeling his breath against her lips, she closed her eyes.

"We should get to swimming now that you're warmed up," he murmured.

Snapped out of the moment, Autumn eased herself out of his grasp and kept her gaze on the shoreline.

"After you," she said, trying not to think of how she wanted him to kiss her and how he had been the one to pull away. She wanted out and away from him.

She started swimming along the shoreline, going at her own pace, and he swam beside her. It didn't take long for her to tire, but the weight of the water washing over her body felt glorious. Elijah asked if she wanted to get out, but she couldn't bring herself to leave the water immediately. The shore reminded her of all the stresses waiting for her. He assured her they could leave whenever she wanted.

Together, they floated until the air grew colder and her exhausted body told her it was time to go. Once they had changed, they spent the journey home in a comfortable silence.

Chapter Seventeen

Elijah

Elijah took the long way home to prolong the journey, angry at himself for not kissing her when he'd had the chance. He hadn't wanted it to seem as though he was taking advantage of such a vulnerable moment. He could see how hard it was for her to open up, and he wanted her to feel comfortable with him and go at whatever pace she needed. Perhaps getting her to come with him to the beach was victory enough for one day, but he'd loved the feeling of Autumn's arms wrapped around him.

He didn't want the day to end—he wanted to draw it out for as long as possible—but as home came into view, he knew it couldn't last.

"Dibs on taking the first shower," Autumn said, opening the front door. She smiled back at him as if daring him to follow her. There was something light in her demeanour that he hadn't seen before. It was like the water had washed the weight from her shoulders.

"Nice try. You just want to use up all the water," he argued playfully, grabbing her around the waist as she tried to run up the stairs. He wasn't going to give her a chance to run away from him, to put up another wall between them.

"I won't! We called a truce." She squirmed in his grasp, but the way she placed her hands over his told him she didn't want him to let go.

"I don't think I believe you," he whispered in her ear.

"You'll have to trust me." She glanced up at him over her shoulder and kissed his cheek.

The sudden contact surprised him enough to release her. He beamed, watching her hurry up the stairs, but it only took a few long strides to catch her before she reached the landing.

"Nice try." He held her close, and she gazed up at him through her long lashes.

"I think a cold shower would do you good," she said, pressing her hips against him.

She might be right.

"We could always...share?" His lips gently brushed against her neck, a silent question, not wanting to push her too far. He heard her breath catch, and he had to swallow his desire to pin her to the wall and consume every inch of her.

"We could, but..." she teased.

He loosened his grip, giving her enough room to break free if she wanted to. She stepped up onto the last step, but with her focus on him, she slipped onto the carpet. A small gasp escaped her as he caught her. They landed on the carpet at the top of the landing.

"Are you okay?" Elijah worried, leaning over her and searching her body for any trace of injury.

Autumn burst out laughing. "You should see your face! I won't break." She rested a hand against his cheek, and he leant into her touch. "I'm fine. You caught me."

Elijah picked a grain of sand from her cheek, and with her eyes lingering on his lips, he couldn't resist.

"I want to kiss you," he said, trying to keep his words even.

She took a moment to reply. "Why didn't you kiss me earlier? I thought you didn't want me."

"I was afraid that if I started, I wouldn't stop. Is that a yes?" he asked, running his thumb along her lower lip.

She nodded, and he brushed his lips against hers. She tasted like salt. Her quiet moans made him want nothing more than to strip her naked and taste every inch of her skin.

"Do you want me to stop?" he rasped, trailing kisses along her jaw, and she shook her head.

"Don't you dare," she breathed, and he reclaimed her lips made rosy from his kisses. A whimper parted her lips as he slipped his hand into her hair and tugged at the roots.

"God, I want you," he whispered against her lips. She tugged at his T-shirt, pulling him closer. "To know you—every part of you." He tipped her chin up with a finger, forcing her to meet his gaze. Staring into her green eyes, seeing how much lust lay within them, was enough to nearly send him over the edge.

"I won't do anything unless you feel the same," he whispered, hoping she would tell him what she wanted, *needed,* from him.

Autumn's cheeks flushed, and he could feel her pulse hammering as he pressed his lips against her neck. Her hands slipped from his hair and settled on his chest.

"I can't think with you on top of me like this—it's distracting," she told him between gentle kisses.

"Your wish is my command." He sighed, easing off her to sit on the stairs, putting some distance between them to steady his own heartbeat. Being so close to her was dangerous.

"I'm sorry. This is happening too fast. I need to think—we live together, it could get messy." She sat up, not meeting his eye.

Elijah knew she was right, but it wasn't what he wanted to hear.

"You should shower. We have all the time in the world to figure this out," he said, helping her up. Autumn didn't release his hand, and he could hear her doubts spinning in her mind. "You don't need to be sorry for making the right decision for yourself, not for me. I'll take only what you are willing to give." He brushed her hair over her shoulder, unable to resist the urge to touch her, the fire within him still burning. She was right, he would need a cold shower.

Her eyebrows pulled together as though fighting an internal battle. "I wanted you to kiss me, I just—"

The last thing Elijah wanted was for her to think he was upset with her.

"It was a lot for one day, and I'm patient. Like I've said before, you won't get rid of me easily," he said, kissing her palm.

She surprised him by standing on the edge of the step and placing her lips against his.

"When I'm done, I can cook?" she offered, staring at him as though she were trying to gauge what he was thinking. He could see her mind going a mile a minute. He wanted to reassure her not to overthink what was happening between them, but he figured that giving her some space would be the right thing for now.

"Sounds great." He winked, and she closed the bathroom door.

Alone, he ran his hands through his hair. *What did you do, Elijah?* He wished he hadn't moved so quickly. She'd admitted so much to him at the beach, and he didn't want to move too fast and scare her off.

However, he meant it when he said he'd be patient. She was worth waiting for.

Chapter Eighteen

Autumn

"What happened to you? You're all smiley—it's making me uncomfortable," Nina said when Autumn greeted her at the car on Friday morning.

"I'm not," she lied, sensing the interrogation coming. She was just surprised her best friend had resisted so long after Elijah's phone call before asking her about her weekend.

Before either of them could say anything else, Elijah came out of the house behind her with Brinkley on her leash. Autumn was surprised he was up so early; she'd heard him working late into the night. She wondered if he had work to catch up on since he'd lost half the day taking her to the beach. Elijah was the only person she knew who had a worse sleep schedule than she did.

"Have a good day," he called.

Autumn waved, feeling her stomach knot.

"Oh, we will!" Nina spoke in her place.

Autumn wished her friend could rein it in for five minutes. "You're undressing him with your eyes," she hissed as he came down the path towards them.

"I would have no problem doing it with my hands," Nina teased, keeping her voice low, and Autumn stifled a laugh. If only she knew what had happened between them on the stairs.

"I'll see you later," Elijah said, kissing Autumn on the cheek. She froze, surprised by the gesture. She tried to tell herself that the butterflies in her tummy were just her anti-inflammatory pills and not her feelings for him.

"Nina, it's a pleasure to finally put a face to the name." He was all charming this morning, and though she wanted to make some smart retort, his lips against her skin had turned her brain to mush.

I'm a strong, independent woman! But his lips...

"The pleasure is mine," Nina giggled.

"I'll see you tonight?" he asked Autumn.

"Mmm...huh," was all she got out.

Elijah stared at her in amusement. "I'll take that as a yes."

∽

IT BEING THE SECOND FRIDAY of May, Nina drove Autumn to see Tim. She would pay her rent while Nina got her nails done, as usual. The sense of routine gave Autumn some comfort.

They only made it to the first set of traffic lights before Nina couldn't resist any longer.

"Did something happen? Something *has* to have happened. Last time we spoke, you hated him, and now he's kissing you goodbye." Nina's eyes narrowed, studying Autumn, who avoided looking at her, afraid that Nina would know she was lying. She wasn't ready to talk about it yet; she wanted what had happened to stay between her and Elijah for now. It was complicated enough that they lived together; telling others would only add undue pressure. *I should probably talk to Elijah before I tell her anyway.*

Although there won't be much to tell if he keeps kissing me in public.

"We went swimming. As for the rest...I don't know yet. There is something happening between us, but it feels too soon to say what exactly..." she said, trying to give her friend something to chew on. "When I know, so will you."

"You went? I can't believe he got you to go," Nina exclaimed. "When he asked me for your size, I didn't think he would convince you." "You didn't think of giving me a heads-up?" Autumn asked as they waited for the lights to change at the end of her street. "What size I am wasn't exactly a normal thing for him to ask."

"I thought he might have been getting you a gift; things haven't been easy between the two of you. At least he respected your privacy. He could have just gone into your room."

Nina had a point. She hadn't thought of that. "Fair enough. But in the future, please tell me if he asks you any strange questions."

Nina laughed. "Okay. Since we're on the topic, he asked me for tickets to our next show."

Autumn felt her chest tighten. She didn't want him to see her perform. Why did the idea bother her so much? *He's heard and seen me rehearse.* But the thought of him watching her on stage made her shuffle in her seat. It felt too intimate. She hadn't even let people she'd casually dated in the past come to her shows.

"You didn't tell him you would, did you?" she demanded, gripping the pastry box on her lap a little too tightly.

"No," Nina said, too quickly, and she could breathe again.

"Good." She sank back into the chair.

"I just put his name on the list."

"You're both determined to drive me crazy," Autumn muttered.

"I saw you blush when he kissed you. I don't think I'd call that crazy."

"I didn't blush," she argued, trying not to think of his kisses or her hands in his hair as he nipped and sucked on her neck like he was a starving man and she was his favourite dessert.

"Agree to disagree," Nina said. "Are you going to tell me how it went, or is your day at the beach a secret?"

"It was good. Just the distraction I needed," Autumn conceded, unsure of how much she wanted to share. Elijah had confided in her about his relationship with Tim, and she wanted to respect his privacy the same way she wouldn't want him to expose what she had shared with him.

"Have your feelings for him changed?" Nina pried.

"Yes," she admitted. After what had happened on the stairs, she couldn't really call them enemies any longer.

"One less thing to stress about. He might be the medicine you need."

Autumn wasn't so sure. Remembering how safe she'd felt as he held her in the water, she wasn't sure where they stood, and the confusion was worse than the loathing. "Hating him was a lot less complicated."

"Whatever you need to tell yourself," Nina said, pulling into the underground parking on Randell Investments.

"Focus on the road and your own relationship." Autumn rolled down the window to give the security guard her security pass. Once it was checked, they were cleared to go in.

"I'm very happy in my relationship, thank you very much," Nina said, but Autumn noticed how she clenched the steering wheel. She was sure Nina was still heartbroken about her ex, even if she didn't want to admit it. "I think

Elijah is good for you; it's been a while since I've seen you smile like that," she went on, parking close to the lifts.

"And *I* think he's bad for my blood pressure," Autumn countered, getting out of the car. The underground car park was wall-to-wall luxury cars.

"My nails should take about an hour," Nina said, locking her car. "I'll meet you back here and then we can head to afternoon rehearsals."

"Alrighty. I won't be too long," Autumn replied, walking to the lifts. As she waited, she picked at the corner of the doughnut box she was holding. She wasn't sure how Tim would react if he knew Elijah had told her about their connection.

Upstairs, the doors opened to reveal white offices and grey marble flooring. She couldn't imagine working somewhere that appeared so sterile. Then again, how cheery was an investment company supposed to look? She headed through the glass doors to the executive offices, where she found Tim's receptionist, Anne, talking on the phone. Seeing the doughnut box in Autumn's hands, Anne ended the call rather abruptly.

"Mr Lionel on the third floor complaining about not getting promoted again—as if I can do anything about it!" she said, pushing her glasses up her nose.

"Nothing doughnuts can't cure. I got your favourite, extra sprinkles," Autumn said, handing her the box.

"You didn't have to, but thank you. Tim is finishing up a meeting, but you can go ahead," Anne said, already reaching into the box with perfectly polished red nails.

"I couldn't come without treats."

"You spoil me. I can't thank you enough for the musical tickets you gave me for my daughter's birthday. She loved the show," Anne enthused.

"No thanks necessary. I know one of the cast members and he gave me a couple of free tickets," Autumn reassured her. She'd been delighted to give someone the tickets since she hadn't been able to attend herself.

The phone rang.

"Randell Communications, please hold," Anne said, motioning for Autumn to head into Tim's office through another set of glass doors.

"Morning," Autumn started, seeing Tim at his desk. The rest of the sentence caught in her throat when she saw Elijah sitting across from him, with someone by his side.

Elijah rose to greet her. "It's a bit early in our relationship to be visiting me at work," he whispered as she stood frozen.

"Are you going to come in or continue to stand by the door?" Tim said abruptly, standing by his desk in a grey suit that was only a shade darker than his hair.

"I didn't mean to interrupt. I can come back," she said, already backing up towards the door.

"Don't be silly, we aren't strangers. Elijah and Francis were just briefing me on some reports," Tim said.

How had Elijah beaten her here? She supposed that traffic had been terrible, and they *had* stopped for coffee and doughnuts.

Elijah motioned to Francis. "This is my lead designer, Francis. This is Autumn, my..."

Autumn wondered how he was going to finish the sentence, but Francis got there first. "I've heard plenty about you. Thanks for cooking for our last meeting. It was incredible! My husband wants your recipe for the quiche."

Autumn stifled a laugh. *Does he know about the credit card incident?* She shook his hand.

"I'm so glad you enjoyed it. I'd be happy to share," she said warmly. She'd only learnt so much about cooking during her recovery because it was something she could do without taking too much energy and had the benefit of helping boost her health. With Francis here, she wished

Nina had come up with her to level the playing field. She felt outnumbered.

"Lovely to meet you, but I'll leave the three of you. Have to get home before my son revolts," Francis said, and Elijah followed him to the door.

"I think I should be off too; you two can have your time," he said.

"I look forward to the next report," Tim called, and Elijah mocked a salute before closing the door behind them.

Autumn noted the tension between them. She wouldn't have been able to tell they were father and son just by looking at them. Tim wasn't all that tall, and his hair, though now grey, had once been a sandy shade of blond, unlike Elijah's. He must take after his mother, whom she realised she knew nothing about.

"Were you going to tell me he was your son?" she blurted out, her mind overwhelmed with questions, then her stomach dropped. *Shit, that wasn't my secret to share!*

Tim relaxed in his chair and offered her the opposite seat, which she took. "Nice to see you too, Autumn, but my family is my business." He buttoned his jacket.

Movement caught the corner of her eye, and she looked through the glass office to see Elijah standing with another worker. They seemed to be talking easily enough, and she didn't know why she felt a spark of discomfort.

"Our relationship is complicated, and within these walls, I'm just an investor in his company." Tim sighed, rubbing his jaw.

Autumn knew she was prying into private matters, but she was desperate for more context. "Why let him rent my house? Why not give me a heads-up?" she asked, desperate to know why he had paired them together.

"Elijah needed a place to develop a game we're investing in. I didn't think it would be an issue since you were planning on going on tour," he said, but she noticed him rubbing his thigh—his tell for a lie. "I was so sure you would get along well. You're both as stubborn as each other."

Autumn ignored the last part. "The tour wasn't a done deal, but I understand. Do you invest in games now? I didn't think you got involved in that type of work." Maybe he wanted to get close to Elijah and was using the game as an excuse.

"I'll invest in anything that provides a return." He shifted in his chair, the line of questioning obviously making him uncomfortable.

"You want to support him?" she asked, noticing a flash of sadness in his eyes.

"Yes, though he would be surprised to hear me say as such," he admitted.

She got the feeling he *was* trying to make amends, even if his pride wouldn't let him say it outright.

"Makes sense, because forcing me to share a house with a complete stranger would be a little troubling," she said wryly.

"I would never put you at risk. I trust him, and you can too. I also trust you not to tell others of our familial ties. This venture is tricky, and the other investors aren't so sure. The last thing they need is to think I'm being led by nepotism. Bear with him a while longer? You might be travelling soon anyway."

"He isn't completely intolerable," Autumn said, relieved that Elijah clearly hadn't told him what had happened between them.

"He has his mother's charms, and I did think you might benefit from some company," Tim agreed, and she didn't know why his words sounded so sad.

"I appreciate your good intentions, but next time, warn me?"

"Deal. I heard your next show is donating some of their profits to St. Helen's children's hospital. We've also got a charity dinner coming up soon, and the charity hasn't been nominated yet. How about I host the auction in honour of St. Helen's to make up for springing my son on you?" Tim asked eagerly.

St. Helen's was where she had spent most of her recovery, and the nurses there were criminally underfunded. Autumn always tried to raise and donate as much as she could for them.

"Thank you—that's a wonderful idea! We could auction tickets to the show to sweeten the deal," she suggested, preferring to offer something in return. It might help the theatre gain new investors.

"It's next Friday," Tim said. "I can add your item to the list of prizes. I look forward to seeing you there; I'm sure there are many who would want to meet you," he said, writing down the details.

"Bribing me with charity…that's a new tactic for you," she teased, fidgeting. On stage with her piano, there was a barrier between herself and her audience, but being praised for her work, past or present, always made her skin itch.

"Then we have a deal," Tim said, and she took his hand in concession.

"We do," she agreed, taking out her phone to transfer him the rent.

He picked up his phone as it beeped to confirm the transaction. "Now that we've talked about my son and my charitable contribution, how are you?"

"I'm fine," Autumn said, though sitting in the hard office chair was reminding her that she wasn't quite right yet. She looked forward to her heat blanket at home, though she had to make it through practice first. She could go to the hospital for an injection to relax the muscles, but she didn't want to be groggy for rehearsals.

"Nice try. Sasaki already called me—don't roll your eyes. He's concerned."

"He shouldn't have. You're my landlord, not my dad," she said, though she was reminded that her dad had never called her back when her mum had said he would. "I'm perfectly fine. I even went swimming to help."

"That's great. Whatever helps." Tim slapped the desk, pleased. "If you ever want to talk, I'm here. Your parents would want me to make sure you're okay. Have you spoken to your parents recently?"

Guilt washed over her. "I text them every few days to check in. If they want to call, they can," she said, and it was the truth.

"It's hard for them, especially your dad. He just wants to protect you. Don't give up on them," Tim advised, and she wondered if he was trying to convince her or himself.

"I will. I even sent them tickets to the next show." *Even though they'll never come, just send chocolates like they always do.*

"I have a meeting in ten minutes, but I'll have Anne send you an invitation to the dinner," Tim said, leading her towards the door.

They said their goodbyes, and she made her way to the lobby. When the lift doors opened onto the lobby, she came face to face with Elijah.

"Done so soon?" he asked as they walked towards the doors.

"Yep, all caught up."

The way he was looking at her made her shiver. It felt as though he could see just how much he affected her no matter how much she fought the attraction.

"I have to go. Nina's waiting for me."

"We could grab a coffee if you want? We didn't get to talk this morning since you ran out the door," he said, and she stopped in her tracks.

"I didn't run." She kept her voice low, not wanting others to hear.

"Really? I thought I saw your smoke trail out the door." He smirked.

Her phone buzzed. Nina was in the car.

"I'm not avoiding anything. We'll talk later," she promised, rising on her tiptoes to kiss him. It wasn't like her to make public displays of affection, but after he'd thought she'd run away this morning, she thought he deserved some reassurance. She thought the floor would melt out from under her feet as his hand brushed her cheek.

They were interrupted when Francis returned and cleared his throat. She pulled away from Elijah's grasp.

"Nice to meet you, Autumn, but I have to steal him away for a meeting," Francis said with a grin.

Elijah didn't move from her side. Autumn flushed, embarrassed to be kissing him in the middle of the lobby. He had the power to make her do things she would never dream of doing with anyone else.

"I'll see you at home," he called across the busy lobby as she made her hurried escape. She knew he enjoyed watching her squirm and being the one to make her do it. She turned her back, not letting him see the reaction he was so desperate for.

Chapter Nineteen

Autumn

On Saturday afternoon, a crash distracted Autumn from her reading, and she slid open the conservatory door to hear a series of cries or giggles. Putting down her book on the kitchen counter, she knocked on Elijah's door. He must have come home recently.

"Is everything okay?" she called out.

When he didn't respond, she opened the door to find a toddler in navy dungarees playing with Brinkley's tail and crying when Brinkley wouldn't let him grab it. Autumn crossed her arms over her chest as Elijah tried to distract the toddler, who was determined to torment the poor dog. She bit her lip to stop herself from laughing.

"Do I even want to know where you got a toddler? First a dog, and now this. Should I be expecting a wife to arrive next?" she asked, noting his untucked shirt and what looked like baby powder in his hair. Seeing him so dishevelled made her day.

"Do you get paid for every sarcastic remark you make?" Elijah said, attempting to pick up the toddler, who cried the further he was taken from Brinkley. The dog had the patience of a saint.

"No, but I'll certainly look into it," Autumn shouted over the child's screams. "Are you going to tell me where you got the kid? I don't feel like being an accessory to kidnapping."

"Todd is Francis's son. Francis had to fix some last-minute details for our game, and Aiden is busy with a case. I said I would look after him," Elijah explained.

"Why would you agree to mind a toddler when you clearly have no idea what you're doing?" Autumn wasn't the most maternal person. She could barely look after herself—the thought of childminding terrified her.

"He's my godson, and because I'm a good person and they had no one else." Elijah tried to soothe Todd by rocking him, but it only made him worse. The crying was beginning to grate on Autumn's ears.

"Just put him down," she pleaded.

Elijah rose from the carpet with Todd in his arms. She backed up as he approached her, reaching the wall. "What are you doing?"

"See if you can do a better job," Elijah said, handing Todd to her and then crossing his arms so she couldn't hand him back.

"I don't know what to do." She panicked as Todd wriggled in her arms, afraid she would drop him. "Please take him back."

"No. Use those maternal instincts since you're judging *my* skills."

Autumn held Todd out in front of her, and he finally stopped crying, too busy frowning at the stranger who held him. His giant blue eyes stared at her, pale eyebrows scrunched together.

"Just because I'm a woman doesn't mean I'm maternal. I can't even keep plants alive, remember?" She held Todd like he was a bomb—which, strangely, he seemed to enjoy.

"He's stopped crying," Elijah pointed out, beaming. Todd's blue eyes stared at her wide in wonder.

"Because he's trying to figure out who I am and why I'm holding him." She awkwardly rested him against her hip. Her back twinged, but she had to ignore it. Todd pulled at the thin gold chain around her neck. "Or he's trying to strangle me."

"Toddlers don't think that much. If anyone in this house was going to strangle you, it would be me." He winked.

"I didn't know you were so kinky," she teased.

"Not in front of the kid," he protested.

"Does he talk?" Autumn asked, as Todd squirmed up her and pulled the pen securing her hair in place.

"Not yet. He can say a few words," Elijah told her. "Stay still a second, otherwise he'll pull your hair."

Autumn paused as he went to his desk and pulled out a hairband.

"Why do you have that in your desk?" she asked, wondering what else he was hiding in there that might surprise her.

"Because you have them littered all over the house and I pick them up before Brinkley can eat them," he explained, standing behind her. She made a mental note not to leave them around anymore. She never knew where they went or ended up; they just seemed to vanish and then multiply.

He combed his fingers through her hair and against the sensitive skin at her neck. The pleasant sensation made her shiver.

"Makes sense. I thought you might have been sneaking women in while I sleep," she joked, and he tugged gently on her hair. "Careful, I'm attached to that!"

His sigh made her smile. She enjoyed teasing him.

"Is that too tight?" he asked once he'd secured the band. The weight of his touch relaxed her as he rested his hands on her shoulders. She hadn't realised she was so tense.

"It's fine, thank you." Her words came out far softer than she'd intended. Not wanting him to see the effect he had on her, she lowered Todd to the floor before her back could give out. "Can you say 'Autumn?'" she asked him.

Todd frowned as he tried. "Ah...Aw..."

"It takes him a few tries. Todd, who's this?" Elijah pointed to Brinkley, who was hiding under Elijah's desk.

"Puppa," Todd squealed, reaching for Brinkley, who quickly scampered out of the room before she could be made the plaything.

"Who's this?" Elijah said, pointing at Autumn.

"Aw—Auttyyy," he warbled, scrunching his face adorably.

"Very cute! Good luck. I have to get back to work," Autumn said, trying to hide how choked up she was. Todd made a dash after Brinkley as she left only for Elijah to catch him and follow Autumn into the kitchen.

"Not so fast. We're in this together now," he called.

"Not a chance. Your godson, your responsibility," Autumn told him, picking up her book.

Holding Todd in one arm, Elijah picked up a toddler seat with the other and placed it on one of the stools, strapping it in place before putting Todd in it. Autumn pretended to read, but from the corner of her eye, she watched Elijah chop up the overly generous portion of spaghetti bolognaise she'd prepared for dinner.

"Are you sure you aren't giving him too much?" she asked, looking at the heaped plastic kid's bowl.

"I thought you said my godson, my responsibility," he retorted. "Unless you want to help, go back to your reading." He warmed it up and checked it wasn't too hot.

There is no way Todd is going to eat that much. I get the feeling this is the first time Elijah's looked after him on his own before. Autumn was about to ask him if he was sure Todd was old enough to eat solids when Todd tossed the bowl of spaghetti. Brinkley ate it up happily from the floor.

Must resist the urge to say 'told you so.' Elijah sighed, and she hid her amusement behind her book.

"Good job," Elijah said, and Autumn's head snapped up.

"I told you it was too much, and don't encourage him to throw food. He'll keep doing it, and I doubt his parents will thank you."

"I was talking to Brinkley. I thought you were reading," Elijah said, picking up the bowl.

Autumn closed her book. There was no way she was getting any reading done while Todd was here. She'd only been reading to distract herself from playing and rest her back. Now, with Elijah trying his best to handle an infant, it seemed she didn't need the distraction. They were providing all the entertainment she needed.

"What are you going to feed him now? I only prepped tonight's dinner with the groceries we had left, and Brinkley just enjoyed your portion," Autumn said.

Elijah groaned, looking at the empty fridge. "I have to feed him," he protested, taking off Todd's dinosaur bib.

"We don't have any food for him. You'll have to go to the shop around the corner," Autumn told him, but she didn't want to be left alone with Todd. "Did Francis not give you anything?"

"No. I told him I'd figure it out," Elijah said, stretching his arms behind his head in frustration, exposing where his T-shirt met his jeans. Autumn glanced away; it seemed only a hint of his skin affected her more than seeing him entirely shirtless.

"A kid is not something to 'figure out.'"

"Can you mind him while I go?" Autumn was already shaking her head, but he added, "If we don't feed him, he'll cry and you won't be able to read in peace."

She squeezed her eyes shut. "No, but I can come with you."

"Really?" He seemed surprised. "I don't have a car seat."

"I have to go for a walk anyway after sitting for so long, but twenty minutes max. In and out, and you feed him." He didn't need to know she had already walked back from practice. Another short trip wouldn't do her any harm.

Elijah clapped his hands, which Todd copied. Elijah picked him up out of his chair and rocked him back and forth.

"Hear that? Ms Grouch is going to come with us," he said to Todd, who snuggled into his shoulder.

Cute.

***

THE SMALL SHOP WAS QUIET, and Elijah took Todd from his baby carrier and tucked him into the trolley seat. Once they'd passed the luminous fruit section, Elijah went to find the baby food while Autumn picked them up a few things for the week. When she had enough for the next two days, she took Todd and the trolley to the baby section in search of Elijah.

At the start of the aisle, there was a carefully stacked pyramid of nappies. Autumn watched in slow motion as Todd slapped one of the bundles on their way past. She tried to catch them before they all fell, but she moved wrong and landed hard on her knees beneath a rain of nappy packs. Todd giggled in triumph. She sighed, wondering how in the hell she had ended up in this position.

"Funny," she said, pushing the packs off just as Elijah appeared. She could see he was trying to contain his laughter, but she resisted the urge to glare at him. It wasn't his fault she was buried in a pile of nappies.

"I was only gone for a second! Are you okay?" he asked, offering her a hand.

"Fine," she grumbled.

He pulled her up while the others in the aisle stared at them like they were the worst parents in the world. A teenager in a work apron appeared, not amused by the ruined display, and started to fix their mess.

Autumn reached down, picking up one of the fallen packs. "Do we need nappies?"

"I have some at home," Elijah said, apologetically handing the worker a pack before they moved to the next aisle.

Hearing him call the house 'home' was jarring, but it didn't bother Autumn as much as she might have expected. These days, when he wasn't home, she felt his absence, making her realise how alone she'd felt before.

Todd distracted her by grabbing the end of her ponytail and trying to chew it. She gently pried it away from him and handed him a cuddly giraffe from the shelf before he inflicted any more damage on the store.

"I think this kid wants to make us suffer," she grumbled. He was awfully cute as he snuggled the giraffe.

"Yeah – a real evil genius," Elijah agreed, adding some juice bottles to the cart. "And you're paying for that."

They made it to the checkout without incident, though they had been far longer than the twenty minutes Autumn had negotiated. It was already dark by the time they left.

"I'm exhausted," Elijah said, carrying a bag in one hand while he held a sleeping Todd in the other. Autumn managed the rest of the bags and opened the front gate, closing it after them. He let her go first so she could open the door, but she paused on the steps when she saw a red rose lying on her doormat.

"Who is it from?" Elijah asked, coming up behind her.

Autumn picked up the rose and tossed it in the bin. "I don't know," she said truthfully. She unlocked the door, not wanting to have this conversation. Hurrying inside, she put away the groceries while Elijah put Todd in his sleep chair.

"You don't know? Someone gives you a rose, and you don't know who?" Elijah pressed, putting Todd's food away.

"No. They just appear sometimes," Autumn said, taking a bag of frozen peas from the freezer. She wished Todd would wake up so they wouldn't have to keep talking about the roses. "Make sure you check the food isn't too hot when you give it to him," she added, putting the bag of peas beneath her back as she lay on the couch. Unfortunately, it was clear that Elijah wasn't going to let it go.

"Aren't you worried?" he demanded, sitting on the table by the couch.

"No – they probably just go to the wrong address," she said, soothing herself with the lie she told herself every time they appeared. She had managed just fine without him; she didn't need his concern now.

"I found one the other day. I thought it was a mistake," he told her.

"You found one?" Huh. They were coming more frequently.

"Have you ever found one inside?"

Autumn couldn't meet his gaze, thinking of the dozen roses she'd found in the conservatory last year on the anniversary of her accident. She'd figured Tim might have dropped them off for her, too afraid to think of another possibility. "Was there a note on the one you found?"

He ran his hands through his hair, frustration emanating from him. "I can't remember—something about the past. I didn't think anything of it at the time."

Autumn felt uneasy. It was harder to ignore the incidents when she wasn't the only one who knew about them.

"Have you told the police? You might have a rogue fan," he suggested.

"I don't think I need to get the police involved. A few flowers are hardly something to worry about." She had already told him enough about her past; how much more did he need to know? *I can't handle any more chaos in my life right now.* "We aren't a couple, you don't need to act concerned." She instantly regretted her words.

"What has being a couple got to do with anything? I'm concerned because it's creepy if you don't know who sent it," he said, taking her hands in his.

"Can you drop it?" She pulled away to turn on the TV, but he stood in front of her, blocking her view.

"No, we should talk about this," he insisted. "Who do you think it could be from?"

"Just look after the kid. I can look after myself," she snapped. "I've managed for years without you."

He drew back, stung. "Of course. There's no way Ms Perfectly Fine could ever need help."

There was a moment of silence and then Autumn pulled out of his grasp, ignoring the way he reached for her. Trying to swallow her hurt, she ran up to her bedroom before they fought about something even she didn't understand. She threw the bag of peas on her bed and rested her head in her hands. When she heard the front door open and close, she figured Elijah must be taking Todd home. She hoped he would come back; she wanted space, but not for him to stay away.

It's not his fault he discovered my weakest point and dared to ask questions I'm not ready to answer. All Autumn knew for sure was that the flowers had first appeared when she'd returned to the stage and appeared every year since on the anniversary of her accident. At first, she'd hoped they were from her parents, wondering if even though they weren't supporting her publicly, maybe they were trying to support her in secret. However, when she'd tried to thank them, they'd had no idea what she was talking about. She'd never mentioned it again. Now, she never accepted flowers at the end of her performances. When it only happened once a year, it was easy to forget about it, to rationalise someone trying to sympathise with her in remembrance of the day.

Maybe whoever is sending it means no harm. They're merely trying to mark the day. She reached under her shirt, her fingertips grazing her scars. *As if I ever need reminding. My body reminds me every day.*

Chapter Twenty

Elijah

On Monday, Autumn left for rehearsals first thing. Working with Francis on the final demo was a great distraction, but all he could think about was getting home to Autumn. He couldn't believe she might have a stalker, or at the very least, a fan that was far too comfortable getting too close. The thought that someone might want to harm her emotionally or physically made it hard for him to breathe. When he chatted to Aiden, it took all his will not to tell him about what was happening with the roses, but it wasn't up to him to go to the police behind her back. He resolved to wait until Autumn was ready.

That evening, he was greeted at the door by Brinkley, who scampered in from the kitchen. With no music or the sound of cooking, it was eerily quiet. *Maybe Autumn is already asleep?* he mused, disappointed because he wanted to talk—to apologise for last night.

Flicking on the kitchen light, he found beer bottles and an empty bottle of wine on the kitchen table. *Nina must have been over while I was out. They could have gone out together?* He changed into a T-shirt and sweats before making a cup of coffee. Only when he went to sit down did he notice Autumn's bag on the couch. Brinkley barked as he knocked over her favourite stuffed panda.

"Shhh! She must be sleeping," he said, putting her keys in her bag so she wouldn't have to look for them in the morning. Cleaning up the mess, he opened the recycling bin to dump the bottle of wine. His blood ran cold when a whole bundle of roses stared up at him. Had someone got into the house?

"Autumn!" he called, rushing upstairs to find her door open and the room empty. The fairy lights were on and her shoes were by her dresser, but the bed was made.

Elijah fisted his hair, his heart hammering as he panicked. He was about to head back downstairs when Brinkley pawed at the bathroom door. The door was unlocked, and there sat Autumn, fully dressed, in the bathtub.

"Are you okay?" He braced himself against the door, letting out a sigh as he realised she was safe.

"You can't come in, I'm in the bath!" Autumn laughed at him, sinking lower into the bathtub as if trying to hide even though there was no water and she was dressed. "Why are you home?" she slurred.

He'd thought she didn't drink, but clearly, he was mistaken. She was holding a glass of white wine in one hand. Though she was smiling, her eyes were puffy from crying.

"Because I live here," he said, leaning against the sink.

"Invader!" Autumn pointed at him, lying back in the tub. *Thank God she didn't fill it with water,* he thought. "Did you see the roses? Fifteen for the fucking fifteenth of May. Every year." She put down the bottle and picked up the ripped-up rose petals covering her legs.

Elijah wanted to wring the neck of whoever was tormenting her like this. He prayed he never met them face to face for fear of what he might do.

"Let me help you out," he offered, not wanting to further her pain by discussing her latest gift.

"No! I'm happy here," she said, pulling her knees beneath her chin.

He knew it couldn't be good for her to sleep in the tub with her back, but as her tearful eyes settled on his, he decided not to force her. Instead, he knelt by her and tucked a strand of hair behind her ear as a single tear slid down her cheek.

"I couldn't hear her. I was pinned, and I couldn't get to her. They found her first. I remember every detail. The smell of the burning wood, the heat. I tried to call her, but I couldn't breathe." Autumn's eyes closed, and he knew she was lost in a memory. Her breathing steadied as she relaxed into the porcelain tub.

"Don't drown yourself in the memories. You can't get stuck in the past," Elijah said softly, though his chest felt tight.

"Being in the sea made me feel better, so I thought I would take a bath." She leaned towards the tap, but he gently took her hand in his, preventing her from turning it on.

"I don't think wine and water is a good combination," he said, reaching for her drink. Autumn watched him remove a second, half-empty bottle from the bath.

"I didn't take you for a wine drinker," she joked, making no move to stop him.

"I'm not," he said, placing it on the tiles.

Autumn rested her head in her hands, and her hair covered her face. "I finished one bottle, and it just didn't hit the spot. Then I remembered I had another. It was a gift from my last performance. I hate wine. I'm going to have the worst hangover ever." She chuckled. Elijah gently tried to help her out of the bath, but gave up when she slapped him away. "But I'm alive, so I suppose I have the luxury of suffering." Autumn hugged her knees tighter as the sobs came hard and fast.

Elijah stood over her, unsure of how to help her. He couldn't leave her like this. He scratched the back of his head, unsure of how she would welcome his presence, but as her sobs wracked her body, the urge to comfort her took priority. He climbed into the tub behind her—it was barely large enough to hold both of them—and stretched out his legs on either side of her body.

"I'm here, I'm not going anywhere," he whispered, kissing the top of her head.

Her sobs began to ease, and she snuggled into his chest. "I'm scared. I don't know what to do." Her words were merely a whisper.

His heart clenched. He desperately wanted to say the right thing to ease her sorrow, but sometimes all you could do was be there. "Just sleep. Everything will be fine tomorrow," he whispered back, feeling her breathing even out. "You're safe with me."

When she fell asleep, he considered carrying her back to her bed, but with Brinkley sleeping in the doorway, he was afraid to wake the dog in case she woke Autumn. Glancing at the towel on the hook beside the bath, he tried to reach for it, but Autumn placed a hand over his heart and gripped his shirt. Elijah cursed himself for thinking how good it felt to feel her pressed against him. Seeing her so vulnerable made him want to protect her from anything and anyone who'd caused her so much hurt. *If only she could trust me this much when she was sober and awake...*

When she settled, he carefully freed the fluffy towel from the hook. The strain caused him to groan, but in her drunken slumber, the sound did nothing to wake Autumn.

Elijah let out a deep breath once his neck was supported and settled in for the night. Finding a semi-comfortable position, he brushed his fingers over her hair, comforting her. As he was listening to her soft breathing, sleep took him.

Chapter Twenty-One

Autumn

Autumn woke cocooned in a warmth she wanted to lose herself in. She struggled to open an eye and she was greeted by a sharp pain running through her temples as the skylight tormented her with the morning sun. She tried to sit up, pressing her hand against what she thought was her mattress only to find herself lying against Elijah, who was still asleep, a pink fluffy towel tucked between his head and the porcelain bathtub. Gently, Autumn eased off him before she peered over the edge to notice the empty bottle of wine.

That explains the pounding headache. She sighed. *Please tell me nothing happened between us!* Her hands drifted over her wrap dress, and she realised everything was in its place. *Thank God. I don't want our first time together to be a consequence of one too many bottles of wine.*

His long legs dwarfed hers. All she wanted was to snuggle back into his chest and go back to sleep. Just his body against hers made her feel more than any kiss she'd ever had.

Cradling her aching head, she let out a low groan, wondering how much nonsense she'd said last night. She eased her legs slowly away from his, careful not to disturb him. Though he was sleeping peacefully, his position looked incredibly uncomfortable. *I can't believe he stayed with me. I should let him sleep a bit longer...*

She tried to remove herself from the tub and gasped when an arm hooked her waist, pulling her flush against him.

"It's rude to watch someone sleep." Elijah's voice was husky from the long night.

She pushed against his hold, and he grimaced. "I preferred it when you were unconscious," Autumn said, struggling out of their entangled limbs to stand up. The head rush nearly caused her to fall over.

"I'm surprised you can stand at all after last night," he said lazily as he stretched his arms above his head.

"Why did you sleep here?"

"You were crying."

There was no pity in his voice, which she appreciated, but the way he looked at her made her feel so seen that it unnerved her.

"Sorry you had to witness that. Wine...tends to make me sad." She tried to step out of the bath. "At least I didn't ask you to get in."

He smirked. "Are you sure?" he asked, pulling himself out of the tub with a loud grunt.

She wanted the ground to swallow her whole. *Did I ask him to get in? I don't think I did. Oh God, please tell me I didn't beg him to stay.*

"Even if I did, you didn't have to," she pointed out, though her body certainly thanked him for letting her use him as a mattress. Lying against the hard tub all night would have not only set off her back, but would have earned her some choice words from Charli. At least she had the wine to thank for keeping her muscles relaxed. She yelled at herself internally for not just thanking him and moving on.

Last night, she'd felt like an exposed nerve, and he'd witnessed it.

"Noted." Elijah put the towel he had used as a pillow back on the hook. "Forgive me for trying to help."

He went to leave, but she stepped in front of him. His eyes roamed over her as if he was unsure of what she was about to do. Hell, *she* didn't even know why she had stopped him. In the tense silence, she folded her arms across her chest, hating how defensive she was being.

"Thank you for staying with me," she said, avoiding his gaze.

"I wish you had just spoken to me about what was going on. I know we haven't known each other that long, but I hate seeing you hurting," Elijah said, leaning against the shower wall in the corner.

"I'm used to handling things myself," she admitted, not liking the space he had put between them.

He ran his hands through his hair, and it was obvious there was something he wanted to get off his chest. "You might not want to hear this, but you're ignoring the roses. I don't think you're handling anything. You don't have to avoid your fears. Let me help you," he pleaded.

His words started a storm within her. "You're right. I don't want to hear it. My problems are my own. I was fine before you and I'll be fine after you."

"I don't want to argue! We can talk when you've calmed down," he said. "I need a shower." Removing his shirt, he turned his back to her and stepped into the shower.

Autumn followed him. He stared down at her, clearly wondering what she was about to do. She didn't give him a chance to ask.

"I might need to calm down, but I think *you're* the one who needs to cool down," she snapped, and yanked the shower tap on and to freezing. Elijah howled as the cold water made contact with his skin.

"I'm sure that's better," Autumn laughed, stepping back to dodge the spray.

"Where are you going?" Elijah grabbed her before she could flee the bathroom. She squealed as the cold pierced her clothing.

"Let me go!" She struggled against his strong arms, but it was no use.

"No. You're keeping me warm."

His words made her shiver more than the water soaking through her clothes. She squirmed only to feel his chest rippling with laughter, deep and rumbling. The warmth emanating from his body cocooned her from the cold. He held her waist with one hand and wiped the water from his eyes with the other.

"Give up?" he asked.

Seeing the water drip from his eyelashes to his lips, she tried to repress the desire to kiss him. "Never." The overwhelming desire to touch him and taste the water droplets on his skin made her bite her lower lip.

Elijah reached up and stroked his thumb over her lip, freeing it. "Want something?" he breathed, resting his forehead against hers.

Autumn's breathing grew heavy as his hands traced her ribs. She opened her mouth to speak, but no words came out. The tension had grown so thick she worried they'd do something they'd regret—but she suddenly realised she feared doing nothing even more.

"I think I like you wet and speechless," he murmured, pinning her against the tiled walls, his fingers encasing hers over her head. She shuddered under his gaze. "Still want to leave?" He studied every inch of her curves, exposed by the dress clinging to her skin.

Her teeth started to chatter—she wasn't sure if it was from the cold or her nerves—but all she could do was shake her head.

"I'm not hurting you?" he asked, trailing kisses along her jaw, his hips pinning her against the cool tiles.

"No. I'm fine." The words came out as more of a whimper.

"I could make you feel *so* much more than fine." His dark eyes settled on her lips, and Autumn swallowed as he licked a droplet from the scar on his lip.

Elijah's eyes flicked from her eyes to her lips, and she knew what he was asking. She nodded ever so slightly, just enough to give him permission, and his lips brushed hers so gently that it nearly caused her to moan. She groaned in frustration as he made her beg for more. His grip loosened on her pinned hands, and she slipped her hands into his hair, crushing his lips to hers.

Needing no further encouragement, his arms clutched her soaking body to his. Any thought of the night before disappeared; all that mattered was his hands and the taste of his lips. His hand slipped beneath her T-shirt, his fingers grazing her abdomen until finally cupping her breast. She fit in his palm so perfectly she was sure she was designed for him.

"You can tell me to stop," Elijah whispered, and she shook her head, bringing his lips back to hers. She felt him smile against her as her nipples peaked, responding to his touch. "Glad to see your body is in agreement."

All the anger, frustration, and passion spilled into their caresses. He groaned against her lips as she ran her nails down his back, trying to pull him even closer. His hand hooked her leg around his hip, allowing her to feel how hard he was. She reached for the band of his sweats, desperate to touch him, but he grasped her wrist.

"Not now," he said, his eyes so darkened by lust they were almost black. "This is about you."

Autumn gasped as his fingers slipped between her legs.

Arching against his hand, she bit her lip to stop herself from crying out. She threw her head back, grasping his shoulders as he stroked and teased her. Her underwear, the only barrier to his touch, added to her frustration. His lips claimed her moans as she was about to meet her edge.

They stilled as an alarm sounded on her phone, killing the moment. Elijah withdrew his touch, resting his forehead against her as he caught his breath. Autumn's eyes fluttered open, but her body ached for them to continue.

"You can't stop," she rasped, greeted by a devilish smile.

"Such words could kill a man. But I wouldn't want you to be late for rehearsals, and if you keep going, you won't make it at all," he told her, jaw clenched.

"Right—rehearsals," she agreed. She straightened up, trying to regain her composure, and silenced the buzzing that had pulled her from the heavenly abyss of Elijah's touch. He stood beside her, and resisting the urge to touch him was almost painful. It almost didn't feel real. How had the man she'd wanted out of her house turned into the very person she didn't want to be more than an inch away from?

"Did that really just happen?" she panted, pushing her fringe out of her eyes.

Elijah slipped a finger beneath her chin. "It did, and it's just the beginning," he promised. The desire in his words made her want to skip rehearsals for the first time in her life.

"I have to g-go," she stuttered.

"If you keep looking at me like that, I won't be able to stop myself," he warned, watching her avert her gaze from his dripping body. "I'll see you later, then."

"Later," she said, hiding her deepening blush as she scampered out of the bathroom. She hesitated in the doorway. She didn't want to leave him like this. It wasn't fair to keep leaving him in the dark about her feelings when he had been so open about his.

"I like living with you, and not because of what just happened," she blurted out. He stared at her like she had gone mad. "I don't want you to leave."

"I'm not going anywhere," he said, striding forward to wrap his arms around her. She buried her face in his chest.

"I yelled at you. I know you were just trying to help," she said.

He pulled away to look at her. "People yell at each other all the time, and it was an emotional night. I could have been more tactful. You can blame a night in the tub for that," he said, kissing her one last time.

"Okay," she said, happy to know they were good, and not just physically.

"Okay. Are you going to let me shower, or do you want to join me and finish what we started?" He winked, hooking his thumbs into his waistband.

Autumn hurried out of the bathroom, only to trip over Brinkley in the doorway. She barked, but too flustered to think, Autumn dashed away and closed her bedroom door on both of them.

"What the hell did you just do?" she groaned quickly. Sitting on the edge of her bed, her fingers brushed her lips. Every fibre of her being wanted to go back to him, but her alarm going off again wiped away any hope of it.

Before long, she was ready for the day in a dry dress with her hair pinned up in her favourite claw clip. Downstairs, she grabbed her bag from the couch and beamed when she noticed that Elijah had cleaned up her mess from the night before. Lingering by his door, she contemplated thanking him, but hearing him on the phone with who she guessed was Francis, she decided not to interrupt. She had already disturbed his sleep. Some space between them would probably do them good.

Autumn wasn't too far from the theatre when the skies decided to open up. Usually, she would have groaned and worried about the cold making her back tense, but today, the cool droplets only made her think of her morning shower. She hurried through the sea of umbrellas until she reached the theatre's side entrance, and for the first time in a long time, Autumn realised she was walking with a smile.

"When I saw the rain, I stopped by your house, but Elijah said you had already gone," Nina said outside their dressing room.

Autumn dropped her sheet music at the mention of his name. Even though she was sure Elijah wouldn't have said anything, she felt like a criminal caught in the spotlight.

"I wanted some air, and it only started raining just before I arrived," she said, trying not to overthink.

Nina nodded, slicking back her wet hair in the mirror. The gesture highlighted her perfect winged liner and red lip. Autumn wished she'd put in more effort than just filling in her eyebrows and using some lip balm, but in the rush to escape Elijah, she hadn't had time.

"How was your weekend?" she asked as they waited on the stage for everyone else.

Nina sighed. "Went for dinner with Garrett. We haven't been right since he found the photo. All night, he kept asking what was wrong when I was fine. The more I said nothing, the more he pressed. On the way home, we fought because he keeps talking about moving in, and I'm not ready. He stormed out, and now I don't know where we stand."

"I wouldn't worry too much—every couple fights. It's just growing pains," Autumn whispered reassuringly as Heather joined them.

"Welcome back. Sasaki wants you to lead us; he has some bits to wrap up," Heather said.

"Good to be back. No problem," Autumn said, letting everyone get settled while Heather returned to the wings.

"She gives me a weird vibe," Nina whispered.

"She's just quiet," Autumn disagreed, though Nina didn't look convinced.

"You didn't tell me how your weekend was. You seem more relaxed," Nina said quietly.

"There was plenty of time to relax," Autumn told her, "but the house was busy. Elijah was looking after his godson, so I read in the conservatory most of the time."

"How is my favourite intruder?" Nina asked, leaning a little too close.

"He's fine. Working away." Ignoring Nina's stare, Autumn went to her piano and arranged her music.

"Is that a glow? Dare I say, a smile?!" Nina circled her before hissing, "Did you do the dirty? I mean, if I had someone that fine under my roof, I would gladly use it to my advantage."

Autumn's eyes darted around the stage. "You're imagining things again, and we didn't do the dirty!" She took her seat, but Nina lingered.

"Who did the dirty?" Aimee asked, handing Nina a coffee.

Autumn sighed. "No one."

"Do we believe her?" Nina said to Aimee, who narrowed her eyes at Autumn.

"I think we would need more information before we can make a decision," she decided, but the conversation was interrupted by Heather at the head of the stage.

"Autumn is going to lead you this morning." Heather clutched her clipboard tightly, clearly nervous to address everyone, but Autumn thought it was good to see her stepping out of Sasaki's shadow.

"Ready?" she called.

Together, they lost themselves in the music. Autumn

was playing much better, and she didn't know if it was because of the break or Elijah. Or perhaps it was simply finding a trace of happiness in her life, when contentment had taken its place for so many years.

"That's more like it." Sasaki clapped as he finally joined them. She felt secure in her playing for the first time in she didn't know how long. "I think we're ready for a full run-through." Everyone grumbled. "Don't act like I'm torturing you. We don't have much longer to work out the fine details."

Thinking that his rehearsal style could certainly be considered torture, Autumn looked to the roof. The rain had stopped, so she would be able to get some walking in before they returned to practice. In her hurry to escape Elijah in the morning, she hadn't taken the time to stretch.

"Autumn, how are you feeling?" Sasaki asked as everyone was busy placing their lunch orders with Heather.

"Much better. You were right, I needed the rest," she said, rising from the stool and putting away her music. The 'much' was a bit overkill; the run-through combined with her night in the bathtub caused the ache to thread up and down her spine, begging her to acknowledge it. Luckily, she'd had an emergency heat patch in her bag and managed a quick awkward stretch in the dressing room while everyone took a bathroom break.

"I'm relieved to hear it. Also, I had a call from Tim Randell. He was asking for tickets to auction off at a charity dinner next Friday."

"Sorry, I meant to call you. I think it would be a great idea to spare a few tickets for the auction. It might attract the attention of those with deep pockets."

"I already agreed—you don't have to sell me. It was a pleasant surprise. I've been trying to find new investors."

Autumn grinned, glad to help the theatre. Without Sasaki, she might not have found her way back to the piano.

Chapter Twenty-Two

Autumn

By that evening, they'd finished their first run-through of the entire show, and to Autumn's relief, her piece was sounding much better. She felt like she was no longer chasing the music. Despite her own relief, when she glanced around the stage, everyone was looking rather haggard.

"Coffee?" she called out, and everyone's grim faces brightened.

"Want to come with me?" Nina asked, and Autumn couldn't resist.

"Absolutely. I could do with the walk," she said, stretching her arms.

Soon, everyone was calling out their orders.

"Latte, extra espresso," their cellist requested.

"Dragon fruit smoothie," Aimee added, and the others followed in quick succession.

"Maestro?" Autumn said to Sasaki, whom she knew wouldn't be able to resist a caffeine fix, taking out her phone.

"Flat white," he said. "And since we have completed our first run-through, I will treat everyone to pizza."

He was met with loud cheers, and Heather was dispatched to get everyone's order.

"Just a large pepperoni for us," Nina told her as she and Autumn left to get the drinks.

Outside the theatre, they spotted Garrett waiting with an armful of flowers. He looked as glum as Nina had been all day.

"I think someone wants to make nice," Autumn said, nudging her friend. Nina remained calm, not giving anything away. Half the mistakes they had been forced to stop for during the run-through had been because Nina was either playing too fast or couldn't keep up. She hated watching her struggle because of a guy who didn't know how lucky he was to have her, but seeing him arrive with flowers made her think a little better of him.

"You can stay and talk if you want to, or we can pretend he doesn't exist and go about our business," Autumn said, pulling her tote bag onto her shoulder.

"You can't manage everything by yourself," Nina protested, then looked to him, waiting, and Autumn saw her friend falter. "Maybe I should talk to him...he did come."

"Then talk. The coffee shop is only across the street; I can take two trips."

Nina hesitated, while Garrett waited for her to make the first move. Autumn was surprised he would stand so close to the puddled street in his chinos for fear of getting a stain, then reminded herself he was trying to make a grand gesture for her best friend.

"I can go with you. I'm sick of being in the back office all day," Heather said, coming out of the theatre behind them. "I was coming after you anyway; I forgot to give my drinks order. Aimee is going to order the food."

"Great! We're sorted, then." Autumn looked to Nina. She hesitantly walked over to Garrett, whose grim demeanour suddenly evaporated.

They all walked across the street to the coffee shop. It was past six already, so the place was rather deserted except for some working on their laptops or reading in the corners. Garrett and Nina sat at a table, talking quietly, while Autumn stood with Heather, waiting for the dozen drinks.

"Do anything nice this week? You had a couple of days off," Heather said, breaking the awkward tension.

"Nothing much, just took it easy," Autumn said as the barista handed her the first tray.

"I suppose you were resting. It must have been awful not to be able to play," Heather said.

"Did you get up to anything?" Autumn asked, unsure of how to reply. She ripped open a third packet of sugar to pour it into her drink. She couldn't stand the taste of bitter coffee.

Heather raised her eyebrows at the sugar content. "Not this weekend. It's always—"

She was cut off when Nina joined them to collect the rest of the tray. Autumn caught a glimpse of annoyance in Heather's eyes, but it was quickly replaced with her usual blank stare as she took the next two trays. Autumn got the impression she'd wanted to talk about something, but with company, she clammed up. Maybe Heather was just socially awkward.

"I got pastries; I think everyone could use a sneaky treat," Nina said, holding up a box of whatever the coffee shop had left after the long day.

"You're just trying to bribe your way into everyone's good graces," Autumn teased, adding money to the tip jar as Garrett held the door for Heather. She always felt sorry for the baristas when they came in with their long order.

"I was messing up so much this morning. I think I owe them."

Nina was the most confident person Autumn knew, and she hated seeing her beat herself up. "I was messing up for months. One bad day is nothing," she reminded her friend, earning herself a small smile.

"You're right. Also, everything is fine with Garrett now. Don't let on that I was so upset earlier. I don't want him to feel bad," Nina whispered as they followed Garrett and Heather, who seemed to have no trouble talking to him. Autumn wondered what they were even talking about.

"It was nice of him to bring flowers. I didn't think he would want to give it another go," Nina said, smiling to herself.

"Of course he would! He's lucky to have you."

They chatted about the run-through until Garrett interrupted.

"Here, let me carry those," he offered, hanging back and taking the tray from Nina.

"Where's Heather?" Autumn asked.

"She just started walking ahead, so I thought I was bothering her," Garrett said. When they rounded the corner, they caught a glimpse of Heather heading into the theatre.

"Is she okay?" Nina whispered to Autumn.

"I don't know. I can't figure her out. She's nice, but there's just something I can't put my finger on," Autumn said with a shrug.

"Maybe she struggles to make friends and gets awkward?" Nina suggested.

Autumn didn't get a chance to reply before Garrett butted in. "Listen, I wanted to ask you, since Nina doesn't think you will."

"Will what?" There wasn't much Autumn and Nina didn't discuss.

"Go on a double date with us," Garrett said smugly, and she nearly stumbled.

"But I'm not seeing anyone."

"Nina said you're living with Elijah Wells."

Autumn didn't like how he said Elijah's full name. *He must have looked him up.* "We just live together. I doubt he would want to go," she said. Why did Garrett want to go on a double date so badly?

"Bring him anyway; we'll have a good time," Garrett said. "I've been thinking of buying some stocks in Nirosoft, but since he left the company, I'm not sure. I'd love to pick his brains before I make a final decision."

Autumn resisted the urge to scoff. Garrett might like to think of himself as a businessman, but all he did was reinvest money he'd earned through his inheritance and surround himself with successful people to make him seem more important.

"I don't think Elijah has the time; he's really busy with work." *He doesn't even know Elijah and he wants to use him for his own gain?* She wanted to slap him and keep Elijah as far away from him as possible. *I can't believe I'm protecting the man I wanted to get rid of only two weeks ago. I blame his aftershave.*

"But there's only another week before the concert and then you might be going on tour. We should all go to dinner and celebrate all the hard work you've both put in," Garrett insisted.

"I guess I can ask him." *When he says no, then I can at least tell Nina I asked.* Anything to stop Garrett from pushing. She didn't know how Nina could deal with him. Elijah wasn't perfect, but Garrett had a slimy aura that made him intolerable.

"Really? I didn't think you would say yes," Nina exclaimed. Garrett held the door for them. Autumn couldn't wait to get back to the stage and away from him.

"It's a maybe. Like I said, Elijah is rather busy at the minute. I'll have to let you know."

"Let's say Little Forest, the Italian 'round the corner from the concert hall—they're supposed to have the best pizza. Nina can text you the reservation. Say next week? Thursday at seven?" Garrett said, obviously not planning to leave until he got the answer he wanted.

Nina gave Autumn a nervous look. It was obvious that Garrett wanted to meet Elijah more than he was interested in a double dinner date.

"Sure. If we can't make it, at least you can use the table yourselves," Autumn agreed, giving herself an out. She didn't like being forced into plans. She never knew what physical state she would be in, and anyway, she didn't want Elijah to have to suffer a night of Garrett's inane questions.

"Great. I'll book the table for next Thursday." Garrett's decisive tone rubbed Autumn the wrong way. She wondered if he was only bringing this up because he and Nina had been fighting; he was the type who liked to prove to everyone else that their relationship was perfect.

Garrett kissed Nina goodbye, and when the theatre door closed, she noticed Nina fidgeting.

"I don't want you to feel any pressure—it was only an idea. I didn't mean to tell him about Elijah. Before we fought, I was just thinking it would be great if you two got together so we could double date. I didn't think he'd jump on the idea."

Autumn didn't want her to be apologising on Garrett's behalf. "Don't worry about it. I'm not sure if I can convince Elijah; he really is busy with work," she said, trying to put Nina at ease. She didn't want them to have another fight because of her. Still, she didn't like another person knowing they lived together. She liked the secrecy of her and Elijah's little bubble without outside pressure. The world already knew so much about both of them. The accident was public knowledge; all someone had to do was Google her.

"I'm sure Elijah won't mind. It might be good to get to know the man who is making my friend glow." Nina nudged her, and Autumn nearly dropped her tray of coffee. Heather was already on stage, handing out the drinks.

"There is no glow! And even if there was, it has nothing to do with Elijah," Autumn lied, though she couldn't help smiling. It had everything to do with Elijah, and even if she wasn't ready to tell Nina, she suspected her friend already knew what was developing between them.

The rest of the orchestra called out to them, eagerly waiting for their coffees.

"We shall see. You can lie to yourself, but you can't lie to me," Nina teased, before joining the others on the stage.

Chapter Twenty-Three

Autumn

Much to Autumn's disappointment, the rest of the week came and went without a repeat of what had happened between her and Elijah in the shower. Since that morning, they'd been like ships passing in the night thanks to their work schedules. Brinkley kept her company while Elijah worked—she was the perfect source of never-ending happiness. If Elijah did ever leave, Autumn didn't think she could bring herself to part with the dog.

Even the thought of him leaving made her chest tighten, though. She felt safer with him around. No more roses had appeared since the anniversary, putting them both at ease. Thankfully, Elijah being so busy meant their conversation about going to the police had also been shelved. The last thing Autumn needed or wanted was to involve the police right before the showcase. She also didn't want to be responsible for distracting Elijah from his own work. With the show a week away, she had about all the stress she could handle, and opening Pandora's box wasn't going to help.

"Why aren't you ready? We have to leave in thirty minutes," Elijah said, standing outside his bedroom. He had been out all day; Autumn had assumed he'd crashed early.

"Ready for what?" she asked, sitting on the couch with her favourite crisps on her lap and a tub of Ben and Jerry's on the table. She was about to start another true crime documentary.

"It's Friday. Tim's charity dinner?" he said, blocking her view of the TV. "I meant to remind you yesterday, but you were asleep by the time I finished wrapping up the contract with Nirosoft's lawyers." He was wearing a criminally well-tailored black shirt and trousers. It reminded her of how nice his body felt beneath her fingers.

Autumn stopped eating mid-spoonful, suddenly remembering the invitation Anne had sent, sitting in the bottom of her tote bag.

"I've been rehearsing all day. I just want to relax. I'm not going. I already told Tim I wasn't. Only a zombie apocalypse would move me from this couch," she told him. "You've been just as busy as I have; I've heard you up at all hours. I think we should just stay on the couch." She held out her ice cream to him. "I'll even share my treats with you, and if you're extra nice to me, I'll even share my blanket."

"As much as I want to explore what's under that blanket, the invitation has both of our names on it. If I have to go, so do you," he said.

She watched him thread a black leather belt through the loops of his trousers. *I shouldn't be attracted to this,* she thought, wondering why him using his hands to do anything was so appealing.

Elijah clicked his fingers to regain her attention. Autumn diverted her attention back to the ice cream—not as satisfying as his touch, but they hadn't spoken about what had happened, and she certainly wasn't going to be the first to bring it up.

"I would rather not spend my evening submerged in mindless chit chat, but you have fun." She smiled, eating a spoonful.

"Either you get up off this couch, or I'll give you a helping hand." He sat on the table in front of the couch and rested his elbows on his knees, clearly waiting for her to move. She took the spoon from her mouth. The last time he'd looked at her like this, they'd ended up knotted together in the shower.

"Don't get any ideas," she said, thinking of his lips against hers. She didn't need his ideas; she had plenty of her own.

"My only idea was seeing you dressed, but if you have the opposite in mind…" Elijah ran a hand up her thigh. She shoved him away, and he chuckled, then grabbed her legs as though to toss her over his shoulder. She knew from previous experience that it wasn't an empty threat.

He pulled her slightly towards him, and she winced a little as her back protested the quick movement. She caught a flash of worry in his eyes, and she didn't need to say anything before he eased his grip on her. She loved that he knew just by her expression when to be gentle.

"Okay, stop!" She raised her hands in submission. He stilled, his hands on the back of her thighs making her heart race. "Okay," she squealed, and he released her.

"Was that so hard?" he asked, taking a tie from the table.

"But you have to go to dinner with Nina and her heinous excuse of a boyfriend next Thursday," Autumn negotiated, putting the lid on her ice cream.

He squinted, clearly thinking it through as he tried to fix his tie in the kitchen mirror. "What's wrong with him?"

"Who?" Autumn asked, admiring how good he looked in the tailored black suit. *It should be a sin to look that good.*

"The heinous boyfriend," Elijah said, folding his arms across his chest.

Autumn dropped her gaze, embarrassed by her blunder. "Heinous might be too strong a word. Garrett is just rather pushy," she said, not wanting to sound too harsh.

"I take it the dinner was not your idea?" He fiddled with his tie. Watching him butcher a simple Windsor knot was driving her crazy. Once her ice cream was safely tucked away in the freezer, she crossed the kitchen to help him.

"No, definitely not my idea to spend an evening with him." She swiped his hands away and took the ends of the tie. "He makes me uneasy."

"How long have you known him? Does he know where you live?" Elijah stared at her while she worked and tried to ignore his tantalising aftershave.

"Nina started dating him about a year ago, so he's been here once or twice. He's friends with one of the theatre's investors. Why do you ask?"

"You've been getting the roses for over a year, so we can probably rule him out," he said, almost to himself.

She yanked the tie to distract him. "Can we not talk about the roses? I promise I'll deal with it once the showcase is over."

Elijah placed his hands over hers with a sigh. "Sorry. I just hate the thought of not knowing who's doing this to you. If I went to this dinner, would you be more comfortable? I don't want you to have to go alone if he makes you uneasy."

"I don't want to go, but I don't want to let Nina down," she said, running her hands down his jacket to smooth out the lapels and trying to hide her smile. She couldn't believe he would go out with her just to put her at ease. Her hands settled on his chest. "Are you sure? I also have to add that he knows who you are, and he's the type who collects successful people," she added.

Realising she still had her hands on him, she snapped them away as though she had been burnt. *If the suit is a sin, then the aftershave is downright murder.*

"As much as I don't like the idea of being collected, if it gets you to come tonight, I'm in."

"You're serious? You'll really go?" Her eyes went wide as he loosened the tie a little. She hadn't seen him wear one before; as good as it looked, she preferred him sans shirt. Even the thought caused her to redden.

"I will, but you have to keep your promise about dealing with the roses after the showcase." He placed his finger under her chin, forcing her to meet his gaze.

She nodded. "Seems fair."

Elijah clapped his hands, breaking the tension between them. "You need to get ready; I don't want to be late. I think only arseholes are late to charity dinners."

"You go, I'll meet you there," she said, but he shook his head.

"We go together," he insisted.

Wondering why his words made her stomach flip, Autumn hurried upstairs to get ready. *I might have to suffer through an evening of schmoozing, but at least I can save face with Garrett.*

She opened her wardrobe and looked over her performance dresses, the only formal dresses she owned. However, in the corner of her wardrobe, she spotted the suit from her last performance.

Perfect, she thought. The black suit hugged her curves perfectly; it was tailored to perfection, and the suit jacket crossed at the waist so she didn't have to wear a shirt. *If I'd said no to the dinner, I could have spent the night on the couch with* Mindhunter, she thought as she pulled it out. She sighed, but as excitement curled inside her, she realised she was actually excited about going out with the man she had sworn to get rid of.

The low neckline did wonders for her cleavage, which she emphasised with a long silver chain. She wore her favourite satin purple heels, which added some height, though she knew they would do nothing to help her back. *Worth it for a night.*

"The taxi will be here in five," Elijah called up the stairs.

"Ready in two." Quickly, Autumn redid her winged liner and added a nude lip.

Elijah was waiting at the end of the stairs. When he turned around, it was the first time she had seen him speechless.

"Will this suffice?" she asked.

It was his turn to redden. The reaction she had been hoping for made getting up from the couch worth it, even if the heels were already causing her back to ache. She still preferred her leggings and *The Thing* T-shirt.

Brinkley barked, breaking the tension. Autumn rubbed her ears and thanked her for her enthusiasm while her owner continued to stare at her.

"If you don't say something, I'm going to assume something is wrong," she said, growing nervous under his intense gaze.

"I'm fine," he started, clearing his throat as he pushed her lightly waved hair over her shoulder. Autumn shivered as his fingers grazed her collarbone.

"That's my line," she teased as Brinkley circled them.

"You look...the suit is..." he started, eying the deep V that told him she wasn't wearing a bra.

"I thought a shirt would make us too matchy," she said, playing with the silver chain.

"It's..." He pulled at the back of his neck.

The honking of a horn outside interrupted them, and Autumn's smile deflated.

"We should go—the taxi won't wait forever," said Elijah, but he surprised her by taking her arm as they made their way down the steps. The gesture did more to her than any caress.

They spent the first couple of minutes of the taxi ride in silence, but she couldn't help but fidget under his gaze. If she had known how anxious she was going to feel attending with him, she wouldn't have come. He only stopped staring at her long enough to give the taxi driver directions to the museum where the dinner was taking place. *Trust Tim to rent out an entire museum to entertain his guests.* But the more generous he was, the more generous the patrons would be, and the more the hospital would get.

"It's rude to stare," she muttered, looking at her hands and wishing she'd had time to touch up her nail polish.

"I didn't realise I was." Elijah pulled at his tie as though it was suffocating him, and she leant over to loosen it. He stilled as her fingers brushed his neck, and watching him swallow was her greatest triumph of the evening.

"I haven't worn this since my last performance," Autumn said, smoothing her hands over her immaculately tailored trousers.

Elijah eyed the taxi driver before leaning in. "I would much prefer to have stayed home and see what it would look like on the floor," he whispered, and she wondered if he was just trying to get a reaction from her.

"A bit late to tell me now. I would have happily obliged," she whispered back pointedly.

He rested a warm hand on her thigh. As he spoke, lips grazing her cheek, he tightened his grip. "Don't test me. When I get you home, you won't be wearing it for long. However, I might let you keep the heels on."

Autumn's heartbeat quickened, and she placed her hand over his.

"Pervert," she muttered, focusing her attention ahead so he wouldn't see the effect he had on her.

"Only when it comes to you. Next time, don't play a game you can't win." He winked, intertwining his fingers with hers.

"You don't play fair," she said, looking at their bound hands, still uneasy about the comfort she found in his touch. The moment felt far more intimate than it should have as he brushed his thumb back and forth over her hand. They fell into a comfortable silence.

Chapter Twenty-Four

Elijah

"How good of you both to come! I don't know how you managed to convince her to attend – she never RSVPS to my events," Tim said, greeting them when they arrived at the steps of the National Museum.

"It took some negotiating," Elijah said, resting his hand on Autumn's lower back. She looked stunning; it was hard for him to keep his hands off her. It had almost been a week since he'd got to hold her, and that was far too long for his liking.

"He's exaggerating—I was more than happy to attend. It's for charity, after all." Autumn smiled up at him.

He pinched her butt, and she squeaked, trying to cover it with a cough.

"Sorry," she said, covering her mouth, "swallowed the wrong way." Glaring at him through her long eyelashes, she tried to step out of his reach, but he held her close as other arriving guests passed them on the steps to head inside. As Tim chatted to her about the showcase, Elijah wondered if she was trying to keep her distance because she didn't want Tim to know about their evolving relationship. *He's going to find out sooner or later. I'll keep her by my side no matter what I have to do.*

"Anyway, you should both get inside," Tim said, letting Autumn pass him, but he held Elijah back for a moment, leaning in. "I'm delighted to see you're both getting on so well. Seems my scheming has paid off."

Elijah peered 'round him to see Autumn waiting for him at the main entrance, her arms wrapped around herself.

"I don't think you can take the credit," he said. He didn't know how someone could spend their life on stage and still be nervous in a large group. *Once we've shown our faces and the auction concludes, we can leave early.* He didn't want to prolong her misery when she hadn't wanted to be here in the first place.

"Speaking of credit, the board is growing nervous. When can we see your final demo?" Tim asked, suddenly all business.

Never, Elijah wanted to say. The final demo was already safely with Nirosoft, awaiting final approval, and once they signed on the dotted line, he would be able to pay off his investment. His dad wasn't the only one in the family with a knack for schemes.

"Next week. Everything should be wrapped up nicely by then," he said, slapping his father on the shoulder before Tim was called away by other guests.

INSIDE, THEY WERE GREETED WITH champagne and told their assigned table. "You and your dad seem to be getting on," Autumn commented as Elijah guided her to their table.

"Have I told you how amazing you look?" he asked, wanting to change the subject. The last thing he wanted to talk about was his relationship with his father.

"Nice deflection," she said, taking her seat.

He glanced around the already full table; the other guests, dressed to the nines, eyed them up to make sure they were one of their own before offering polite smiles. They said quick hellos before drifting back to their own conversations and expensive champagne.

"Can I ask why you picked this charity?" he asked, picking up the leaflet with stories of those who had been treated in the hospital. Her expression faltered, and he didn't need to be told it was a personal reason.

"It's where I was treated and where I met Charli."

"Ah. Then I should make a big donation when my deal closes."

"Why?" she asked, taking a sip of champagne.

"For looking after you so well when I couldn't." The words just tumbled out. Although they hadn't known each other back then, he wished he had been there to hold her hand.

Noticing the sudden tears in her eyes, he gave her hand a reassuring squeeze. She was about to say something when an older woman came up behind her.

"Sorry to interrupt. I'm Claire Wright, and I just have to ask—are you Autumn Adler? The concert pianist?" she asked, offering her hand.

"I am," Autumn said, shaking it.

"I knew it! My husband didn't believe me, but I had to come over and check. I've already made a bid on the tickets to your first solo performance in the auction, but I didn't think we would have the pleasure of your company," she said breathlessly.

"The pleasure is all mine, and thank you. I hope you get the chance to see us play," Autumn said kindly.

"I don't know, your ticket is currently in the top position," Claire told her. "If I'm outbid, is there any chance of getting tickets?"

"We're sold out, unfortunately. With only a week to go, there isn't much I can do," Autumn said, leaning slightly away from the woman as she loomed over her.

"I don't want to play favourites, I just heard you play last year, and I always think back on it. Tim mentioned that your theatre is looking for investments. My company would be more than happy to make a contribution," Claire said slyly.

Elijah wasn't surprised by her attitude. Those in attendance were used to getting their way. Tim handled the investments of many in the top one percent, so it wasn't a surprise to find the room full of CEOs, CFOs, and a sprinkling of politicians.

"That's very generous of you. How about you give me your details and I'll see if I can arrange something?" Autumn offered. Elijah guessed they kept some seats for family and friends.

Claire wrapped her arms around Autumn, who stilled at the sudden contact.

"That was kind of you. I can't thank you enough." Once she released Autumn, she handed over her business card. "I'll let you and your partner get back to your conversation."

"He isn't—" Autumn began, but Claire was already heading back to her table, having got what she wanted.

"I'm not what?" Elijah smirked.

Autumn ignored him, downing the rest of her champagne.

"That was an awfully kind gesture," he said, giving her a break.

She leaned in so the rest of the table wouldn't hear. "Claire Wright is the CEO of ClearSkin. If she comes to our theatre, she'll bring the press. The least I can do is get her a ticket."

"How calculated of you," he teased, resting his elbows on the white-linen-covered table.

"I'm not the only one," she said, and he followed her eyes to Tim, getting ready on stage to start the auction. "Maybe this would be a good time to tell your father you're meeting with Nirosoft. If he knew that you felt so caged by him, he might let up." He had told her the night before on a walk with Brinkley.

"Touché. But if I told him what I was doing, he would pull out immediately. He doesn't like being beaten at his own game," Elijah said, offering her a second glass of champagne from beside their name cards.

"The auction is about to start. Make sure to be generous!" Tim announced. "Now that everyone has placed their starting bids, we can begin."

Everyone picked up their paddles in preparation, and anyone not already in their chairs took a seat.

Elijah sat as close as he dared to Autumn while she talked with the others at their table. He could have watched her talk and laugh all night long; many stopped by their table to talk to her, to get her signature, and ask her about her next showcase. Her success inspired him.

He realised the bidding had already begun. He wasn't sure for what, but Autumn was clearly interested since she kept raising her paddle.

"You're feeling generous," he whispered, and she chuckled.

"You could say that."

When the next bid hit €5,000, she lifted her panel again. He wondered if the champagne had gone to her head.

"Five thousand. Going once, twice, and...sold!" Tim announced, and the room broke out in a round of applause.

"Thank you to our generous patron, paddle one thirty, Elijah Wells. You've bought yourself a night at the royal ballet!"

Elijah's head snapped up, and his eyes darted between his paddle and Autumn. She waved it in front of him and winked.

"You swapped the paddles," he said quietly, since everyone at the table was watching. He shook his head, pretending to be irritated with her but finding that he couldn't really be angry. He loved seeing her mischievous side.

"I don't know what you're talking about. If you'll excuse me, I have to go to the ladies' room," she said sweetly, making a quick getaway.

Elijah waited a minute or two before following. *If she wants to play games, let's play,* he thought, unbuttoning his jacket.

"If you'll excuse us," he said, though the rest of the table barely even noticed him leave, too distracted by the ongoing auction.

There was only one private bathroom off the event hall, much to his relief, since he didn't fancy sneaking into the women's. Luckily, there was no one else inside.

"I thought we were past the games," he said, finding Autumn leaning over the sink, reapplying her lipstick.

Her eyes flicked to him in the mirror. "Oh, c'mon, it's just a bit of harmless fun. The money *is* going to charity."

Elijah walked to the door and clicked the latch. He stood behind her in the mirror, watching her intently.

"Now who's playing games? You can't lock us in here for the night," she said.

"I don't need the whole night. I thought you'd want your prize." He swept her hair behind her ear and brushed his lips against her neck. He could smell her floral perfume as he watched their reflection, seeing how perfectly she fit into his embrace.

"Someone could come in and get the wrong idea," she breathed as his hand trailed down her ribs to her hip. Her suit was so tight, he was sure she could feel every caress.

"Do you want me to stop?" he asked, trailing kisses along her neck. She rested her head back against his shoulder.

"No," she sighed, closing her eyes as his hand slipped inside her jacket and palmed her breast. She gasped as her nipples hardened under his touch.

Autumn turned around to face him, and in a flash, Elijah's hands gripped her behind and sat her on the counter. Her body arched against him, and she ran her hands down his chest as he tasted her lips. When she moaned, it was such a sweet sound that he nearly lost control.

"You *had* to wear a suit," he groaned, running his hands over her thighs as they wrapped around him.

"You think I'd let you have me in a bathroom?"

"Who said anything about letting? I'd have you begging me to do it," he told her, slipping into the front of her trousers.

She gasped as he brushed his fingers against her, only to surprise him by leaning back.

"Why do you get to have all the fun?" she asked, trailing kisses along his jaw.

"Do tell." He slipped his hand into her hair and twisted it into his fist, forcing her to look at him with eyes so hungry he wanted to bend her over the sink and forget about everyone outside.

"I'd rather show," she purred, and slowly undid the zip on his trousers.

Elijah hissed as she slipped her hand inside his trousers. Her grasp was such bliss that it was almost painful. Her smile told him how she marvelled at his response. He gripped her wrist, stopping her from stroking him before he lost all self-control.

"Not fair! You get to touch me all you want." She pouted as he pulsed within her grasp.

He rested his forehead against her as she released him. Her touch had nearly broken him, but without it was even worse.

"Touch me like that and you'll start something I want to finish with you writhing beneath me, and we can't do that here."

Autumn's swallow made him feel utterly victorious even if she was the one torturing him. He released her wrist to redo his zip before he changed his mind. But then his arms were around her, his lips on hers in a hot, possessive kiss. Her soft moans rocked him to his core.

A sudden knock on the door shocked them both out of the moment.

"You've got to be kidding me," Elijah panted.

"Oh my God, we can't get caught. This is a charity dinner! You should unlock it," Autumn exclaimed, sliding off the counter—though not without pressing her body to his, letting him know exactly what he was missing out on. "It was nice playing with you," she added, heading towards a cubicle to hide.

"What if I don't want to play anymore?"

She paused and turned to face him with startled eyes. "What do you mean? You want to move out?" she asked, her words so vulnerable that he wanted to open the door and tell whoever was interrupting them to piss off.

"No, that's not what I meant." He ran his hands through his hair. *Why did I have to pick this moment to say this?* "I...I want to trade our truce for a real go at it," he said only to be greeted with her confused frown. "I want to date you, fight with you, then enjoy every moment of making up."

Autumn's eyes went wide. "I don't know what to say," she whispered.

The knocking intensified.

"Can we talk about this later? I can't think with someone banging on the door."

Elijah wanted to go to her, but he couldn't force her. *I have to work on my timing!* "Later is fine. This isn't how I wanted to tell you. Just...think about it," he said, and she nodded, clearly lost in her own thoughts.

Once she was concealed in a cubicle, he went to the door and unlocked it.

"Sorry, I don't know how that happened; the lock must have jammed," he said to the stranger, who ignored him and headed for another empty cubicle.

Elijah thought about waiting for her; the bathroom was unisex, so it didn't matter if they were seen together so long as it wasn't in a compromising position, but he figured that she might need a minute to compose herself after he had blurted out his feelings at the worst time. *I'll see her back at the table. The last thing I want to do is crowd her.* He let the door close behind him.

He hadn't reached the table before Tim stopped him.

Chapter Twenty-Five

Autumn

Autumn let out a sigh of relief when she heard Elijah leave. Resting her back on the door, she attempted to gather her thoughts.

I don't know how I've gone from hating him to letting him do the most delicious things to me in a public place, she thought, using her fingers to detangle her hair before straightening her jacket. Shame and excitement coiled within her. *Maybe the hate our relationship started with is what makes him so irresistible. I thought a week apart would distance us, but it only made me want him all the more... and clearly he feels the same, or he wouldn't have confessed his feelings.*

When she heard the other guest leave, she made her way down the hall. *What am I supposed to say to him? I don't want him to leave, but he really has the worst timing. Between moving in and confessing—what is wrong with him?* Lost in thought, she was about to turn the corner to re-enter the main room when she caught sight of Elijah and his father talking. Autumn lingered out of sight, but just about able to make out their conversation.

"You must tell me how you bribed Autumn to attend," Tim said, and she rolled her eyes. *Why does everyone care what events I attend and don't attend?*

"I didn't have to bribe her. She clearly cares about the hospital, so I was more than happy to accompany her," Elijah said, and she watched him straightening his tie, clearly uncomfortable at his father's line of questioning.

"And the fact that you both disappeared at the same time?" Tim's question was barely audible, but it made her blush, mortified to know that their absence had been noted.

"I suggest you mind your own business. What Autumn and I do is between us," Elijah snapped, and she buried her face in her hands.

"Treat her right. I won't have you disrupting her life; she's been through enough," Tim said, squaring up to his son.

Autumn was taken aback by his tone and the hypocrisy of his statement. He was just as responsible for disrupting her life as Elijah was, if not more so. Elijah never would have moved in without his permission. She wasn't used to seeing this side of Tim. *I can't believe he's taking my side over his son's! Elijah wouldn't hurt me. I'm the one who's more likely to doom whatever is happening between us.*

The realisation made her heart ache. She could only imagine how much Tim's words hurt Elijah; for a father to treat his son this way made her want to wrap her arms around him and protect him.

"It's *our* relationship. I would never hurt her. Unlike you, I treat the woman I love with respect."

Elijah's words make her pulse quicken. *Love?*

The word washed over her. At first she wanted to go to him, but her feet wouldn't move. Suddenly, a chill rushed through her. She felt like the floor was going to open up and swallow her whole. She didn't want to come between father and son, especially when Tim had always looked out for her, while her own father couldn't accept her return to the city. She certainly wasn't ready, nor did she think Elijah was ready, to share with others what was developing between them—which Elijah had confirmed was love. *Does he really* love *me? We barely know each other!*

She placed a hand over her stomach as it flipped. She couldn't face returning to the table to sit beside him and pretend that she hadn't heard his conversation with Tim.

You just need some air. Give yourself a few minutes, she thought, and though it was cowardly, she slipped past the men and into the crowd of guests, making her way to the entrance before Elijah could notice her leaving.

You can't just run after he told you he wants to be with you, her conscience scolded her as she tasted fresh air. The cool breeze was a welcome distraction from her burning skin.

She knew she was running away from her feelings as much as she was running away from him. His touch had set her on fire and she needed to extinguish it, for both their sakes. She knew from first-hand experience that playing with fire got you burnt.

I'm such a coward, she thought as she found refuge in a taxi. She froze when the driver asked her for the address. *If I go home, I'll have to face Elijah, and I don't think I have the willpower to not give in to him.* She gave the driver Nina's address and hoped her friend would be alone.

The guilt of abandoning Elijah weighed on her heart, but she desperately needed to figure out the mess they had made. She thought about leaning in to her feelings for him, but it was too complicated. They lived together; it was like moving ten steps forward in their relationship.

Once she'd paid her fare outside the flat complex, she buzzed her friend's number and prayed that she didn't have company.

"Hello?" Nina's voice was an instant comfort as it came over the intercom.

"It's me," Autumn said, shivering in the cold as others out for the evening passed her on the city street.

"Autumn? What are you doing here? Did Garrett call you?" Nina said in a flurry.

"Garrett? No, why would he call me?" Now she was not only feeling guilty about abandoning Elijah, but worried about what was going on with her best friend.

"I'll buzz you up and we can talk," Nina said, and the buzzer sounded.

The lift took her to Nina's flat on the second floor. Autumn couldn't reach the door fast enough.

"Is everything okay? Not like you to just turn up," Nina said, in her pyjamas. Autumn noticed her puffy eyes. She had been crying again.

"I didn't want to be alone," she said simply, knowing that she could have just stayed at the museum and gone to Elijah to talk things through. She could still taste him on her lips, and the guilt churned up her stomach.

"Good, because neither do I." Nina sighed, closing the door.

"Do you want to start?" Autumn asked, sitting next to her on the tangerine-coloured sofa in the middle of the sitting room.

"We broke up," Nina told her, clutching a cushion to her chest.

If she hadn't been able to see how upset Nina was, she would have cheered. "Why? I thought everything was fine."

"We were, except he kept talking about moving in together. He thought since my lease is up next month, it would be perfect timing." Nina sniffled, and Autumn reached for a tissue on the unicorn-shaped side table. "I said no, and he said it was only because I was nervous about living with someone."

Autumn guessed where this was headed. "But you lived with Sophia."

"Yep, and when I let it slip, he stormed out and told me we could either move forward or move on. So...I told him to move on." Nina shrugged.

"It sucks to have your heartbroken, but I'm proud of you for sticking up for what you wanted. You can't bully your way into living with someone," Autumn told her, only to realise the irony of the statement. But her own situation was different. They had been strangers—though it still wasn't the best start to a relationship, she had to admit.

"I almost had sex with Elijah on a sink," Autumn blurted out.

"Good for you, but I'm going to need a bit more context."

"We went to the charity dinner I was telling you about, auctioning tickets for the showcase. I thought it would be funny to use his paddle to bid on something."

Nina's eyes narrowed. "Okay, how do we get to the sink?"

"He wasn't too pleased, but it was all in good fun and for charity."

"Sure, expensive flirting, I get it," Nina said, lapping up every word. "I'm intrigued."

"After I won, I went to the bathroom because the others at our table were starting to stare." Autumn tried to suppress a smile at her small victory.

"I see where the sink comes in. There are worse places. At least it wasn't outside—that I wouldn't recommend."

"Yep." Autumn buried her face in the side of the couch. "I don't know what came over me...when he gets close, my brain turns to mush."

"I need wine for this conversation." Nina left her for the small kitchen the colour of cotton candy. "Want some?"

she asked, and Autumn could hear her looking through her shelf dedicated to alcohol and mixers. Cocktails and movie nights were a staple ritual.

"No, but do you have some ginger beer? My stomach is in knots. I feel so bad for leaving him there." Autumn grabbed the stuffed panda beside her and snuggled it under her chin.

"When you say you left him there, what do you mean, exactly?" Nina asked, handing Autumn the glass of fizzling ginger beer. Even the smell helped. She sipped until her stomach calmed down.

"We were interrupted, but he told me he wanted me. Not just for tonight, but he wants to trade our truce for a relationship," Autumn told her.

Nina covered her squeal with her hand. "That's great! I think he's good for you. Though I'm not understanding how his confession is a bad thing or how you ended up here." She frowned.

"I ran." Autumn muttered her admission into the pillow, hiding her face in shame.

Nina choked on her drink.

"You what?" She smirked. "*I* would never run away from that man."

"Elijah went out first, and when I was on my way back to our table, I heard him talking to Tim. Hearing how he spoke about me, about his feelings...I panicked. I'm terrified I'll let him down." She felt like an idiot now that she was saying it aloud, but it was the truth. They had only known each other a short time, and she worried they were moving too fast. She loved her bubble, but since he'd arrived in her life, he'd popped it.

"How could you let him down? You don't have to be perfect. He's lived with you for three weeks, and to live with someone is to see every side of them," Nina reasoned. "He hasn't run away—you did."

"I'm not proud of it."

Nina's phone vibrated on the table.

"Are you going to answer that?" Autumn asked.

"Nope. This is too juicy." Nina sat back and took another drink.

"It might be Garrett calling to apologise," Autumn pointed out, thinking that her friend was revelling in her misery a little too much.

"Then I'm definitely not answering."

Autumn admired her for standing her ground. She was fairly sure that if Elijah appeared in front of her, she would crumble.

"So, what are you going to do? You live with him, and you can't hide here forever," Nina said, her eyes filled with sympathy.

Autumn squeezed her panda cushion tighter. "That's my point. There's no escaping each other. With anyone else, I could have my own space, but he's everywhere. There's no time to breathe."

"Maybe he's exactly what you need because you *can't* get away. He won't let you push him away, and geographically, you can't either. The universe works in mysterious ways." Nina wrapped an arm around her.

"You might be right. Maybe I'm just freaking out because, for the first time, I don't want him to leave, so I left first," she grumbled. He wasn't the problem—she was.

The phone rang again.

"Just answer it, or he might appear at the door," Autumn said. The last person she wanted to see her like this was Garrett. Selfishly, she hoped it wasn't him; if he did appear and they made up, she would have to go home and face the music.

Nina started, sitting on the edge of the couch. "Elijah, hi, how are you?" Autumn didn't dare look up to meet her eye. "Yep, Autumn is with me. She wasn't feeling well, so she came over."

If anything, she had been feeling too good when they were together, and it was leaving that had made her ill.

"No, don't worry. You don't need to come and get her, she's fine," Nina said. "Ha, good point—when *is* she not fine?"

Autumn glared at her, but was grateful he didn't have the address. To find it, he would have to go into her things, which she hoped he wouldn't do even if she had poked around his.

"Don't worry, I have it covered. She's going to spend the night with me," Nina said before ending the call.

"How did he sound?" Autumn asked, peeking over the pillow.

"Like a worried, overgrown, sexy puppy," Nina said, and Autumn groaned, guilt and embarrassment merging within her.

"Can a puppy be sexy?" She frowned, trying to make light of the situation.

"With that voice, yes. If I were you, I wouldn't walk home, I would run," Nina teased, leaning over the couch.

"You aren't helping." Autumn knew she was only saying it to get a rise out of her, but it was working. She looked at the door and considered going home, but her fear froze her to the spot.

"What's it going to be? Going home and facing life, or hiding for the night and facing it tomorrow?" Nina asked as she hesitated.

"I'm going to sleep here with Mr Panda, and pretend my invading hunk didn't do things to me no human being should do in a public space," she muttered. Nina's laughter was utterly infectious. "Tomorrow, I will put my big girl pants on and act like an adult."

"Sounds like a plan. You pick some girly movie. If I'm not mistaken, I have some cookie-dough ice cream in the freezer with our name on it, and we can forget about the men in our lives."

Nina fell asleep on the couch first. Despite what had happened with Elijah, Autumn was glad to spend some time with her. She hadn't even realised how much she'd missed her friend. Between work, relationships, and getting through every day, it was becoming clear to her how often she neglected fun. They only saw each other at work or on their pre-rehearsal coffee dates. Before Elijah, Autumn couldn't remember the last time she'd done anything off-schedule. She certainly wouldn't have gone swimming, got a dog, or attended the charity dinner.

But even if she enjoyed those things, her routine was her safety net. As she drifted to sleep, she considered what might happen if that safety net no longer existed. Even if losing it would benefit her, it terrified her to change what had kept her going, surviving, since her accident.

Chapter Twenty-Six

Elijah

"What about getting home? Does she need a lift back later?" Elijah asked Nina, pretty sure he heard Autumn groan on the other end of the phone. He much preferred being the reason for her moans. He tried to contain his smile as he remembered her head resting on his shoulder as the pleasure of his touch took over her body. But the smile vanished quickly as the truth of it punched him in the gut. She'd run away from him.

He paced in the street in front of the museum, trying to work out some of his pent-up energy.

"Don't worry, I have it covered. She's going to spend the night with me," Nina said.

Elijah shook his head. He knew Autumn wanted space from him, and it hurt far more than he'd thought it would. "Tell her I'll see her tomorrow," he said, because what else could he say? 'I miss you, come home, let's talk?'

Talking isn't our strong point, but God, do our bodies know how to communicate, he thought, and gritted his teeth as Nina hung up. If he knew her address, he'd go after Autumn and insist they talk things out.

He hadn't meant to get carried away. When he'd realised she'd left, his stomach had dropped. If he hadn't been talking to Tim, he would have noticed her leaving the bathroom, but he hadn't wanted to be rude and he didn't want his father to think about what was going on between them. Not yet, anyway—though he was quietly determined to make Autumn his. He wanted to be her partner, for her to trust him with her secrets the same way he already trusted her with his. Over time, he hoped to show her he could be a part of her life and that she wouldn't have to lose the independence she clung to so tightly.

Instead, I blurted out my feelings at the worst possible moment and drove her away. He rolled his neck, trying to ease the tension.

"What are you doing out here, son?" Tim asked, joining him on the steps outside the museum. Elijah put his phone back in his jacket pocket.

"Nothing. Getting some air," he said, trying to sound casual.

"Where's Autumn?" Tim asked, looking up and down the street. "Did you fight?"

"No, nothing like that." If they had, it would have been much easier to sort out. "She wasn't feeling well, so I put her in a taxi."

"If she wasn't well, you should have gone home with her."

Elijah sighed. That was exactly what he had wanted to do, but getting Autumn to do anything he wanted was damn near impossible. Tonight, something had changed, a crack in her facade had exposed itself, and he'd stupidly torn it wide open.

"She insisted I stay," he lied.

"She was probably overwhelmed. She doesn't like being recognised since to know of Autumn Adler is to know of her tragedy. I think it's why she loves that small theatre so much—lower expectations to be met," Tim said, putting his hands in his pockets.

"At the rate she practises, I don't think the expectations are any less," Elijah scoffed. "Not their expectations of her."

"Her expectations of herself. She doesn't think she deserves the attention."

"I don't think you know her at all. She doesn't enjoy the attention," Elijah snapped, not liking Tim making assumptions about her. Only he saw how damn hard Autumn tried, even if it was a lot of effort for what Tim considered a 'lesser' theatre.

"Forget I said anything. As long as she's playing, I'm happy," Tim said, trying to make peace.

"Why do you care so much?" Elijah asked. He was grateful for all the care and support his father had shown Autumn, but it still hurt that Tim seemed to care so much more about the daughter of his friend than he'd ever seemed to for his son.

Tim opened his mouth and then shut it. He clearly didn't know how to answer, and Elijah no longer wished to discuss Autumn with him. The last thing they needed to do was fight when he was so close to being free of his father.

"Let's head back inside," he said. "I'm sure there's someone you want to introduce me to."

His father perked up, clapping him on the back. "There is. Also, you have to settle your bill for the auction."

He had to resist every part of him that wanted to call Nina back and demand she tell him her address. *She can't avoid me forever; she has to come home at some point,* he thought, writing a cheque at the auction table.

Once he'd settled his ridiculous bill and been introduced to what felt like fifty of Tim's friends, he decided he'd had enough socialising for one night. He cursed himself for attending in the first place, wishing he had just stayed on the couch with Autumn. He hailed a taxi, gripping the back of his neck as he thought of going back to an empty house. *I didn't mean to scare her off. But what did I expect by confessing my feelings in such a way?*

His phone vibrating in his pocket distracted him.

> Apartment 28,
> Hillvalley Street,
> Harlow 4.

Elijah smiled as he read the address from Nina. Suddenly determined to go get his girl, he told the driver the new address.

When they pulled up to the right street, it was already drizzling, and Elijah hesitated as he lingered at the door. He figured that Autumn might not be happy for him to turn up on the door. *When has she ever liked my surprises?* he thought wryly before buzzing number twenty-eight.

It was only a matter of seconds before it buzzed, and he took the lift to the second floor. Shifting anxiously, he knocked on the door and waited for her to answer.

After what sounded like a scuffle inside, Autumn opened the door, her eyes wide with surprise.

"Oh! Sorry, I thought you were..." she mumbled, before glaring over her shoulder at Nina, who was on a sofa.

"Thought I was who?"

"Hi, Elijah." Nina waved.

Autumn stepped into the hall, leaving the door open a crack behind her. She stared at her feet, chewing her lip, and he knew he had to say something to put her at ease.

"I'm sorry for turning up like this. I just couldn't leave things the way we did."

She nodded. "I would have answered your calls, but my phone died," she said, finally looking at him.

As soon as her sad green eyes met his, he couldn't be upset with her. "Remind me to get you a battery pack for your birthday. That damn phone of yours is going to be the death of me," he said, and even though he meant it, it earned him a smile.

"I feel terrible. I panicked, but there's no excuse for leaving you like that. I just went outside to get some air, and the next thing I knew, I was in a taxi headed here," she explained, and he could see how guilty she felt.

He took her hands in his to stop her fidgeting. "It's okay. It was a lot for one evening. Hell, I wasn't expecting to say what I said."

"Seems like neither of us could control ourselves," she muttered.

"Can we go home and talk? I don't really want to do this in the hallway," he said, unable to breathe until she agreed.

"Okay," she said, and he brought her hand to her lips.

"I'll be on my best behaviour." He made a cross over his chest.

"Ha. I don't think you know how."

He laughed. "But I can try."

"Let me get my things. I'll meet you at the lift." Her words were music to his ears. With a sigh of relief, he released her, letting her head back inside. She left the door open a crack, and he couldn't help but listen in.

"I can't believe you texted him," Autumn said, though she didn't sound angry.

"One of us might as well get a happy ending this evening," Nina replied. "Don't let your fear ruin a good thing."

Elijah hated the thought of Autumn being afraid of their feelings for each other. He could only hope that affection for him outweighed her desire to protect herself from what might happen in the future. *If she isn't going to leave, then neither am I,* he thought, and then chuckled to himself, because it was that very logic that had got them into this position in the first place.

"Thank you, but are you going to be okay? After everything with Garrett?"

Elijah wondered if they had broken up. Autumn had mentioned that their relationship wasn't on the best terms.

"I'll be fine, and you can tell me everything on Monday," Nina promised, and Elijah couldn't hear their last exchange. He paced before the lift, and seeing Autumn's soft smile as she walked towards him caused his chest to tighten.

"Your house or mine?" he asked, pressing the button.

"To be decided," she said, surprising him in the lift by reaching on her tiptoes to brush her lips against his. "I'm sorry I overreacted. I shouldn't have left you like that."

"You're apologising?" he asked dramatically, wrapping his long coat around her as they walked out into the street.

She rolled her eyes. "Don't get used to it."

"I think you owe me for such outrageous behaviour," he said, opening the door to the taxi waiting outside and giving the driver the original address once again. It felt easy, almost too easy, to fall back into their usual pattern of risqué banter. Elijah knew they needed to talk, but right now, he felt safer on familiar ground, and perhaps it would help Autumn relax too.

"And what exactly do I owe you?" she demanded.

Elijah tugged her close by the lapels of her borrowed jacket before she stepped into the taxi.

"I have several things in mind, but none of them are suitable for our current environment," he told her, loving how she flushed. "Now get in so we can go home."

Autumn gripped Elijah's hand, stopping him from opening the gate. His eyebrows pulled together, worried she was changing her mind.

"Yes," she said, staring up at him.

Yes?

"To giving it a go. I wanted to answer you before we go inside."

She took a deep breath and he waited, giving her the time she needed to continue. He tried to contain his excitement and elation, but he couldn't stop smiling.

"I'm not used to having someone around all the time, and you drive me crazy in every which way, but I want us to try."

Elijah saw her shoulders relax as she finished, and he wrapped his arms around her. Letting him in was a big step, and he couldn't express how grateful he was for her trust.

"That's all I ask. We can take this one step at a time." He placed a slow, lingering kiss on her lips.

"And what about several other things you mentioned?" She returned the kiss with more urgency than he'd expected. Flirty Autumn was a threat to life itself, but he was determined to go at her pace.

"I don't think the public would approve," he said, looking up and down their street.

"We'd better get inside, then," she teased.

"Your wish is my command." Before she could escape, he tossed her over his shoulder. He slapped her butt as she squealed.

He didn't release her until they reached the door of her bedroom. He watched as she slipped off his long coat, letting it fall to the floor. She stared at him with eyes that told him she wanted this, *needed* this, as much as he did.

"Are you sure? I'll wait for as long as you need," he told her, tucking a strand of hair behind her ear, listening as her breath caught.

Autumn sat on the edge of the bed and unbuttoned her jacket, baring herself to him. He heaved a deep breath, admiring how beautiful she was.

"Before I say yes, there's a long scar on my lower back. You don't have to touch it, but it's fine if you do," she said quietly, looking down at the circular scar on her abdomen. "You can avoid them, but I just wanted to say that touching them won't hurt me," she added with more confidence. He loved how confident she was with him. It was that fire that had made him fall for her.

"There is no part of you I'd ever want to avoid," he assured her. "You've no idea how much I've longed to touch and taste every inch of you. Scarred or not, it's part of you and deserves to be cherished."

She sighed softly, as if to let his words sink in. "Yes. I'm sure." Her eyes, so beautiful, glistened with trust.

It was all he needed, but she made it all the sweeter by gripping his shirt and pulling him close. Elijah kissed her hair and her cheeks until her lips parted for him. He wanted to savour every moment, but he wanted her so much that he didn't know how long he could last.

"I'll never get enough of your lips," he said, feeling her smile against his lips as she worked his shirt from his shoulders.

"You never wear a shirt. I don't think you should start now." Autumn nipped at his neck while she worked on his buttons and slipped her fingers inside. He pulled her flush against him, and though he tried to be gentle with her, it took all his willpower to restrain himself when she brought her lips to his chest.

"You're playing with fire," he breathed, and she looked up at him through her long lashes.

"Then burn me."

He loved it when she challenged him. This time, they wouldn't be interrupted; he would show this woman ecstasy when all she knew was pain. The giggle that escaped her when he pushed her back onto the mattress nearly ruined him.

He settled between her legs, thrusting his hips forward roughly, and she met him with eager movements.

"You've no idea how much I've been aching for you," she rasped.

He unbuttoned her trousers. "Not for much longer. Lift your hips for me."

Autumn happily obliged, and he pulled her trousers and her underwear down the perfect curves of her legs. One of his hands slipped to the back of her neck. "Do you have any idea how beautiful you are when you smile?" he murmured, kissing her cheeks as she blushed. He deepened the kiss. She moaned, giving him better access to her mouth.

He traced kisses over her neck and her breasts until she shivered beneath him. She sucked in a breath when his tongue traced the inner curve of her thigh, then lay back, closing her eyes. Elijah smiled against her skin, tracing his name with his tongue on her inner thigh. She was his—she just didn't know it yet. He teased her until she gripped the back of his head, her hands in his hair telling him exactly what she needed. She pushed her hips forward, trying to tempt him, as if he needed any encouragement.

He licked and sucked until she was wet and panting. He needed to make sure she was ready for him, and as she writhed beneath his lips, he couldn't wait any longer. She pulled at his shoulders until he made quick work of his trousers and settled over her. He fisted the sheets as she grasped him. If she kept touching him like that, he didn't think he would last another minute. He thrust her hands over her head, pinning her wrists with one hand so he could torture her with the other.

"I need..." she pleaded, rolling her hips against him. Her eyes were hazy, lost in the sensation of his body against hers.

"Need what?" he asked, tasting her tongue as she rolled her hips, trying to entice him again. He wanted to hear it.

"You," she said.

Desire coursed through his veins, the blood rushing between his legs almost painful.

"You'll never get rid of me now," he said, his hips holding her hostage against the bed as she tried to bring a satisfying end to what he wished to draw out forever.

Her nails dug into his hips. "Elijah, move, please…" She wrapped her legs around his waist, which nearly drove him over the edge. He rewarded her by trailing his fingers between her legs, smiling at her shyness as she tried to move away. After a moment, she rocked her hips against his hands instead, her knees widening, welcoming him.

"Is this okay? I don't want to hurt you," he groaned, trying to remain in control.

She smiled up at him. "I'm perfect."

Her body shook with pleasure beneath him, and hearing her call out his name was all he needed to lose his grasp on reality, sure that she was ready for him. First, he reached into the drawer beside the couch and pulled out a condom. Autumn's eyes widened; they'd both been so lost in the moment, they'd almost forgotten. Once it was secure, she pulled him towards her with a cheeky grin.

Elijah tucked a hand under her thigh, opening her up to him. Autumn tilted her hips while he filled her. She gasped, reaching her limit and tightening around him.

"God, Autumn, you fit me so perfectly, like you were made for me." He groaned, kissing a path from her neck to her mouth.

Her breath hitched, and her nails clawed down his back as he rocked into her. Her hips twitched, rolling beneath him as she moaned his name hoarsely. He desperately wanted to take it slow, to savour every moment, but desire won out. Their movements became more frantic, both lost to pleasure. Autumn gripped his hips as she pleaded with him not to stop. The sensation was almost too much; he knew what they both needed. His lips engulfed her pleas as he slipped his hand between them, and her gasp against his lips nearly undid him as his thumb circled her clit. She arched into his touch, spasming around him. A low groan escaped him when he finally released all that was pent up inside him. Pinning her to the bed, he gently circled his hips, drawing out the moment of sheer bliss between them.

"I have no words," Autumn panted as he rested his forehead against hers for a moment before rolling off her so he wouldn't crush her. The sound of their heavy breathing filled the silence.

"That's a first," he teased, placing gentle kisses on her forehead and temples before cradling her to his chest. He ran his fingers through her hair, listening to her breathing soften.

"How about we just stay here forever?" she asked, snuggling closer.

He didn't think he would ever get used to the effect her touch had on him. "I think that can be arranged."

He kissed the top of her head. Both too exhausted to talk, to think, they fell asleep, happy to be lost in each other.

Chapter Twenty-Seven

Elijah

After a blissful weekend with Autumn, Elijah woke up in the early hours to find himself alone in her bed, which he much preferred to his own. He didn't need to wonder where she had escaped to for long because the sound of music drifted up the stairs.

At the piano, he found her wearing his shirt with her hair loose over her shoulders, clearly too lost in her playing to notice him. He leaned against the doorframe, admiring how beautiful and peaceful she was. How had he got so lucky?

"Are you going to stand there and stare?" she asked as she finished the piece, turning to look at him.

Elijah clapped, loving the way she buried her head in her hands when embarrassed.

"That was incredible. I can't wait to see you on stage." He sat beside her on the bench, tracing her fingers on the keys.

"This was for fun. I was feeling inspired," she said, resting her head on his shoulder.

"Oh, really? Would I have anything to do with that?"

He kissed the side of her head. It was as though the last wall between them had finally come down, and he never wanted to feel it there again.

"Maybe," she said, slipping her fingers between his.

"Is there something on your mind?"

"Just thinking about Nina. I hope she's okay. As much as I've enjoyed our weekend together, she just broke up with Garrett, and I feel bad that I haven't seen her."

Elijah understood her concern. "I would have thought you'd be relieved they've broken up," he said, silently relieved they wouldn't have to go to dinner and that Autumn would no longer have to be around someone who made her uncomfortable.

"I am, but I don't want her to hurt."

He loved how much she cared. He would have felt the same way if it were Francis. "Sadly, it's Monday. You'll be reunited with her in a few hours," he reminded her, taking her chin in his hand. "You've got a big heart, Autumn Adler."

She looked up at him with those big eyes that made him weak. "Are you sure you can look after it?"

"Let's get you back to bed, and I'll think of a way."

She slapped him playfully. He carried her back upstairs. *If she isn't going to look after herself, I'll take great joy in doing it for her.*

∽

"Have you seen my keys?" Elijah asked as they both got ready to leave in the hallway. "I think I gave them to you last night."

Autumn searched in her bag as he opened the front door, and then he felt her freeze beside him. She reached down slowly to pick up the red rose on the doormat. There was a message with it this time. Elijah felt the blood drain from his face as he picked it up.

"Let's not let it ruin our day," Autumn said, putting the rose in the bin outside, but he had to know.

Enjoy your performance.
You never know when it might be your last x

Son of a bitch. Elijah's jaw clenched, and he walked down the front steps to her. He read the note over and over until the paper crumpled in his grasp. "This is a direct threat. We have to go to the police! This is about your safety." His heart was pounding.

"I don't think it's anything to get worked up over," Autumn said. She placed a reassuring hand on his heart. "Please don't worry about it. You have a meeting and I have morning practice; we can talk about it later."

He stared at her, wondering how she could remain so calm. Maybe it was because the alternative frightened her too much. He noticed she settled a protective hand on her lower back and wondered if it was just an instinct to protect her most vulnerable spot or if she was in pain.

"Autumn, please. This letter has no envelope; they were outside while we slept. You don't have to ignore this. I won't let anything happen to you." The thought of someone standing on their doorstep drove him crazy. Why had Brinkley, who went insane for the post, never reacted to the rose being delivered? The dog was trying to say her goodbyes to them, but they were too wrapped up in the conversation.

"What if all this person wants is a reaction?" Autumn suggested, but he wasn't going to risk her safety on that reasoning.

"Francis's husband is a detective. At least let me consult with him."

She shook her head. "No, please don't. I can't handle a circus right now," she pleaded, reaching for him. She stepped into his arms, and he never wanted to let her go.

"You have a stalker," he said, kissing her hair. "You might be able to brush off the roses left on the anniversary, but this note is an actual threat. To know where you live, they have to be someone who knows you." *How anyone who knows her could think she deserves to be treated this way after everything she's been through is a crime in itself.*

Autumn stepped out of his reach, running her hands through her hair. "It isn't necessarily someone I know. Anyone could know about the accident. All you have to do is Google me to discover my tragic backstory. Even if we call the police, what will we tell them? I've received roses on the fifteenth of every month for the last three years—"

He stopped her. "Every month? You've been getting roses every month for three years? I thought it was only once a year!"

"You jealous?" she teased.

"Please don't joke. I have a mind to lock you inside and not let you out until I catch this prick." He huffed, pacing. "Three years...that's oddly specific. Tim told me you've been back playing for six."

She listened while he played detective, folding her arms across her chest.

"What about an ex?" It hurt him to even ask. They hadn't opened the ex files yet, and he hoped they never had to.

"No. The last person I dated is touring, and they aren't the type to get hung up on anyone," she told him.

"What about any fans hanging around after performances?" he asked, trying to think of any and all possibilities.

"I don't think so. I wouldn't know what to look for."

"How can you be so calm about this? If I was getting gifts from a stranger, I would be freaked out."

Autumn laughed, and it terrified him. "Trust me, when you've been to hell, everything else appears dull in comparison," she said. "There's nothing this person can do that can outweigh anything else I've been through."

Hearing her so content in her suffering tore at Elijah's soul. A car horn stalled their conversation, and she gripped his jacket, forcing him down to her level.

"Thank you for caring so much." She kissed him, and he let out a long sigh, knowing he wouldn't be able to stop her from leaving. The horn sounded again. "That's Nina. And please listen to me. I have to get to rehearsal, and you have to go or Francis will blame me for keeping you. Let's not give whoever the hell is doing this the satisfaction of ruining our day."

He was a minute away from going full protective caveman, but he knew her comeback meant everything to her, and he wasn't going to stand in her way. Pulling her into his embrace, he let the smell of her perfume ease his worry. She tried to worm out of his grasp, but he wasn't going to let go until she conceded one point.

"I won't call the police, but let me tell Francis's husband what's happening and see what he suggests. You don't have to fill out a report until you are ready," he said. Negotiating usually worked for them when they couldn't agree.

Autumn's eyes narrowed, telling him she was considering it. "If I agree, will you let me go?" she asked, looking over the gate to Nina.

"Probably," he mused before tilting her chin up so he could taste her one last time.

She sighed into his embrace. "You are exhausting."

"And I'm beginning to think you have a death wish."

"Keeps life interesting." She winked.

He raised his eyebrows, still waiting for her answer.

"Fine, talk with him. I have to go." She squirmed away from him, and he waited until she was in the car before he took Brinkley back inside.

"Aiden Grimshaw's office. Is he in today?" Elijah asked the receptionist at the front desk of the police station.

The man in his sixties eyed him above his thick glasses. "What is the reason for your inquiry? If you are here to report a case, you need to talk with an officer first."

"No, I'm here to see a friend," Elijah said. He didn't want to get stuck with a junior officer.

"Detective Grimshaw should be back soon. Detectives are on the third floor; last door on the right." The receptionist diverted his attention back to the computer.

Elijah was making his way up the stairs when his phone went off. It was Francis calling.

"Hey. Sorry, I can't talk," he whispered, finding Aiden's name at the last door. He knocked but there was no answer, so he took a seat outside and decided to wait.

"You'd better talk! Where the hell are you?" Francis hissed.

Elijah winced. He knew he should have gone to the station after the signing with Nirosoft, but he wouldn't be able to focus until he spoke with Aiden about Autumn's stalker. The note was burning a hole in his pocket.

"The contract signing will have to wait. Push the meeting an hour and I'll get there," he said, keeping his voice low so he didn't attract attention from the passing officers.

"I'm beginning to think you're sabotaging this deal on purpose! Since you moved into that damn house—"

Aiden appeared in the doorway.

"I'll be there. Take them out to lunch on the company card," Elijah said in a desperate effort to stall. Francis groaned, and he hung up.

"Elijah? What are you doing here?" Aiden said, closing the file in his hands.

"I need to talk to you about something."

"Is everything okay with Francis?" he asked, his eyes wide with panic.

"No, Francis is fine, although he might want to murder me right now because I'm meant to be halfway across town, signing papers. This is about something else."

"Okay. Come in."

It was the first time Elijah had ever seen him at work. He led him to his office; there was a picture of Todd and Francis on his desk.

"Are you in trouble?" he asked, getting right to the point.

"No. It's about Autumn."

"She locked you out this time? Francis told me about the stunt you pulled."

Elijah wished it was that simple. "No, we're fine, but someone has been leaving items at her door for years and she hasn't done anything about it," he said.

Aiden frowned. "What type of things?"

"Roses. Autumn was in an accident a decade ago, and the roses keep arriving on the date of the anniversary," Elijah explained.

"Flowers? Could it be someone she knows trying to do something nice for her? Surely, the day must be hard for her."

Elijah shook his head, knowing that it sounded like he was making a big deal out of nothing. "They never sign a card. When they started, she asked everyone she knew, and they said they hadn't sent anything. Autumn doesn't know who is sending them."

Aiden opened his notepad. "She doesn't want to file a report herself?"

Elijah sighed. "I wanted to ask your advice first, and she's terrified to admit whoever is doing this is a threat. She's using her rehearsals as an excuse, but I can see how worried she is. She has a performance coming up, and I'm worried it could be some crazy fan." He checked his phone to find another missed call from Francis.

"I can see that you're concerned, but without her filing a report, I can't do much. She may come around, but it's better not to press her."

"I don't want to force her, I'm just worried," he said, running his hands through his hair.

"I have to be clear. You're in an intimate relationship with her? Could it be a jealous ex?" Aiden asked. Now it felt like he was talking to a detective, not his best friend's husband.

"Yes, we are, but she says it couldn't be an ex," he said firmly.

"Do you have any of the evidence? Any of the roses? The note?"

"The roses she threw away, but I kept this morning's note. They've arrived on the fifteenth of May for the last three years, but recently, it's been happening every month, and this morning she found this." Elijah took the note from his pocket. He'd put it in a sandwich bag in case there were prints on it. Aiden took a glove from his desk before he handled it.

"'Enjoy your performance. You never know when it might be your last.'" Aiden's brow furrowed as he read the note slowly.

"I think they mean her next show, which is only a few days from now. I'm worried they're growing bolder. Maybe the roses weren't getting enough of a reaction?"

"Okay. I'll send it off to check for prints and see what comes up, but I'll need to speak to Autumn at some point if we go any further," Aiden said.

Though Elijah was glad for his help, he wished Autumn had come and explained herself. There might be details he didn't know about or that she might have overlooked.

"If you find anything, please ring me. I feel in my gut it has to be someone she knows doing it." He needed to hear someone else's opinion on the matter because if he kept going over it in his head, he thought he would go insane.

"Why do you think that?" Aiden asked.

"They knew she moved to the city six years ago but the roses only started arriving in the last three. They know the date of her accident and that she has a concert coming up."

Aiden looked uncertain. "The move, maybe, but the rest could be gathered from the internet. Please don't try and solve this yourself; you'll only end up hurting yourself and putting Autumn at risk." The detective's tone told Elijah how serious this was and that he was right to be concerned for Autumn's safety. The thought of waiting on the results made his skin itch. "It should take a couple of days, but I'll contact you with any word. Until then, make sure you lock up and don't leave any windows or doors open. We don't want anyone who might want to get in to have any access."

Elijah nodded. "I installed an alarm which contacts the station when I moved in—I have expensive equipment. We have Brinkley as well, but she's more likely to love someone to death than protect us."

"The alarm should be enough to deter intruders, but I would install an outer camera as soon as possible. If they left the note, they might leave something else between now and the show."

Elijah didn't know why he hadn't thought of installing one sooner. "I'll get on it."

Aiden's phone rang, and he stepped out for a moment. In his absence, Elijah thought of Autumn having dealt with years of being harassed alone.

"Sorry, but we have to leave it here for now. I have to get to court," Aiden said, returning.

"Thank you for your time. I appreciate any help."

"If anything else happens, call immediately—my number or the station—and we'll dispatch someone to you."

"Do you think there's any chance they might just give up?" Elijah asked.

Aiden rested a hand on his shoulder. "I'm sorry, but they have held their focus for three years. I don't think they're going to leave Autumn alone any time soon," he said sadly.

The statement crushed Elijah. He didn't want Autumn to hurt anymore; he saw how much she struggled, how much she wanted to live her life as normally as possible. The thought of someone wanting to take the last ounce of peace she had made him want to spill blood.

All he wanted to do was go to her, but his phone buzzed in his pocket, telling him he had to get to the signing before Nirosoft backed out. He couldn't help Autumn if his focus was elsewhere, and the sooner the deal closed, the sooner he would be able to focus. *She's safe at the theatre; her friends will protect her,* he thought, getting on his bike outside the station. Francis and Nirosoft would be waiting.

Chapter Twenty-Eight

Autumn

"Have a nice weekend?" Nina asked as they pulled away from the curb.

Autumn watched Elijah head back inside with Brinkley and hoped he was okay. Seeing him so worried troubled her more than any pathetic attempt from a stranger to frighten her. He had his own company to deal with, and she didn't want to add to the weight on his shoulders. He never made her feel like a burden, but she hoped she could be there for him in the future as much as he had been there for her.

"One of the best, but I don't want to talk about me," she said, not wanting to rub it in while her best friend was going through a breakup. "How are you? Did you hear from Garrett?" She tried to suppress her guilt for getting wrapped up in Elijah, both physically and metaphorically, and not calling her over the weekend.

Nina gripped the steering wheel before answering. Autumn realised she'd forgotten to take her phone off silent in case Elijah rang her after talking to his friend at the station.

As she reached for her bag at her feet, her fingers grazed something soft.

"A rose petal?" She rolled it between her fingers, the red staining her fingers a bright pink.

"Must have missed one. Garrett came over last night and tried to make it up to me," Nina said bitterly. "As though some flowers are going to make everything right."

Autumn dropped the petal and took her phone off silent, remembering how Garrett had brought flowers to the theatre before. "Are you going to hear him out?" she asked, watching as Nina gripped the steering wheel.

"No way. He picked his side, and I'm not going to change just because he wants something from me," Nina sneered, and Autumn could hear how angry she was. She'd expected her friend to be upset, but there was an anger emanating from her that made Autumn uneasy.

"I'm sorry it didn't work out, but you deserve someone so much better who won't pressure you into anything."

"Don't talk about it," Nina snapped. "I just want to get to practice and forget about him."

Autumn nodded. They spent the rest of the journey in silence, and it was a relief to get out of the car. She couldn't blame her for being angry, but she had never seen Nina that way.

∽

When they arrived, Aimee told Autumn that their costume maker had finished her dress for the showcase and it was waiting for her in her dressing room.

She couldn't wait to see it; she had fallen in love with the lilac chiffon the moment she had seen it. She'd opted for a full-length dress with tiny straps and a corseted bodice to support her during the long performances, since the showcase would run for a week. She usually went for a suit, but this was her comeback; she wanted to celebrate it and feel as confident as possible when she took the stage.

She didn't wait even a moment to say hello to everyone before darting off to her dressing room. When she opened the door, only the dressing table's mirrored lights highlighted the dark room. She jumped when she saw Heather lingering by the dressing table.

"God, you frightened me," she exclaimed, placing her hand over her thudding heart.

"I swear it wasn't me," Heather blurted out, moving away from the dresser.

"What wasn't—"

There was a glass vase of dead roses on her dresser.

Autumn's bag dropped from her shoulder. In shock, she stepped closer to get a better look.

"They were here when I came in. I was looking for you," Heather babbled.

Ignoring her, Autumn leaned in. Her hand covered her mouth as she realised the roses were sitting in what appeared to be blood. Tears pricked her eyes as years of pent-up fear rose to the surface.

She rounded on Heather, standing by the costumes. "How could you do this to me?"

Heather shook her head, not saying a word.

"Autumn?" Nina called. "What's taking so long? Sasaki wants to get started." She walked in, and Autumn grabbed Heather before she could leave.

"Call the police – ask for a detective called Aiden," she said urgently. "She has been harassing me ever since—"

"I haven't, I swear! Please," Heather pleaded, but Autumn didn't believe her false tears.

"I'll get Sasaki," Nina said, her words shaky, and she took off.

"Autumn, please believe me, it wasn't me. I have no

reason to do this!" Heather attempted to reach for her, but Autumn evaded her grasp.

"Stop lying. It's been three years since the roses began, and you joined the theatre three years ago. I'm so stupid—how could I not have seen it?"

Heather tried to leave; Autumn blocked her path.

"I won't let you run away from this. If you weren't the one to deliver these, then you can explain it to the police," she growled, backing her up until she was forced into the chair by the dresser.

Heather pulled at her sleeves. "You don't understand—"

"Then explain it to me," she demanded, but they were interrupted before Heather could answer.

"The police are on the way. What the hell is going on?" Sasaki asked, entering the dressing room with Nina close behind. Heather sat at the dressing table, wiping the tears from her cheeks.

"What's going on is that Heather has been stalking me for three years," Autumn snapped, finally admitting it to herself and those who cared for her the most.

Nina, standing by Autumn, shook her head. "Heather? Why would you want to harm her?"

"I don't!"

Autumn clenched her jaw, trying to contain herself, but failed. "Then you just give blood-soaked roses to *all* your friends?"

Sasaki got between them. "Calm down. We will figure this out when the police get here. Heather, did you deliver these flowers?"

Autumn stared at him, unable to believe he was taking Heather's side.

"No. I found them when I was dropping off the dress for the show."

Sasaki rubbed his brow, letting out a sigh. "Autumn, wait in my office. Heather, you will stay here." He turned to Nina. "Go outside and wait for the police. When they arrive, we'll sort this out."

"I'm not leaving," Autumn argued, not wanting to let Heather out of her sight. For years, she had kept her face hidden, but Autumn wasn't going to let her hide again.

"Yes, you are. I don't know what's been going on or why you choose to keep such an important matter to yourself for so long, but we will get to the bottom of this. If you don't go to my office now, I will send you home."

Autumn stormed out of his office as he crouched to talk quietly with a sobbing Heather. Tears—he was going to believe tears over what she had seen with her own eyes! She paced in his office, trying to calm down, trying to stop herself from going back to her dressing room and shaking the truth from Heather herself.

At last, she sat down at Sasaki's desk, resting her head in her hands. Removing her phone from her pocket, she thought about ringing Elijah, but she couldn't bring herself to pull him away from such an important day.

Nina jolted her from the thought anyway as she guided a man in plain clothes with jet-black hair tied back out of his face into the office. He was younger than she'd expected; she'd thought all detectives were old and haggard. However, he was probably in his late thirties and not at all haggard. Francis had good taste.

"Autumn?" he asked, and she nodded. "I'm Aiden, Elijah's friend. You asked for me?"

"I'm sorry, I know we haven't met, but Elijah said he was going to talk to you. I don't know if he got the chance because I knew he was signing today with Francis—" The words came out in a hurried tumble as she jumped to her feet.

"Take a breath. There's no hurry. I have an officer taking Heather's statement," Aiden said, his eyes warm and trustworthy.

"She's the one who's been leaving roses. I don't know why, but I knew something was off. I feel so stupid. She must have just been laughing at me every day." Autumn cursed herself for not going to the police sooner, but she'd never expected the sender to be someone so close.

"Please take a seat," he said gently.

Nina took Autumn's hand. "Do you want me to call Elijah?"

"No"—she shook her head—"please don't; it's an important day for him." She didn't mention Francis; she didn't want to embarrass Aiden by highlighting their personal connection any further when he was obviously so determined to be professional.

"Why didn't you tell us someone was harassing you? We would have helped you," Nina said, sitting on the arm of the chair to comfort her.

Autumn couldn't give an answer that would matter now, and Aiden didn't wait for a response. "Can you tell me what happened? Elijah has already filled me in on the roses."

"I went to my dressing room and Heather was just standing there, frozen. When she realised I was there, she looked shocked and started to back away, then I noticed the flowers. She said it wasn't her. Then I noticed what was at the bottom of the vase—I think it was blood."

"Blood? We can test it to make sure," Aiden said gently, writing everything she said down on a notepad.

Autumn nodded, resting her head in her hands. She felt like bees were buzzing in her ears with all the questions she had.

"But you didn't see her enter the room with the flowers?" Aiden asked.

Autumn's head snapped up. "No. Does that matter?" Suddenly, she was afraid her discovery would amount to nothing.

"I'm afraid so, if she says she found them and there's no evidence of her purchasing or delivering the flowers. But don't panic—we'll check her accounts to see her recent purchases."

Autumn took a deep breath. "What happens now? Will she be arrested?"

"We'll take the vase in to get the prints. Elijah already gave me the note you received this morning, and we'll send them both to the lab," Aiden told her.

Her shoulders relaxed with gratitude that Elijah had already spoken to him so she wouldn't have to explain everything right now. Her limbs felt numb, which was a change for her. She guessed it was the shock.

"How long is that going to take?" Nina asked for her. Autumn squeezed her hand, relieved to have her friend here since Elijah couldn't be.

"I'll put a rush on it, but I can't be certain."

"Can you hold her?" Autumn asked, afraid that Heather would come after her now that she knew her identity. Then again, part of her couldn't believe she was even thinking of quiet, shy Heather as dangerous.

"We'll hold her for twenty-four hours and see what she has to say, but without more evidence, that's all we can do for now," Aiden said, closing his notepad.

"And then she's free to come to work and be around me?" Autumn asked, her nails digging into her palms. How was she supposed to focus with Heather around?

"No," Sasaki said from the doorway. "I've told her she can only return once she's been cleared."

"What about the showcase? Surely, Autumn can't perform—for her safety," Nina said.

Autumn stared at her in horror. Even though her friend meant well, the last thing she wanted was to be locked away in her house.

"That's up to Autumn," Sasaki said, "but either way, I will support her decision."

"No. I want to perform. She didn't want me to make my comeback, and I'm not going to give her the satisfaction of keeping me off the stage," Autumn said, determined not to let fear stand in her way.

"Can you give us a minute?" Aiden said to Nina and Sasaki.

Both left without protest, but they didn't go far; Autumn could see them outside the office window.

"I'm sorry this is happening, Autumn. This isn't how I would have liked us to meet," Aiden said, now as more of a friend than a detective.

"Thank you for coming. I just needed someone I could trust."

He smiled softly, and she recognised Todd's eyes. "I will handle everything personally."

She was grateful to have met Elijah if all his friends were this nice. "You have no idea how much I appreciate it. I wish I had listened to Elijah and gone with him this morning." Why had she ignored what was right in front of her?

"If you had, you wouldn't have been here to catch her, and we wouldn't have two pieces of evidence to inspect," he pointed out.

"Can I ask you a favour?"

"Anything."

"Could we keep this to ourselves for now? I don't want to make today about me when they're finally closing with Nirosoft."

Aiden looked unsure.

"We could tell Elijah together when we do," she suggested. "I want him to have all the facts, and I think it would help him to know we've spoken."

"Sure. It's up to you, but I will need to stop by tomorrow and take a full report from you. Is that all right?" he asked, heading for the door.

"Tomorrow is fine. I just don't want to take their night from them. They've both worked so hard on this deal."

"That's awfully kind of you. Francis and Elijah wouldn't want you to keep this to yourself, but I thank you for thinking of them," Aiden said, squeezing her arm gently.

He opened the door just as his colleagues were leading Heather outside. Autumn caught her pleading gaze. She wanted to speak to her, to demand answers, but she was too raw, and she wanted to confirm it first so Heather couldn't lie any longer.

Aiden left with the other officers, and Sasaki joined Autumn in the office while Nina went to inform the others that practice would be delayed until the afternoon.

"I wish you had told me you were being harassed," Sasaki said, sitting on the edge of his desk.

Far too overwhelmed to be scolded, she rubbed the tears forming in her eyes. "I thought if I kept it to myself, then it wouldn't be happening."

He swallowed her up in his embrace. "I want you to go home and get some rest. You can practise at home if you like, but you need some time to collect yourself," he said gently.

Autumn found herself welling up, grateful for the fact that he always put her first. She wiped a tear with her sleeve.

"This is all in the past now. There's no need to be hard on yourself."

"Will you still let me play on Friday?" she asked, hoping he wouldn't stop her.

"If that's what you want, then yes, but I will be increasing security just in case," he said, rubbing his forehead.

She hated to put more pressure on him, but it couldn't be helped. "I never expected what was happening at home to spill into the theatre," she told him.

The lines in his brow deepened. "I'm afraid it was the other way 'round. To put you through this after everything makes me doubt whether I should have brought you back."

His concern broke her heart. "Please don't say that! I can't live without music. You know that as much as I do. I've never been anything but grateful to you for giving me the courage to return. I won't let her or anyone else stop me."

"Okay," he sighed. "If you want to perform, then I won't get in your way; the show must go on."

She laughed, almost in a daze. "Thank you for always being on my side."

"Always. Now, go home and get some rest. I'll see you tomorrow."

When she left his office, Nina was already waiting with her things.

"Please tell me you aren't being suspended?" she exclaimed, fretting by the stage door.

"Suspended? I haven't done anything wrong." Autumn didn't know where she would have got such an idea from. She didn't think anyone had been suspended from the theatre since she'd joined.

"Of course. Sorry. I just worried because you didn't tell us what was happening and now the showcase is at risk." Nina pretended to zip her lips. "Sorry, ignore me. It's all been a shock, but as long as you're okay, that's all that matters."

Autumn swallowed her guilt, hating the thought of affecting the showcase. The last thing she wanted was for people to find out what was happening behind the scenes and not attend the show.

"No need to be sorry. It's a mess, but I can't talk about it anymore," she said, putting her bag on her shoulder. "I'm going to go home and forget for a while." She couldn't face telling the others what had happened.

"Are you okay to get home?" Nina asked, opening the front door for her.

Autumn nodded. "I could do with some air."

Nina gave her a quick hug before heading back inside.

On her way home, Autumn glanced up at the clear blue sky and shining sun, suddenly realising that she felt safe now that she knew who was behind the roses. For the first time in a while, she didn't fear what might be waiting on her doorstep.

Chapter Twenty-Nine

Autumn

Autumn made up a batch of white icing to put the final touches on Elijah's cake before he got home. Francis had mentioned how awful Elijah was at celebrating big events, so she thought she'd surprise him. She'd picked up the ingredients while walking Brinkley. She couldn't bring herself to practise after the morning's event, and she figured she probably should have rested her back while she could, but the thought of lying around only made her more tense.

Baking was a welcome distraction from Heather and the roses. In the kitchen, with her favourite music blaring and Brinkley ready to catch any crumbs at her feet, she'd finally let herself get excited about Elijah's news.

"Wait! Don't come in yet," she called out when she heard the door open. Brinkley scampered out from beneath her legs to greet him.

"Should I be worried? Did you kill some plants again?" Elijah asked, laughing.

Autumn grabbed the confetti popper from her bag, not caring that she was smearing icing everywhere.

"Surprise," she yelled, releasing the confetti with a pop as he stepped into the kitchen. The sound made him jump, hands raised as if to defend himself, and she giggled at his startled expression. "Congratulations!" On her tiptoes, she kissed his cheek.

"You know?" he asked, kneeling down to soothe Brinkley, who was barking at the loud bang.

"Francis texted me. He said everything went well with Nirosoft—you're now a free man!" she said, heading back to the counter to hide the cake and hoping he would go into his office to change so she would have time to finish it.

Elijah tossed Brinkley's stuffed panda into her bed to distract her, then reached into his jacket pocket and pulled out the folded papers. "All done and dusted, once I've paid off the investors. I'm free to run Kyloware with no interference!" He beamed, joining her at the counter and trying to spy what she was concealing with a tea towel.

"You've worked so hard; you deserve it," she said, delighted at one thing going right today.

"What's all this? Baking?" Elijah asked, distracted by the messy kitchen while he picked the confetti out of his hair.

"It's not ready! You weren't supposed to be back yet. I told Francis to try and keep you," she said, blocking the cake from his vision. She had to finish putting the Kyloware logo on the top.

"You can't blame him. I wanted to get back to you, and he deserved to get to spend some alone time with Aiden," he said, hugging her from behind. He rested his chin on her shoulder, his hands on her hips. She couldn't help leaning into his embrace; after the day she'd had, having him home was a relief. Something she never would have said three weeks ago.

"You made me a cake," he said, removing the tea towel to see the black icing covering the vanilla sponge cake.

"A half-finished cake! I was going to put the Kyloware logo on it. Right now, it just looks like a black splodge."

Elijah squeezed her tight against him. "Splodge or not, I love it. How did I get so lucky?"

He turned her to face him. She rolled her eyes, wondering if he would think so if he knew about today. Seeing him so elated, she couldn't bring herself to tell him—not yet, anyway.

He wiped a smudge of icing from her cheek with his thumb and brought it to his lips. "Delicious. Now that I've had a taste, I need more." His smirk told her he wasn't talking about the cake.

"You have to wait until I'm finished," she said, crossing her arms over her chest to put some space between them.

Autumn knew what he was about to do a second before she did it, but still squealed as he grabbed her by the waist and tossed her over his shoulder. He was the only person who didn't treat her like she was going to break.

"Where are we going? Shouldn't we celebrate?" she panted as he carried her into his office and placed her on his desk. She tried to squirm away, but Elijah held her flush against him.

"I plan on celebrating," he said, running his hand up her thighs. "I love these jeans, but they're covered in flour. I think we should take them off." He undid the button at her waist.

"What's a bit of flour? You were the one who covered them in paint," Autumn retorted, watching him trace the paint blots with his hands. Her thighs started to tremble beneath his touch. However, before they went any further, she needed to know something. She looked him in the eye. "Now that you're free, are you going to move out?"

She had to know the answer before she fell any deeper.

Elijah rested his forehead against hers, brushing her hair over her shoulders, not answering immediately. Autumn rolled her hips impatiently, grinding against him as if daring him to deny her. His reply was a low groan against her lips; he gripped her hips to pull her harder against him, confirming that he needed her as much as she needed him.

"That's not the answer," she panted as he nipped at her jaw, her neck.

"I already told you. There's no getting rid of me," he growled, fisting her hair and forcing her to look at him. He leaned down and engaged her mouth in a slow, erotic kiss that went straight to her toes, sparking every erogenous zone in her body. "Is this what you had in mind for the celebration? Or...should we go back to the cake?" His head dipped for another kiss, eyes dark with desire.

"Since we're celebrating freedom, I'll give you the freedom to do whatever you want with my body," Autumn told him, running her lips along his jaw.

His hands swept over her, demanding and possessive. He loved her, and she felt it. Even if they hadn't said those words yet, their bodies did the talking.

"Again with words that will be the death of me." His palm slid under her white T-shirt, and she delighted in his sharp intake of breath as he felt that she wasn't wearing a bra.

"Then we're even, because your touch will kill me," she rasped as shockwaves of pleasure spread down between her legs. Her hands settled over the impressive bulge in his trousers. "Don't make me wait," she breathed, and a wide grin stretched over his lips.

"No need to ask twice."

He groaned as she undid his trousers and gripped him tight, stroking leisurely until he pinned her arms behind her back. He yanked off her jeans and underwear so impatiently she nearly came off the desk with them. Her laugh was stifled by his kisses.

He made his way down her body, kissing her ribs and dipping his tongue into her belly button; the sensation caused her to clench around his exploring fingers. She tore at his shirt, desperate to feel his skin against hers. With eager fingers, she guided him inside her. His kiss swallowed his name as he filled and stretched her until she thought she could take no more.

She moved with him until their movements were frantic with need and she felt herself splinter. She cried out as the convulsions tore through her, surprised that pleasure could feel so violent. Elijah rocked his hips, drawing out the aftershocks of her ecstasy until he arched his back, and she watched him, completely lost in his own pleasure.

They held each other, saying nothing, as they caught their breath. At last, he reached beneath her thighs and lifted them around his hips, kissing her shoulder as he carried her over to the couch. Together, they lay on the couch in his office, Autumn on his chest.

"This really is a hideous blanket," Elijah said, and she glanced at the fluffy yellow blanket he covered them with.

"You could have bought a new one," she said, feeling content with the warmth of his body and the softness of the blanket cocooning them. She'd never felt safer.

"But this one smells like you," he sighed.

"Pervert," she muttered playfully, and he squeezed her tight.

"Only for you." He kissed her hair.

"How do you feel now that the deal is closed?" She'd meant to ask him over the cake. He had to be conflicted; his victory meant possibly furthering the gap between him and Tim.

Elijah rested an arm behind his head, and she saw the wheels turning in his mind. "Relieved, but a little guilty. I didn't want to have to go behind Tim's back. Regardless of our personal relationship, the game would have taken three times as long without his investment," he said, sounding deflated.

She nodded. From what she knew of him, he prided himself on honesty. "Maybe if Tim has no control over your company anymore, you can both move on," she reasoned, hoping they could repair their relationship. Tim wasn't perfect, but it would be nice if Elijah got the chance to see how kind he could be.

"I don't know. It will depend on how he reacts. I want to forget the past—I'm tired of carrying it with me," he said, looking down at her. "Seeing how you've been able to put your past behind you, how strong you are, has encouraged me to do the same."

"I don't think I'm strong. I don't have a choice but to keep going, and I couldn't carry about the anger or blame with me, or it would have tormented me far more than any physical pain did," she told him. "What happened to me was an accident. I can't change it the same way you can't change your past relationship with Tim; but you have a chance, if you want to try."

His thumb brushed the scar on her abdomen. "You have no idea how resilient you are. You could have stayed in Islacore and never touched a piano again or got back up on stage. You didn't give up."

She swallowed the emotions rising in her throat. "I have to tell you what happened today, but promise you won't be mad that I didn't tell you sooner?" She sat up, wanting to look into his eyes as she told him about Heather.

Elijah cupped her cheek. "You don't have to tell me anything. I talked to Aiden."

"What? I asked him not to tell you. I didn't want to ruin your day."

"You could never ruin my day. It wasn't his fault. When Francis and I finished signing, Francis called Aiden to join us but he said he was at your theatre, so I knew something had happened. He told me you went home and were safe and not to let on until you were ready to talk about it."

Autumn buried her head in her hands. He pulled them away. "You never have to hide anything from me."

His earnest eyes, so loving, steadied her breathing. She didn't know how she was ever going to show him how much his support meant to her. "I wanted to be the one to tell you, but...I don't think I can go over it again," she said, exhausted by the reality of it all.

"We don't have to talk about it now. Aiden will be round in the morning. I just need to know if you're okay."

"I'm afraid." She chewed her lips, worried she would burst into tears. He snuggled her close, letting her talk. "What if facing it only makes it worse? You didn't see how pleading Heather was. I'm beginning to question whether it was her, and...if it isn't, then I don't know what I'm going to do."

"Why don't we face it together? You don't have to do it alone," he said, pulling the blanket tight around them as if it would shield them from what was to come. "I'm right here beside you."

"Okay. Together," she agreed, finally accepting that she wouldn't have to face another hardship alone.

Secure in each other's embrace, they drifted off.

Chapter Thirty

Autumn

The following morning, Autumn sat on the counter while Elijah made eggs Benedict. They'd barely got any sleep after spending most of the night talking about nothing and eating the cake she'd made. She was already on her second tea but she had never felt better. Waking up beside Elijah was her new favourite ritual.

A part of her worried it would have to come to an end eventually. But she didn't want to ruin what time they had together and had decided to follow her heart, even if she was terrified he would break it.

Any thoughts of heartbreak were quickly forgotten by her fascination with his bare forearms as he finished making the creamiest hollandaise she had ever tasted. *Why is it so sexy when men cook?*

"I thought you couldn't cook?" she asked, watching him put the toast under the grill.

"My roommate in college was studying culinary arts. It's the one thing I make well," he told her, slinging a tea towel over his shoulder like the professional he wasn't. "Plus, I had to thank you for making such a delicious cake."

MS PERFECTLY FINE

He caught her staring, and she couldn't help but laugh.

"See something you like?" he asked, standing between her legs at the counter. She wrapped her arms around his neck, bringing her lips to his, not minding the scrape of his morning stubble. He groaned as she nipped at his lower lip. "Do you want breakfast or not?" he asked, his voice husky with desire.

Though she thought she would never get enough of his lips, she was hungry for more than him. "I'm starving."

His eyes ran over her body like she was the meal, and she nudged him away.

"For food," she clarified.

He winked. "Food—right."

They were interrupted by the doorbell, and Autumn groaned, annoyed by the interruption as he left her to answer it. Elijah reappeared with Aiden, who, from the dark circles under his eyes, hadn't slept much.

"Thank you for coming so early," Elijah said.

"No problem. It's best if we can get started right away," Aiden said, and Elijah led him to the couch.

Autumn thought of all that had transpired between them since he'd moved in and hoped Aiden hadn't heard everything. Stealing Elijah's credit card might have been a joke, but it was a crime.

"Thank you for handling this personally; I'm sure you have a lot on your plate," she said. Francis had mentioned to Elijah how he was already dealing with two big cases; she didn't know how he did it with a toddler in the mix.

"No need to thank me. Elijah is like family. Hopefully, I can help make this less of a daunting experience for you." From the way he was looking at her, she sensed Elijah had told him about her accident.

She wasn't sure where to begin. She'd kept everything to herself for so long, it felt weird to talk about it out loud. Elijah put together the eggs Benedict as Aiden talked and gave it to Autumn. Though she didn't have much of an appetite, thanks to the subject matter.

Aiden opened his laptop and placed it on the glass table. "Who knew about what was happening? About the roses?"

"No one. I kept it to myself. Well, the first time one appeared three years ago, I asked around the theatre, but no one said they'd sent it. I assumed it was just sent to the wrong address, so I didn't dwell on it. Then, the following year, on the date of my accident, another appeared, so I thought it might have been someone trying to do something nice." She shrugged, feeling stupid now.

"What about your parents? Did you tell them what was going on?" Aiden asked, typing her responses.

Elijah took her hand, sitting beside her.

Autumn shook her head. "Are you kidding? They would be on the doorstep and have my bags packed within the hour. They never got over my accident. They hated the thought of me returning to the stage, but they've come around some in the last two years."

"And it's only been in the last year that the roses have started to appear more frequently?"

Relieved that he hadn't urged her to tell her parents, Autumn thought it over. "I think it was after it was announced that I would be making my solo comeback, about two months before Elijah moved in. Does this matter when we've already caught Heather?"

Aiden leant on his elbows. "The vase was wiped clear other than Heather's prints, which should confirm it was her, but because the rest was wiped clean and she says she only touched the vase to see what was in it when she found them, we can't be sure."

Autumn's stomach dropped, and she tried not to fidget.

"However, we did find a partial print on the inner rim that the culprit might have left by accident. It usually takes about two hours to identify when we have a print to compare it to; however, we are having a problem with our processing system, and unfortunately, we have to wait for tech support, so it may be a while before we get an answer. Before everyone left the theatre yesterday, they consented to have their prints taken. Heather said she never touched the rim, so if it matches her, good chance it was, but we need to know for sure."

"What about the letter?" Elijah asked while Autumn gathered her composure, her mouth dry. *If she was smart enough not to leave prints, why would she not wipe it down again? Maybe I discovered her before she could?* The questions gnawed at her certainty that Heather was the culprit.

"The only prints we found on the letter were yours and Autumn's," Aiden said. "Is there anything else you can give me that was left?"

"I threw out the roses. They would be long dead anyway, and they never came with a note," Autumn said, wishing she had kept everything.

"Were any of the roses labelled or de-thorned?"

Autumn had to think. "They didn't have a label, but I think they were de-thorned—I didn't really pay attention. Why does that matter?"

"Most florists would label them and make you sign for them, which leads us to believe they were all hand delivered. Florists also usually de-thorn them before sending them out; the fact that the culprit took the time to trim some of them might mean they don't wish to harm you," Aiden reasoned.

"That might be a bit of a stretch. The note was clearly a threat, and this isn't the first," Elijah said. "When I first moved in, I found a rose with a note but I threw it away, thinking it was just the wrong address. I don't recall what it said."

Autumn placed her hand on his knee to stop it from shaking. "Why didn't you mention this before?"

He ran his hands through his hair. "I didn't think—it just came back to me."

"Okay, so this would make this the second note you've received? Has anything changed since you received the last rose that had no thorns or note?"

Autumn was about to say no when she realised that there was a six-foot change sitting beside her. "Elijah moved in—and Brinkley," she added, smiling at the pile of fluff who was sniffing at Aiden.

"And in three years, has anyone else come and gone that they might have become aware of?"

"My friend Nina, my landlord, and my physio. All female, except my landlord. I don't think Tim would be sending me roses," she said, noting how the last part caused Aiden to look at Elijah. Clearly, he knew Tim was his father.

"Any other visitors?"

"No. I mean, Nina's boyfriend Garrett was here once or twice to pick her up? I don't like strangers in my house." She noticed that Aiden tried not to smile. Elijah must have told him everything.

"Do they have keys to the house?" he asked.

"Nina does for emergencies, and so does Tim, but that's it," she said. "Neither one would do anything to hurt me."

"No one-night stands? Partners?"

"Not in the last year or so, and they wouldn't have come here. I don't like people knowing where I live." She glanced at Elijah, but he didn't react. It was nice to know he didn't judge her. She was a woman in her twenties living alone, not celibate.

"And apart from that, your schedule was routine?" Aiden asked. "It would be easy for someone to figure out your comings and goings?"

"Sadly, yes. Rehearsals or the same weekly appointments...and I do my groceries in the same place around the corner on the same day. It wouldn't have been hard for Heather to know when I was going to be out if she watched the house for a week or two, and she'd know my address from my personal file; she literally made my work schedule." That would have also given Heather her number and her parents' information.

"That could explain the escalation. Stalkers can obsess over a routine to make them feel connected to you, and when Elijah moved in, it could have felt like a threat to them."

The thought of being watched for so long sent shivers down her spine.

"Have you seen anyone pass repeatedly or cars lingering?"

Autumn shook her head, but Elijah perked up. "Yes, about two weeks ago. I saw someone parked outside. I thought it was Nina coming over since they usually drive to and from rehearsals together, but it could have been Heather."

Aiden typed away. "Any details about the car stand out?"

Elijah shook his head. "It was late, could have been anything. Should we stay in a hotel for a few days?"

Brinkley settled at the detective's feet, wanting all the attention. Aiden stroked her absentmindedly.

"No, continue as normal. Heather will be held for another twenty-four hours since we have her prints on the item, and we will arrest her if the partial one belongs to her. There have been no purchases on her card for anything related to flowers, so hopefully, we will get more from questioning her."

"What about the show?" Autumn asked, wondering if it *was* a good idea to perform in case Heather was released by then.

"I've spoken with Mr Sasaki. He has agreed to some of our officers being posted at the exits and entrance, but it's still a risk," Aiden warned. "Your safety is more important, but it's your decision, and we will do everything we can to protect you."

"If I had come forward sooner, would it have helped?" Autumn had to ask, wondering if she had brought this onto not only herself but also Sasaki and the others at the theatre.

He let out a slow breath. "Well, it's possible that we could have tracked when the roses appeared, tried to figure out when they would make the next drop. However, there's no point in dwelling on ifs. We're working on it now," Aiden reassured her. "Try to take it one day at a time."

Autumn nodded. "Can I ask what was in the vase? Was it real blood?"

"No, it was fake. Stage blood, only meant to frighten you," he said.

Her shoulders relaxed. No living thing had been harmed to hurt her. "That's a relief."

"There is something else that came up, but it might be a bit of a shock," Aiden said carefully, clasping his hands. "When we scanned Heather's prints, we noticed that she changed her name three years ago."

Autumn frowned.

"Her real name is Lena Garvey."

Autumn felt a cold sweat break over her. "No way. There's no way Mollie's sister would do this to me." She rubbed her palms against her thighs, trying to calm down. "Surely, I would have recognised her...she was a couple of years younger than me and Mollie. How could I have forgotten her so easily?"

Heather was so different, so meek and quiet, where Lena had always been so loud and confident. She hadn't worn glasses like Heather did, and her hair was darker and longer now. When Autumn pictured Lena, she was still a pre-teen chasing after her older sister, not the woman she had known the last three years. *I suppose a lot can change in ten years, and Lena was only about twelve when we lost Mollie.*

"You never thought she looked a little familiar?" Elijah asked, distracting her from her thoughts.

"No...maybe once? When she was dropping me home, I thought there was something about her, but I never expected this," Autumn said, trying to come to terms with this revelation.

"Can I ask about your accident and your connection to the Garvey family?" Aiden interjected.

"There's a police report..." She didn't want to go over it again.

"Would you mind giving me a brief summary?"

She sighed, sensing the detective wasn't going to let it go. Telling the story never got easier. It always felt a knife slowly twisting in her gut, her nerves remembering the day her mind longed to forget. "I was performing outside at a winter festival. The stage floor was old and needed maintenance because of the bad snow that year, but there wasn't time. During the performance, the stage collapsed, and then the lights came down. The broken wood caught fire. I was protected by my piano, but I was pinned by a bar." She lifted her shirt a little to show the scar that connected her front and back.

"And Mollie Garvey was with you?"

"They found Mollie first, but she was closer to the fire. She was knocked unconscious in the collapse, and the smoke inhalation killed her in minutes. My lungs were hurt from the smoke, but I survived. I had to learn to walk again. I have some tissue and nerve damage, which leaves me in chronic pain, and sometimes it's a struggle to use my left leg." Even talking about it seemed to spark the nerves in her back, as if they were remembering the trauma.

"And the family?" Aiden pressed.

"I haven't heard from any of them in years. Did Heather—Lena—tell you why she changed her name?" Autumn asked, wondering why she would keep it a secret, why she wouldn't just tell her who she was. *She shouldn't have had to tell you—you should have recognised her!* her guilt scolded her.

"When we confronted her, she said she changed her name when she went to college. Her parents divorced, and her dad gambled away the settlement received from the accident. Her mum has remarried and started a new family, and Heather said she didn't fight for custody. She said she wanted to start anew."

Autumn thought of her own settlement. She'd never touched the money. She hadn't wanted it, so her parents had used it to buy their home and on her rehab and medical bills.

"What has that got to do with Autumn? Why would she go to such lengths to get close to her?" Elijah asked.

"I don't understand why she would come after me like this. I never would have done anything to hurt Mollie!"

"Our working theory is that to Lena, it's the tenth anniversary of her sister's death but it's your return to the stage. My guess is that she needs somewhere to put her blame," Aiden said gently.

Autumn swallowed hard. She had never thought this would be the outcome of her wanting to play again. *Why didn't she just confront me? Was she sending me the roses to try and get me to quit? Surely, confronting me and telling me who she was would have been far more effective. We could have talked it through, understood one another. The secrecy doesn't make sense.*

"Lena, or her parents, never tried to contact you after the accident?" Aiden asked. "If her parents harboured resentment, it could have been transferred to her."

"No, never. They were nothing but kind after the accident. Mollie and I first met because our mums were really close. That's how we both ended up playing for the same company," Autumn said, hating to think they might resent her for surviving. She had punished herself enough for years; she didn't need someone else to do it for her.

"I think that's enough for now." Elijah squeezed her hand, and though no amount of comfort would fix her, she was glad he was with her.

"Can I see Heather? Could I talk to her? I need to hear what she has to say for myself. Even if she did all this, Mollie would want me to make sure she was okay." What Heather had done in hiding her identity was wrong, but Autumn couldn't imagine how hard it had been for her friend's sister. At only twelve, she'd witnessed her sister's death and her family breaking apart. The thought of the ever-smiling kid she'd known having changed so much was heart wrenching.

"Are you sure?" Aiden asked. "She might not give you any answers."

"I know, but I have to try," Autumn said, suddenly wanting to protect the person who had made her life harder for years. She hadn't been able to save Mollie, but she was going to try and help her sister, if only for the memory of the kid she'd known growing up.

"I can set up a short interview for tomorrow morning. We might have more results by then." Aiden closed his laptop. "You should take the day to digest the information I've given you and prepare."

"Thank you. I really appreciate it," Autumn said, following him towards the door with Elijah behind her.

"Call me if you can think of *anything* else, or if anything happens."

"Thank you," Elijah said, giving him a hug. Autumn opened the door for him.

"I'm always here to help. Congratulations on the game—Francis is over the moon!"

"I'm sure he is now that he has a break from me nit-picking at his designs," Elijah said with a grin.

Autumn was glad they were so close. It made the experience with Heather—or Lena—far less daunting knowing Aiden was on their side.

"That's what family is for," he said before turning to Autumn. "I'll see you tomorrow. Look after each other."

Autumn let Elijah walk him down the path to give them some time to talk while she headed back inside for a quiet moment to gather herself. She took her cup of tea out into the garden, desperate for some fresh air. She felt like the walls of her past were closing in.

"You okay?" Elijah asked as she sat in the garden, surrounded by untamed plants, with her favourite Rambunctious Raccoon mug.

"Peachy," she said.

He snuggled in beside her, and she placed half her blanket across his lap. He wrapped his arms around her waist and rested his chin on top of her head. Though she hated going over her past, having him with her gave her strength she hadn't known she needed.

"Thank you for being with me. I don't think I would have ever faced it without you."

"Yes, you would have. You don't give yourself enough

credit. But I'll be here whenever you need me or want me," he said, kissing the side of her head.

She relaxed into him, the last of her lingering anxiety leaving her.

"How about we go back to bed and I make you forget about this morning?" he whispered in her ear, placing a gentle kiss on her neck.

She rested her hands on his. "Don't you have work to do?"

"Now that everything is sorted with Nirosoft, I only have my meeting with the Randell board on Thursday. So I'm all yours," he told her, running his fingers through her hair.

"I can't wait for this to be over. Your deal, the showcase, Heather..." Autumn sighed, wishing they could hide from the world.

Elijah smiled reassuringly at her. "Like Aiden said, one day at a time. We have each other."

Chapter Thirty-One

Autumn

By Wednesday morning, there was still no news about the partial print. Autumn spent half the night tossing and turning, trying not to wake Elijah, hoping someone would confirm it had been Heather sending the roses before she faced her at the station.

After forcing down what she could of the breakfast Elijah made for her, Autumn arrived at the police station with Elijah following close behind. Sasaki had messaged to say he wanted to come, but with final rehearsals, there was no time to spare. Nina had agreed to help him handle the fallout; the press had somehow learnt that an unnamed culprit was harassing the returning child prodigy, Autumn Adler. She hated seeing her full name in print; it made her feel more like a product than a person.

Aiden greeted them outside the station before leading them through to his office. At his desk, Autumn eagerly took the cup of coffee on offer as the detective prepped her for seeing Heather.

"Are you sure you don't want to wait until Aiden gives us more news?" Elijah asked, but Autumn squeezed his hand. If she didn't go in now, she didn't think she would ever sleep again.

"It's fine. I want to get this over with," she said, and he kissed the back of her hand, reassuring her.

"This won't be easy, and she's still maintaining her innocence, so please don't get your hopes up about getting the answers you want," Aiden said, a file laid out before him.

"Does she know I'm coming?" Autumn asked, glad she had Elijah's hand on her knee to stop her leg from shaking.

"We told her this morning. She's been asking to see you since we brought her in, but we didn't think it was wise until we had more evidence. Since you want to speak to her, we can give you fifteen minutes."

It wasn't much time, but she was grateful for anything. "I don't think she wants to hurt me. I think she just wanted someone to see her, listen to her. She had plenty of opportunities to hurt me and she never did," Autumn said, though part of her wondered why Heather didn't just confess.

"If it's too much, there's still time to back out," Aiden said, guiding her towards the interview room.

"I have you and Elijah on the other side of the door, I'll be fine," she promised. "Heather wanted my attention, and like you said, when she saw Elijah move in, it tipped her over the edge. She must have thought I was moving on and forgetting about the accident. As much as I would love that to happen, it never will."

"I could be wrong, but I think she just wanted to be close to someone who had been in the accident. Someone who understood her pain. It might have been the threat of losing that that spurred change," Aiden mused. "Heather claims she tried to talk to you numerous times about the accident. I wanted to confirm with you that she never talked to you about the accident, never tried to tell you who she was?"

Autumn hesitated. "I'm not very open about my private life. I don't remember, but if she had brought it up, I probably would have brushed her off," she admitted. If she had been more open, not so obsessed with her bubble, would she have recognised Heather?

"Can you tell us about your relationship with the culprit before and after the accident? She gave us some details yesterday and I want to corroborate them."

"Lena and I didn't really have a relationship since there are four years between us. I was best friends with her older sister Mollie, but sometimes, Lena would come to movies with us. We didn't have much free time; we went to the same school, and both of us were accepted into the same orchestra. We were doing our first tour that winter when the stage collapsed. You know the rest."

"Heather said you didn't attend Mollie's funeral?" Aiden asked.

Autumn cleared her throat to stop herself from choking on her guilt. Elijah squeezed her hand.

"I was too sick to attend. I had to have multiple surgeries on my back. I spent months in St Helen's Rehabilitation hospital, and by the time I had a chance to even think, my parents told me her parents had got divorced. To be honest, I was pretty wrapped up in my recovery, and I didn't notice much else around me. Our mums were close, but when we moved, I don't think they kept in contact." Autumn glanced at Elijah; he hadn't known that part of her story. But he didn't look at her with pity, only admiration. If she hadn't loved him before, she did now.

Aiden gave her a sympathetic look, but Autumn was distracted as two officers led Heather by the window. She was pale, her head hung low; with her glasses on the table, Autumn saw how much like Mollie she had become.

An officer came into the office and whispered something to Aiden before handing him another file.

"All right, she's ready for you. She's handcuffed, so she can't harm you. If you need something, there'll be cameras on you and I'll be right on the other side of the glass," Aiden said, leading them from the office.

"Have you called her parents?" Autumn asked before heading in.

"We couldn't get hold of her father, but her mum is driving up now. She shouldn't be too long," Aiden said.

Autumn watched Heather through the window. Hunched over the table, she looked broken. She turned to Elijah, who looked like the last thing he wanted to do was let her go in alone.

"I'll be outside when you've finished," he told her, giving her one last squeeze. Her resolve weakened in his embrace, but she took a shaky breath and stepped away from him, gathering the last of her strength.

"Fifteen minutes," Aiden reminded her.

Autumn nodded in agreement, stepping through the door before she was left alone with the person who had been watching her for the past three years.

"I'm so glad you agreed to see me," Heather said softly, resting her cuffed wrists on the table.

Autumn took a seat, leaning away from her. "I just want to say something first," she said, taking a shaky breath.

Heather bowed her head, waiting for her to start.

"When I first got the rose, I thought it was an accident. When I received it the next time, I was happy. I thought you might have been a silent supporter, someone who wanted me to get back on stage. It gave me hope. Then, when the third rose came on the anniversary and followed every year, I knew it wasn't meant to be a show of support. I knew whoever was sending me the roses was taunting me." Autumn's voice cracked, and Heather's head snapped up.

"The only reason I came to the theatre was that I wanted to support you. I just wanted you to remember. I didn't want anything else, only for you to remember her."

"You think I'd forget my best friend?" Autumn demanded. "Not a day has passed when I haven't been reminded of what happened to us. I didn't need roses to remind me of what my body screams every day."

"Please, Autumn, you can't think I did this to you! I'm her sister. I don't know anything about the roses. The only thing I did was put a photo of the three of us with a note on the back in your dressing room. But you didn't even go to her grave. I waited to see if you would show up. I was going to tell you who I was, but when you didn't show, I thought you didn't want to see me. You just wanted to move on with your life, so I let you be."

Autumn had no clue what she was talking about. "What photo? I never got one, only the roses. When did you send it?"

"About three weeks ago. I even tried to talk to you after rehearsals when I dropped you home, but I couldn't bring myself to tell you. I thought you would be angry at me for not telling you who I was sooner or for coming back into your life."

"I swear I didn't see any photo or note in my dressing room. If I had, I would have gone to the grave. It's not like I just forgot about her; I visit her as often as I can. Lena—do you mind if I call you that?" Autumn wanted to be respectful, in case disguising her identity wasn't the only reason she'd changed her name.

Heather nodded.

"If you had reached out in any way, I would have never been angry at you," she continued, trying to steady her breathing.

"You were doing so well. I thought if I told you I would ruin it," Heather said, her eyes reddening as though she was about to cry. Autumn ran her hands through her hair, trying to steady herself.

"My life will never be normal. Every day, my body reminds me of what I survived and what Mollie didn't. There isn't a day that a part of me doesn't wish your sister and I didn't walk out onto that stage. I could have saved myself years of mind-numbing pain and Mollie would still be with us. But we did. I'm here. And though I wish with every fibre of my being that Mollie was too, we can't change the past. I can only try to do the best I can."

"I never knew you felt that way," Heather said, not meeting her eye.

"You never asked."

Heather picked at her nails.

Autumn needed to get her to open up. "But...say I believe you. Why did you change your name?"

Heather perked up. "I changed it when I was in college to get away from my past. My dad has debts and when he couldn't pay them, they would come looking for me in college. It had nothing to do with you."

"Why were you always hinting that I was going to lose my seat?" Autumn asked, remembering all the times when Heather had made her panic about it.

"I never wanted you to lose your seat at the showcase. I always tried to adjust your work schedule so you could get some rest days. All I wanted was to see you play. The only reason I even thought it was a possibility was that I heard Nina suggesting you weren't ready because of your recent flare-up," Heather explained.

"Nina told Sasaki I shouldn't play in the showcase?"

"Yes. She said we should have her headline just in case you had to back out," Heather said. "I tried to tell you, but every time we had a chance to talk, she would interrupt."

Autumn was taken aback. Nina had been nothing but supportive of her solo. Sure, she was always concerned about Autumn's health, but so would be any friend. To hear she was talking to Sasaki about it in private didn't sit right. It was Autumn's life, Autumn's career—it wasn't Nina's place to intervene. However, it wouldn't have been the first time; sometimes Autumn had trouble gauging how much she could take on. She got lost in the passion and love for music, and sometimes she needed someone to remind her of her limitations. However, this was different. This time, Nina had gone to Sasaki behind her back.

"This isn't about Nina," she said, not wanting Heather to deflect the blame.

"Sorry. I know you don't want to hear such things about her. I see how close you are."

"I don't know what to believe," Autumn murmured, trying to take everything in.

"Because I lied about who I was?" Heather asked, still picking her nails.

Autumn nodded. "But I do believe that Mollie would hate to see you like this, living your life chasing her memory rather than embracing your passion."

"She would be so ashamed of me for not telling you who I was, but being close to you felt almost like I had her back," Heather said, wiping the tears sliding down her cheeks. "It hurts so much without her. How do you do it?"

Autumn shrugged. "I take each day as it comes."

"And it gets easier?" Heather asked, looking hopeful.

"Yes, but you can't do it alone, hiding in the shadows. Look...if you did do this, I want you to know I forgive you." Autumn meant it. She didn't want to be angry or resentful; she wanted, *needed,* to move on.

The door opened. "Her mum is here," said Aiden.

Autumn got up, but Heather reached for her, only to be stopped by her cuffs.

"I know you have no reason to believe me. I lied about who I was for three years, but I swear on my sister's memory that I never sent the roses," she said desperately.

Autumn paused and nodded, not sure what to say, then let Aiden lead her from the room. Autumn felt like he was closing the door on her soul. She didn't know what to think anymore; all she wanted was to get out of the station and get some fresh air.

Heather's mother, Lori, was pleading with an officer to see her daughter. Seeing her brought back so many memories—some good, others painful. Suddenly, Autumn felt like she was sixteen again and expected Mollie to appear at her side at any minute. The last thing she had wanted was to bring the family more hurt.

"I don't think she did this," she whispered to Aiden.

Aiden looked grave. "I think we should wait for the prints. She could be playing up your connection with her sister."

Autumn looked back through the glass to Heather, crying softly to herself. "Hiding her identity was wrong, and though she might have wanted to be close to me, I don't think she would have gone this far."

"And the photo she mentioned?" Aiden asked.

"I don't know. I never saw anything in the dressing room," she said, wondering why Heather would lie about something like that.

"Autumn, I'm so sorry, but she can't have done this—you were like a sister to her," Lori said, tears in her bloodshot eyes.

Autumn took her hands, trying to comfort her. "She needs you. She's stuck in her grief, and she won't get the help she needs in a cell. I truly want to believe it wasn't her," she said, and the colour returned to Lori's cheeks.

"I'm sure she'll be proved innocent. I'll do anything she

needs! When she left school, I thought she moved to the city. I had no idea she went to look for you." The way her eyes darted around told Autumn she was ashamed of how she had let her only living daughter slip away.

"You can see her now," Aiden said. Autumn sighed, grateful for the interruption. She didn't know how much longer she could bear being here.

Elijah was waiting outside, leaning against his bike. Taking a few breaths, Autumn felt her heartbeat steady. Just seeing him helped her shoulders relax, and all the anxiety drained from her body. Seeing Heather get lost in her grief and pain had reminded her that she had to be grateful to have people she loved supporting her.

She didn't even need to say anything before he closed the gap between them and held her close. There were no words to make it better, but it was enough just to have him there, waiting. He kissed the top of her head, telling her silently she was safe. She couldn't find the words to thank him for giving her the space to let her figure out the situation for herself.

He wiped a stray tear from her cheek. "I know this is a stupid question, but are you okay?"

"No, but I will be," she said, offering him a faint smile.

"Let's go home," he said, and she nodded, taking the spare helmet from the back of the bike. She glanced at the station as they drove off, gripping Elijah as tightly as she could, relieved that he was willing to stand with her and not run away at the first sign of trouble.

Autumn spent the rest of the day practising at home, trying to focus on her upcoming solo. All the emotional trauma from the last few days—weeks, even—seemed to compound itself, and Autumn found herself just wanting to sleep. To let her brain and body rest and reset.

Dragging her fingers over the keys, she wished she'd taken Sasaki up on his offer to have Marcus Lerou fill in for the rest of the showcase and only have her perform her solo. The emotional exhaustion was only heightened by her pain. Every time her foot pressed the pedal, it radiated up her leg as though the music was singing to her injured nerves. Staring at her phone atop the piano, she considered calling Sasaki and telling him her concerns, but she worried that the moment he heard the doubt in her voice, he would try to get a decision from her in an effort to protect her. And right now, if she had to make a choice, she felt like giving up entirely.

"Maybe I should just remove myself from the situation," she said to herself, letting the weight of her emotions win over her desire to play. She picked up the phone and held her thumb over Sasaki's number.

Just as she was about to hit it, she thought of Heather and Mollie, about the photo Heather had mentioned. She straightened and took a deep breath, reminding herself of all she had done to make this comeback happen, and decided not to give up at the last moment—not when she was so close. Resting her elbows on the piano, she swiped past Sasaki's number to call Aimee. She couldn't go to the theatre herself; the last thing she wanted to do was appear and disturb everyone with only two days to go before the show. She waited for her to answer, pacing, with Brinkley following her back and forth.

"Is everything all right?" Aimee asked, picking up after the first couple of rings.

"Sorry if I'm interrupting rehearsals; blame me if Sasaki gives out," Autumn said, pulling at the back of her neck.

"No, don't worry. A few officers arrived to go over security for the night of the showcase, so Sasaki has given us a long break," Aimee told her.

Autumn winced, hoping the others weren't too put out by the interruption. Then again, by keeping her safe, they were also ensuring their own safety. "Could you do me a favour?"

"Absolutely, what do you need?"

"In the dressing room, at my table, could you look around and see if a photo has fallen behind the back or sides of the dresser?" Hopefully, Aimee wouldn't ask any questions.

"Sure. Give me five minutes, and I'll call you right back."

Aimee hung up, forcing Autumn to wait in silence. It was the longest five minutes of her life, and that was saying something, but if Aimee found the photo, it meant Heather was telling the truth. And if she was telling the truth about the photo, she might truly be innocent.

If she's innocent, then whoever is sending me the roses is still out there. Autumn jumped when the phone buzzed beside her.

"Find it?" she asked before her friend could get a word in.

"No, sorry. There were no photos that I could see, and I checked the drawers as well. Is it important?" Aimee said.

Autumn sat on the piano bench, unsure of whether she was disappointed or relieved.

"Don't worry about it. But while I have you, can I ask if Nina has said anything about my solo seat to you? I heard she was worried I wasn't up to it." She couldn't ask Nina in case her friend didn't want to admit she had been talking about her behind her back, even if it was out of concern.

"I think she's just worried. A solo is a huge undertaking. She's been the only big-name soloist in the showcase for the last five years; she's worried about you and the theatre in case you have to drop out at the last minute, especially considering how the press reacted to your return," Aimee told her.

Autumn chewed her lip, surprised that it was true.

"Please don't take it to heart; it was all said out of care for you," Aimee said when she didn't respond. "I mean, you are headlining the posters. We sold out in minutes because of your return, and if we don't pull it off, it could ruin the theatre."

"You don't need to explain. I understand exactly what my absence would mean. I will be there on Friday, you can be damn sure of that." Autumn didn't mean to sound so defensive; Aimee was only the messenger. However, she couldn't help her frustration from spilling out.

"I have every faith in you. I know you wouldn't agree if you weren't able, and you deserve that seat. You've earned it," Aimee said, ever the cheerleader.

Autumn tried not to dwell on the thought of others gossiping about her. It wasn't like it hadn't happened before, but having her friends' doubt stung. "One last thing—don't mention this conversation to anyone else?" She didn't want to cause more drama.

"Sure thing," Aimee said. "Sorry, but I have to go; we have a run-through in five."

Autumn barely got the chance to say goodbye before she hung up. She wished she was there rather than at home, slowly losing her mind over whether Heather could be believed or not. She threw her phone against the couch, trying to work out her frustration. It didn't matter how hard she worked; they would always doubt her. *I've never given them any reason to think I would back out of the showcase. I've never been late to a rehearsal, nor skipped a day. Any time I missed practice was because Sasaki sent me home, but if it were up to me, I would have stayed.* Rolling her neck, she tried not to let it get to her.

"Maybe she didn't leave the photo and she just wants to distract me?" she asked herself.

Brinkley snuggled up to her legs, sensing her unease.

"What do you think? Did she leave me the photo or not?" She hunkered down face to face with Brinkley, who couldn't answer but did eagerly accept ear scratches.

"Who might have left you a photo?" Elijah asked, coming out of the office wearing a hoodie Autumn hoped to one day steal.

She sat at the kitchen counter while he took one of her smoothies from the fridge. She didn't care about him eating her food anymore; she now considered it theirs.

"When I was in the interview room with Heather, she mentioned she left a photo of the both of us with Mollie in the dressing room, but I had Aimee check and she couldn't find anything. I don't know why she would lie about something like that when admitting to leaving me anything might get her in more trouble."

Elijah wiped the green stain from his lips and left without saying anything. Watching him disappear into his office, she swung around in the chair and got up to follow him, wondering what he was up to. He was kneeling by his desk.

"Either you're sick of me, or you're looking for something—and trust me, at this point *I'm* sick of me," Autumn said, sitting on the couch.

He glanced over his shoulder at her and winked. "I could never be sick of you." He pulled out a small packing box. "When I had the movers gather your belongings from this room, they accidentally left a box under my desk that was meant for storage. I thought it was one of mine. When I opened it, there was a photo of you on top, but it might not be the one you are looking for."

"It might be. I keep all my old photos in the attic. It's too hard to have them out, but I don't know how it would have ended up in the house," she said, staring at the box he placed on the table before her. "I guess Heather said she left it three weeks ago, which is around the time you moved in."

Elijah didn't rush her, merely waited until she was ready. Not wanting to be there all night, she swallowed her nerves and removed the lid.

There they were: Autumn, Mollie, and Lena, with toothy smiles and bright eyes. The sight of their younger selves took her breath away. She couldn't remember the last time she'd looked at a photo of her younger self. Reaching for it, she almost stopped herself as though it could hurt her, but she had to know if there was a note on the back. Autumn gripped the corner and turned it over. There it was, just as Heather had said it would be.

Millbrook Cemetery Saturday 2:30 pm
Lena x

"Lena told the truth...about the photo, about Nina talking to Sasaki," she whispered to Elijah, who was looking over her shoulder. "Why would she tell the truth about those things but not confess to the rest?"

He studied the photo. "I don't know."

"Either she didn't send the roses or she's messing with me." Autumn's mind swarmed with questions. She placed her head in her hands to try and focus.

"But she said she left it in your dressing room. How did it get into the house?" Elijah asked.

"Maybe it got caught up in my things when I was taking stuff home from the theatre? But I'm sure I would have noticed a photo, especially this one," she said, looking at Mollie's smiling eyes staring up at her. She hadn't realised how much time had distorted her memory of her best friend.

"Why this photo? Is it special?"

Autumn rested her hand over her aching heart as the memories flooded through her. "It was taken about an hour before the accident. Lena took it with the camera she got for Christmas."

"You all look so happy," Elijah said, tracing her smile.

"We were," she said, looking at her sixteen-year-old self, who knew nothing of pain or grief. All she was worried about was getting a good review in the paper and being selected to go on the national tour. *I wish he knew me then; he could have seen me before the scars, physical or not.* Despite having the same red hair and dimples, she barely recognised the girl staring up at her. That version of herself had died with Mollie.

"There's nothing I can say to make this better, but I'm here, and you won't have to go through anything like this again alone," Elijah said, sitting on the table across from her.

"Being here with me is more than I could ask for." Autumn let him take her onto his lap, and she rested her head against his chest, eased by the sound of his steady heartbeat.

Elijah's embrace and the intense emotions the photo had brought up helped her realise something. She *did* want to play her solo; she wanted to do it for so many people— for Mollie, for her old self, and the broken-but-healing self of today. For Elijah, to show him what she could do when he supported her. For her parents, even if they still didn't understand her dreams. But here in Elijah's arms, still feeling the tension of the last few weeks twinging in her back, she made a decision. She didn't have to do everything. It was okay to acknowledge her limits. It didn't mean she was any less of a person or that she wasn't trying as hard.

She felt a sense of peace as she reached a conclusion in her head. This felt like a good compromise.

"I know what to do about the showcase," she said.

Chapter Thirty-Two

Elijah

Elijah kissed Autumn's cheek, and she stirred in her sleep. He decided to let her sleep, having heard her up again in the night. He'd wanted to go to her and comfort her, but after her interview with Heather and discovering the photo, he thought she probably needed some time to herself to digest everything she'd learnt. When she'd finally come back to bed, she'd tossed and turned until finally settling in the early hours of the morning.

He wished he could push out the meeting with his father and the board of Randell Investment and stay home with her. However, for the sake of his company and those who were relying on him, he couldn't put it off.

"Stay with your mum," he whispered to Brinkley, curled in at the end of Autumn's bed. She had to go into the theatre in the morning for the final run-through of their showcase, and he hoped to be home before she got back. But if he got held up, Brinkley would be with her at home, so she was in good paws.

With the cheques secured in his navy suit jacket pocket, Elijah straightened his tie in the elevator on the way up to the executive floor. He'd hoped to arrive early so he could update Tim on what was happening with Autumn, knowing he wouldn't want to be the last to know. However, he'd got caught up in morning traffic and had to go straight to the boardroom. The board were expecting Francis to attend with him, but he didn't want to put his friend on the firing line. Being Kyloware's CEO, he would take responsibility for buying out their investment, and he had been generous with the interest to avoid leaving a sour taste.

He opened the glass door. A dozen sets of eyes fell on him, and he was greeted briefly with handshakes and a quick good morning before he took a seat at the right hand of his father.

"With everyone here, how about we get started?" Tim said, turning to his son. "We are all excited to see the completed demo."

"Actually, there's been a change of plans," Elijah said, straightening in his chair.

Tim's jaw tightened, and he addressed the board before Elijah could reveal his partnership with Nirosoft. "If you will excuse us?"

The board members seemed hesitant.

"Please?" added Tim.

Elijah knew his father wouldn't want to be humiliated in front of his board.

The board left without protest, but their whispers of what might be happening lingered after them.

"What's this about?" Tim demanded as Elijah moved his chair out from under the table so they could face each other.

He pulled at his tie, unsure of how to have this conversation. He didn't want to completely ruin their relationship, but he also needed to sever the chains Tim had on him.

Tim frowned when he produced an envelope from his pocket. "You didn't need to bring me a report today; we were expecting to see the final demo."

"Just open it," Elijah said, placing the envelope in front of his father.

Tim removed the cheques. The first returned his investment with interest. The second was for the house Autumn had been renting for the last six years.

"What is this?" Tim scoffed, his eyes narrowing.

Elijah leaned against the table and spoke calmly; the last thing he wanted was an argument. "I sold the game to Nirosoft to buy out your investment. My company now has the capital to stand on its own."

Tim looked as though he would rip up the cheque. Not that it mattered; Elijah would write another. He doubted his father would want to bring the contract to court and have it revealed that he was his son.

"Is this a joke? We had an agreement," Tim protested, tossing the cheques to the table.

"We signed a contract stating that Randell Investment would invest in Kyloware Inc. Nowhere in the contract did it say you had rights to the game or anything my company produces," Elijah said.

Tim shook his head. "You would do this to your own father?"

Elijah took a deep breath before he continued, careful not to react. "You have your money back, plus a healthy amount of interest. Your board will be happy; many weren't keen on the investment in the first place. Real estate and tech aren't exactly in the same lane."

"Why would you prefer to sell your work to your biggest competitor rather than work with your own blood?" Tim asked, pulling at his tie.

"My own blood? You put my company in a chokehold to force a relationship with you," Elijah said, clenching his fists beneath the table. "I won't have the company I've spent my life working towards be used as a bargaining chip."

Tim put the cheques back in the envelope, not bothering to even look at the second cheque, which Elijah was sure he would have got a kick out of if he hadn't been so pissed off about the other.

"I never wanted to force you to do anything. I never thought you could despise me so much as to do this. I wanted to help you because I wasn't there for you in the past," Tim said.

Elijah felt his chest tighten. He wanted to believe that his intention was pure, but after years of being pushed into the shadows and now only being addressed because of his success, he just couldn't fully trust his father.

Tim put down the envelope and began to pace behind his chair. Elijah had thought he would feel relieved, even satisfied, at seeing his father blindsided, but instead his scheme felt shallow, leaving an ashy taste in his mouth.

"Please sit. I don't want to fight about this. I understand if you wish to sever ties after this, but I won't be forced into your life."

Tim ran his hands over his face. "Your company is your own. I won't interfere any longer, but should you need help in the future, I will help you," he said at last. "I...I did force your hand, and I apologise."

Elijah thought he must be dreaming. "And the strings?" he asked. There had to be a catch.

Tim shook his head, shoving his hands in his pockets. "No strings. Is it really so bad to want your son in your life?"

Elijah felt like he had been slapped. He tried to keep his voice steady. "Where were you for the first thirty-odd years of mine? You've never acknowledged me as your son, and if my company wasn't ranked the next tech company to watch, I doubt you would have even picked up my call."

"I can see how my actions have hurt you. Tomorrow, I'll tell the board of your decision and that you're my son. I'll inform them that it was in both of our best interests to dissolve our working relationship," Tim said gruffly.

"You expect me to believe that?" He had to be bluffing. "That simple?"

Tim reclaimed his seat and leaned towards him. Elijah could see how serious he was, and suddenly felt like he was the one being blindsided.

"I admit I handled the investment poorly. I didn't know how to approach you; I didn't know where to start," Tim began. "When you asked for my help, I knew I wouldn't get this chance again to make amends with you. I'm an old man. I don't care as much as I used to about the opinion of others, and I wish I had cared less in my youth. You and your mum deserved far better than me." There was genuine sadness in his voice.

"I understand wanting to make amends, but you forced me to live with Autumn to keep an eye on me," Elijah said. He'd felt as though he was on house arrest—though Autumn with him *had* made his jail time sweeter.

"Yes, I went too far in trying to keep you close. In all honesty, I really didn't think it would be an issue. You both needed a bit of push; the pair of you only think about work and take no time for yourselves," Tim said, leaning back into his chair.

Elijah rubbed his forehead, trying to figure out if his father was being sincere or whether he'd been possessed. He was right, they had both been stuck in their bubbles.

"Speaking of Autumn, you might enjoy what's left in that envelope," he said, looking at the envelope.

Tim removed the second cheque and tilted his head. "What's this for? Don't tell me you're trying to buy me out of my own company?" He chuckled.

Elijah smirked. He had no interest in investments. "The house. I want the house for myself and Autumn." He couldn't wait to see Autumn's face when he told her. It would no longer be her house or his, it would be *theirs*.

"This is far above the asking price," Tim muttered, and then settled into a laugh. "Well, it seems I did something right when it comes to you."

"Even if I don't appreciate the method, I have to thank you for bringing us together," Elijah admitted. They had started out roughly, but he couldn't imagine life without her.

"Have you spoken to Autumn about this?" Tim asked, with an edge of concern.

"I will, but I want it to be a surprise."

"Autumn hates surprises, but she loves that house. I could see how she looked at you at the dinner." Tim sighed. "I hope you are both very happy."

Elijah had never expected this was how the meeting would go, but he had to ask one more thing while his father was in such an honest mood. "Can I ask why you helped Autumn? You asked nothing from her in return, and yet for your son, you never gave without asking for something back." He wasn't trying to be hurtful; he only wished to understand what had changed.

Tim hung his head. "Autumn was my penance. Her dad asked me to look out for her. I wasn't the villain in *her* story; I wasn't the asshole who disowned his child and abandoned his mother. To her, I was like an uncle who wanted to see her dreams come true. When you told me you were coming back and asked me for my investment, I wanted to help you. The door was open a crack, and I was afraid you would close it again."

Elijah could see how hard it was for him to admit, and he didn't want to punish him for his past decisions. They were both adults. What happened in the past was best left there. Autumn had taught him that.

"Going forward, how about we separate business from our relationship? It'll take time, but I want to move forward," he said, seeing how much it meant to his father. The future was yet to be determined. If Autumn could forgive and put the past behind her, so could he. She was right when she'd said he would regret not trying.

Tim nodded slightly, as though trying to accept what Elijah had said. "I'd like that very much. I won't interfere, and the house is yours. I'll transfer the deed to you first thing Monday."

Elijah leaned back in his chair, surprised by how easily Tim had relinquished control. If anything, he seemed eager to help. "And the board? Are you sure you don't want to talk to them?" he asked, happy to take responsibility for his actions.

"I'll tell them I changed my mind and you returned the investment with a bonus each should be satisfied with," Tim said.

Elijah was surprised he would take the hit and risk his reputation. *Maybe he really has changed.*

"You should get going. I have my own dragons to face," Tim said, placing a hand on his shoulder. They weren't at the hugging stage yet, but it was a good start. "Tell Autumn I'm thinking of her, and I'll be there to support her tomorrow night."

"Will do. With everything going on, she'll be glad to hear you're coming," Elijah said, buttoning his jacket.

"Sasaki called me last night and told me what was happening with the investigation. To think she was keeping it all to herself breaks my heart." Tim led his son towards the door.

Elijah's shoulders relaxed, relieved he didn't have to explain everything to him. He had been afraid Tim would be angry with Autumn for not telling him sooner. "I think it's one of the reasons why she was so hostile about my moving in. She wasn't ready to admit what was happening."

"All we can do is be there for her and try not to make it worse," Tim said as they walked to the elevator.

"Thank you for being there for her," Elijah said, but Tim waved him off.

"It's your turn now. Look after each other."

Elijah suspected Tim would spend the rest of the day deep in damage control. The first time he had stepped into Randell Investments, he'd wanted revenge, to see his father shrink, to embarrass him in front of the board. Yet as the elevator doors closed, all he saw was a tired old man who wanted his son in his life. Elijah removed his tie and smiled to himself, eager to start a future without the pain of his past.

Chapter Thirty-Three

Autumn

Autumn glanced out at the chattering audience as they filtered down the aisles. The theatre shone like a golden beacon with the chandeliers above the audience lit up. The glistening lights highlighted the red velvet seats and golden statues on the private boxes. She couldn't believe they had sold out five nights and then had enough demand to add two more; she had a feeling it had something to do with Claire Wright, the CEO from Tim's auction, mentioning their showcase in her latest interview, stating she was looking forward to seeing Autumn Adler's comeback. Sasaki had emailed her the article, stating such publicity couldn't be bought.

They'd added two more nights to the original run to meet the demand, but it was the most they could do since many in the company were going on tour within the coming weeks. Seeing the theatre thrive was all Autumn had hoped for, a way of paying Sasaki back for all his support and patience over the years.

The lights dimmed, giving everyone a five-minute warning before the showcase began. Autumn adjusted one of the gold pins holding up her curls to stop it from digging into her scalp as she watched everyone take their places on stage. She wished she could be on stage for the whole show, but having seen how exquisitely Marcus had played when she'd arrived yesterday for the final run-through, she'd been assured that it was okay to share the stage with him. She knew, given her emotional and physical state, it would do the show greater justice to let him play the group pieces. What mattered to her most was her solo comeback to close the show, and since the audience had come to see her, in those last minutes, she would give them her whole heart.

After talking it through with Elijah last night, she even felt somewhat relieved. With all the stress behind the scenes, her pain had increased. Autumn decided to look on the bright side; she still got to close the show and watch everyone else in their element.

"I'm so glad we get to share the stage tonight," Autumn said to Nina, who was about to go on stage. Her solo opened the showcase.

Nina smiled, patting her shoulder. "With everything going on, it must have taken a lot of strength to get here. Everyone is so proud of you."

Before Autumn could wish her luck, Sasaki announced the show.

The audience applauded when Nina appeared, and Autumn watched her friend, in awe of her. Having carried the showcase for the last few years, her performance had an air and grace Autumn aspired to. Watching Sasaki conduct the opening, she tried to let the music silence her anxiety, but with the heat in the wings, she could feel beads of sweat on the back of her neck. The thought of taking the stage alone caused her mouth to dry.

Suddenly worried about who might be watching her if Heather wasn't the culprit, her eyes drifted to the officers in plain suits lingering in the shadows at the stage entrances and emergency exits. She was protected. Thanks to the adrenaline coursing through her, the dull ache that should have been radiating through her body after so many rehearsals was practically gone.

Elijah tapped her shoulder, disrupting her thoughts.

"How did you get back here?" she demanded, noting how handsome he looked in his black tux. His presence gave her an extra boost of confidence.

"One of the officers let me in through the stage door since Aiden added me to the cleared list."

She rolled her wrist. "I can't seem to get them to steady."

Elijah glanced at her hands and took them in his own. "You don't need to be nervous. If you play how I heard you last night, no one will be able to take their eyes off you—not that they will anyway, considering how beautiful you look." He brought her hands to his lips as she heard the next movement begin. Autumn wanted to compliment Nina on how well she'd done, but she must have exited off the other side of the stage.

"Thank you for coming back here. I didn't realise how much I needed it," she whispered. The love in his eyes almost killed her.

"Nothing makes me happier than standing by your side."

They watched the next two movements with his arm around her shoulders. The winter movement was coming up, and she wanted him to see her from the audience.

"I go on after this movement. Take your seat. I don't want Tim to be lonely," she said. Sasaki had sat them together now that they'd agreed to work on their relationship. Elijah kissed her cheek before disappearing back to his seat.

Sasaki announced her name, and Autumn took a deep breath and straightened her shoulders. All her worries disintegrated when she stepped into the spotlight.

Everything went silent as she took her place at the piano. This was her moment to let everyone know that this was her space, and no threat, injury, or trauma was going to take it away from her. From the small pocket in her dress, she removed the picture of herself and Mollie and placed it on top of the piano.

This is for us. She smiled, feeling as though her friend was sitting beside her.

Autumn's fingers grazed the keys, and she glanced at Sasaki, who nodded curtly, telling her to begin. With a slow exhalation, she let the music flow through her. No longer caring about being perfect, all she wanted to do was make the stage hers again.

The spotlight blinded the audience from her view, and she finally felt she was home. She could hear nothing but the music; she didn't miss a note or try to speed through it. She savoured every moment, and when it was over, she felt her tears slide down her cheeks.

We did it. We finished, she thought as Mollie smiled up at her. She placed the photo safely in her pocket.

She didn't even notice the applause until Sasaki offered her his hand, breaking her from the trance. Staring out, she smiled through her tears and saw the audience rise to their feet, cheering and clapping. Quickly wiping her tears, she bowed in thanks. Sasaki embraced her, and she thought she would pass out from the relief. The moment that she had longed for, and been terrified of, was over.

"I'm so proud of you," Sasaki said, releasing her. "Welcome back."

Autumn laughed as the adrenaline left her. "I can't believe I did it."

Together, they bowed again, and she searched the audience for Elijah, scanning the front row. Tim gave her two thumbs up, but she noticed Elijah's seat beside him was empty. *He must be backstage waiting for me.* She left the stage as the others passed her with quick congratulations to do their own bows.

"Autumn, sorry—your phone wouldn't stop ringing," Aimee said, passing over her phone before jogging on to join the others.

Autumn frowned at her phone. Elijah was calling.

"Where did you disappear off to?" she asked, heading backstage to her dressing room. The ongoing applause distorted his voice.

"I'm sor—I had...out. Aiden...they got... print...-ack." His words were broken and mixed with static.

"Elijah? I can't hear you. The reception is terrible back here. Just come in the stage door," she said through the static.

"Wait! The...-int wasn't—" Her phone went dead as soon she entered her dressing room.

"Elijah?" she called, but the signal went dead. She cursed under her breath and shoved her phone into her pocket, reminding herself to call him back as soon as she left.

Closing the door to the changing room behind her, she tried to turn on the main light, but the bulb must have blown. However, the lights from the mirrors meant she could see, and all she wanted was a chance to gather herself before she rejoined the others for a glass or three of champagne.

At her dressing table, a bouquet of white roses waited for her. She touched the crisp white petals, smooth beneath her fingers. *At least they aren't red,* she thought, only to notice a shadow lingering behind her in the mirror.

Autumn froze. "Heather?"

It wasn't Heather who came forward, but Nina. Autumn relaxed and started reapplying her lipstick.

"You frightened me! I was wondering where you went after your solo," she said, watching her friend in the mirror.

Nina didn't say anything. She merely stared at Autumn until she capped the nude lipstick and turned to face her.

"Did you enjoy your standing ovation? I don't know how you can stomach it. Or do you think you actually deserve it?"

Autumn stared at her, dumbstruck. Even though it was Nina talking, it sounded nothing like the friend she had known for the last six years. "Are you okay? You...don't sound like yourself."

Nina laughed in a way that made the hairs on Autumn's arms stand up.

"You know they just pity you, right? Poor Autumn Adler, making her comeback after such tragedy. You're like an animal in the zoo to them," she said, stepping closer.

Autumn recoiled, clutching her phone in her hand. "Why are you talking like this? This isn't you!"

"Me? For the first time in a long time, this *is* me," Nina said, stabbing her finger hard into her own chest.

Autumn felt as though all the warmth had left the room.

"It was you this whole time. You sent the roses. Heather was telling the truth." Autumn's words were so low she barely heard herself; she thought her throat would close up as the betrayal ripped through her.

Nina clapped slowly. "Finally! I was beginning to think you weren't going to catch on."

Autumn didn't want to hear another word, let alone be in the same room with her, but when she tried to push past her, Nina shoved her back with such force she hit the dressing table. She swallowed, realising Nina had another idea of how this conversation was going to end.

Her thoughts raced. If she couldn't leave, then she had to buy time and keep Nina talking until Elijah or the officers realised she was missing.

"Caught on? Forgive me for never considering that my best friend would want to hurt me when I've done nothing to deserve it." Autumn tried to keep her voice calm. If she didn't know Nina at all, she had no idea what she was capable of.

Nina scoffed, blocking the door. "Always the victim. Do you think you're innocent in this? Think again! I would never have had to go so far if you had just stayed in the background. When you first joined us, you were so fragile; no one thought you would last long. You even collapsed on stage after one performance! I figured I had nothing to worry about."

Autumn tried not to react to the pain her words inflicted. "If you hated my arrival so much, why did you come with me to the hospital?"

Nina sighed, seemingly bored of her questions.

"Know thine enemy, keep your friends close and enemies closer—take your pick. We're in a very competitive line of work, and I had to figure out how much your injury affected you. I figured it was easier to go to the source since you never talked about it. There wasn't much online."

Autumn couldn't believe the moment that had solidified their friendship for her had been nothing but a scheme for Nina's benefit. Pushing down her terror and agony, she had an idea. Carefully, she held a button on the side of her phone so it would record their conversation. She usually used the short-cut to record her practice sessions; she'd never thought she would need it to record a confession.

"But why wait three years?" she asked, watching Nina pace. "If you hated me so much, why not make my life a misery from the start?"

If she had a confession, she could get Heather released immediately. She dropped the phone on the chair and stood up to protect it from view and so she wouldn't be caught with it in her hands.

Nina rolled her eyes as if the answer were obvious. "Because you were attracting people to our shows, which meant more eyes on me. But you were getting stronger, and when Sasaki mentioned a comeback, I knew he would offer you the next solo. I had to do something. I thought once I started sending the roses, you would be put off, and with some slight influencing about 'not being ready,' you always declined his offer."

"You still opened the show. What exactly have you lost? I took nothing from you!"

Nina walked over to the wall and tore down their latest poster, shoving it in Autumn's face.

"It's *you* standing before all of us. It's *your* name highlighted. You took my place! I've been discarded—as though I haven't sacrificed everything for this place," she barked, tearing the poster in two.

"The sad truth is that you never had to do any of this. I would have stepped out of the show if you had just asked, but Sasaki would have just replaced me with another headliner like he did today. I've already lost one best friend; I never would have wanted to lose another," Autumn said quietly. It was the truth. She had to fight enough with her own body every day, she didn't want to have to battle for a position she'd never thought would cause strife in the first place.

Nina's grimace faltered, and Autumn thought she might have got through to her for a moment, but as she stepped towards her, Nina's gaze hardened once again.

"This is why you don't deserve to lead our theatre. You're pathetic. I would never give up my seat. It's who I am," Nina said. "Lerou was an oversight on my end, but he won't stay. He'll leave, and I'll be the only named headliner again."

Autumn shook her head. She'd never known this was how Nina felt, how far she was willing to go to make a name for herself. "Pretending to be my friend for so many years... wasn't it exhausting? All the lies, the sneaking around?"

"It was rather troublesome. Initially, I hoped you would tell Sasaki about the gifts and he would dissuade you from playing entirely, but you were so stubborn. You refused to bring them up. No matter how much I pried after I'd made a delivery, you were so determined to be damned *Ms Perfectly Fine.*" The resentment flowed out of Nina so fiercely, Autumn didn't know how she had contained it for so long.

"So you decided to escalate things? You went from once a year to once a month to frighten me?" she said, making sure her voice was clear for the recording.

"I couldn't let you just come out of oblivion and take everything I've worked and sacrificed for." Nina shook her head before a slick smile spread across her lips. "Then I found the photo of you and that dead girl in here. It didn't take me long to figure out who Heather was. Kind of creepy to change your name just to be close to your dead sister's friend, but her lie was a golden opportunity—the perfect scapegoat."

"Don't you dare speak about either of them that way," Autumn hissed, taking a step closer, and then stopping short with a jolt of fear when Nina raised her hands. She retreated, then realised how Nina had got into the house. "You had a key and the alarm code, but you forgot to set it when you left. That's how Elijah was able to move in without my noticing!"

"He nearly caught me too." Nina smirked, walking back and forth in front of the door. "He came in just as I left the photo. Even broke the back door on my way out trying to get it open. Then he ruined my endgame by changing the locks. I was going to leave the bloodied roses in your kitchen for extra flare. I had to settle for the dressing room." She laughed. "Surprisingly, it worked out even better for me, because you caught poor, shy Heather. I did tell you she was nothing to worry about—probably one of the only honest things I told you—but you always had a weird feeling about her, and it played beautifully into my hands. She was always *so* willing to help you. After she picked you up that morning, she was so worried. She even told Sasaki about you taking painkillers. In fairness to her, she really didn't mean you any harm, but with the doubts I'd been pouring into Sasaki's ear all season, it was just so easy to get you sent home." She turned a glare at Autumn. "But you're like a damn weed, always springing back up."

"You're truly sick. So much effort just for a showcase," Autumn said, nauseated by how far she had gone just to see her own name in bold instead of Autumn's. Guilt washed over her as she thought of how she had wronged Heather.

"It's not 'just a showcase!' The fact that you even had to consider whether or not to go on tour when Sasaki asked drove me crazy. No one who truly belongs on that stage should even have to question it."

"How did you think you would get away with this?" Autumn asked. "Were you just going to torment me forever?"

"No. My plan was perfect. I figured with all the commotion, Sasaki would suspend you, and then you wouldn't be able to go on tour. With only one show under your belt, you'd be forgotten before the next season," Nina said, smiling at her own genius.

"But it wasn't perfect, because he didn't do what you wanted. I still got to play, and you left a print, which they now have. You'll never play on a stage again." Maybe if Nina realised how much trouble she was in, she would admit she had been wrong.

Nina pulled at her suit jacket. "That wasn't my fault. I always wore gloves, but you came over after the auction and I was forced to hide the vase. I thought I'd wiped it clean. Why do you think I encouraged you to go home with him? Elijah was the perfect distraction, and it also meant I could make my delivery the next morning."

Autumn sighed. "Brinkley never barked because you had met her."

"Right on the money. Garrett even tried to break up with me because he found the photo and the receipts—he's smarter than I gave him credit for. When he stormed out, I went straight over to yours because I thought he was going to tell you," Nina said.

"Elijah saw you that night. That was you outside the house." Autumn clenched her fists, wishing she had listened.

"Guilty. I had to make sure Garrett didn't turn up after I left. Elijah really was a pain in my ass, always there, getting in my way. Thankfully, I managed to convince Garrett I was doing it for your own good. I thought he, of all people, would understand. Or at least I *thought* he understood, but then when he wanted to go for dinner, I knew he was going to warn Elijah because I had already convinced him you would never side with him over me. You're loyal to a fault." Nina smirked. "I had to end it with him, though, because of course he felt *sorry* for you after he spoke to Heather the other day. Threatened to go to the police, and in order to keep him quiet, I promised to stop. I told him I had to end it with him to get my head straight, and he believed my tears and blubbering. It's not you, it's me—a classic."

Autumn used all her inner strength to stop herself from slapping the smug expression from the other woman's face.

"I never wanted anyone's pity," she started, but Nina's laughter cut her off.

"Who are you kidding? Everyone made allowances for you. Sasaki bent over backwards to accommodate you the way he never would for the rest of us, just because of your tragic backstory. But I have to say, you did an excellent job at selling tickets. Don't think it was because of your talent, though. People just feel sorry for you." Nina's face was so distorted by rage, Autumn barely recognised her.

She took a breath, tired of being insulted. "Why shouldn't there be allowances for those of us who will never get to be normal again, those of us who spend every day with pain so nagging it threatens to drive us insane? You want me to apologise because Sasaki brought me back when many others would have discarded me? Never. I won't apologise for the kindness he has shown me!" Autumn trembled as years of frustration escaped her. "The world isn't built for those of us with chronic issues. Do we get some sympathy? Yes, but once the novelty wears off, that's it. We're told that our suffering has happened for a reason, that we are so strong and an inspiration, but it's all bullshit to make them feel better because soon, they get bored! They lose interest in people who can't keep up, who cancel and spend most of their time worrying about whether tomorrow will be a bad or good day. As you said, we're seen as a burden, something to be pitied, and sooner or later, we're pushed aside. You want me to feel sorry for you because I dared to pull myself back from nothing and play through pain you could never even imagine? No! Sure, everyone has their issues, but try adding a body that fights you every step of the way and then you might have my sympathy." She dared to step closer, forcing Nina to look her in the eye. "Until then, I think all that's left to say is fuck you, Nina, you pathetic, jealous bitch."

The words dripped from Autumn's lips with venom she didn't know she had within. It was the weight of everything she had ever wished to say to those who turned their backs on people who needed them the most.

And then Nina pulled a knife from behind her back.

"I think we've both said our piece," she mused, "and I think the obvious conclusion is that there's only enough room for one of us." Her eyes were so wide, they chilled Autumn to her bones. "And since I don't expect to get away with this and I probably won't get to step on a stage again, I think I should finish what that stage started ten years ago. Who knows? You might even thank me for putting you out of your misery." She pressed the tip of the blade to her fingertip.

"Give it your best shot. At least you aren't hiding in the shadows any more like a coward," Autumn spat.

A wicked grin on her lips, Nina lashed out with the knife and caught Autumn's palm as she held her hand up in defence. She cried out, clutching her bleeding hand to her chest.

"Autumn?" Elijah called, and both Autumn and Nina whirled around.

Elijah! He's here! It sounded like he was trying to break down the door.

"Nina, they have your prints on the vase. If you give up, they'll go easy on you," he pleaded, but Autumn knew it wouldn't work. She glanced at the vase of white roses as Nina eyed the splintering door. *I'll never be a victim again. Not without a fucking fight.* She backed up to the dresser and reached for the vase behind her back.

"Don't worry, this will all be over soon," Nina called out to Elijah as Autumn picked up the vase.

As Nina turned back to face her, she smashed it over her head.

Glass and roses littered the ground. A rivulet of blood trickled down Nina's forehead before she dropped the knife and crumbled to the floor.

Autumn could hear Aiden and Elijah calling out to her, but she couldn't find the words to speak as she stared at the woman she'd thought was her friend. Dazed, she thought to kick away the knife from Nina's hand, just in case.

The door finally gave way, and the bang woke Autumn from her shock. Aiden came in and quickly checked Nina's pulse. Elijah hurried towards Autumn.

"Is she...?" Autumn trembled, unable to finish the sentence.

"She's just knocked out. Call the paramedics," Aiden said to another officer by the door.

Elijah gently led Autumn from the room and out the stage door. The fresh air eased her anxiety, and she leant against Elijah to keep herself warm.

"It was Nina this whole time," she said, too stunned to cry as a paramedic called them over to one of the ambulances.

"I know. Garrett called the police and tipped them off. With his testimony and Nina's print, she won't be released any time soon," Elijah told her, gesturing for her to sit in the back of the ambulance.

"Are you hurt anywhere else?" the paramedic asked, and Autumn shook her head.

"Just my hand. I can't really feel it, though."

Elijah's brow furrowed, but she was used to far worse pain.

"That's the shock. It'll probably hurt more tomorrow," the paramedic said, examining her hand. "It doesn't need stitches; I'll clean and dress it."

"Did you say Garrett knew she was going to do this tonight?" Autumn asked Elijah.

He took a seat beside her, resting a hand on her thigh.

"No, he just said he suspected she was harassing you and he didn't want to get caught up in it if she did something stupid."

"Trust Garrett to cover his own arse," Autumn sniffled, though she thanked him silently for plucking up the courage to tip them off, or they might not have come looking for her when they had.

Elijah wrapped his jacket around her shoulders as the shock finally set in, causing her to tremble. "You're safe now," he said, kissing her hair. Autumn rested her head against his chest and heard his heart pounding. He must be doing his best to seem calm.

"Can we go home?" All she wanted to do was go home and sleep. She didn't think her body or mind could take much more.

"I'll find out."

Sasaki was talking to an officer nearby. Autumn couldn't believe how the success of the night had been so totally ruined for the others because of Nina's jealousy. Aiden came by while she watched the paramedics carry Nina out and load her into another ambulance. Seeing her friend unconscious, part of her couldn't help but worry. The friend she cared about had clearly never existed, but it still caused her heart to ache far more than her injured hand.

"Can I take her home?" Elijah asked Aiden.

"Sure. We can take her statement tomorrow," Aiden said.

Autumn remembered what she'd put in her pocket before striking Nina.

"I don't think you need it. Here," she said, showing them her phone clutched tightly in her hand. "I think I got everything, but I can't be sure." She handed Aiden the phone. He pressed it against his ear, listening to the recording, his eyes wide.

"You got it; it's all here," he marvelled after a moment.

Relief allowed her to rest against Elijah, but then she remembered. "Can you let Heather go? Nina was just using her to cover her tracks."

"I'll call the station and have her released immediately," Aiden agreed. "I'm sorry you were injured. I should have had some officers escort you backstage."

"Thank you, but there's no reason to be hard on yourself. Nina was the last person I thought could have been behind it. Does everyone know?" she asked, hoping they didn't blame her.

"We've got everyone gathered inside, taking their statements. Thankfully, the audience was already clear when Elijah notified us that he couldn't find you. They were all very worried about you and wanted to make sure you were okay. It took half a dozen officers to keep them from checking on you when we told them you were safe."

Autumn smiled, her eyes welling with tears, grateful for their concern and assured of the fact that Nina's venom wasn't contagious. Despite all that had happened, hopefully the audience would remember the night positively. She didn't want all this to affect the theatre.

"Where's Sasaki?" she asked.

"He's gone back inside with the others. We thought he would be the best person to tell them what was happening," Aiden said, and she nodded in agreement. "He'll probably want to assure them the show will continue, but I don't know how. With my hand and without Nina, we're down two soloists." She hadn't expected her first solo run in ten years to be over in one night.

"This isn't the time to worry about that. You just need to focus on yourself right now," Elijah said gently.

"I can't help it. Nina was wrong in thinking I don't love the theatre as she did. I love it enough to protect it from myself, whereas Nina was willing to burn it down in order to protect her place on the stage." Autumn pulled his jacket tighter around her shoulders. Strangely, now that she knew Nina had been behind the roses, her fear had disappeared.

Elijah looked to Aiden. "What happens next?"

"Go home and get some rest. I'll keep you updated, but with the evidence we have, possession of a weapon, and the intent to do bodily harm, she won't get out for a long time," Aiden said grimly.

Elijah shook his hand. "Thank you for helping us."

"No need; I'm just relieved you're both safe. Francis would have divorced me if anything happened to either of you."

Aiden's smile put Autumn at ease. She would never have thought that by meeting Elijah, the circle of those she cared for would expand so greatly.

Once Autumn was bandaged to perfection, Elijah brought her home.

They were barely through the door when Sasaki called Elijah, who assured him that she was okay. Autumn was grateful for him dealing with the call; she didn't have the energy to talk anymore.

Brinkley followed her upstairs, and she turned on her bedroom light. Stripping off the dress she'd so been looking forward to wearing, now covered in blood, she let it fall to the floor. She climbed under the covers, and the weight of her sheets felt like safety.

Brinkley snuggled in beside her, rested her head on her thigh, and comforted her. Autumn stroked her ears as the final threads of anxiety eased.

In the hall, she heard Elijah say goodbye to Sasaki. The bed dipped as he climbed in beside her, and she rested her head on his chest. The sound of his heartbeat steadied her own, and she closed her eyes as he ran his fingers through her hair.

"I was so terrified I would lose you. I wish you could know how much I love you," he whispered, kissing the bandage on her hand before laying it back on his chest.

"I know because I love you too. Thank you for coming for me," she said, then smiled. "I didn't know busting down a door could be so sexy."

"Always. I'll happily bust down any door that tries to get in between us."

Though she'd been trying to make light of the situation, his words were spoken with such sincerity that Autumn sat up and brushed her lips against his before settling back in his embrace.

After such an exhausting night filled with adrenaline and terror, they fell asleep in a matter of minutes, secure in the knowledge that tomorrow there would be no rose waiting, no looming threat. They were free to live as they saw fit without the interference of others, and it was the best night's sleep either of them had had in a long time.

Chapter Thirty-Four

Autumn

Two Weeks Later

The days following the showcase were a blur. Nina was arrested, and with further evidence discovered in her flat and the conversation Autumn had recorded on her phone in the dressing room, she pleaded guilty.

Autumn didn't go to the sentencing; she didn't want to waste another moment of her time on anyone who wanted to hurt her. Despite having to drop out of the showcase with her injury, her opening night received rave reviews, and it wasn't long before offers from other companies started pouring in. She considered going on tour, but she wasn't sure what she wanted anymore. For the first time in a long time, she was genuinely happy. She had her other friends at the theatre, Elijah, and of course, she couldn't forget Brinkley. Though Elijah told her she should tour and follow her heart, she wasn't sure it was what her heart wanted anymore.

Standing in the kitchen with the morning sun drifting

in, Autumn noticed the photo of Mollie on the fridge tilting, so she added another magnet to the photo. She wanted to see it every day to remind herself how lucky she was to be here, how lucky she was to have had a friend like her. She didn't want to erase her anymore, in hopes of freeing herself from painful memories. Heather had reminded her that not all their memories were painful, and she was determined to remember her for all the good times they'd had together.

She picked up the letter pinned beside the photo that invited her to tour with the National Orchestra as lead chair. Chewing her lip, she placed it on the counter. The decision she'd made she had done so for herself, but as she heard Elijah come in with Brinkley after their morning walk, she hoped he would be supportive.

Sadly, the first person Autumn had wanted to tell about the National Orchestra and seek advice from, the friend she had shared the stage with for six years, was the very person who'd tried their best to prevent her comeback. There were moments she yearned for their friendship and grieved for the good times they'd shared. Yet at the same time, the memories were forever tainted by the knowledge that the friendship had been based on a lie.

She was sure it couldn't all have been false—they had spent too many hours laughing and consoling one another for it to have been a total fabrication—but she needed to put it behind her, to mourn the version of Nina she'd known, and move on. Despite the betrayal and hurt she felt, she contented herself in knowing that though she had lost a best friend, she had gained a sister. Heather had been released from the station the day after opening night, and Autumn had been the first to greet her. Heather had decided to go back to college and pursue her own dreams. She was proud of Heather making a fresh start, and she hoped they kept in contact.

"I thought you would be packing," Elijah said, coming into the kitchen. The smell of the fresh morning air wafted around them. Brinkley rubbed against Autumn for her morning cuddle.

"Not right now," Autumn told Elijah, kneeling down to wrap her arms around the fluffy beast, not caring that she would end up covered in fur.

"Don't forget to give me some loving," he quipped, putting Brinkley's leash on the counter.

"I think Dad is getting jealous." Autumn scratched Brinkley's ears before she took a dog treat from the jar on the counter. Brinkley took the bribe and made her way to her bed in the conservatory, her tail wagging happily as she went. Once Autumn was free, Elijah embraced her. Even though it had only been an hour or two since they'd left each other's arms, she'd missed the feel of his lips against hers.

"Satisfied?" she asked, only to chuckle when he lifted her onto the counter.

"Never," he said, placing his hands on her thighs. She rolled her eyes, knowing she had to talk to him before they got carried away.

"I have something to tell you," she began, trying not to make it sound too daunting.

"Should I be sitting for this?" he asked, resting his hands on either side of her on the counter.

Considering all they had been through together in the last few weeks, she didn't blame him for assuming the worst. She placed her hands on his shoulders and gave them a squeeze to try and lighten the mood.

"No. It's good news—well, it depends on your perspective, really," she added, unsure of how he was going to feel about it.

"How intriguing. I'm all ears," he said, staring into her soul, which only made her more nervous.

"I've decided I'm not going to go on the national tour. I called them while you were out," she confessed.

Elijah's smile slipped into a frown. Worried by his expression, she dipped her head.

"But I thought that's what you wanted?" he asked, lifting her chin gently to look at her.

She shook her head. Before she even had a chance to explain more, she was in his arms, his lips crushed against her smile. *That's more the reaction I was hoping for.*

"Are you sure this is what you want? I don't want to hold you back." He rested his forehead against hers.

"It *was* what I wanted, but I've had time to think, and after talking with Sasaki, I've decided to take some time off after everything. Maybe try my hand at composing."

"Composing?"

"I believe you once called one of my pieces 'cats being murdered?' But the week of the showcase, those nights you heard me playing, they were my own. I was always too afraid to share them."

"I would never have said such a thing," he protested, pulling at the back of his neck, but she wasn't offended—not anymore, at least. "I can't believe you never mentioned it. Aren't you just full of secrets?" He brushed her hair over her shoulder. She shivered as his fingers grazed her skin; she loved it when he played with her hair.

"This means I won't have to leave for three months and I still get to do what I love, but at my own pace for once," Autumn said, swallowed up in his embrace.

"I don't like the idea of being separated from you for more than a day, but I'd never have asked you to give up the tour. I told you before, I'll still be here if you want to go. You couldn't get rid of me before, you certainly won't now."

Autumn smiled. His love and support for her only made it more impossible to leave him and the home they had built. His words reminded her of how rockily they had started. All the petty squabbles and attempts to drive each other crazy she could only look back on now with fondness.

"I know how much you support me, and I promise I'm doing this for me, because I want to, and not because I feel like I have something to prove or have some greatness to achieve. I just want to play," she said. He kissed her nose as she continued to explain all she had been plotting. She would have told him sooner, but she'd wanted to figure out everything first. "Sasaki has already told me he thinks a show with original pieces would be an even greater success, but I have months to work on it, so I can finally give my body a break."

"So long as you're happy, I'll support you. Whether it's here or the other side of the world, you aren't getting rid of me," he promised.

Autumn leant out of his embrace. "But we have one small issue outstanding."

"What's that?" he asked, his eyes narrowed in suspicion.

"What are we going to do about living arrangements?" she asked, then was surprised by his nervous smile.

"I have something for you. I was going to wait until you came back, but since you're staying…"

He led her outside and turned her towards the gate. Thankfully, it was dry, because she was only in her socks, but she hadn't wanted to interrupt him by stopping to put on her shoes. Brinkley hurried out the open door, clearly wondering what they were up to.

"Should I be worried?" Autumn asked, hearing something clink behind her.

"Turn around," he said, and she could hear how shaky his voice was.

She found Elijah holding a set of keys with a paw-shaped keychain. Her eyebrows pulled together in confusion as he placed them in her hand. When she looked inside the golden keychain, there was the picture of the three of them they had taken on a walk a few days prior.

"A key? Please tell me you didn't change the locks *again?*"

"To our house," he said, placing the key in her hand, and her chest tightened.

"You want to keep living together?"

"If you'll have me," Elijah said, and Brinkley barked. "Us," he added.

Happy tears prickled Autumn's eyes.

"Please don't cry! This is meant to be a good thing." He wiped a tear from her cheek.

Autumn gripped the keychain in her hand, not wanting him to misunderstand. "These are happy tears. I thought now that everything was settled with your company and with Tim, you would move out," she explained. Her fears seemed silly now, but she'd known that just because she was willing to stay didn't mean he was. Everything had moved so fast between them; she would have understood if he'd wanted to slow down.

"I've told you, there's no getting rid of me. I'm giving you this because I want to move forward. Since we've already lived together, anything less and we would be going backwards. The house is ours. Both our names are on the deed."

"It's really ours?" she asked in wonder, closing the gap between them.

"Tim signed over the deed. We're stuck with each other."

His smile was so infectious she reached up on her tiptoes and kissed him, not caring if the neighbours saw.

"I love you too much to ever be separated from you, but I need you to know that I'll never ask you to pick between your music and me," he added, but all she heard was love. The last time they'd uttered the words was after the showcase, when they had both been so exhausted and flooded with emotion that it almost hadn't felt real. Hearing them now, in the warm light of day, felt all the more special because it wasn't said in response to the fear of one losing the other. He would never question her music; she hoped she could be there for him as he built Kyloware into the vision he'd dreamt of.

"You love me?" she asked, tugging at his grey jumper to pull him in closer. She had spent so much time wanting him to leave and now she was never going to allow him to escape.

"With every fibre of my being," he breathed, picking a fallen cherry blossom from her hair. He snuggled her close, and she could hear his heart pounding.

"I love you too," she sighed quietly against his chest. She pulled back, letting herself breathe, and she could see the longing in his eyes. He looked at her as though the world didn't exist around them.

"What was that? I couldn't hear," he drawled. Her cheeks flushed pink as he kissed her forehead, her cheek, and then her lips.

"I love you," she repeated against his lips.

He showered her in kisses until she melted into his arms.

"We should go home before we gross out the neighbours," Elijah said when they breathlessly broke away from each other.

"Yours or mine?" Autumn teased, looking up at him.

With a tight squeeze, he kissed the side of her head and led her up the steps to the front door. "Ours."

Other Completed Works by The Author

Young Adult Dark Fantasy
A Hellish Fairytale Series

Crowned A Traitor I
Where Traitors Fall II
When Traitors Rise III

Towerwood | Novella
Stepmother | Novella

Adult Fantasy Romance

The Naughty Or Nice Clause

Romantic Suspense

Ms Perfectly Fine

Discover more from Kate Callaghan...

Get the FREE first chapter of
The Naughty Or Nice Clause **when you sign up for Kate Callaghan's Mailing List.**

https://dl.bookfunnel.com/16mngr0ok8

Being Naughty Has Never Been So Nice!

When Lyla's father retired as CEO of the toy company which has been in their family for generations, she was meant to receive his shares. Instead, she discovers the company is bankrupt and her father has given her shares to Mason Klaus, an investor known in the corporate world for his cold and callous nature. Much to Lyla's frustration, her only option is to run the company with him, despite their evident loathing for one another.

When Mason cancels the annual Christmas party, Lyla throws it anyway—only for the event of the season to result in a terrible fire. With the offices and Lyla's credibility ruined, Mason offers her a deal: he'll forget her part in the disaster, but she must join his family for the twelve days of their Christmas holidays.

ACKNOWLEDGEMENTS

This book has been my Everest, and I wouldn't have been able to climb the mountain without all of YOU. I have to start with my fabulous partner in crime: my editor, Emma. My books would be absolute chaos without her. She deserves a medal for putting up with me and my characters. Thank you so much to my cover designer, Pru Schuyler; not only is she a fantastic author, but she also creates the most beautiful covers. To Enchanted Ink Publishing, thank you for turning my stories into books. Thank you for helping me bring my books to life. To RaeAnne, thank you for putting the finishing touch on this story.

Thank you so much to everyone, my Bookstagram family, BookTok, reader group, and those who have requested my stories from Netgalley, who helped spread the word about my books and supported me as I try a new genre. I will never be able to thank you enough for taking a chance on my stories. I wouldn't be able to do what I love without you, and I'll never take any of you for granted.

KATE CALLAGHAN

released her debut YA dark fantasy trilogy, *Crowned A Traitor: A Hellish Fairytale* in 2020. While the Hellish Fairytale universe is being expanded, she is also writing adult romance and fantasy. She loves dark tales, villains, and happily-ever-afters—something you will find in all of her books. Chatting with readers and getting to share many different stories is her favourite part of being an indie author. Currently, she lives in Dublin. She loves dramas with subtitles (to silence the characters), coffee, and reading too many dark romances. If missing, please check your local coffee shop. You will find her with her computer and an iced beverage.

Follow below if you want to learn more about future stories! Signed copies are also available on the author's website.

Facebook Reader Group
Become A Rambunctious Raccoon
facebook.com/groups/rambunctiousraccoons

Mailing List | Gain Access To Exclusive News

WWW.CALLAGHANWRITER.COM

Instagram | @callaghanwriter

Tiktok | @katecallaghanwriter

Milton Keynes UK
Ingram Content Group UK Ltd.
UKHW011016301023
431590UK00002B/6